THE
GATHERING
STORM

Peter Sma[...] Australia, and hails from a sea[...] [ca]reer in advertising he became [...] [an]d novelist. He lives in London [...]

D0335629

Praise for Peter Smalley

'Salute a new master of the sea. Smalley is intending to appropriate the capacious mantle of the late Patrick O'Brian and, on the strength of this book, it should prove a snug fit. Smalley has written a real page-turner, engrossing and enthralling, stuffed with memorable characters. Highly recommended.' *Daily Express*

'What these books are about are old-fashioned concepts such as duty, honour and standing by your friends and knowing what bravery is . . . They are typically exciting, compulsive action adventures. Take one on holiday this year.' *Esquire*

'Following in the wake of Hornblower and Patrick O' Brian . . . there is enough to satisfy the most belligerent armchair warrior: cutlasses, cannibals, as well as a hunt for buried treasure. All this plus good taut writing.' *Sunday Telegraph*

Also available by Peter Smalley

HMS Expedient
Port Royal
Barbary Coast
The Hawk

THE GATHERING STORM

PETER SMALLEY

arrow books

Published in the United Kingdom by Arrow Books in 2010

3 5 7 9 10 8 6 4

Copyright © Peter Smalley, 2009

Peter Smalley has asserted his right under the Copyright, Designs and Patents Act,
1988 to be identified as the author of this work.

This novel is a work of fiction. Names and characters are the product of the author's
imagination and any resemblance to actual persons, living or dead, is entirely coincidental

This book is sold subject to the condition that it shall not,
by way of trade or otherwise, be lent, resold, hired out,
or otherwise circulated without the publisher's prior
consent in any form of binding or cover other than that
in which it is published and without a similar condition,
including this condition, being imposed on the subsequent purchaser

First published in the United Kingdom in 2009 by Century

Arrow Books
The Random House Group Limited
20 Vauxhall Bridge Road, London, SW1V 2SA

Addresses for companies within The Random House Group Limited can be found at:
www.randomhouse.co.uk/offices.htm

The Random House Group Limited Reg. No. 954009

www.rbooks.co.uk

A CIP catalogue record for this book
is available from the British Library

ISBN 9780099513643

Penguin Random House is committed to a sustainable future for
our business, our readers and our planet. This book is made from
Forest Stewardship Council® certified paper.

Printed and bound in Great Britain by Clays Ltd, St Ives plc

Typeset in Janson by Palimpsest Book Production Limited,
Grangemouth, Stirlingshire

An horrid stillness first invades the ear,
And in that silence we the tempest fear.

John Dryden

Frigate in the navy, a light nimble ship, built for the purpose of sailing swiftly. These vessels mount from 20 to 50 guns, and are esteemed excellent cruisers.

Falconer's *Dictionary of the Marine*

As ever for Clytie, my heart's companion

ONE

Spring 1791

Captain James Hayter, RN, raised his fowling piece, aimed, and pulled the trigger. The flint snapped home in the pan, there was the flash of a spark, then nothing. The fat wood-pigeon soared up, wings clapping, and disappeared into the trees across the meadow.

'Damnation.' Muttered.

Captain Hayter lowered the gun, and examined the lock and pan.

'Damp powder, old fellow.' To his dog. 'That is what comes of pushing too eagerly through foliage after rain, d'y'see. Without putting the lock under my arm. Carelessness, Tam.'

The dog looked at him, head tilted on one side at the sound of its name.

'And disappointment.'

The dog's tongue lolled as if in agreement.

'No pigeon pie, that's what.' A breath, and he shouldered the gun, and adjusted the strap of the empty game bag. 'But we've come far enough today, and walked off our fat. Hey?'

The dog watched him, waiting and alert, one ear cocked, the other half-cocked.

'Time to go home, I think.' He set off to the south, along the winding path at the edge of the meadow. Sharp sunlight gleamed on the metal furniture of the gun, and along the barrel. The dog tarried a moment, having heard the word 'home' and become reluctant.

'Come on, Tam.'

And now the dog bounded after him. Cloud shadow followed them across the field, hiding the sun, darkening the copse on the hill above. Presently a shower of rain came sweeping and billowing, and the man and his dog became indistinct as they reached the stream and the line of low trees on the far side.

When they reached Birch Cottage, Captain Hayter's home, about thirty minutes after, both were very wet. James crossed the stable yard and went in at the rear of the house, left the dog in the scullery, and put his gun and bag in the dark little parlour beyond the kitchen that he used as his gunroom. He took off his wet coat, shook his wet hat, and now turned his head to the kitchen with a frown. The kitchen was empty. The whole house had a curious atmosphere of emptiness, and quietude. He strode out into the passage, glanced again into the kitchen, then went through into the living quarters. Silence.

'Catherine!'

He glanced up the staircase, then went into the library, opening the door wide. The fire had not been lighted. The room was empty. He went through into the drawing room, and found that empty. Turning out of the room:

'Catherine!'

From the scullery the aggrieved barking of the dog, echoing through the lower part of the house. And the subdued tick . . . tock of the long-case clock in the library. No other sound.

He stood a moment in frowning puzzlement, then ran quickly up the stairs, gripping the banister to lift himself along, just as he would have gripped the shrouds of a mast to aid his going aloft. As he came to the top of the staircase:

'Cathy! Are you there?'

No answer. And now he was beginning to be anxious, a little. A muffled voice, from the bedroom at the far end of the passage. The boy's room. A man's voice. Fear gripped his guts, and dug in its claws. He hurried there, to the door of the room, and saw that it was ajar.

'Cathy . . .'

He went in. Catherine stood at the foot of the boy's bed, and Dr Harkness, the new local practitioner, stood at the head, bending over the small form of the boy, who lay with his head on the pillow. The doctor adjusted the pillow, and under the rustling movement was the rapid shallow rasping of the boy's breath.

'Oh, James . . .' Catherine's terrified, distraught face as she turned to him. He moved to her.

'What is the matter?' As he took her hand, dreading the answer.

'Perhaps it would be best, Mr Hayter, if you was not to come farther into the room.' Dr Harkness, holding up a cautionary hand. 'I have already said so to Mrs Hayter.' A brief glance, and he returned his attention to the boy.

'Not come in?' The truth flooding in on James even as he asked the question. 'Is it a fever . . . ?'

'Aye, it is. Typhus.' Plain, matter-of-fact. 'He must be kept isolated. We must make a quarantine of this room, this quarter of the house entire.'

'There can be no doubt . . . ?'

'None. Y'will observe the petechial eruptions upon his neck.'

James leaned, peering at his son, and saw on his neck and on the upper part of his shoulder visible above the covers, small roseate eruptions on the sweat-sheened flesh. The claws in his guts dug deep, and he bent nearer.

'Nay, do not venture too close, if y'please.' The doctor's black coat hung over the back of the chair by the bed, and his black instrument case stood on the seat. The doctor's spectacles, perched precisely halfway down his nose, gave his face a particular severity of expression, even as he sought to be calm and factual in his pronouncements. He was a young man of twenty-eight or -nine, who looked a dozen years older. His hair was already grey at the temples, and his forehead bore a chevron of deep lines.

'I had no notion he was ill,' said James. 'I did not see him this morning, in course, before I went riding over to talk to Mr Brimley about his hunting meet.' Mr Brimley was their nearest neighbour, across the hill. 'I was up and about and gone so early. And then straightway when I returned . . .' as if explaining things to himself as much as to Catherine and the doctor '. . . I went to examine some papers, and then I was gone again with my gun and the dog. It did not cross my mind that he—'

'He could not eat anything, poor little boy . . .' Cathy, tears now on her face. 'He had seemed listless a little, all these last days, but I had thought it was only a spring chill. And then today he could not rise from his bed after his rest. Oh, could not I soothe him, doctor? Could not I cradle his head a moment . . . ?'

'Nay.' Not curtly. 'He cannot be aided by that, just at present.' He did not say the word quarantine again, but James heard it under the other words.

'Where is Tabitha?' he thought to ask now. 'There was no one at all in the downstair part of the house when I came in. Where are the other maidservants?'

'I have advised members of your staff to remain in their own quarters for the moment. I must make arrangements.' Dr Harkness wiped the boy's forehead with a wet cloth, and wrung out the cloth in a basin. Catherine began again:

'But, Doctor, if you are close by him, and will take the risk of fever, why cannot I, his mother—'

Dr Harkness cut short her pleas with not quite harsh authority and directness. Laying the cloth on the edge of the basin he said: 'Madam, I am a physician. I think your husband will understand me when I say that it is my duty to take such risk, and I hope that you will understand me, in turn.'

'I thank you for your kindness in warning me, Doctor, but I think you must know that I have already had such proximate contact with my child all the morning that I cannot be in any greater danger now, if I sit close to him, and bathe his forehead and hold his hand. Is not that so?'

'Nay, it ain't, I fear.' With the same directness. 'The petechial eruptions have appeared only in the past hour. You will do very well to keep clear, now. Both of ye.' A glance at James.

'Who will care for him, poor little boy?' Catherine's tears again spilled. 'He must be nursed.'

'There is a young woman in the village that has already been exposed, when her younger brothers took ill. She has shown no sign of fever, when she tended to them as their nurse.'

'Have they returned to health?'

'Alas – no.'

'They are dead?' Aghast.

'Neither child survived, but their sister is hale. She—'

'She will never come into this house while I draw breath.' Catherine drew herself up, lifting her head, and looked at Dr Harkness very direct. 'I thank you again for all your kindness, Doctor, and for your advice. I shall nurse my own son.'

'Madam, is that really—' began the doctor.

'Cathy, I do not think—' began James.

'I shall nurse my own son!' Fiercely, staring straight ahead. 'Do you hear!'

And the thing was settled. Both men knew that it was, and that they had better say nothing further. The doctor permitted himself a very small sigh, and shrugged into his coat. James stood back from the bed to let him pass, then followed him along the passage and down the stairs, leaving Catherine alone with the ailing boy.

'What treatment should my wife apply, d'y'think?' James asked Dr Harkness as they came to the bottom of the stair.

'If she is to stay by his side, what physic should she give to him? And when? I mean, how often should she—'

'There is very little may be done for the boy. I should advise prayer, was I a priest. I am not.'

'There is nothing *at all* can be done for him?' James, his voice very low in spite of the vehemence of his question.

'We are practical men, I think, sir. We know what life is. Your wife, his mother, will be by the boy's side. If he has strength enough to resist and fight the disease, then the fever will break. If he has not . . .'

'He is going to die.' Flatly.

'Nay, I have not said so.'

'But that is what you mean, ain't it, Doctor?'

'While ever there is life there is hope.' Sincerely.

'Damnation to pieties! Tell me the truth!' His voice cracking.

'If the boy lives through the night, then we may hope for a gain on the morrow.'

'That is all you can say . . . ?' His voice again very low.

Dr Harkness looked James in the eye, made to touch his arm, and then hesitated – for fear of contaminating him – and withdrew his hand. A moment, and:

'I hope with all my heart that your boy may live.'

James met the doctor's honest gaze, read in it what he already knew, and nodded. The doctor fastened a last button on his coat.

'If there is any change this evening, or during the night, do not hesitate to send word. I shall come at once.'

'You are very kind.'

'And I must iterate – no one of your household, other than your wife, is to venture into that part of the house where the boy lies.'

'Very good, Doctor. Thank you.'

He saw the doctor to the door, and his waiting gig. The rain had ceased and evening light lay angled across the paved forecourt as the doctor climbed into his gig and drove away, the sound of the horse's hooves fading on the quiet air.

*

In the days following, James went over and over in his mind all of the events leading to the culmination. The papers he had paused to examine when he returned from Mr Brimley's house, and later in the morning, papers he had read and reread in the library, and had then sat long in answering, because he had thought himself obliged to take great trouble with his reply. The walk he had embarked upon thereafter, taking with him a wedge of pie and a flask, his gun, his game bag, and the dog Tam. The afternoon he had wasted, largely in sheltering from showers of rain, in pursuit of elusive wood-pigeons. His late return, thoroughly wet and disappointed, and caught up in his thoughts. Could he have done different, on that day? Should he have? And what of the days preceding? Had he been inattentive, when Catherine remarked on the boy's less than energetic demeanour?

'Rondo is a little out of sorts, I think.'

'Is he? Is he? Then he had better go out into the fresh air, hey?' As he searched for and found his riding crop.

'I wonder if there is not a draught in his room? The chimney—'

'Do not fret about him, my love. He is a boy, and boys are hearty creatures. I shall say a word to Albert, and we'll have him up on Danny Boy this afternoon. Now, where the deuce have I put my gloves?'

But he had forgotten to speak to the stable lad, had forgotten about the pony Danny Boy, and his son, in pondering his own future. Should he have accepted his new commission, after all? Should he have accepted the ship-sloop *Eglantine*, 22, merely to attain the rank of master and commander? When Captain Rennie, his erstwhile commander and friend, had wanted James to return with him into HMS *Expedient* frigate as his first? Should not he write voicing his doubts to Their Lordships, and request further time to come to his decision? Good heaven, no. Certainly Their Lordships would look very unfavourable on a fellow that ... And so his thoughts had dashed hither and thither in his head, until the letter had come – the sealed, official, absolute and unignorable letter:

> ... you, the said Master & Commander so appointed, shall proceed forthwith to Portsmouth, there to Receive from the port admiral's hand your Warrant; thence to His Majesty's Portsmouth Dockyard, where you will go aboard the said Vessel, His Majesty's ship-sloop *Eglantine*, 22 guns, & duly commission her, & assume your duty of Command, and with all Despatch make her ready for the sea ...

His doubts had arisen from something that had happened during his previous commission – his first as commander – in HMS *Hawk*, cutter. A thing that had haunted him ever since. He had been obliged, in most pressing and distressing circumstances, to shoot dead a horribly injured man. It was a very shocking thing to have had to undertake, and he knew that his people had been shocked. He had seen it in their eyes. And yet he had had to do it, there had been no alternative if the poor wretch was to be delivered from his agony. He had fired the shot, and at once thrown the pistol into the sea.

'God forgive me.' He had said it then, and an hundred times since, as he rode his horse, as he shaved himself in the glass in the morning, as he strode to the top of the hill behind the house – at any moment when he was alone with his thoughts.

'God forgive me, I am not fit to command men any more.'

Even when he had replied to the letter, informing Their Lordships that he would go to Portsmouth, he was not free of nagging doubt, but in least now he knew his duty; duty had freed him of indecision. And then came the blow.

Dr Harkness's face, never handsome, was a grim mask of self-control, framed by deep lines, as he came into the library on the day following:

'We have lost him. I am very sorry.'

James got up out of his chair, and had to grip the back. 'But he ... he had seemed to recover. There was a gain, earlier today ... was not there?'

'There was, a little. It was not enough. I am so very sorry, Mr Hayter.'

'Is Catherine with him?'

'She has not left his side. You should go to her, and bring her out of the sickroom.'

'Yes ... yes.' Gripping the back of the chair still, and looking out through the window.

'And we must – forgive me for being so hard, at such a moment – but we must remove the body without delay.'

'The body.' Looking at the doctor. 'Yes.' His boy, his son, a body. Lifeless in the bed. 'Yes, a body cannot be left to lie, when fever has struck. It is the same in ships exact, you know. The bodies must be got over the side, without delay, if there is fever below.' Explaining the thing to himself as much as to Dr Harkness. 'But in course you know that, Doctor. I shall go up to her, and bring her out of the room.' He released his grip on the chair.

'I should say also – she must remain in a separate room herself, for a day or two. As a precaution. You – you should not embrace her, just at present. Nor touch her at all.'

'I cannot be with her? To comfort her?'

'I am sorry to be so hard. I would not place these strictures upon you, was there an alternative.'

'Nay, Doctor, you cannot help what is fact. I shall go up to her.' Taking a breath and moving towards the door.

'I'll send Marcus Freeman from the village, at once.' Laying down his bag a moment, and shrugging into his coat.

'Freeman?' James, pausing in the doorway.

'The undertaker. He must come today.'

'Oh. Yes. Yes, you are right. Please to make it so, Doctor.'

He went upstairs and found Catherine sitting on the chair by the bed, very pale and still, a shawl round her shoulders, her eyes closed. The boy, his son Rondo, that was no longer his son, no longer a boy with life in his limbs and a voice in his throat to cry out in excitement as he sat his pony and trotted through the gate to the grassy paddock, Albert running alongside at the bridle . . . lay now at peace. James stared a moment, and swallowed, and made himself breathe.

'Catherine . . .'

Opening her eyes. 'He is asleep.'

'Yes . . . he is asleep.'

'I shall wait here until he wakes.' Adjusting the shawl.

'Nay . . .'

'There is no need for you to stay with me. I shall wait with him until he wakes.' A pale smile.

'My love – Cathy – he will not wake again . . .'

'In course he will wake. In a little while. He is much better.'

'Oh, my poor darling Cathy.' He made to come toward her, and:

'Do not come near! He is asleep! I do not wish him to be waked, when he is so very tired . . .'

Utter despair rose in James's breast, and threatened to unman him. His eyes filled with tears, his throat was constricted, he wished to fall to the floor and weep. He overcame this sense of helplessness and grief by pure effort of will, lifted and shook his head, and was resolute.

'Catherine.' Not loudly, nor harshly, but with authority of tone. 'Come with me now, and we will go along to your bedroom.'

'I cannot leave him alone. What if he should wake?'

'There is someone to care for him.'

'To care for him? Who?'

'I have arranged it. Come.' He held out his hand. 'We will go to your room, where there is a fire, and fresh linen.'

'Fresh linen . . . ?' Looking at him, uncomprehending.

'Come.'

She rose, and came towards him. He wished to take her in his arms, and hold her close to him, and kiss her. He wished to show her all the profound love he felt for her, and to share with her in long embrace the grief of their loss, and to reassure her with all his heart that he would love her always and for ever, but never so deeply as at this moment. He wished it with all of his being, and knew that he could not do it. Could not even touch his beloved wife, for fear that she was herself infected, and would infect him in turn.

She came to the door, with a last glance over her shoulder at her child in the bed, and as James went ahead followed him to her bedroom. A fire burned bright in the grate, the flickering flames reflected in patterns on the ceiling. The curtains had been drawn, and the room was pleasantly warm. A fresh nightgown lay on the bed, and covers had been turned down. James had seen to all this himself, since the maidservants were not permitted to come into this part of the house.

'I will leave you to undress, my dear.'

He stood aside to allow her to go in. She walked to the fire, and turned anxiously:

'Are you going away, now?'

'There is much for me to do—'

'You are going to Portsmouth?'

'No, no – I am not. I must go downstairs and—'

'You will not leave me alone in the house?'

'I will not do that.'

'I could not bear it.'

'I will not go away from you.'

'That is well . . . I could not bear it.' Turning to stare into the fire.

Had she accepted it? Did she understand that Rondo was

dead? He did not know. Her expression, lit by the glow of the fire, was not one of bewilderment or confusion. She seemed sad, but calm. Presently he left her, and went down.

When he returned with bread and broth on a tray, twenty minutes after, she was fast asleep, her hair spread on the pillow. He put the tray down by the bed, and pulled up the covers gently, so as not to wake her.

'She has accepted it,' he murmured to himself. 'She knows the boy is gone from her.'

He watched her a moment longer, her breath fluttering a strand of hair on the pillow, her face ghostly pale with the exhaustion of her vigil, now relieved.

'I love you, my darling Catherine.' Whispered.

*

The undertaker came with his assistant from the village, and the removal was conducted with the minimum of upset. James took no part in it. He remained in his library while it was done, and allowed one of the maidservants to direct the men at their work. Dimly he heard the wheels of the covered cart and the hooves of the horse as the body was taken away through the stable yard at the rear. Had they brought a coffin with them? He did not know. He did not want to know anything of how it was managed.

Dr Harkness had said he would inform the vicar, and James had not had the presence of mind to tell the doctor to say nothing at the rectory, that he would call there himself on the morrow, and make the necessary arrangements for the interment. He tried to read, and could not. He attempted to write a letter or two, and put the quill aside. A thought came to him.

'The bedding must be removed, and burned. I must see to it at once.'

He went upstairs to his son's bedroom – and found that the bedding had been removed with the body. Only the frame of the bed remained, stark and small upon the floor.

'Gone.'

And now James felt the terrible loss of his son, and he sank down on the floor by the open door. He did not know how long he had lain there when there came the sound of an arrival below. Hooves, wheels, voices. One of the servants at the door. A man's voice, enquiring. James roused himself, wiped his eyes with his kerchief, and tidied himself – and went down.

It was the vicar, the Reverend Constant, a full-figured man, ruddy-cheeked, in usual a very genial fellow as he drove his gig about the lanes of his parish, or rode to hounds, not in the least like some of the more modern clerics, that were pallid, gaunt men, very black in their coats and breeches, and inclined to sermons quoting direct from the Old Testament. 'Thou shalt not' was none of the Reverend Constant's purpose. He liked good food and wine, and made no secret of it. His wife and numerous children were fond of him, and he of them. He was not a man for profound thoughts, or deep philosophies. He was a convivial country parson with a good living. But at times like this he felt it incumbent upon him to strike an attitude of dolorous sympathy quite out of kilter with his usual self. James had been dreading it.

'My dear Mr Hayter,' he began, as James came into the library. 'That is – Captain Hayter.'

'Vicar.'

'My sincere condolences, sir, in your very dreadful loss.' Holding his hat before him. Had he withheld it from the maidservant in order to appear more pious? wondered James, and then was ashamed of himself.

'Thank you, you are very kind. Will you drink a glass of sherry?'

'The loss of a child is always a very dreadful thing, and we cannot all of us readily understand why God has permitted it, why he has allowed the taking of so young and vibrant a life, in the full flower of innocence. That is his mystery, in his infinite wisdom. It is our sorrowful portion to pray for the souls of those departed, and obediently to trust in his divine judgement, always tender, and merciful. When we reflect—'

'You are kind.' James did not know how much more of this rank nonsense he could bear. He was fairly certain the Reverend Constant did not believe in it, either. That he was doing his duty as he saw it, going through the motions, being pious and gloomy and platitudinous, and would sooner be drinking a glass of warming sherry, and dealing with the arrangements in a suitably practical and kindly way – a decent, sensible, better way. James made it easy for him. He poured sherry into glasses, handed one to the vicar, and:

'To my son Rondo, and what he might have been, and become.'

The vicar put his hat on a chair. Relieved of ponderous obligation, he lifted his glass and:

'To Rondo, indeed.'

When they had drunk their sherry, James and the vicar fell to discussing the arrangements. All pieties and solemnities were forgotten, and the form of the service and the time, and that of the burial, were soon agreed. The Reverend Constant drank a second glass of sherry, and was on the point of departure when:

'My dear Captain Hayter, I am remiss.'

'Eh?'

'I have not asked after Mrs Hayter. Is she . . . ?'

'She has took it hard, certainly. It will take time—' A sharp thudding sound, beyond the door. Both men turned.

The door of the library was now flung open, and Catherine appeared, her hair in disarray, her nightdress trailing on the floor. Her skin was very pale, and her eyes shone over-bright.

'Where have you taken him!'

'My darling, you should not be—' began James, moving toward her.

'Where is he!'

'He has – he is being took care of.'

James glanced at the Reverend Constant, who took up his hat and and began a sideways-stepping movement toward the door.

'Is that you, Vicar?' Catherine now swung on him. 'Why have you come?'

'Dear lady, I am just going—'

'Nay, do not fly away on my account, Vicar. I will like to hear all your news. As an example, will you tell me what you and my husband have done with my son?'

'Done with him? Why, we was discussing the—' Breaking off as he saw James's frantic signal: Say nothing.

'Well?' Catherine, an imperious stare.

'I must leave these – these family matters to your husband, madam. They ain't my business.'

'No? Are not they?'

'No, indeed. And now, if you will excuse me, I shall—'

'I do not excuse you, Vicar. You see, I have listened at the door.' A wild, glassy, triumphant smile, now turned on James.

'Listened?'

'Hah! You did not think me capable, neither of you, of such subterfuge and cunning! But I am a woman, and women are cunning in defence of their children!'

'Catherine, my darling, you are not quite yourself.' James moved toward her again, holding out a hand.

'Do not lay a hand on me, sir! Stay away from my person! I will not allow you to steal *me*!'

'Darling, dearest – I am only concerned for your health. You will catch cold.' But he did not try to go any nearer to her, fearful that she would plunge away from him, fall and injure herself.

'You wish to send *me* away! I will not go!'

'My darling, I have no wish to send you anywhere. This is your home, where you—'

Abruptly breaking down: 'Oh, why did you do it! Why, why, why, why? Poor little boy, poor little boy . . .' She collapsed, as if her bones and sinews had turned to sand, and her head hit the the edge of the door with a thud as her body tumbled slack. Her head lolled to one side, and she lay still. James ran and knelt beside her, and cradled her head, careless of his own health now.

'Oh, my love . . .'

The Reverend Constant, shocked and anxious, peered over his shoulder. 'Has your poor wife injured herself?'

'You came in your gig, Vicar?' James, urgently, turning his head.

'I did.'

'Will you do me a service? Will you fetch Dr Harkness?'

'I will, I will, gladly. She is injured?'

'I fear so.' James's hand, when he lifted it from the back of her head, was covered in blood. 'I fear she is gravely injured. Please hurry, will you?'

'You may rely on me.' Another glance at the prostrate Catherine, and the vicar hurried away.

Dr Harkness came, and bathed Catherine's cut and bruised head, and wound a bandage round it. He helped James to carry her upstairs to her bed, and pronounced her free of any greater damage from her fall. She had regained her senses, but was dazed and unable to converse, or to understand what was happening to her. The doctor gave James physic, with instructions, and came downstairs with him.

'You will need to keep a close eye upon your wife, Mr Hayter, these next few days. I do not mean the abrasion on her head, which will heal quickly. There are more cases of typhus in the village, and I am concerned that your wife had such close contact with her son when he was suffering the worst eruptions of the disease. You yourself must also be vigilant. Any headache, any sudden flux of the bowels, any sudden onset of fainting weakness – and you should avoid contact with other persons, now, even your own servants.'

'But the vicar has been here today. We were together some little time, in the library.'

'The Reverend Constant asked me to alert him in all cases where the disease has struck. Like myself, he wishes to do his duty.'

'But surely he has young children of his own?'

'He has.' A sigh. 'I cannot prevent him from tending his flock, you know. He knows what risk he takes, I assure you.'

'How many cases altogether, Doctor?'

'In Winterbourne Keep, seven. And five in the neighbouring village.'

'Will there be more, d'y'think?' As they went out on to the front court.

'It is entirely probable.'

'Should I send the servants away?'

'How many servants have you here? Three?'

'Aye. Tabitha, that is very elderly now, and the two young maidservants. Oh, and the stable lad.'

'It will be better, I think, for them to stay here.' He did not elaborate, but James was wholly aware of what he meant. If the servants were themselves already infected, sending them away, among other people, would do more harm than good. As the doctor drove away:

'Perhaps we are all infected. Perhaps we are all doomed to die.' But he did not say it loud enough for Dr Harkness to hear.

On the morrow a letter came for James, from Portsmouth. He did not reply. He did not even read it.

TWO

Captain William Rennie, RN, and his bride Sylvia – a handsome naval widow he had met months since, and had been immediately and greatly drawn to – were living for a few weeks at Portsmouth, far from their home in Norfolk. They had taken rooms at the Marine Hotel while Captain Rennie's ship – HMS *Expedient*, frigate, 36 – was refitted. The ship had lain in Ordinary most of the previous year, and had now been recommissioned because of the worsening situation in France.

Expedient was at present shored up in the dry dock having her copper examined. Rennie moved about the dockyard, visited the port admiral's office, returned to the yard, fretted, enquired, took the wherry over to Gosport to chivvy his purser Mr Trent as he made his requests and purchases at the Weevil, visited his tailor Bracewell & Hyde, and was full of the energy of renewed command.

'Yes, yes, but what of the buttons?' he said in Mr Bracewell's shop. 'Have Firmins sent them?'

'I am still awaiting them, I fear, sir. The—'

'What? Still? Good heaven, Bracewell.'

'Firmins are very taxed at present, sir, with many orders. So many ships coming back into commission, so many officers that wants new buttons, not to mention new lace—'

'Yes yes, very well. Let me know the moment you have the buttons to hand, will you? The full set, for my dress coat. Do not forget.'

'I will not likely do that, sir.' Mr Bracewell, politely, tape measure draped neatly about his neck.

'Very good. I am at the Marine Hotel.'

'I have the address in my book.' Politely, as Rennie strode out to the clinking of the above-door bell.

Rennie had gone aboard *Expedient* as soon as he had come to Portsmouth, and before she had been given her number for the dry docking by the master shipwright. He had formally read his commission on the cluttered deck, surrounded by indifferent artificers, his standing officers, and those few men of the ship's complement already berthed in her. The bulk of her people had not yet been gathered, leave alone entered in the ship's books. And now that the ship was out of the water, her standing officers and those few others attached were living in a hulk moored upstream of the dockyard, until she could be refloated.

The boatswain Mr Tangible and the carpenter Mr Adgett had followed Rennie to the dockyard gate, caught him up there, and vehemently complained about this arrangement.

'Why cannot we live decently ashore, sir?' demanded Mr Tangible.

'Surely a port hulk is decent enough these days?' Rennie, knowing the answer to that.

'I am not a man to complain, not in usual, but that damned hulk is intol'ble, sir. Rats, filth, the cook is senseless drunk, and her people bring whores into her at all hours, and – well – conduct themselves very licentious. It is altogether very hard for both Mr Adgett and myself.'

'Yes?' Glancing at Mr Adgett.

'Yes, sir, as I say.' Mr Adgett, nodding.

'Well well, we must see what can be done.'

'Thank you, sir.'

'Thank you, sir.'

'I shall say a word to the master attendant. He may know of lodgings—'

'I could save you that trouble, sir, if you please. We have

lodged at my sister's all the while the ship was in Ordinary, and would wish to go there now.' Mr Adgett.

'Y'didn't live aboard – at all?'

'We did *go* aboard her regular, sir.' Mr Tangible.

'By the by, where is the gunner? Where is Mr Storey?'

'He is presently ashore, sir.' Mr Adgett, nodding.

'Ashore? Where?'

'I believe he has took a room at the Pewter Inn, sir.'

'The Pewter! Good God.'

The Pewter Inn at the point was one of the most notorious dens in Portsmouth.

'It is under new management, sir.' Mr Tangible, hastily. 'The prev'ous landlord was took by the Revenue. The Pewter is altogether more respectable now, sir.'

'What you are saying to me is that none of you lived aboard *Expedient*, when ye've been paid to do so by the Board all these months, as her warranted standing officers. Hey?'

'Not – at night, sir. Only at certain other times.' Mr Tangible.

'During the day.' Mr Adgett. 'As I say, sir, we thought it prudent to be present when the assigned artificers was aboard, but we—'

'Christ's blood, gentlemen.' Rennie, very severe. 'The artificers are paid by the commissioner to move from ship to ship as required by tendered reports of inspection. Their place is not in a particular ship, but in any ship in need of running repair. Your place, as required by the Navy Board, is in your ship, at all times. Pray do not interrupt me, Mr Adgett.' Holding up a hand. 'Y'will both of ye kindly attend to your responsibilities now by remaining in the hulk, until *Expedient* is refloated. You will then live in the ship. I will find Mr Storey at the point, and say so to him. Should any of you wish to go out of *Expedient* for *any reason*, you will seek my express permission. Do I make myself plain?'

The two standing officers straightened their backs.

'Yes, sir.'

'Yes, sir.'

'Very well. Good day.' Turning abruptly on his heel and marching out through the gates.

There was a note waiting for Rennie when he returned to the Marine Hotel from a fruitless trip to the point to find his gunner. Would Captain Rennie attend upon the port admiral at his earliest convenience?

Rennie went to the port admiral's office. Admiral Hapgood greeted him with the bleak grimace that in that officer was the warmest attempt at welcome he was capable of making. His beetling brow and forbidding features did not disguise a gentler, pleasanter man. They reflected exactly his character and attitudes. He was known widely and sardonically in the service as 'Happy' Hapgood.

'Captain Rennie.'

'Good morning, sir.'

'Do you know the whereabouts, sir, of Captain Hayter?'

'James Hayter? I have been expecting him to get into touch with me, you know, but he—'

'Why has not he done so?'

'I – I could not say, sir, for certain. I know that he accepted his commission in the *Eglantine*, 22, and that he was due to come here to Portsmouth to make her ready for the sea. However, I have been so caught up with my own commission that—'

'In little, y'don't know where he may be found?'

'Well, sir – I imagine that if he ain't here, he—'

'Imagine? It ain't my purpose to imagine, since I am not a fanciful man. Is he at home?'

Rennie had endured a difficult morning, and had to curb his tongue now. He replied, having taken a steadying breath:

'I do not know, sir. I expect so.'

'He don't reply to letters sent to him at home. Why not?'

'I do not know that neither, sir.' Politely, a slight lifting of the eyebrows.

'Ye've heard nothing from him then, yourself?'

'I have not, sir, no. My wife and I have come direct from Norfolk. I am hard at work refitting my own ship, and have had no time for anything else since we came to Portsmouth.'

'Captain Hayter was your first, was not he, in previous commissions?'

'He was, sir.'

'You know him well?'

'Aye, very well.'

'Then y'may go and find him, Captain Rennie.'

'Eh?'

'Go to Dorsetshire, without the loss of a moment, and bring him here, the fellow.'

A booming thud rattled the windows. The noon gun. Rennie glanced at the windows, took a moment to consider his best response, and:

'Sir – Admiral Hapgood. I cannot in all conscience, I think, ignore the wishes of Their Lordships and abandon my duty at Portsmouth.'

'You refuse, sir?' A beetling glare.

'It ain't my wish nor intention, sir, to refuse a direct order, but you must understand that—'

'Must? Must?'

'I mean that I hope you will understand me, sir, when I remind you—'

'Y'may remind me of nothing, Rennie. Your first may undertake your duties while you are gone. That is quite usual in refitting ships, I believe.'

'With respect, sir, my first ain't here.'

'Not here? Why not? Who is he?' Rapped out.

'Lieutenant Makepeace, sir. He is on his way to us, and should be—'

'Who is your second, then? He will do.'

'Lieutenant Merriman Leigh, sir. He is not here, neither. Nor is my third, Mr Souter.'

'*None* of your officers is at Portsmouth?'

'No, sir. They—'

'Your standing officers are present, I hope? Are they?'

'Yes, sir.' Confidently.

In addition to Mr Tangible, Mr Adgett and Mr Trent, and the elusive gunner Mr Storey, the ship's newly appointed cook, Allway Swallow, had appeared with his dunnage and gone aboard the hulk only yesterday.

'Then they may reasonably undertake the work, governed by your master.' A nod, a grimace.

Expedient's sailing master, Mr Loftus, had yet to join the ship. Rennie said so to Admiral Hapgood, who:

'*Expedient* is damned odd for a commissioned ship, Captain Rennie. I have yet to receive your final instructions from Whitehall. Your officers are not here. Everything about her is wanting in purpose and compliance. Are your people assembled, and placed on her books?'

'Not quite yet, sir.'

'Then she ain't ready for sea, won't be for some little while, and will not be greatly disadvantaged by your absence. Y'will go to Dorset, remind Captain Hayter of *his* duty, and bring him forthwith to Portsmouth.'

'Very good, sir. May I have that wrote out?'

'Wrote out? Ain't it plain?'

'Oh, indeed it is, sir. But I will like to have something in writing to show to James Hayter. If you please.'

'Very well, very well.' Lifting his voice: 'Pell! Pell, there!'

And when his clerk had come he dictated the letter. Presently Rennie returned to the hotel, and his wife helped him to pack a valise. As a naval wife she was used to absence; however:

'Why don't the admiral send a letter, William?' Folding a shirt.

'He has sent letters. James has not replied.'

'Then why don't he send a paid messenger?' Handing him his small shaving glass.

'My darling Sylvia, I do not wish to go away from you, but go I must.'

'How long will you be gone?'

'A few days at most.'

'I shall miss you.' Kissing his cheek.

'And I you.' Fondly turning.

*

A twilight hush had fallen across the paved forecourt at Birch Cottage as Captain Rennie drove down from the road in his hired gig. The trees surrounding the house had become shadows, and those shadows were now fading into darkness. The first stars stood in the clear pale sky above the chimneys, and the air was chill. The hush became melancholy silence, broken only by the horse's hooves. Rennie drew up, and sat quiet a moment before descending. The sweet pink-pink of a last blackbird echoed across the front of the house, and the grey outline of the roof absorbed the sound. A breath of blossom floated. Rennie shivered.

He could not see a light in the house, and for a minute or two he wondered if he had not come to the wrong address. He had hired the gig at Blandford in the afternoon, driven south to Winterbourne, and enquired in the village for Birch Cottage. He had been given directions by a boy, and – thought Rennie – strange looks. He had told himself that very probably all visitors were treated with suspicion in these remote rural districts, and had put the strange looks from his mind.

'Should I knock?' Murmured to himself. 'If it is the wrong house perhaps they will take it ill . . .'

Then his sea officer's sense of purpose asserted itself, he stepped down and strode to the door, and lifted the knocker. As he was about to let it fall the door was opened, Rennie stepped back in surprise, and a fan of light spilled out.

'Who is it? Is that you, Dr Harkness?' A woman's voice, young and untutored.

'No, it ain't.' Rennie stepped into the light and removed his hat so that his face might be plainly seen.

'Oh. Sir.' The maidservant, startled, lifting a candle-holder.

'I am Captain Rennie, come from Portsmouth to see Captain Hayter. May I come in?'

'The house is quarantined, sir. I fear that—'

'Who is it, Mary?' A man's voice, James Hayter's voice. 'James?'

And now James came forward into the glow of the light.

'Good heaven, sir. It is you, I thought I heard your voice.' He stepped past the girl. 'I will just take the light, Mary. Return to the kitchen.' Standing now in the doorway: 'I fear I must turn you away, sir. We are quarantined here.'

'I see.' Rennie thought that his friend looked gaunt and thin in the candlelight, and older than his years. 'Is it fever? You have had fever in the house?'

'Yes. Yes. Fever.' A single nod.

'I am very sorry, my dear James. Had I known in course I should not have come.' Looking into his face. 'Is Catherine—'

'Catherine is – she is recovered, a little. A bad bout, you know, but she will come back from it.'

'I am very sorry. Had I known—'

'You could not know, sir.'

'And your boy Rondo?'

'We have lost him.'

'Christ Jesu . . .'

'He died very quick, very sudden, when we had thought . . .'

'My dear James. You poor fellow. I deeply regret intruding on your grief—'

'No, sir, do not apologise. I can guess why you have come. I have not replied to the letters, and you have come as an emissary of Their Lordships.'

'Well, not quite. The port admiral.'

'Admiral Hapgood?'

'Aye.'

'And you have another letter from him?'

'I have, yes.' Bringing the sealed letter from the pocket of his coat.

James hesitated a moment, standing in the doorway, then he came to a decision. Standing aside:

'Sir, if you will take a risk – and I must iterate, there is a small risk still – I will like you to come in, and sit with me a minute or two in the library. I have not suffered from the fever myself, nor have any of the servants, and the library is in least warm – warmer than standing out here in the night air.'

'Thank you, James. Then I will come in.'

He followed James into the library, where a fire glowed in the grate and the air was pleasantly temperate after the chill of the paved forecourt. James poured Madeira, stoppered the blue decanter, and the two men sat before the fire. Rennie gave his friend Admiral Hapgood's letter. James read it through quickly, then put it aside.

'I cannot go there, now.'

'No, no, you must stay here until Catherine is better, in course.'

'I mean – I cannot take up the commission.' Glancing at Rennie briefly, then staring into the fire.

'Not take it up, James . . . ?'

'It means nothing to me now, d'y'see? I have lost my only son . . . and Catherine will not wholly recover before the summer. Dr Harkness is of the opinion that she may never get back all of her former strength. So you see – I cannot possibly go away.'

'In course that is how you feel, just at present. It is entirely natural that you should. You have suffered a terrible loss, a dreadful loss, and Catherine must now be your first concern. But in a few weeks—'

'I shall not go back.' James turned his glance again on Rennie. 'I have made my decision.'

'Well well, I will not press you now, my dear James. Not at present.'

They sat mute for several minutes, and drank their wine, each buried in his own thoughts. The fire whispered and settled, and occasionally sighed as a flame flared up, and the glow flickered across their faces. At last, James:

'I cannot erase it from my mind . . .'

'Nay, James, do not speak of it now, when it is so painful to you.' Rennie, thinking to aid his friend by enjoining his silence.

'No – I wish to speak of it. I have not spoke with anyone but Harkness in many days – and he is a busy fellow, with other duties, and has not time to listen.'

'Then – I am here.'

'It is the sound . . . the sound in my head.' Quietly.

'Sound?'

'The sound of a handful of earth, falling on the lid of the coffin. Just a brief rattle, you know, a light sprinkling rattle – and yet it echoes in my head like a horrible thunderclap – over and over again. I cannot rid myself of it.'

'It will pass, in time.' Not knowing what else to say.

'Often, you know, I fear that I shall go mad. It is there every day, all the time.'

'Perhaps your physician could give you a potion—'

'I asked him for something to aid sleep. It provoked a worsening of the sound – crash, crash, crash, in my head. I cannot rest, I cannot find a moment's respite but the damned abominable noise returns.'

'You have been under a great strain. Your nerves are frayed.'

'Nerves? Hah!' Bitterly.

Rennie looked across at his friend, took a quick, deep breath, nodded, and:

'Listen now, James. I will speak, after all. The moment

Catherine is well enough you must take her to your father's house at Shaftesbury, and then come on to Portsmouth and take up your duty of getting *Eglantine* ready for the sea. That is the cure, James. That must be your course—'

'No! Will no one listen to me, in God's name! I am not fit to command! I have turned my back on the sea for ever!' Vehemently, standing up and walking away from the fire.

Shocked into silence Rennie stared at his friend's back, at the tensed shoulders and rigid neck, and saw a man at breaking point. At length:

'You are not yourself, James. I shall go away now to the inn in the village, and return on the morrow.'

He put down his glass, and stood up. James now faced him again, and lifted a hand to his head to push back a lock of hair.

'I beg your pardon, sir, I shouted at you. You will return to Portsmouth, did y'say? Tomorrow?'

'Nay, I shall return here, to Birch Cottage.'

'Ah. Yes?' Distractedly.

'Yes, indeed.'

'Well, as you wish. I will – I must go to Catherine now, and see if she needs anything.'

'Of course, very good. I'll see myself out, James.'

'Thank you, sir.'

And James left the room, with a half-turning, sidelong glance as he reached the door and went out.

Rennie stood still a moment, in genuine dismay. 'The poor fellow.' He shook his head. 'Poor dear fellow.'

*

'No, sir, I could not persuade him.'

'Persuade him?' Admiral Hapgood was contemptuous. 'I did not ask you to persuade him, Captain Rennie. I gave you an order to bring him back.'

'He would not come.'

'He read the letter? You are certain he read it?' Admiral Hapgood stood at the window, and looked bleakly at the world.

'He read it in my presence.'

'It is beyond reason.' Returning to his desk. 'What is the matter with him? Has he gone mad?'

This was so nearly the truth that Rennie was obliged to look away lest his eyes betray him.

'I – I do not believe that he has, sir, no. As I have said, his family—'

'Yes, yes, fever.' Over him. 'He lost a son, and his wife was ill. Such things are not uncommon in England, Captain Rennie. Typhus is a curse everywhere, from time to time. But good heaven, sea officers of all men must face these things and continue to do their duty. We cannot allow private difficulty to interrupt the king's service.'

'I am very sorry, sir, but Captain Hayter has made his decision. Naturally, I attempted to dissuade him. He is my valued friend, and we have sailed three hazardous commissions together. Nobody could more greatly regret his departure from the service than myself, and I said so to him very sincere. However, he was adamant. It would have been ungentlemanlike to press him further, under the circumstances.'

'You think that, do you?'

'I do, sir.'

'Ungentlemanlike?'

'Just so.'

'You are a bloody fool, Rennie. You have allowed him to hoodwink and bamboozle you.'

'Eh?' Outraged.

'Self-approval is his fault, sir. Self-approval and damned self-pitying pride. Many men lose sons, sir. Life is fraught with such peril. But they do not then lie down to sulk and snivel in defeat. They lift up their heads, and behave manly, and courageous. That is how they may father other sons, and rise to their responsibilities.'

'Well, sir,' Rennie kept his temper, 'well, you was not there to see how hard the blow fell upon him. Men are not all the same—'

'Pish posh, Captain Rennie. You will like to make excuses for the fellow because he is your friend. His behaviour is very reprehensible, very foolish and weak.'

Tears of rage pricked Rennie's eyes, but he held himself in. The admiral grimaced and gave a furious sigh, throwing up his hands.

'However – if he will not return, he will not. I have done everything that is in my power to help him. I shall write to Their Lordships immediate. His ship will go to another officer.'

'I cannot argue with you, sir.' Rennie, angry and sad, conceding the inevitable.

The admiral looked at him, and in spite of his contempt for what Rennie's friend had done, he could not find it in him to blame Rennie any more. Rennie perhaps lacked certain qualities of imagination, but he had stood loyal by his friend, whose faults were not his own. The admiral relented.

'Very well, Captain Rennie. He is your friend, whatever his failings, and I will not like to say any more against him in your presence.'

'That is kind in you, sir.' Surprised.

'I am not kind, you know. I am merely trying to be – gentlemanlike.'

'It is the same thing, in a way – ain't it?'

'Hm. Perhaps.'

Rennie made his back straight, and:

'Good day to you, Admiral.'

'Good day, Captain Rennie.'

Rennie walked stiffly to the admiral's door, put on his hat thwartwise and settled it firm on his head. He went down the stair to the entrance, and out into sunlight and the sharp fragrances of the Portsmouth air: dung, tar, tide. He breathed them in, and was restored.

Captain Rennie had met his wife Sylvia on an overnight coach journey between Norwich and London. She was then Sylvia Townend, a naval widow, and he had been able to be of some service to her. They had later renewed their acquaintance at Porstmouth, where she was staying with her sister, and had grown fond of each other. There had then occurred – not by his making – a diversion of their paths. Subsequently, when he returned to his home at Middingham in Norfolk, Rennie learned that she was staying nearby, had at once sought her out and proposed, and had been accepted.

At first glance, seen together emerging from the Marine Hotel, or walking down the High, they did not make a very likely pair. Rennie was spare, his face and forehead were lined, he looked older than his thirty-six years, and could not be described as handsome. His wife was very comely, with a fine figure, and a hint of the voluptuous in her eyes and mouth; she chose her dresses and bonnets with care, and was always handsome in appearance. Had he not been dressed in the uniform of a senior post captain, Rennie could have been taken for a passed-over curate, or an ageing clerk, faded, desiccated, resigned to his lowly station, who had been permitted to walk beside the lady a few moments to acquaint her with minor parish business, or to convey a lawyer's message. Even in his naval coat he did not look like a man with near connection to his radiant companion. Closer scrutiny, however, revealed an intimacy of glance, and conversation, and confidence, that bespoke their condition of life. They were a loving couple.

When he returned to the Marine Hotel from the port admiral's office, Rennie went straightway to their rooms in the expectation of finding his wife.

She was not there, and Rennie was disappointed. He had missed her during the days of his absence in Dorsetshire, and there was much he wished to say to her. He had thought it prudent to make his report to Admiral Hapgood as soon as he returned to Portsmouth, and had accordingly gone straight from the George Hotel, where the coach had set down its passengers in the afternoon, and climbed the stair at the port admiral's office.

Now he set down his valise on the chair in the bedroom, gave a penny to the boy who had carried it up, and took off his coat. He called for an ewer of hot water, washed, and shifted into a clean shirt. Then he went downstairs to enquire about his wife.

'Mrs Hayter went out earlier today, sir.' The head porter.

'Ah. Ah. My wife did not say where she was going, did she, by any chance?'

'Not to me, sir, n-ho. Perhaps she may have said something to her maid . . . ?'

'My wife did not bring a maid with her from Norfolk.'

'Ah, yes, sir. Most ladies do travel with a maid, and it had quite escaped my memory that—'

'Yes yes, well well, never mind. I dare say I shall discover my wife's whereabouts before long.'

'You are going out yourself now, sir?'

'Yes, I am. I have much to attend to at the dockyard.'

'And if Mrs Hayter should return whiles you are absent, sir, shall I say that—'

'I will just write a note to her, and leave it with you.'

Rennie scribbled the note in pencil, folded it and left it with the porter, and went away to the dockyard. When he returned in the evening he found Sylvia there, and was more profoundly glad and relieved than he had expected. The visit to Dorset had affected him deeply, and he was grateful not simply to be reunited with his wife, but for his untroubled and purposeful life, aided and shored up by her love.

We are such fragile creatures, you know, my love.' Holding her.

What do you mean, William?' Curiously, pulling back her head a little to look into his eyes.

And he told her about his friend's loss.

THREE

Weeks had passed, *Expedient* was now refloated, rerigged and stored, her boats had been got into her, and her guns, and she had been trimmed. And now most of her people – her required complement of 260 souls, as per the scheme attached to Rennie's commission – had been put on her books.

As in a previous commission her people had not been gathered by Captain Rennie's efforts of recruitment, nor those of his officers, but had been – as it were – produced out of a hat. Tom Makepeace, Rennie's erstwhile second lieutenant, now his first, said to his captain:

'I don't know where the order came from, sir, or how it was managed, but they have come here, all properly provided with conduct money, a few dozen at a time, from Woolwich and Deptford and Chatham, all along the estuary – and assembled at the Marine Barracks here at Portsmouth, all within a week or two.'

'Are there any Expedients among them, Tom?' Meaning, were any of the gathered men former members of the ship's crew.

'Not that I have been able to discover, sir. All of them are faces new to me. But in course I was not with you on the Jamaica cruise.' Referring to *Expedient*'s second commission, when by a muddle of communication he had been left behind.

'I am nearly certain that none of them has served with me before.' Rennie, a sniff. 'No, a person behind has arranged this crew for us.'

'A person behind, sir?' Puzzled. 'D'y'mean, at the Admiralty?'

'No no, not exact, Tom, not exact. Never mind, they are right seamen, by the look, and they will do. Must do, we have no more time.'

Since gaining this commission Rennie had been puzzled by other things. At first there had been a certain urgency about it, and he had come to Portsmouth full of bustling energy. Then there had been the inevitable delays of bringing a ship out of Ordinary, examining and refitting her, &c., then a curious hiatus while he waited, and the port admiral waited, for his final instructions, his sailing instructions, to be delivered from the Admiralty in London.

Rennie knew only what had been mentioned in his preliminary instructions. That *Expedient* was to make a general survey of the coast of France. No other details had been vouchsafed him. Why not? He had enquired at the port admiral's office. Admiral Hapgood had shaken his head in pretended misunderstanding:

'Ain't the word plain to you, Captain Rennie?'

'If you mean—'

'Survey, sir. Survey.'

'Aye, sir, it is plain enough I suppose. But nothing else is plain.'

'What else should be made plain?'

'I was once required to make such a survey of Jamaica, you know, but in the end the duty was quite other.'

'Eh? Other?'

'Well well, I should not speak of – it is of no matter, sir. All I meant was that I wish to understand whether or no I am to be thrust into something other than a duty of survey, now.'

'Thrust? Other? I do not understand you, Captain Rennie. If I was you, sir, I should do exactly as I was told. When your sailing instructions arrive, I will tell you. Good day to you.'

'Yes, sir. Thank you.' Coming away entirely unenlightened.

* * *

Rennie's two junior lieutenants had joined the ship. Lieutenant Merriman Leigh, RN, was a pleasant fair-haired young man from Suffolk. He was the youngest son of a retired admiral, and both of his brothers were in the service. Lieutenant Leigh had not spent more than a month or two on the beach in the last several years, due to family interest. His last commission had been as fifth in the *Caesar*, 74, in the Channel Fleet. In all his service he had managed to avoid duty in West Indies, where three of his former middy shipmates had died of yellowjack. It was clear to Rennie that his second was a man protected, destined for high things in his future.

His third was Lieutenant Renfrew Souter, RN, a Scot from the Borders. Rennie was not quite sure about Mr Souter. He was a taciturn young man of one-and-twenty, with auburn hair and a certain dourness of demeanour. He had until now been without a commission, having passed his Board two years ago, and lived at home on half-pay ever since. Certainly Rennie had Mr Souter's papers, with details of his service as a midshipman, but he knew nothing else about him, and decided to ask. He sent for him.

In the great cabin, in the smell of new paint:

'Mr Souter, thank you for attending so prompt.'

Mr Souter stood very correct, back straight, hat under his arm, the buttons of his undress coat gleaming clean.

'Sit down, Mr Souter, sit down. I wished to speak to you informal, so to say, and since we have not yet begun to give dinners in the ship, I felt this was our best opportunity. Will you drink a glass of wine?'

Thank you, sir, I do not take alcohol.' Sitting down opposite Rennie at the cabin table.

'Not? Ah.'

Light glanced and danced on the deckhead timbers, dazzling through the stern gallery windows as the ship eased on her mooring cables.

Rennie sniffed in a breath, and:

'Now then, Mr Souter. Tell me something of your experience of the sea, will you?'

'D'ye mean when I passed my Board, sir?'

'No no, I meant – your time in ships. Your experience in ships.'

'D'ye mean generally, sir? Or d'ye wish to know about particular ships?'

Was he being deliberately dense? wondered Rennie. The brogue was not obtrusive, but there was a disconcerting austerity of pronunciation. Rennie felt in need of refreshment before he tried again. Only yesterday his former steward had returned destitute and in rags to the ship, and Rennie had not had the heart to turn him away. He summoned him now:

'Cutton! Colley Cutton!'

His steward appeared. His appearance had been transformed. He was fresh-shaved, his hair had been combed flat, his shirt was clean, and his breeches – and he was carrying something in a wicker basket.

'Bring me a bottle of Madeira wine.'

'Yes, sir.'

'What is in that basket?'

'It is a person of your acquaintance, sir.'

'A person of my—'

A plaintive miaow from the basket.

'Good God.'

The steward placed the basket on the decking canvas, and opened the lid. A small, delicate creature, all black but for a patch of white over one eye, jumped out on the squares, and fell to cleaning its fur with quick nodding movements of its head.

'Dulcie.' Rennie, in delighted astonishment. 'I thought she was lost after our last commission.'

'Mr Adgett found her, sir, and has kept her fed, like.'

'Mr Adgett? Why did not he say something to me?'

'Don't know, sir.'

'Well well, no matter. She is here, she is restored to me.'
Adopting a soft, ingratiating tone: 'Dulcie . . . Dulcie . . .'

The cat ignored him.

'. . . Dulcie . . . ?'

The cat stood, stretched, padded away to the stern gallery
windows, sprang up easily on the bench, curled up in the
corner and shut herself away in sleep.

'She don't know me . . .' Rennie, chagrined.

'Hit will take her a day or two to come round to you, sir,
I expeck.'

'Come round to me?'

'Well, sir, cats is very particular about neglect. They do
not like it.'

'Damnation, how am I guilty of neglect? I believed the
creature lost. I wished to take her home with me, but she had
disappeared. What was I to do?'

'No, sir, yes . . . but she don't ezackly see it in the same
hillustration, sir. As a cat.'

'Ah? Does she not? Ah. Madeira, Cutton. Jump, now.' A
breath. 'Mr Souter, I beg your pardon. Where were we,
exact?'

*

A further week, and *Expedient* was ready for the sea, except
in one – vital – component part. She lacked a surgeon.

In her first three commissions *Expedient*'s doctor had been
Thomas Wing, the diminutive disciple of Dr Stroud of the
Haslar Hospital at Gosport. Rennie had liked Thomas Wing
from their first acquaintance, when he came into the ship as
surgeon's mate, and had come to know him, and trust him,
better than almost any other man on board. Now, in spite
of letters, and other urgent enquiry, Dr Wing could not be
found.

Rennie had tried at Gosport, making two journeys there
to consult Dr Stroud as to Thomas Wing's whereabouts.

'He ain't here, Captain Rennie,' Dr Stroud had told him, on the first occasion. 'I have heard nothing from him these last few months. Has he gone abroad, I wonder?'

'Abroad? Why should he go abroad?'

'He has been abroad with you, has not he?' Mildly.

'I do not know that I would call attachment to a ship "going abroad", you know. He was my warranted surgeon, and extremely valuable to me.'

'May not he have become attached to another ship?'

'In the Royal Navy, d'y'mean? No no, I should certainly have heard of it. We had always agreed between us that he would come with me in any subsequent commission. He would not desert me, I am certain.'

'He would have to gain the appointment to you by warrant, though, wouldn't he? From the Sick and Hurt?'

'Yes yes, Doctor, but that in course is a mere formality.'

Rennie had fretted, written further letters, and grown anxious that Wing had been lost to *Expedient* now, and that he would have to ask for another, inferior, man.

'Perhaps he has died, sir,' suggested Lieutenant Makepeace.

'Died?' A fierce glare.

'Men do die, sir, after all. Just because Thomas is a doctor – albeit a very fine one – don't mean that he is immune to—'

'That will do, Mr Makepeace.'

'I merely suggested it as a possibility, sir, that—'

'Be quiet, sir!'

The day following that conversation with Lieutenant Makepeace, Rennie had formally requested another surgeon for his ship. And on that same day, shortly after the noon gun, Dr Wing appeared. He had himself rowed out to the mooring by a ferryman, and brought his dunnage aboard. Rennie, working on innumerable vexing lists in the great cabin, was informed of his arrival, and at once went on deck.

'Dr Wing! Thomas!'

'Captain Rennie!'

They shook hands warmly.

'You got my letters, then? I had thought—'

'Eh? Letters? No. I heard nothing about the new commission until I came to Portsmouth late yesternight. And naturally – faithful to our understanding – I have rejoined the ship.'

'You had received none of my communications? Nothing came to your London address?'

'My dear Captain Rennie, I have not been in London since last year.'

'Not in London? Oh.'

'No, I have been – elsewhere, on private business.'

'Private, hey? Are you wed, Thomas?'

'Matrimony was no part of the matter. The farthest thing from my thoughts.'

'Well well, I will not pry into your private affairs, Thomas. Let us get ye berthed, and so forth, and your dunnage stowed.'

'Thank you, sir. I . . .' Hesitating.

'Yes, Doctor?'

'I am not in possession of my papers, I fear. That is, I was so taken up with the business just mentioned that I thought of little else, and I have come to the ship without any official—'

'Pish pish, Thomas. A mere formality. I know who you are, good God, and that is all that's required for me to put you on my books.' Quite forgetting the formal request he had made for another man. 'When you have settled in comfortable, come to the cabin, will ye?'

Later, in the great cabin, as they drank tea together, Dr Wing:

'I see that you are inundated with documents, sir.'

'That is the price we pay for going to sea, alas. Every last nail and length of twine must be entered, checked and signed for, and—'

'Surely that is your clerk's work, ain't it?'

'Alan Dobie, d'y'mean?'

'That is his name. I had forgot it. Alan Dobie. Yes.'

'Well, Dobie was my clerk in *Expedient*, yes. But then he joined John Company as a clerk when we paid off our last commission, and was sent away to India. I have not been able to find a comparable man to replace him.'

'May I interpolate?'

'Eh?'

Dr Wing, with the careful enunciation of the autodidact: 'May I make a suggestion as to his replacement?'

'You, Doctor?' Rennie raised his eyebrows.

'I would not wish to overreach myself, sir, but I believe I do know of a person that would suit.'

'As my clerk?'

'Indeed, sir, as your clerk.'

'Well well . . . who is this "person", Thomas?'

A knock at the cabin door. Rennie frowned, and:

'Cutton! Cutton, there! See who that is, will you.'

A further knock, and Colley Cutton came hurrying from his spirit kettle in the quarter gallery, and opened the slatted door.

Mr Loftus, the sailing master, stood waiting. Rennie beckoned him in:

'Come in, come in, Mr Loftus. Look who is here.'

'Why, good heaven, it is Dr Wing! I am right glad to see you, Thomas!' Dr Wing rose from his chair and was little taller than when he had been seated, but he wished to shake hands. Mr Loftus came to the table and pumped the surgeon's hand with enthusiasm. 'Right glad, indeed.'

'You wished to see me, Mr Loftus?' Rennie, when the greetings had been dispensed with.

'Yes, sir. There has been a late delivery of casks by a hoy. I am not entirely certain where they may be stowed.'

'What casks? I know of nothing that has not been stowed days since.' Rennie, getting up on his legs.

'Beer, sir. And a hogshead of wine.'

'No no, Mr Loftus.' Coming round the table, his coat

brushing and dislodging sheafs of lists, which now tipped
and scattered on the canvas squares. 'The hoy has clearly
mistook us for another ship. We have our full allowance of
beer—'

'These are not part of our allowance, sir.' Over him. 'They
are by way of being a – a gift to the ship.'

'Gift! Whose gift, Mr Loftus?'

'Mine, sir,' said James Hayter, and he walked into the
cabin, removing his hat.

Hours passed before Rennie was able to speak to James alone
– as he knew that he must. Quite apart from his lists, and
his interrupted and now postponed conversation with Dr
Wing, Rennie had to deal with a great many minor exi-
gencies in the ship. One of the six lately arrived midshipmen
had fallen ill, and had to be taken off in a boat to the Haslar
at Gosport. Three seamen, absent without leave from the
ship, had returned drunk in a stolen boat with three young
women, and been discovered *in flagrante* in the forepeak. Mr
Trent complained that half a tier of salted pork was spoiled,
and wished to have it replaced as a matter of urgency. The
boatswain Mr Tangible was unhappy that he had not received
his full allowance of Stockholm tar, &c., &c. Without saying
so to James, and with a heavy heart, Rennie had ordered the
hoy to stand away, taking the beer and wine with her. And
at last he returned to the great cabin, having allowed all of
these matters to occupy him until the sun was low in the
west, when he could avoid the interview no longer.

'My dear James, I do beg your pardon for leaving you
alone so long. So many damned distractions, you know, for
a commanding officer awaiting his sailing instructions.'
Bustling into the great cabin, removing his hat, striding to
the table and glancing briefly and purposefully at his lists.

'There is no need for apology, sir.' James, rising from his
chair. 'I came uninvited aboard, after all, and took you by
surprise. It is I that—'

'Has Cutton looked after you?' Tapping a list. 'No, that has not been done. Damnation.' Distractedly, then: 'Has he given you wine, and a biscuit?'

'Thank you, sir, I wanted nothing.'

Looking up from the lists: 'He did not bring you wine, the wretch? I'll soon—'

'Nay, sir, nay, he is not at fault. I did not want anything, and said so to him.'

'Ah. Oh. Very good. Sit, sit, dear fellow. Will you drink a glass of wine now? Say that you will, a glass of wine with me – hey?'

'Thank you, sir, then I will.'

As they waited for Cutton to bring the wine, Rennie cleared his throat, and:

'I may as well say at once, James . . . I had to send the hoy away, you know.'

'Send it away?'

'It was generous kind in you, James, to think of giving us such a quantity of beer – and wine, indeed – but the plain fact is that we are fully stored, and the ship trimmed for sea. Mr Loftus was very unhappy with me, and I could not—'

'Bernard Loftus objected?' James, surprised. 'He seemed pleased enough when I came aboard.'

'Yes, did he? Well well, that was before the other trouble, about the tiers of pork. It is all a question of trimming the ship, as I'm sure you will grasp – as a sea officer.'

'In course, sir. I do see that, now.'

'Hm. Hm. – Ah!' With relief, as Cutton brought their wine on a tray.

'Yes, I . . .' Pouring wine. 'I had been promised – or rather, Mr Trent and the cook had been promised – fresh meat, d'y'see. But there was an interruption about that ashore, and then the trouble about the spoiled casks of pork . . . Well well, y'don't want to hear all these irksome things, James, when ye've come aboard as a guest. Let us be convivial over our wine.' Handing him a glass. 'Your health.'

'Your health, sir. In truth, I had hoped to discuss with you—'

'How is Catherine? That is a question I should have asked at once, good God. How is she?'

'She is much better, thank you, sir. Nearly restored to full health, and staying at Melton House with my mother.'

'That is excellent good news, excellent. I am so very glad, James.'

'Thank you, sir. May I – may I come to the matter which brought me to the ship, sir?'

'In course, in course – by all means.' Dreading the next few minutes.

'I am come to ask a very great kindness of you, a very great favour . . .'

'Go on.'

Putting down his glass: 'As you know, I did not take up my commission in the *Eglantine* sloop. She has gone to another officer now, Captain Edward Semple.'

'Yes – I had heard.'

'Subsequent to that decision, which I now deeply regret, and consequent on it – I am left on the beach.'

'Yes – on the beach.' A sympathetic nod, disguising great discomfort.

'Therefore, sir, I am come here to ask if you will intercede with Their Lordships on my behalf, and take me again as your first.'

'Indeed. Indeed. I had thought as much. I knew it as soon as you came aboard.' A wry grimace, an apologetic nod. 'I cannot pretend I did not.'

'Then – you are willing to consider—'

Holding up a hand: 'James, before you say any more, my dear friend, I must tell you that it cannot be so.'

'Cannot . . . ?'

Both hands laid flat on the table. A deep sniff. 'Nay, nay, it cannot. You are master and commander, now. Your rank prevents it, leave alone any other consideration. I am very sorry, James, but there it is.'

James looked away a moment, himself took a deep breath, and then leaned forward: 'Sir, I think you know me very well, and understand me. I was foolish to have declined the *Eglantine*, and greatly regret having done so. The world looked very dark, and I could not see beyond my own grief and despair. But that is not the man I am. I am a sea officer, to the marrow of my bones, and I think a good and brave one. As are you.' A breath, then: 'As one sea officer to another, I ask this of you. As a trusted friend I ask it. Intercede in my behalf, and ask that an exception be made. Give me this chance to save my career. Will you?'

*

Rennie returned to the Hard in his launch, as he had done every evening since the ship had been refloated and given her mooring number. Until his instructions came he was determined to live ashore with his wife, even if his people were obliged to live aboard. James had already departed in his hired boat. Rennie had come on deck to see him go down the ladder. It had been very painful for Rennie to turn him out of the ship, and James had been very subdued as he stepped over the thwarts into the stern-sheets of the boat. He did not again look up at the rail, nor did he even lift a hand in farewell as the boatman pulled away from the side.

Rennie told his wife the story, concluding:

'I fear it may be the end of our friendship.'

'I have never met your friend, William, but you have so often spoke of him that I feel I do know him. I don't think he will wish to turn his back on you. I don't think he is that kind of man.'

'I have turned my back on him, have not I, my dear?'

'You have not, you have not. You told him the truth. It was the honourable thing to do, the only thing to do.'

'Aye, it was.' A sigh. 'I know it – and yet I feel so damned guilty, all the same. I refused his gift of beer and wine. I turned him out of the ship. The poor fellow, after all he has endured . . .'

'But that was none of your doing, William. You did your best for him in going to Dorsetshire, and begging him to return.'

'Yes, yes, I know – but to see him sitting so quiet in that damned boat, knowing that in all likelihood his career in the navy was finished . . .'

'William, it was not your fault.' Earnestly, looking into his face, her hand on his.

'I wish with all my heart I could have said to him: "In course, James, we'll simply ignore your new rank. I will send away my third – a fellow I don't much like, anyway and ask Tom Makepeace to go down to second, and my second to third, and give you back your old berth. We will stow your dunnage and drink a glass of wine on your reappointment." I wish that I could have, but I could not. Their Lordships would never permit it, under any circumstances, and it would be entirely foolish to entertain the notion that they would. It was made clear to me when I returned from Dorset that James was to be froze out. I could do nothing at all for him. Nothing.'

'It was not your fault.' Gently.

'You are right.' Kissing her cheek. 'You are right.' A moment, and: 'He asked if he might come into the ship as a supernumerary, and reminded me that he had took me into the *Hawk* cutter when he commanded her. And again I was obliged to refuse. I could not ask my junior officers to be complicit in that kind of deceit. If discovered it could lead to court martial and disgrace. It is one thing to slip aboard a cutter in a civilian coat to chase smugglers up and down the Channel. It is quite another to go into a frigate, in plain defiance of Their Lordships, following on the deliberate refusal of your own command. No no—'

'William, my dear, I am going to forbid you to speak of it any more. Let us go down to the dining room, if you please, and eat our supper. I have ordered it.' Linking her arm with his.

'You have? What did you order?'

'We are to have broth, then fish, and then duckling.'

'Ah. Ah. Very good.'

'You are hungry?' A smile.

'To say the truth, I am. It has been a long and difficult day, and I am hungry, indeed.'

And he put away his guilt, and the pain of the afternoon, and went downstairs arm in arm with his wife.

But later as he lay abed Captain Rennie could not sleep. James Hayter's drawn, crestfallen face haunted him, and accused him, and he was ashamed of himself in the quiet dark.

FOUR

The wave, blue and undulating, rose to its riffling height and struck the cutwater as the ship pitched heeling into the wind. There was a solid thump of water against wood, and a shock of spray flew up white and fell in a cloud of glittering shards over the forecastle. The whole ship shuddered. The seaman clinging in the forechains as he attempted to swing the lead for a sounding streamed from head to foot. He shook himself, blew water from his nose and mouth, and tried again. Shoals lay close.

On the quarterdeck, close by the helmsman at the wheel, Lieutenant Makepeace lifted his voice against the wind, and:

'Keep your luff! Hold her so!'

Relayed from the forechains, the cry: 'Five fathom, pebble and shell!'

Tom Makepeace lifted his silver speaking trumpet. 'Stand by to tack ship!'

Thump, and again a shock of spray, and the sea frothed and hissed along the wales. Creaking timbers, and the groaning, gnarling, stretching complaint of shrouds, and stays, and braces. The slide of water along the deck, and the sluicing gush of scuppers as the ship lifted herself, and ran on.

'Weather braces!'

Feet slipping on the sloping deck. A midshipman vomiting over the lee rail.

'Lee braces haul through!'

Boom-thump, and a further storm of spray.

'Helm's a-lee! Fore sheet, foretop bowline, jib and stay-sail sheets – let go!' Bellowed.

The jib flapping and snapping emptily as the ship rolled and pitched closer to the wind.

'Off tacks and sheets!'

And as the ship came through the eye:

'Mainsail haul!'

Presently, shuddering and thrusting, streaming water and creaking in every part of her, the ship passed through the critical moments, and:

'Let go and haul!'

Foresails braced round, tacks and sheets trimmed. Broad canvas took the wind, bellied and filled, and the ship heeled true on her new heading.

At Lieutenant Makepeace's shoulder, another voice now:

'Very good, Mr Makepeace. Neatly done. Let us run right quick across to France, and show them how we handle ships in the Royal Navy.'

HMS *Expedient*, frigate, 36, with her full complement of 260 souls, ran close-hauled on the larboard tack, buffeted by a stiff easterly, across the white-flecked blue of the Channel toward the faint grey wandering line of the French coast.

Getting her to sea had not been a pleasure for Captain Rennie. It never was, he had reflected in the preceding days. His sailing instructions had failed to arrive, and in a quandary he had again called on Admiral Hapgood.

'You had better make use of the available time,' the port admiral had allowed.

'In what way, sir?'

'Weigh, and take her out. Ye've been idle at your mooring far too long.'

'Thank you, sir.' A relieved nod.

'I do not mean that you should follow your preliminary instructions in full, or anything like. Y'will put your people through their paces, so to say, and find out the ship's strengths.'

Rennie knew his ship's strengths perfectly well, and her weaknesses, but he did not say so to the admiral. He did say:

'How long may I keep the sea, sir?'

'No no, y'will not keep the sea at all, Captain Rennie. Take her out, run before the wind a board or two, then bring her about and return to your mooring. You apprehend me?'

'I would wish to exercise my great guns, sir, I think.'

'Yes yes, that is for you to say, and I will not interfere – except that you should not *fire* your guns. We must not waste powder.'

'Very good, sir.'

On the day following Rennie had been preparing to weigh when a boat came to the ship with a message. Would Captain Rennie kindly repair ashore, to the port admiral's office?

With great but concealed irritation Rennie did as he was asked. At the office he was introduced to a gentleman of thirty-five or -six, in a dark coat, very slim and neat in his appearance, and with what Rennie took at first for a diffident manner. He was introduced as Mr Brough Mappin.

'May I apologise, Captain Rennie, for inconveniencing you? Most kind of you to come here at such short notice.'

'Mr Mappin. How may I be of service, sir?'

'Service, yes. That is the word. I do seek a service.' Turning his head. 'I wonder, Admiral, if you will permit me a moment or two alone with Captain Rennie?'

'Eh?'

'A few minutes, if you would oblige me?'

'Hm. Very well. I shall – I shall go downstairs.' A beetling frown, and he moved to the door. 'Pell! Pell, where are you!' And as he trod down the stair: 'Pell, damn you, come here!'

Mr Mappin closed the door with a click of the lock, and motioned Rennie to a chair by the admiral's desk. The gesture, and the brief half-smile that accompanied it, revealed to Rennie the man behind the diffidence and apology. Here was a fellow accustomed to getting what he wanted.

'I will come direct to my point.' Mr Mappin sat down behind the desk, in Admiral Hapgood's chair. Rennie waited, his hat across his knee, in the chair opposite.

'Lieutenant Hayter is your friend, I think?'

'James Hayter? He is now master and commander, you know, and so is known as Captain Hayter. And yes, he is my friend. Why d'you ask?'

'I fear that he is again merely lieutenant. He accepted the sloop *Eglantine*, and then declined to go into her.'

'Yes, I know, but surely they would not—'

Over him: 'He never read his commission aboard, and thus refused quite deliberate to take up his duties. I am informed he could have been dismissed the service. Instead Their Lordships have decided to strip him of the rank of master and commander, and reduce him to lieutenant.'

'Good God, that is nearly unprecedented.'

'He came to you, did not he, and asked that you take him into your ship?'

'You are well informed, Mr Mappin. He did make that request. I was unable to grant his wish.'

'You would not take him, even as – I think you call it – supernumerary?'

Rennie took a breath. 'Mr Mappin, we in the navy are plain-spoke men. I ask that you come to your point, sir. If you please.'

'Yes, forgive me, you are right to chide.' The half-smile. 'I want you to take a supernumerary into your ship.'

Rennie looked at him again, and saw the same man sitting in his well-cut coat, but there was something new in his expression. A hardness had replaced the sudden little smile, and there was a new acuity in his gaze.

'Mr Mappin.' Politely. 'Will you tell me who you are?'

'By all means. I am a man in usual private, with private interests. On occasion I give advice, and assistance, in other circles. Government business.'

'Ahh. Hmm.' Rennie raised his eyebrows. 'I had heard

that Sir Robert had retired, after that unfortunate episode with the Excise. But I was doubtful, myself.'

'You have left me behind, Captain Rennie. Sir Robert? The Excise?'

'Come now, Mr Mappin. Sir Robert ain't a man to allow himself be bested by a pipsqueak like Major Braithwaite, that arrested him on a spurious charge, and then attempted to have him brought to his trial. No no. I don't think Sir Robert has retired quite yet. What say you?'

Mr Mappin tilted his neat head, and shook it. 'I do not know the gentleman . . .'

'Don't know Sir Robert Greer? Ha-ha, that is a capital joke. You work for him! Or in least by his side! Hey?'

'I do not.'

'Not? Hh-hh, I do not think you are being entirely fair to me, you know. I am not such a fool that I don't recognise the attitudes and tactics of the Fund.' An amused jerk of the head.

Mr Mappin brought one finger to his lips, left it there a brief moment, then withdrew it and leaned forward.

'Look here, now, Rennie. I don't know the fellow with whom you so confidently associate me. Nor have I any interest in, nor connection to, any bank or fund in the City. I am here on government business.'

'Yes?' A polite glance, and a nod.

Mr Mappin sat back in his chair. Again the finger to the lips. Again withdrawn.

'Perhaps I was misinformed, after all.' A little sigh. 'Disappointing.'

'What?'

Mr Mappin got up on his legs, and came round the desk. Standing before Rennie's chair:

'Your name was given to me as a reliable officer, that could be trusted to undertake whatever was required of him. I am not—'

'Y'said you wished me to take a supernumerary into my

ship. Since I am to go to France, or in least to the French coast, that can only mean a spy.'

'I have not said who, nor have I said—'

'Christ's blood, man!' Angrily rising. 'I am tired of men like you! Like Sir Robert Greer, and all his works at the Secret Service Fund! I have had more than my fill over the years of your schemes and deviousness and denials! Either tell me what you want, damn' quick, or I shall proceed to the Hard, go into my launch, and return to my ship. In least there I will be where I belong as a sea officer – an *honourable* calling!' Jamming on his thwart-wise hat.

This little display of naval ire had not been impeccably spontaneous. Rennie had wished to discomfit Mr Mappin, and show him that sea officers could not be intimidated. He also wished to make the fellow admit his connection to Sir Robert Greer. Mr Mappin, however, had not been dis-comfited in any way. He had waited for Rennie's tirade to cease, then mildly:

'Yes. The reason I mentioned Lieutenant Hayter to you was because, having refused to take him into your ship as supernumerary, I knew you would likely refuse to take anybody at all.'

'Then you was correct in that assumption.'

'Lieutenant Hayter was an embarrassment to you, was not he? He had behaved foolishly in refusing his own command, and then he came whining to you. What could be his role in—'

'I do not care to discuss that with you, nor with anyone! If you are attempting to make me take on my books some other person, by belittling Mr Hayter, I will not listen to you!'

'No? That is a pity.'

Rennie stood waiting, and Mr Mappin sat him out, until Rennie became uncomfortable. He knew that Mr Mappin very probably had the power to insist. At last:

'What good reason could you give to me, Mr Mappin? What is behind this? Spying? Hm?'

'If you will like to take off your hat, Captain Rennie, and sit down . . .'

Rennie stood silent a moment longer, then sniffed, pulled off his hat and sat down. Brusquely:

'Well?'

'Thank you.' The half-smile, and Mr Mappin turned his head briefly to the door. 'We must not deprive the admiral of his quarters longer than he would like.' Returning his gaze to Rennie. 'When your sailing instructions come, they will make no mention of any name. You are to say nothing of this meeting today to anyone, nor make any mention of an impending arrival. The day before your departure to survey the French coast, the person I have chosen will come to you. He will not appear until after dark. You will take him into your ship, and he will then tell you the reason behind this scheme.'

'D'y'mean that he will carry written orders?'

'I do not. Nothing is to be wrote out specific. Nothing. He will tell it to you.'

'Hm. Hm.' Rennie pursed his mouth, shook his head, sighed. 'Mr Mappin, ye've not told me who you are. Nor admitted who your masters are, though I am in no doubt you are acting upon their instruction. Ye've given to me no written orders. Ye've refused to divulge a single compelling reason why I should accommodate you in this.' A sniff. 'In the absence of a confirming document of some kind, from the Admiralty . . . I must say no to you.'

'Ah. Must you? Again, that's a pity.'

'For you, perhaps. Not for me, sir.' Rennie had again got up on his legs. Seeing that his bluff was not in fact going to be called, he then had no option but to leave Mr Mappin in the office and go downstairs. The admiral was not in the lower rooms, when Rennie glanced into them, nor was his clerk Pell.

With a shrug Rennie had stepped out into the air. He thought of James Hayter, and Mr Mappin's contempt for him, and now regretted that he had not taken James as supernumerary, even if only to thwart the bloody glib-talking little tailor's fop and his wretched requests. And there the matter had rested until Admiral Hapgood gave him permission to weigh and put to sea on *Expedient*'s brief shaking-out run.

When the French coast was clearly in view, Rennie took the con, and ordered that his ship be brought about, to run before the wind on the return to Portsmouth. Boats must be swung out and towed as part of the exercise. As the ship heeled true on the new heading:

'Mr Tangible!'

'Sir?' Attending.

'We will beat to quarters, and clear the ship for action!'

The boatswain lifted his call, and the piercing tones echoed across the deck. Immediate feverish activity. The rattle of the marine's drum. The thudding of many feet. Curses. From below, the crash and clatter of mallets as bulkheads were struck and stowed, and cabin furniture. Lieutenants and middies to their sections. Guncrews assembled. Powder and shot to hand. And now:

'Silence on deck!' Tom Makepeace.

The creaking of rigging, of bolt ropes and canvas, of timbers, and the sighing of the wind; the rinsing, rushing wash of the sea; the cries of seabirds high over the trucktops.

'Cast loose your guns!'

Tackles loosened, sponge rammers and handspikes laid ready.

'Level your guns!'

Quoins thrust in, and bedded.

'Out tompions!'

Red stoppers pulled out of muzzles, and dropped hanging on lanyards.

'Run out your guns!'

Crews at the tackles, heaving. Breeching ropes hauled through and bent.

'Prime!'

Priming wires thrust down vents and cartridges pierced. Horns tipped by gun captains and fine grain poured. Pans primed.

'Point your guns!'

Gun captains kneeling at flintlocks and sighting.

'Larboard battery – FIRE!'

BANG BANG-BANG-BOOM BANG-BOOM
BANG BANG.

The eighteen-pounders.

THUD THUD THUD THUD

The thirty-two-pound carronades.

Shuddering timbers. Whirling clouds of smoke and grit along the deck, and ballooning from the ship's side. Explosions of spray to the south as roundshot smashed heavy into waves.

'Reload!'

'We are ragged, Mr Makepeace. Very ragged.' Captain Rennie paced aft to the tafferel, turned and paced forrard to the wheel, the great shadow of the mizzen and driver falling on the deck as the ship heeled.

A few moments more. Frenzied activity. Shouts. A dropped bucket of sand.

'Larboard battery ready, sir!'

'And slow.'

'Yes, sir – the guncrews have had very little practice as yet.'

'Hm. I have disobeyed the port admiral in firing my great guns, Mr Makepeace. But as a commander at sea I felt it my duty to give the people a whiff of powder. Nothing like the stink of powder to sharpen a crew. Sharpen us all. We will not fire the great guns again, but we will continue to exercise them, until we are fit to call ourselves a fighting ship.' His hand to a back stay as the ship butted into a sudden lifting wave. 'Pray proceed.'

'Very good, sir.' His hat off and on, and he faced forrard to raise his speaking trumpet. Light flashing on silver. The shadow of a rope striping his face.

'Silence on deck!'

*

As he came ashore in his boat at the Hard, Captain Rennie saw a familiar tall figure emerge from the dockyard gates.

Jumping ashore, wetting his shoes: 'Langton!'

The figure hesitated, turned, and began walking rapidly and diagonally away down the wide expanse, toward a boat at the eastern end.

'Captain Langton!' Waving. The figure took no notice. Rennie nodded to the midshipman in charge of his launch, and hurried across the Hard in pursuit of the retreating figure. He nearly tripped on a wheel rut, staggered, and feeling a fool hurried on, raising a hand then lowering it abruptly. Would not the fellow stop, good heaven?

'Langton!'

At last, puffing and sweating, Rennie did catch him up, and an embarrassed Captain Langton was obliged to turn and acknowledge his fellow officer.

'Ah. It's you, Rennie. I thought it was some drunken fellow calling out.'

'Drunken fellow . . . no no, ha-ha, no no. I had wanted – that is, I had meant to seek you out before this, you know, and—'

'Everything was explained.' Over him. 'It was all told to me, the whole thing.'

'Ah. Ah. Very good. Then . . . ?'

'So in course there is no need for you yourself to explain it. Now.'

'Well well, I had thought, you know, that it would – that it would sound clearer, and better, coming direct from me, d'y'see.'

'Yes? Did you? I expect so.'

'I can see that you are still angry with me.'

'Angry? Nay, I am not. You acted as you did because you were under an obligation to do so. It was all explained to me, some time since, as I've said.'

The difficulty between them had arisen when Rennie – required to do so by high official request – had provoked a spurious quarrel with Captain Langton after that officer had sat on a court martial which dismissed Rennie from the service for gross dereliction of duty. That too was spurious, unknown to Captain Langton at the time. Rennie had subsequently failed to appear at the appointed hour, having accepted Captain Langton's challenge to a duel. These actions had brought Rennie to disgrace – expiated only when the reason for his actions was at last made known. He had all the time been acting under official instruction, as part of a plan to overthrow a clandestine attack upon the nation's interest.

Since then Rennie had meant to approach Langton in person, and apologise for having insulted him, but the opportunity had never arisen until now. Captain Langton had of course been apprised of all the facts long since, but harboured a niggling suspicion that Rennie's insults had been after all more than mere play-acting and pretence. Rennie had insulted him so roundly and publicly – a bombardment of drunken epithets in a coffee house – that Langton could not in his heart, in spite of the information he had been given, quite believe in Rennie's innocence.

Rennie took a further breath now, and: 'Then, then, if you ain't angry – the matter is all over and done. Will you have supper with my wife and me, at the Marine Hotel?'

'Supper? I – I do not think I can. I must go aboard my ship.' Stiffly.

'Perhaps – dinner, tomorrow?'

'I do not think I can – tomorrow. We are giving a dinner aboard. A duty dinner.'

'Ah. Ah. Then I will bid you good day. No doubt we will meet again, and perhaps I can persuade you to dine with us another time. You have not met my wife, I think?'

'I have not had that honour.' Stiffly polite.

'Mrs Rennie was a naval widow when we met. Sylvia Townend. I think you may have known her late husband.'

'Robert Townend? Captain Robert Townend?'

'Yes.' Sensing a thaw.

'Well, I did know him, years ago. But he was not then married.' Again stiffly.

'Rennie felt that he must attempt a last time to make Captain Langton understand him, and thus forgive him. A breath, and:

'Look here, Langton, I feel very badly about what happened. You was put to great trouble, and must've felt grievous wronged. All that dishwater about the duel, and so forth—'

'Dishwater?'

'Well well, it was more than dishwater, I grant you. It was deliberate deceit and insult. I wish you would allow me to give you a full explication, if not over dinner, then in least permit me to offer you a glass of wine—'

'Captain Rennie, an explication has already been made. As I have tried to say to you, there is no need for further iteration. If you will excuse me, I must go into my boat.' Making to walk on.

'Oh, good God, man.' In something like despair. 'Will not you unbend, and allow me to offer you my friendship?'

Captain Langton paused, hearing genuine distress in Rennie's tone. He frowned, turned, and now his inherent good nature overruled all else. The frown became an awkward smile, and he held out his hand.

'Very well. Very well.'

They shook hands, to Rennie's great relief – and Captain Langton's. Neither was a man that liked to bear a grudge, or have one borne against him. Captain Langton, with a little jerk of his head:

'You said some damned wounding things at the coffee house, old fellow. But I forgive you, as I should have done months ago.'

'Yes, I was obliged to be inventive. I did say harsh things to you, and regretted them bitterly all the time I was saying them. Well well, what d'y'say we go there now, and drink a glass of wine together, at the very table where I sat on that day. Hey?'

Captain Langton looked at him. 'To the coffee house? You cannot mean it? Go *there*?'

'In course I do mean it, it's the best possible conclusion to a damnfool quarrel, invented by other men.'

'To the coffee house, hey? Ha-ha-ha, yes, by God! To the coffee house, ha-ha-ha, capital. I will like to see their faces when we go in!'

And the two sea officers strode together back across the Hard, laughing and talking as they went.

FIVE

Lieutenant James Hayter, RN, was in London on a private quest. He had heard, as seafaring men do hear these things, that the 800-ton East Indiaman *Dorsetshire* was in need of a mate, and that her master Captain Sprigg sought an officer with a record of service in the Royal Navy. James had got into touch with Captain Sprigg, and a date and time of interview had been arranged.

James was lodging at Mrs Peebles's private hotel in Bedford Street off the Strand, an establishment known for its comfortable rooms, excellent table, and reasonable charges – where he in turn was known and always welcome. On the morning of his appointment with Captain Sprigg a written message was delivered to him at the hotel. As he ate his breakfast in the dining room he read:

By hand
Lieutenant James Hayter, RN, at Bedford Street
Wednesday
Sir,
We do not know each other, & have never met, but if you will indulge me I shld take it as a great favour if you wld meet me at the Admiralty at 12 noon today, upon a matter of vital importance.
Pray ask for me as you go in, & you will be directed to a side room where we can be private & undisturbed.
Yr humble servant
Brough Mappin

Please do not take offence when I say that this is of infinitely greater moment – both immediately, & afterward – than yr intended interview with Captain Sprigg.

James put down his coffee cup, glanced up as the serving girl brought his eggs and bacon, and when she had bobbed and gone he reread the letter.

'Brough Mappin . . . ? "We do not know each other."' Murmured to himself. 'Then how the devil does he know about Sprigg?'

Mrs Peebles, stout in her green dress, came to his table, apologised for interrupting his breakfast, and enquired as to whether James would be requiring his room for longer than the two days engaged.

'I am not entirely sure, Mrs Peebles, just at present.'

'I ask simply because there is a gentleman coming to town tomorrow, with a party of friends, and they wishes to take half a dozen of my ten rooms, for a week. It is just that if you was going to be stopping on, sir, I—'

'Yes yes, Mrs Peebles, I understand you.' Slightly put out. He glanced at the letter again, folded it away in his waitscoat pocket, and: 'I will do my best to let you know this afternoon.'

'Thank you, sir.'

James went to his bedroom and wrote a note to Captain Sprigg, asking that the interview be postponed until the morrow, as urgent family business had taken him elsewhere. He paid a boy to deliver the note by hand to the shipping office.

At noon he presented himself at the Admiralty, in his dress coat, and wearing his tasselled sword. He was shown to the side room mentioned in the letter, where he found Mr Mappin. His hat under his arm James advanced into the room, and Mr Mappin rose from his chair.

'Mr Mappin?'

'Lieutenant Hayter?'

They bowed, and Mr Mappin indicated a second chair. A kneehole desk was the only other piece of furniture in the small, bare, plain room. James placed his hat on the desk, and sat down, easing his sword by his side.

'Thank you indeed for coming, Mr Hayter.'

'Before you say anything further, Mr Mappin, I must ask you a question. How did you know of my interview with Captain Sprigg?'

'I have been trying to get into touch with you for some little time, Mr Hayter. I had thought that in your present circumstances you might wish to make yourself available to John Company, and so I made enquiries, and requests, and your name duly appeared.'

'D'y'mean you bribed various persons in that company to forward my name to you? Clerks, and the like?'

'Bribery is too harsh a word, I believe, for what was done.'

'You think so? Well, no matter. My name came to you, and you found me at Bedford Street. And here I am, now.'

'Indeed. And thank you again for your attendance.'

'Why did you wish to see me? And why here, at the Admiralty? Are you employed here, Mr Mappin?' All with a sea officer's directness.

'Am I? Nay, I am not. I work in another sphere.'

'Then why—'

Quickly, over him: 'If you will indulge me, Lieutenant, I think I will come to my point quicker if you will allow me to ask the questions, without interruption.'

'Interruption?' Astonished.

'I wish to ascertain something at once. You seek employment?'

'As I think you know, else you would not have mentioned Captain Sprigg.'

'And if employment were offered to you – in another quarter?'

'Do you mean – the Royal Navy?' Puzzled.

A brief impatient half-smile. 'No no, not the Royal Navy, Mr Hayter. We are talking, as I thought you had grasped by now, of the Secret Service Fund.'

'Good heaven, why should I wish to join that?'

'Because you are a lieutenant on half-pay, with no other offers of employment.'

'But that is damn' nonsense. When I got your letter I was about to meet Captain Sprigg, who would certainly have offered me the mate's berth in his ship. Who will offer it to me tomorrow, when I go to see him then.'

'No. He will not.' Confidently.

'What the devil d'y'mean?'

'He has been asked to fill the position elsewhere.'

'Asked!' Outraged. 'Asked by whom!'

'By me, sir.'

'Well, God damn your bloody impertinence!' Rising.

'Perhaps we are impertinent, at the Fund.' Mildly. 'We are certainly underhand, and often criminal in our methods. We do not care how we obtain information, nor where. We do not give warning how nor where we may strike. Those who make mischief against us, in dark places, will certainly live to regret it – if they are not dead.'

'And you want me to join you?' In wondering contempt, staring at him.

'We do a great many things behind, that can never be acknowledged. We are devious, merciless, and determined to prevail.' His tone more emphatic. 'But we are not vicious, nor corrupt, nor malevolent men. We are at heart, and in fact, loyal servants of His Majesty the king. As are you.'

'Don't compare yourself to me, sir! I am a sea officer, and everything I do must be above-board, sheeted home true and answered for, upon my oath!'

'You shot a man, did not you, in your last command? That was in pain, and could not live?'

'By God! You know that! And you dare to throw it in

my face?' James drew his sword with a ringing hiss, and put it to Mr Mappin's throat. 'You miserable bloody wretch! Why shouldn't I run you through?'

'I can think of two reasons. No doubt there are others, if I put my mind to finding them.' All with extraordinary self-possession, not a hair out of his place on his head, nor a wrinkle anywhere on his coat. 'First, I should be killed. Second, you would certainly hang, and thus we would both be dead. Not an happy end to our conversation. Hey?'

James looked at the fellow a long moment, and then lowered his sword.

'You take very grave risks, Mr Mappin.'

'I am paid to. Risk is intrinsic to my work.'

'Paid? You undertake your work from that motive?'

'As would you, at least in part – should you join us. A man must live, and pay his tailor.'

James put up his sword, turned away from the desk and chairs, and stood quietly, his head bent. Presently, turning to Mr Mappin again:

'You spoke of what happened in my last command – my first and last command. Yes, it's true I shot a man dead, that could not live long and was suffering very bad. I cannot forget it, and never will.' A breath. 'I had thought to go into the Company, and make my way there as an officer in a blameless duty. But I would still be obliged to command men, and gain their respect, and I am unfitted to it, even in a merchant ship. You have made me see that.'

'Will you not sit down, Lieutenant?'

'Eh? Sit? Why? I have said all there is to say.'

'In course, in course, but if you will sit down one moment I think perhaps you will benefit.'

'Oh, very well.' A sigh, and James pulled the chair to him and sat down.

'I know that you have suffered very hard of late, and I am very sorry for you.' Mappin's voice was lower now. 'I too have lost my only son, two years ago.'

'You?' Looking at him.

'Aye. A riding accident. He was five years old. For a time – many weeks – I was not quite a human being.'

James nodded, and said nothing.

'Had it not been for my work, you know, I think I might have run mad.'

'Yes. That is how I feel, now. But I have no work, Mr Mappin.' James looked away, and was about to rise again, take up his hat and go out, when:

'There is work for you, very worthwhile work, waiting to be done.'

A long moment, and at last James looked him in the eye.

'I do not think I am the man you seek, Mr Mappin. Your world, the world of Sir Robert Greer – a man that in course you know – is foreign to me, and alien to my nature. You have done me a service today in showing me that I do not belong on the deck of a ship, either. I must seek employment in another field.' Rising, and taking his hat. 'Good day to you.'

'Wait, wait. Will you wait one minute more?'

'Well?'

'There would be no official position, no acknowledge-ment of your . . . employment.'

'I don't understand you. I do not wish to take up the position.'

'No, no, and nor would you, because it don't exist.'

'Then what are we talking about?' Shaking his head.

'Let us say . . . an hundred guineas.'

'I see. You are offering me one hundred a year?'

'Oh no. No no. One hundred per quarter.'

'Four hundred a year?' Astonished.

'Guineas.'

James, in spite of himself: 'And . . . what would be my duties, exact?'

'You are interested in the position, then?'

'You have just said there ain't one, Mr Mappin.'

'So I did. So I did.' A breath. 'You would be in a ship, at various times. Not in command. At other times on land, seeking people out.'

'Spying?'

'No no, not that. As you have told me, that is alien to your nature.'

'Whom should I be seeking out? And where?'

'Before we go further, I must know one way or t'other. *Are* you interested?'

'I have not said that.' Stiffly.

'Come come, Lieutenant, the navy is a plain-spoke service. Give me an answer. Yes, or no?'

James looked at him, took a deep breath, shrugged – and nodded.

'Good. I am glad. Your fluent French will greatly aid us.'

'How did you know I spoke French, Mr Mappin?' Tilting his head.

'It is part of my work to discover such things, Lieutenant. You spent time in France as a youth, and you are quite at ease there in polite society. I would not have chose you, else.'

James looked at him again, frowned slightly, then again nodded. 'No – no, I expect you would not.'

And now Mr Mappin rose, and held out his hand. James took it.

'You have made the right decision,' said Mr Mappin briskly. 'And now you must disappear.'

'Disappear? I do not—'

Over him: 'You will say, naturally, that you must tell your wife of your new situation. We will do that for you. A message will go to her, at Shaftesbury.'

'But if I vanish—'

'And you will say that you must return first to your hotel, retrieve your things and pay your bill. That is being done at this moment. And in course there is no need for you to say anything further to Captain Sprigg. As I said, he has been told to look elsewhere for a mate.'

'If I am to—'

'By the by, I will like you to shift your coat.'

Mappin went to the door, put his head outside and gave an instruction. A moment after, a bundle was handed to him, which he brought in and placed on the desk.

'Your new clothes. Let me have your coat and breeches and hat, and your sword, will you?'

'You mean – I am to shift my clothes immediate, here in this room?'

'I do mean that, yes. If you please.'

James began to remove his clothes, first unbuckling his sword. As he did so:

'Where am I to go?'

'To a safe place.'

'Will you tell me where?' Removing his shoes.

'It is quite safe, I assure you.' A nod.

James paused, one foot on a chair as he made to unfasten one of his stockings. 'I think we had better understand each other, Mr Mappin.' He lowered his foot to the floor and stood straight in his shirt and breeches. 'I have agreed to your proposal, but never think I am some meek servant boy, his voice not yet broke, that will go blind and uncurious anywhere he is told.'

'In course I do not think that.'

'Then tell me where I am to go, and why.'

'In due course, in due course.' Opening the bundle on the desk.

'No, Mr Mappin, no. Tell me now.'

Mappin held out a fine linen shirt, and a coat and breeches of dark velvet. 'Here, these are what you will need, exact.' Also in the bundle were a silk waistcoat, dark stock, and new stockings.

James did not take the clothes. Instead, he began putting on his uniform again.

'Nay, what are you doing?' Mappin, frowning. 'Lieutenant Hayter has disappeared from view. You cannot go out in his uniform, now.'

James, his fingers on the buttons of his white waistcoat: 'If I am to remove it, kindly oblige me with a reason, and tell me where I am to go. Either that, or you and I have no agreement of any kind. I never came here today, and tomorrow I will go home to Dorset – to be a farmer, content among his cattle. Well?'

'You have no cattle, since you have no acres on which to graze them.' Mildly.

'Fields may be leased, Mr Mappin.'

Mappin regarded him, head a little on one side. At last: 'Very well. You are to remain here in London. Rooms have been engaged for you at Clerkenwell. You are to have a new name. Henry Tonnelier.'

'Tonnelier? A French name.'

'You are not French, yourself, but your family came to England from France a century ago.'

'What is my profession? Shipping?'

'You are a silk merchant.'

'I know nothing of the silk trade, Mr Mappin.'

'Nor need you. You will not trade in silk. You will do nothing at all.'

'Nothing? At Clerkenwell? How long must I endure this condition of life, this nothinghood?'

'Until we call upon you. Then you will go into the ship.'

'Oh, yes, you said something about a ship. A merchant vessel?'

'No.'

'Then – what? You cannot mean it is a naval ship . . . ?'

'Yes.'

'Mr Mappin, ye've just took me out of the uniform of a sea officer, RN, and now you propose to put me into one of His Majesty's ships of war?'

'I do. That ship will take you to France.'

'When?'

'When your passage has been arranged. Quite soon, we think.'

'And when I am in France, what then?'

'You will meet various persons, gain certain information, and proceed to act upon it.'

A sigh. 'Christ's blood, Mr Mappin.' Looking at him not so much in anger as in resigned exasperation. 'Talking to you is like drawing teeth – no great pleasure for neither party.'

'I assure you, Lieutenant – that is, Mr Tonnelier – when the time comes I shall be right loquacious, and you will become enlightened. For the moment it is well that you know nothing, or next to it.' Reaching into his coat, and producing a silk purse. 'Here is some money. You must live quiet, but y'must live well.' He handed the purse to James, who felt the heavy weight of coins.

'A fitting purse for a silken gentleman.' James, an ironic smile. 'How much have you given me?'

'An hundred guineas.'

'Good heaven.' Looking inside the purse, then: 'And I am to have no sword?'

'I do not think a silk merchant would go about with a sword.'

'Then I want my pocket pistols. They are with my things at Mrs Peebles's hotel, a pistol case—'

'Mr Tonnelier, you are now a man of peace. A trader in luxury goods, not a warrior. There can be no swords and pistols now.'

'If not the pair of pistols, then a single one will do.'

'No, it will not do.'

'I will not go about in London without protection.' Firmly.

'You will not "go about", except where we tell you. You will live very quiet.'

'Look here, now, Mr Mappin—'

Over him: 'I fear I cannot allow you any weapons.'

'You fear! I am the one you wish to act for you, creeping and skulking under a spurious name, carrying a large sum in gold, in a part of London where even the watchmen go fearful at night. Either allow me the pistol, or my sword, or go to the devil!'

'Well, perhaps after all you are not the man we want, Lieutenant.' A languid shrug. 'So bellicose a fellow could not go into France unnoticed. He would give himself away in half an hour. Let me have the purse, and throw on your naval coat. Your sword is on the desk. Take it up, and go on down into Dorset by all means, where you may wave it about in the fields and keep your cattle in check.' Holding out his hand for the gold, and raising his eyebrows.

James frowned fiercely, glared at Mr Mappin, then was unable to prevent a wry smile. 'You have called my bluff, Mr Mappin, by God.'

Mr Mappin lowered his impatient hand and gave a faint reciprocal smile. 'You wish to proceed?'

A conceding nod. 'I am your man.'

'There must also be, I should explain at once, further alteration to your appearance – aside from your clothes.'

'You mean – I am to go disguised, like a player in the theatre?'

'Exact. I do.'

*

Two men were waiting aboard *Expedient* when Rennie returned to her on a bright, breezy morning. As he came up the side ladder and was piped aboard, he glanced aloft.

'Tops'l breeze, Mr Makepeace. A weighing breeze, hey?'

'We are to weigh, sir?' Tom Makepeace, in hope, his hat off and on as the sound of the call ceased.

'Nay, Tom. Not this morning.'

'Oh.'

'Hm. "Oh." Exact.'

'There are two persons waiting on you, sir.'

'Perhaps they have our sailing orders.'

'No, sir, I think not. They—'

'Where are they?' Over him.

'At the door of the great cabin, sir. I have the defaulters list—'

'Yes, very good. Bring it to me in half a glass, will you?'

Rennie went aft to the great cabin and found the Marine sentry in conversation with the two waiting men. One of them was very tall, in a warrant officer's plain blue coat; the other was shorter and stooping, in a civilian frock coat.

'Gentlemen.' Nodding to them, and: 'I will see you first' to the tall man, who followed him into the cabin. Rennie removed his hat, and unbuckled his sword. 'You are a doctor, I take it?'

'I am Edmond Mace, sir, surgeon. Here is my warrant from the Sick and Hurt.' Producing the document.

'Yes, yes, yes.' Rennie, facing him across the table, putting down his hat and hanging his sword on a chair. 'Unfortunately, Dr Mace—'

'Oh, I am not a physician, sir. Only a passed surgeon.' Handing his warrant to Rennie.

'Just so, but y'would be called Doctor in the ship.' Taking the warrant, glancing at the seal. 'Unfortunately, the position of surgeon in *Expedient* is already took. I have my doctor, d'y'see?'

'Oh.' Puzzled and crestfallen.

'Yes, I applied for a surgeon, right enough. But my own man came the same day, and – well well, there it is.' He tapped the warrant on the surface of the table, and dropped it there.

'What am I to do . . . ?'

'Never fear, Dr Mace, never fear. I happen to know that

Captain Langton of the *Hanover*, seventy-four, is in need of a surgeon just at present, his warranted man having took ill of drink. Are ye a drunkard, Dr Mace?'

'No indeed, sir.' A wounded frown.

'Very good. Forgive my bluntness. I'll just write a letter to Captain Langton, introducing you, and then send you over to his mooring number in a boat. He will arrange everything with the port admiral, your warrant will be amended, and all will be well with you.'

'If you are quite sure, sir . . .'

'It ain't that I'm rejecting you on merit, nor the lack of it, Dr Mace. I am arranging for you to go to sea in a ship of the line. You ought be glad of that, you know.'

'Yes, sir, I expect so. Thank you.'

Rennie moved to his desk, sat down and picked up a quill. Finding no ink:

'Cutton! Colley Cutton, where are you!'

Presently young Edmond Mace departed the ship in Rennie's boat, and Rennie interviewed his second visitor.

Removing his hat as he came in, the stooped young man: 'Dr Wing advised me to come to—'

'Thomas Wing?' Puzzled then: 'Ah, in course, in course, you are the clerk! Are you?' Peering at him anxiously. 'I hope you are.'

'Yes, sir. I am—'

'Come in, come in. And sit, sit – after all that is your usual posture, when you are working, hey? Tell me your name.'

'Nehemiah Tait, sir.' Sitting down, holding his hat on his knee.

'Nehemiah. Hm. And how are you called?'

'I am – I am called Nehemiah, sir. Oh, d'y'mean, familiarly?'

'Aye, exact.'

'Enty, sir. As my initials are N and T.'

'Enty, very good. Well well, you will not object if I call you that? Enty?'

'No, sir. I hope that you will.'

'And in course Mr Tait, when more formal address is required. You have served in ships?'

'I have been employed for five years by the Company, sir, and—'

'The East India Company? That is fitting, that is fitting. The man you replace has just gone into service with them. Now then, tell me your ships.'

'Well, sir, you see—'

'There is no need of embarrassment that you have not been in fighting ships, you know. There is no shame in going to sea with John Company, a very reputable—'

'No, sir, you don't understand me. I have never yet been to sea.'

'What? Never?'

'No, sir. Dr Wing – Thomas – said that neither had your previous clerk been to sea your first commission in the ship, nor had Thomas himself, and you had no complaint about neither of them, in fact the opposite.' All in a rush.

'Well, yes – that is true.' A sniffing breath, and: 'But I was obliged to show my clerk the ropes, so to say, and he was so damned seasick the first leg I thought he would die. Are you subject to seasickness, Mr Tait?'

'I do not know, sir.' The formal 'mister' not lost on him. 'Since I have never been to sea.'

'Never *at all?* Never even in a packet-boat?'

'I have been the length of the Thames, sir, from London to Northfleet and back, in the ferry.'

'The Thames ain't the open sea, Mr Tait.' A puffing sigh. 'What other experience have y'had? I take it you was in some sense dealing with ships, at John Company?'

'I dealt with tea, sir, in large. Tonnages of tea, number of bales, and the like.' Lamely, fearing that his chances of employment were rapidly fading.

'Then we have that in common, in least. I am an avid

drinker of tea. Talking of which . . . Cutton! Colley Cutt—Oh, there you are. Is that my tea?'

'Hit is, sir.' Cutton, emerging from the quarter gallery with a tray, and bringing it to the table.

'Well well, put it down, man, so that I may drink it. Where is my cat?'

'She is about, sir, somewheres in the ship.'

'Find her, and bring her to me.'

'I will, sir, if I am able.' Going out of the cabin.

'Can you instruct boys, Mr Tait?' Rennie poured tea.

'Erm – no, sir. I have had no experience of that.'

'Then I cannot put you on the books as clerk and schoolmaster.'

'I expect not, sir.' An apologetic grimace.

'Where on earth did Dr Wing find you? – That is, that is, how d'y'come to know each other?'

'We lodged in the same house in London, and Dr Wing was kind enough to provide medical assistance when I was near crippled with costiveness, which he was able—'

Over him: 'Yes yes, well well, just so. Y'may begin, Mr Tait, by making order out of these lists.' Indicating the mass of papers lying at a dozen angles on the table.

'You mean, I am – I am situated?'

'I must have a clerk, and you are here.' Sucking a mouthful of tea. 'Where is your dunnage?'

'My . . . ?'

'Your belongings, Mr Tait.' Impatiently. 'Your chest and hanging cot, and so forth.'

'I . . . I have my valise, and my writing case.'

'No cot? Then one must be rigged for you, Mr Tait. Say so to Mr Adgett. Sentry!'

'Sir?' The Marine sentry, opening the door.

'Pass the word for the carpenter. He is to attend on Mr Tait at his earliest convenience.'

'Aye, sir.' Closing the door.

'As soon as you go out of the cabin, Mr Tait, ye'd better

look at the ship. Discover all you are able both on deck, and below, since you are to live aboard from now on. Mr Trent will wish to speak to you, also.'

'Yes, sir. Who is Mr Trent?'

'He is the ship's purser, Mr Tait. Without his say-so you will get nothing to eat, and nothing to drink, neither.'

'When am I to look at the lists, if you please, sir?'

'Now, Mr Tait, now. Before you do anything else.'

'I . . . I . . . yes, sir.'

'Very good.' A brisk nod. 'Take up the lists, and go into the hole by the coach. That is where you will work.'

'Coach . . . yes . . .'

'Cheerly now, Mr Tait. There ain't a minute to be lost.' Another sucked mouthful, and: 'Cutton!'

Presently Tom Makepeace appeared with the list of defaulters. 'I'm sorry I did not come sooner, sir, but I saw that you were busy, and so I thought—'

'Yes, Tom, y'did right.' Glancing down the list. 'This is very long. Too long. Twenty names.'

'Yes, sir.'

'That is what comes of lying idle at our mooring, when we should have put to sea long since. The people grow restless, and make mischief.'

'I fear so, sir.'

'But that don't excuse anything, by God. They'd better learn that lesson, right quick.' Running a finger down the list of names. '"Hopeful Lubbock, rated ordinary, answered back when drunk, and raised his hand to a midshipman." Don't say which middy.'

'Richard Abey, sir.'

'Hm. The only one of our former mids that is with us again. A steady, even-tempered lad, too. He'll make a good sea officer one day. I'll warrant he did nothing to provoke the man?'

'Not in the least, sir. Lubbock was very aggressive, and foul-mouthed. Mr Abey gave him an order, which he ignored, and when it was repeated would have struck Mr Abey, had he not been prevented, and held.'

'Very well. Lubbock is to be singled out, and flogged. Two dozen lashes, all hands to witness punishment.'

'Very good, sir.'

SIX

Sir Robert Greer sat up in his bed at his house in Swallow Street in London, and prepared to receive his visitor. The day was warm and sunny, but the covers on the bed were heavy and Sir Robert wore thick flannel, as if it were a winter's day. He was remarkably pallid and skeletal, and very ill, but his black eyes were still penetrating and steady. He heard his visitor mount the stairs, and with an effort sat a little higher against the pillows. The pain returned to his belly, and he thought of reaching for the tincture on the cabinet, but now the door had swung open and his manservant Fender announced:

'Mr Brough Mappin to see you, sir.'

Fender stepped aside, and Mr Mappin came in, dressed in a grey silk coat, with matching waistcoat and breeches, a dark red stock and laced shirt. A gold-and-stone fob seal hung at his waist. His buckled shoes gleamed briefly as he crossed the floor through a muted shaft of sunlight from the high, leaded window. He was, thought Sir Robert, rather too much the dandy, young Mr Mappin, but he did not say it.

'Come in, Mappin, come in. What news have y'brought to me? Is the thing arranged? Altogether arranged?'

'Not quite altogether, Sir Robert. We are—'

'Not? Why not by now, Mappin?' In the querulous tone of an ageing man, that he was not unaware of, and regretted, since it undermined his authority. Had he heard that tone in his own voice not a year since it would have shocked him.

Now it merely saddened and irritated him. He cleared his throat and tried again:

'We must be prepared in all distinctions. There must be no impediment to any part of the plan.'

'Indeed, Sir Robert. However, as I think you know, I was never happy about the denials I was required to make to Captain Rennie.'

'He must have no inkling of my involvement!' With an emphasis that made his voice thin and hoarse.

'I know that is what you advised, Sir Robert. I fear he guessed it at once, though.'

'But that was your specific task, Mappin. To deflect him. To make him believe you was acting on direct authority of the government. The moment he had a suspicion of my involvement he would deny you and thwart you!' His voice again rising thin.

'Yes, as you said. It is a difficulty we must acknowledge, however.'

'No-no-no-no-*no*! You must convince him! You must!'

'Sir Robert, with respect, I think that since Lieutenant Hayter knows of your involvement, and Captain Rennie strongly suspects it, then—'

'Hayter knows? How could he know?'

'I was obliged to tell him that he was joining the Fund.' A little shrug.

'You damned fool!' Nearly breathless with anger.

'Sir Robert, may I speak frankly?' Firmer, his eyes candidly regarding the ailing man.

'I think you are doing so, already.' Controlling his voice, pushing his head against the pillow.

'If I am to have charge of this venture, I think I must behave as I see fit, under any and all circumstance. In course I will like to ask for your counsel, and listen to your advice. But I must deal in facts, else make grave errors. It will be an error, in my view, to continue to pretend to Captain Rennie that the Fund ain't behind this.'

'He will thwart you! He will ruin the whole careful under-taking by his intemperate folly!'

'Surely he was chosen because of his steadiness, and courage, was not he?'

'Not by me!'

'Well, no, Sir Robert. I am entirely aware of that.' Another little shrug.

'Nor would I have picked Hayter, neither.'

'But they were chosen, Sir Robert. Have not you yourself made their shared role in this more difficult, by asking me – nay, obliging me – to be devious?'

'Mr Mappin, you overreach yourself, sir! I am controller of the Secret Service Fund. I *am* the Fund!'

'You, sir?' A tilt of the head.

'Me, sir!'

'Forgive me, Sir Robert, but ain't the Prime Minister the controller of it? Of us?'

'I have always acted independent. The Prime Minister has never interfered with the work I do in the nation's interest. He knows very well that I am the only person that—'

'Nay, Sir Robert.' A finger to his lips. 'You are *not* the only person. Not at all. The Prime Minister has made it clear to me that he wishes me to conduct this venture according to my own lights, from now on.'

'You have the ear of the Prime Minister?' Incredulous. 'You, Mappin?'

'My own lights, and his own.'

'I do not believe you for a single moment, Mr Mappin. I think you have took leave of your senses. You will soon discover, if you seek to inhibit me in any particular, that I am—'

'You are a frail old man, Sir Robert.' With icy candour.

'What! You dare to speak to me like this!'

'I dare because I must. The venture on which we are embarked is too important and delicate a matter to be the subject of internecine division. I wished to spare you this moment, but now that it has come I must be harsh. I followed your advice, and was wrong to do so. I should have said what I am saying now long since. From today I shall proceed on my own course, without further consultation with you. I am very sorry, but there it is.'

'You are sorry! You damned impudent—'

'Good day, Sir Robert.'

'I will have you arrested!' Thrusting out an arm under the fourposted canopy as Mr Mappin departed, closing the door. 'D'y'hear me, Mappin!' As footfalls descended the stair. 'You damned blackguard . . . hnnh . . . ohh . . . Fender! Fender! . . . ohhh . . .'

The sound of the great door below closing with a subdued thud, and now Fender's footsteps as he came running up.

'Fend— Ohhh . . .'

Fender pushed open the door with a bang and a creaking of hinges, and hurried to the bedside. And found the figure in the bed fallen to one side against the pillows, the face ghastly white, the eyes staring.

'Sir Robert . . . ?'

'Hhhh . . .' A last exhalation of breath, and the staring eyes ceased to stare.

Fender peered at him, then leaned in under the canopy and put his fingers to the pallid neck. And felt no pulse.

'He is done.' Whispered.

*

In the midshipmen's berth on *Expedient*'s lower deck, the senior mid and master's mate Edward Dangerfield, a strong youth of seventeen, was discussing with Richard Abey, a boy of not quite sixteen, the merits of flogging. He took a biscuit, and some cheese, and:

'I know it is bloody and all that, but the blood is soon washed away, and the man is subdued without being gravely injured, only his pride, and justice is served.'

'Justice! You call—'

'Pass the butter, will you?'

Richard Abey pushed the butter dish. Dangerfield's family was rich, and the senior mid was thus able to provide heartier and tastier fare at table than the standard stodge that would otherwise have awaited them at mealtimes. Richard did not like to argue with Dangerfield overly forceful, in case he withheld supplies, but in this instance:

'I cannot see that justice is served in any distinction, Dangerfield. A man drunk does not know or care what he is doing. Ain't the real culprit the ration of drink?'

'What? You are not suggesting, I hope, that seamen should relinquish the comfort of their grog, are you?' Taking up his tankard and draining the contents.

'Well, it is beer while we are in home waters, Dangerfield. But grog or beer, I would cut the ration by half, or three-quarters.'

'Oh, would ye? How long is your sermon today, Chaplain? Hey?'

'When we lie at our mooring like this, day after day, the people have nothing arduous to do, and four quarts of beer per diem is far too much. That is why—'

'Sailing on the open sea, watch on watch in all weathers, going aloft, manning the pumps, and so forth – y'would deprive the people of their comfort, when they are wet and cold and tired? Even then? My dear Chaplain, you would provoke a mutiny right quick, if you did that.'

'I did not say in all circumstances, Dangerfield. Heavy weather far at sea, and the fire gone out, the captain will certainly order a double ration of grog, unwatered if the men will like it. I am not against that, good heaven. But here at home, lying idle, where is the good in filling men's bellies with drink that will only addle their senses?'

'You wish to excuse the fellow that attempted to strike you?'

'No no, in course not. He deserved to be punished. But not by flogging him. Cutting off his beer would have been—'

'A simple inconvenience to him, for a week or two.' Over him. 'A flogging ain't an inconvenience, Richard. It is painful, and bloody, and above all else – mortifying. It ain't just the pain of the lash the man feels. It is the pain of his humili-ation. Tied hand and foot, spread upon a grating, made to groan and cry out and soil his breeches, he is reduced to the condition of a wicked child. So that when it is over, and his cuts have healed, he will likely think twice before he trans-gresses again.'

'I had never quite seen it in that light before, Dangerfield. In a way it is even more disgusting.'

'Eh? Why?'

'To reduce a man – any man – to the condition of an infant is grossly unjust to him. And it demeans the chastiser. It makes him a bully.'

'By God, you sound like some damned radical dissenter, stood upon a cart in the marketplace.'

'Surely I am free to express an opinion, Dangerfield, when I was the cause of the poor fellow's flogging?'

'Poor fellow! Pfff! Drunken oaf is the better description. And you were not the cause. *He* was, by his own action in becoming drunk.' Shaking his head. 'Never think, by the by, that he will be grateful for your pity. He will look at you with contempt, and think you puny-hearted. *Are* you puny-hearted, Richard?'

'No.' A frown.

'You are not?' Another shake of the head.

'No, I am not!' Stung. 'I have seen action, Dangerfield, and have never shirked great hazard nor risk at sea! I was senior mid my last commission, in the *Hawk* cutter, that was twice near blown to splinters in the Channel!'

Dangerfield, mild and steady: 'Then for the love of Christ show them all who y'are, Richard, and what you are made of. A quarterdeck man in a blue coat, that must be reckoned with and obeyed. Hey?'

A hailing shout, then the sounds of a boat coming along-side, nudging bumps through the wooden wall, and the wail of the boatswain's call on deck.

'Hello, who's that, I wonder?'

*

It was the port admiral, who had himself brought Captain Rennie's sailing instructions to *Expedient*'s mooring number. With him in the boat came Mr Brough Mappin. Admiral Hapgood could not think of himself as having brought Mr Mappin to the ship; it was simply that Mr Mappin had appeared at the Hard and decided to come. Admiral Hapgood had asked him:

'Why d'y'wish to go to *Expedient*, sir?'

And Mr Mappin had replied: 'To see Captain Rennie.' The half-smile.

'Let me save you the journey. I will gladly convey a message.'

'Ah, no, thank you. I must see Captain Rennie myself. It is a confidential matter.'

'Ah. Hm. Then by all means, Mr Mappin, avail y'self.' Grimly gesturing toward the stern sheets of his launch. The admiral noted with satisfaction that Mr Mappin possessed no boat cloak, nor any other means of protecting himself from the splashings and sprinklings produced by double-banked oars on open water. To the admiral's further satisfaction Mr Mappin arrived at the ship's side with his fine-cut coat near soaked through. There was a brisk breeze, the waves were chopped white, and the half an hour it took the admiral's crew to row out across Spithead to *Expedient* was an eventful time for the landlubber. He was distinctly paler in his face than when he had stepped aft across the thwarts at the Hard.

'Just clap on to the pieces as ye go up.' The admiral to Mr Mappin as the man at the bow held the boat in with a hook to the side of the ship.

'Pieces?'

'The steps of the ladder, man.' With a sea officer's impatience.

'Ah, yes. I have you. I see them.'

'Nay, Mr Mappin. Do not attempt to grasp the ladder as the sea falls. As it *lifts* is the moment . . . *Now!*' Tapping him firmly on the shoulder.

To his credit Mr Mappin did not fall into the sea. He clung to the bottom of the ladder, felt his body lurch one way as the sea rose, then the other as the boat fell on the sea beneath him, and with a supreme effort he swung himself upward and into the waist, his fine shoes slipping on the narrow wet steps.

As the admiral came up into the ship behind him, Mr Mappin was startled by the piercing eagle's shriek of the boatswain's call, and the rigid expressions on the faces of the hastily assembled line of Marines.

Captain Rennie came forward to greet the port admiral, his hat formally off and on, and took him aft to the great cabin. Mr Mappin found himself virtually ignored, and was obliged to bring up the rear as Rennie endeavoured to be affable to Admiral Hapgood:

'I had not known you was coming, sir, else we could have put our boys in white gloves, and so forth, and rigged ropes at the ladder.' As the sentry at the great cabin door stood aside, his back straight, Rennie continued: 'Come in and sit down. I fear we are not quite prepared for guests, but you are in course welcome.' He hurried in ahead of the admiral, and thrust away in a drawer a spread of papers and journals that lay scattered over the table.

'Captain Rennie, I bear your instructions.' Pulling them from inside his coat with a gesture that in another man might have been a flourish, but in Admiral Hapgood was merely an irritable jerk. He thrust them at Rennie, who took them with a little bow.

'Thank you, sir. It is kind in you, indeed, to bring them yourself.'

'What? Why should not I bring them?'

'No no, in course – I did not mean – I merely meant—'

'Mr Mappin has come in the boat.' Not 'with me', Rennie noted, as Mr Mappin now stepped into the cabin. 'I do not know why. You had better ask him, I expect. He would not tell me.'

'Yes, Mr Mappin, come in. Will you both sit down? May I offer you a splash of something?'

'Sherry, if you have it.' The port admiral sat down at the table.

'Nothing, thank you.' Mr Mappin moved to the other side of the table and pulled out a chair.

'Tea, perhaps? Or perhaps you will like grog, Mr Mappin?' Noting his pallor.

'Nothing at all, I thank you.' He sat down.

'As to sherry, Admiral, I can offer you only Madeira. Will that do?'

'Madeira, then.' A nod.

'Cutton! Colley Cutton!'

'I am here, sir.' Cutton, attending.

'Bottle of Madeira wine, Cutton. Jump, jump. Now then, Mr Mappin.' Turning to his second guest again as the steward withdrew. 'How may I be of assistance to you?' A slight emphasis on 'you'.

'Y'will kindly assist me, if y'please, Captain Rennie.' The port admiral.

'I beg your pardon, Admiral.' Facing him. 'Erm . . . now?'

'I will like you to open your instructions, Captain Rennie. Break the seal and read them out.'

'Yes, sir, very good.' A compliant nod, and Rennie broke the Admiralty seal and unfolded the document. He scanned the opening lines, and looked up quickly.

'Ah. I – I fear that I am unable to read them.'

'Unable?'

'That is, I am unable to read them aloud.'

'What? Why not?'

'Well well, Their Lordships do not wish it, d'y'see.'

'They have sent me here to you in my launch, directly obliged me to come, bearing your instructions, and I am to know nothing of their content?'

'I – fear not, sir.' Briefly raising his eyebrows.

The admiral leaned forward. 'Where does it say that? Let me see.'

'Well, sir . . . you will apprehend, I am in no doubt, that I cannot – may not – do so.' Again raising his eyebrows, and folding the document with what he hoped was authoritative finality.

The admiral glanced at Mr Mappin, who sat pale and silent, then looked again at Rennie.

'Is Mr Mappin, by any chance, to be allowed to know what is in those instructions? Hey?'

Rennie tapped the document. 'Mr Mappin ain't mentioned, sir.'

'Not mentioned? Then what is he doing here, Captain Rennie?'

Rennie, embarrassed: 'Mr Mappin, I hope that you will excuse us in talking about you as if you was not in the cabin—'

'Do not apologise in my behalf, Rennie.' Admiral Hapgood was prepared to be severe; they were aboard one of His Majesty's ships, and here Mr Mappin was out of his depth. 'Mr Mappin has chosen to be present without invitation at our interview, and he may think what he pleases about my questions to you, and your answers to me. Now then—'

'Contrary to that, Admiral.' Mr Mappin, raising a finger to his chin. 'Contrary to that, Their Lordships have asked me specific to come here today.' He took the finger away from his chin, tapped the pocket of his coat and drew out a letter. 'So you see I am not uninvited, after all.'

'I beg your pardon, Mr Mappin.' The admiral, stiffly. 'Well, sir, I shall ask you direct. Are you party to what is in Captain Rennie's instructions?'

'Ah.' The finger to his lips a moment. 'Ah. I fear that I am unable to divulge anything of my present visit to anyone but Captain Rennie.' The half-smile. 'I thank you for bringing me to the ship. Good day.'

'Good *day*? Good *day*? You are impertinent, sir, to a serving officer!'

'There is no need of your waiting for me in your boat, Admiral.' Mildly. 'Captain Rennie will send me ashore in one of his, I am in no doubt. Good day.'

'Damnation to that! I will not be dismissed like some bloody little midshipman! Not by you, sir, that ain't a sea officer, nor any kind of serving officer at all!'

'On the contrary, Admiral – and I am sorry to have to use the word again – on the contrary, I serve the nation's interest equal to you, or any officer in uniform. Do not imagine for one instant that I am incapable of defending my own interest, neither. Your boat is waiting. Good day.' He did not stand to emphasise his point, or even raise his voice, but simply sat back a little in his chair, and lifted his head to stare languidly at the admiral.

The admiral glared at him, glared at Rennie, and:

'Well, I'm damned.'

And having thus condemned himself he banged out of the cabin, pushing the sentry aside so vigorously that the man dropped his musket with a clatter. Presently, the sound of the boatswain's call; another moment, then 'Give way together!' and the admiral was gone.

Mr Mappin listened to the retreating wash of oars dragging through water, nodded, and pushed the letter he had brought across the table to Rennie.

'This difficulty arose because Their Lordships would insist upon poor Admiral Hapgood bringing your instructions himself. I tried to demur, and dissuade them, but to no avail.

It was their feeling that your instructions were of sufficient importance to warrant a senior officer as messenger. They could not be persuaded that it would be demeaning to the poor fellow.'

'You have sympathy with him? When he insulted you?' Rennie, in surprise.

'In course, he felt that I had insulted him. He felt himself slighted. A younger man might well have called me out.'

'Well, that would simply have been foolish.'

'Foolish?' A glance.

'Well well, a man in your position, Mr Mappin, will not likely go about accepting absurd challenges, hey? They would be beneath you, hm?'

'You think that? At Cambridge I shot a man in the neck, whose own ball went wide, and he lived by pure luck. My ball missed the principal vein by half an inch. To this day he talks hoarse, though.'

'You have fought a duel? Good God. Forgive me for thinking you . . . another kind of man.'

Rennie took up the letter, opened it and was about to read it; instead he frowned, turned from the table and:

'Cutton! Cutton, there!'

Presently: 'Sir?' Sidling in.

'Where the devil is our wine! You did not bring our Madeira wine!'

'No, sir, I did not, yes. The admiral was so very fierce that I did not like to hinterrup him, sir – for fear that he would of ate me.'

Rennie had to bite his lip to remain severe and keep his face straight. He cleared his throat.

'Hm. Hm. Y'may bring it now, Colley Cutton.'

When the wine had come and Rennie was busying himself with the tray, Mr Mappin:

'Before you read the letter I gave you, Captain Rennie, I should give you a piece of news.'

'News?' Pouring Madeira for himself, and taking a biscuit.

'Sir Robert Greer is dead.'

Rennie dropped the biscuit, and nearly spilled his wine.

'Good God. By God. He is dead.'

'It pleases you?' A tilt of the head.

'What? No.' A gulp of wine. Another. 'No, I . . . I had thought him near invincible . . .' He turned and stared at the stern gallery window.

'Perhaps it saddens you, Captain Rennie. Forgive me for having thought otherwise.'

Rennie, turning back to his visitor: 'I am neither happy nor sad, Mr Mappin. I am . . . took aback, so to say.' Another swallow of wine, emptying the glass. 'So he is gone.' A deep sniffing breath, and looking more closely at Mr Mappin:

'Why did y'tell me y'didn't know him, at first? I knew the contrary at once, in course.'

'That was not my wish, Captain Rennie, and I regret it.' The half-smile. 'Read the letter, if you please.' Nodding at the letter lying on the table.

Rennie looked at him a further long moment, then took up the letter and read:

To be delivered into the hand of

Capt W. Rennie, RN, aboard HMS *Expedient*, at Portsmouth

You are to take into your ship, when he comes to you at Portsmouth, Mr Henry Tonnelier, as supernumerary. However, he may not be entered in the ship's books. The utmost discretion is to be exercised in yr dealings with him, & you are to accommodate him in every particular of his wants, wishes & duties, as they may be explained.

Hood

'And now glance over your instructions again, will you, Captain Rennie.'

Rennie poured himself another glass of wine, taking his time. He did not wish to appear to be acceding to Mr Mappin's demands too eagerly or compliantly. He lifted the bottle and raised his eyebrows to Mr Mappin.

'Will ye join me in a glass?'

'Thankee, nay.'

'You never drink wine, Mr Mappin?' As if slightly dismayed, and disappointed.

'Well, I do. But today I am – I do not want any.'

'Ah. I would not wish you to think that we are not hospitable in the Royal Navy.'

'No, I assure you, I had not thought that.'

'Very good.' Rennie pushed the bottle aside, took a pull of wine, and with an exaggerated frown of concentration took up his instructions and studied them, turning and holding them to the light. In truth he was very interested indeed in what they said, and in what the letter said. In these documents, so long awaited, rested the real purpose of his commission.

In part his instructions read:

. . . and having again given out as your Duty the Survey of the French coast, among your Officers & people, you will proceed to that coastline proximate to the port of Brest, and carry out such observation, examination and calculation commensurate with such Survey, until your passenger requires you to deliver him ashore – which undertaking will be explained to you in due course.

Your commission will follow in all distinctions the purpose contained in yr preliminary Instructions, excepting the matter referred to above, which be the underlying Cause and Reason for it.

You will treat these Instructions as entirely Confidential in nature. They must never leave your keeping at any time, nor will you discuss the matter herein given as the principal purpose with anybody in the ship, nor outside, saving the Govt representative that will vouchsafe to you further explication, as indicated above.

Rennie put the letter and the instructions aside, took another pull of wine, and:

'It is a very great mystery, Mr Mappin, even now, when I have read the letter and my instructions both. Will you enlighten me? Who is Mr Tonnelier? His name is French, if I'm not mistook.'

'His name is French. He is not.'

'Then who is he?'

'He will come tonight. You will meet him tonight.'

'Yes? I hope so. I will like to weigh in the forenoon tomorrow, when the tide is favourable.'

'He will come.' A confirming nod.

'And when he has come, and *Expedient* is at last at sea and we are heading for France, will he tell me why he is to be put ashore there?'

'He will.'

'You cannot tell me now?'

'I think not.'

Patiently, curbing his very great exasperation: 'Mr Mappin. Hm. I cannot understand why I am not be trusted with—'

Over him: 'Until you are at sea, Captain Rennie, the least said will be the safest thing.'

'Very well.' A shrug, a sigh. 'I am a simple sea officer, and I will do as I am told.'

'Thank you.'

'I will do my duty.' Leaning forward a little. 'But if I find that I have been hoodwinked, and muddled, and lied to deliberate, I shall come looking for you, Mr Mappin. You apprehend me?'

Mildly, the half-smile: 'Let me assure you—'

'Do you apprehend me, Mr Mappin?' Without raising his voice.

Mr Mappin lifted his head, and regarded Rennie narrowly. A moment, then a polite nod.

'I do, sir.'

SEVEN

The man who came into the ship shortly after nightfall, introduced himself to the officer of the deck, Mr Souter, and was duly brought aft, was very little like the young Lieutenant James Hayter who had shifted his coat at the Admiralty at Mr Mappin's request. Here was an older man, in beautifully cut clothes, with an air of prosperous *gravitas*. He wore a rather old-fashioned peruke, and a pair of gold-mounted spectacles. He had a neat grey beard. He moved with confidence and assurance past Mr Souter into the great cabin as Captain Rennie was sitting at a late supper with Lieutenant Makepeace. Captain Rennie rose to greet his passenger, who:

'I am Henry Tonnelier, and you, sir, are Captain Rennie, I believe?' His voice deliberately thin and rather hoarse, to disguise it.

'I am, sir, I am. Welcome aboard *Expedient*.'

'Thank you.' A bow, very correct. James was feeling far less confident than his outward manner proclaimed.

'Have you ate supper, Mr Tonnelier?'

'I have, thank you.'

'Yes, we are late tonight, I fear.' Turning. 'My first lieutenant, Mr Makepeace.'

Tom Makepeace, already on his legs: 'Your servant, sir.' A bow, slightly unsteady.

'Your servant.' Another bow, and James began to feel himself slightly ridiculous, but kept this entirely within.

Lieutenant Makepeace was flown with wine. He was about

to resume his seat when something about the newcomer struck him, and:

'Have not we met before, Mr Tonnelier?'

'Nay, I think not.' James sat down in the chair pulled out for him by Colley Cutton.

'Well, if you say so.' Lieutenant Makepeace now sat down, then: 'But I could've sworn to the contrary, you know.' Dragging in his chair. 'You are not a lawyer, are ye, Mr Tonnelier?'

'I am not.' Politely. 'My business is silk. The silk trade.'

'Silk. Ah. No no, in course I am wrong – I am wrong, often – and I . . . I have got you muddled with one of the lawyer fellows that dealt with my father's estate. Thomas Weddle Makepeace.'

'I know nothing of the law, I assure you.'

'A glass of wine with you, Mr Tonnelier.' Captain Rennie pushed the decanter. James allowed Cutton to fill his glass.

'Your health, sir.' Captain Rennie.

'Your health.' James swallowed wine, and was about to open his mouth to speak, when Lieutenant Makepeace broke in:

'Not to confuse the names, you know. That was my father's name, not the lawyer fellow's. His name I cannot recall.'

'No?' James, again very polite.

'No, but it was something like – like Barber, I think it was. Or Penrose – was it?'

'Mr Makepeace.' Captain Rennie.

'Sir?'

'Mr Tonnelier has no very great curiosity about your late father's estate, I think. Nor have I.'

'Very good, sir.' And Lieutenant Makepeace fell silent.

James bit his tongue, suppressed a terrible desire to guffaw, determinedly sucked down the remainder of his wine, and:

'We sail on the morrow, Captain Rennie?'

'We do, Mr Tonnelier. An hour after first light, as the tide aids us then.'

'Yes, the tide. I see.'

Lieutenant Makepeace felt that he had been silent sufficiently long. Swivelling his head:

'Forgive me, Mr Tonnelier, but are you interested in surveying work?'

'Surveying?'

'In ships, you know. We are going to France to carry out a comprehensive duty of survey. I thought perhaps—'

'I am a silk merchant, Mr Makepeace, as I have said.'

'Yes, in course, you did say that. Forgive my inattentive stupidity. Silk. Exact.'

'Another glass, sir?' Rennie pushed the decanter toward James, and glared at Lieutenant Makepeace, who failed to notice, and continued:

'Yes, do forgive me, and all that, Mr Tonnelier, but I do not quite follow what exactly it is that you—'

'Mr Makepeace!' Captain Rennie.

'Sir?'

'Kindly go on deck and relieve Mr Souter.'

'Relieve Mr Souter? But it ain't—'

'Do as you are told.' A freezing grimace of a smile. 'If you please.'

'Very good, sir. As you wish.' Lieutenant Makepeace rose, put down his napkin, nearly knocked over his wine, and pushed in his chair with a heavy scrape. 'Good night, sir. Good night, Mr Tonnelier.' And with careful dignity, walking very deliberate, he left the cabin.

'I am very sorry indeed that you was subjected to such infamous behaviour in one of His Majesty's ships, Mr Tonnelier.'

'Really, there is no need of an apology, Captain Rennie.'

'Mr Makepeace was grossly impertinent and intruding in his questions.'

'I am sure he meant no harm. I was quite at my ease.'

'I had thought to ask him to supper, and introduce you . . .' Rennie paused, frowned, and:

'Excuse me a moment. Cutton! Colley Cutton!'

'Sir?' Sidling from the second quarter gallery, where he kept his kettle, tray, &c.

'Y'may go forrard to the fo'c's'le and smoke, if you wish. I will not need you again tonight.'

'Thank you, sir.' And he sidled across the cabin and left by the door.

'I must correct him of that habit of sidling.' Rennie, half to himself, and turning back to his guest: 'Yes, I wished Mr Makepeace to see that you were a perfectly ordinary sort of supernumerary passenger. Had I known he would very nearly recognise you, James, as I did . . .'

'What!' His mouth open.

'Aye, James, aye. You did not think for a moment, did ye, that I would not see through this damned hocus pocus of a disguise, hey?'

'Good God . . .' Thoroughly bemused, dropping all pretence, and pulling off the peruke.

'Mr Mappin is too fond of deceit. Ye should be wary of the fellow. But that is by the by, now. If we are to keep you in the ship as Mr Tonnelier, and get you safe across to France, we must continue to play along with that sphere of His Majesty's service, and maintain your disguise.'

'I – I am very sorry to have inflicted this nonsense upon you, sir, but Mr Mappin was most insistent. He – he recruited me, you know, when he heard that I was seeking employment, and before I knew what I had done, I had agreed to everything he asked. In course, you are entitled to an explication, and—'

Rennie held up a hand, shook his head, and mildly: 'Good heaven, my dear James, don't apologise, and there is no need for ye to explain your motive to me, neither. We are both caught up in his "nonsense", as ye call it, and must do our best. In least we are serving together again, hey? We had better examine your scheme, while we have this opportunity.'

James, still disconcerted: 'You mean, the—'

'Well well, we must have a plausible reason for your passage to France.' Equably. 'To give out among the people in the ship, and indeed my junior officers. I will like you to keep private in your quarters, but you cannot be wholly invisible in the ship.'

'Yes, sir, very well. It is the silk trade, just as I told Tom Makepeace. I go to France to consult with colleagues in the trade about the supply of silks and stuffs from the great silk industry at Lyons and elsewhere. There has been a serious disruption of supply of all cloths and fabrics coming from France since the events of '89, as you may imagine.'

'Indeed? Yes, well, I expect so.' Nodding. He cleared his throat, and toyed with his glass. 'However, there remains the question, James: why does Mr Tonnelier go to France in one of His Majesty's fighting ships? You follow?'

'It is all quite straightforward. I am acting in my capacity as representative of the London guilds of silk merchants, the British silk trade. France is our principal supplier. France is in difficulty. I go to examine that difficulty at first hand, in the interests of trade, of commerce. To discover what may be required to resolve it. What could be more expeditious than my passage in a fast frigate. In the *Expedient* frigate, hey?'

'Indeed, hm-hm. Most expeditious, James. But are you to go ashore at Brest itself? To be candid, I don't know how kindly one of His Majesty's frigates may be received there, if I sailed direct into their harbour. We are not at war, but Brest I understand is heavily defended. The commanders of those batteries may take it into their heads to see a British warship as an invader, given the dark trouble in which France finds herself. I have heard from fellow officers – Captain Langton, as an instance – that of late the French forces, both the army and the navy, are not close-governed from Paris. There are factions at work. I will not like to risk my ship to factional bombardment, James.'

'You need have no fear of that, sir. I will not go ashore at Brest. I will like you to put me ashore on the nearby coast, at night. Have you charts to hand?'

'Indeed.' Rennie rose and went to his desk, from a wide drawer of which he produced several charts. Selecting one he brought it to the table and spread it out with leaden weights at each corner. Pointing:

'Here is Ushant to the west, and here is the Passage du Four and the Black Rocks. To the east of that Le Conquet, the Pointe de St Mathieu, and Bertheaume Bay . . . and Brest beyond.'

'Mm-hm . . .' James leaned over the chart, peering at it in the light of the deckhead lantern. Rennie brought a candle-holder.

'Now then, where would you like me to put you ashore? The bay, perhaps?'

'No, sir.' His finger traced the intricate outlines of the shore. 'Here it is. The Pointe de Malaise.'

'There? But good God, James, that is a very wild and rocky place, very remote.'

'Exact.'

Rennie straightened, stood holding the candle a moment, peering at James, then:

'James, I am obliged to ask you, now – even if you find y'self unwilling to answer – what is the real enterprise on which you and Mappin are engaged? I take it the silk is dishwater?'

'Sir, it ain't that I don't want to answer – but the truth is, I do not yet know myself. All I do know is that I must go ashore at that place, or as near to it as you may land me. Can we get a boat inshore there, through the rocky shoals, and these damned little islands?'

Rennie made a face, tugged an ear, sniffed. 'We could attempt it – here – or here.' Pointing. 'But there is such variation of depth, I will always be apprehensive how close in I may navigate.'

'Yes, twenty-five fathom here, and only three or four just here.' James, also pointing. 'Which means troubled water close inshore. Hazardous for a boat's crew, with all these rocks. I do understand your reluctance, sir. But I fear I must insist.'

'Very well, James.' Nodding, another sniff. In spite of his earlier assertion of equanimity, Rennie was not happy – but he would do his duty. He was not altogether sure that James was deliberately keeping him in the dark, but he strongly suspected it.

'I am to remain ashore until the twentieth of June, or at the latest the twenty-first. Will you be able to return and take me off then, sir?' James, looking up from the chart.

'At the same place?'

'Aye, the Pointe de Malaise.'

'The twentieth is a fortnight from today. I will proceed with my survey, and then make my best endeavour to take you off on that date, James, or the day following. It may depend on the weather, in course. You will be able to stand by a few nights until the weather lifts, if it is poor at first?'

'None of us can predict the weather in those waters, sir. Naturally, I will stand by if need be.'

They discussed the arrangement in detail, a system of signals by lamp, &c., and came to accord.

Later, when James had settled in his hanging cot in the coach – provided for him as sleeping quarters by Rennie – and Captain Rennie had retired to his own sleeping cabin, both men lay awake, listening to the creaking of cables and the liquid whisperings of the sea, the element that had shaped their lives and made them the men they were.

James thought of Catherine, and tried to imagine lying at her side. Thinking of her made him think of his lost son, and this was so painful to him that he turned on his back and thrust all thinking, all meanderings of the mind, all imagining and wondering and doubting away into the darkness, and made of his head an empty pasture.

Rennie thought first of James and his appearance in the ship in that absurd disguise, and of his surprise and pleasure in discovering his erstwhile lieutenant again at his side, however peculiar and vexing and unlikely the circumstances. Then he thought of Sylvia, his beloved wife, of their leave-taking at the Marine Hotel, her determination not to allow herself tears, and her failure, and his heart was suffused with feeling. How had she come to love him? How had she made of a balding, ageing sea officer, never a handsome fellow, an object of love, and desire?

'I do not know . . .' Sighed. 'And I do not care. Just so long as it is so . . . my dearest darling.'

*

James, in the guise of Mr Tonnelier, and on the advice of Captain Rennie, did not move about the ship, but remained in the coach. It became clear to James that the presence of a guest was an awkwardness for Rennie, not simply because the fiction of Mr Tonnelier must be maintained, but because of his guest's constant presence. Rennie had made available his quarter gallery for the comfort of his guest, but James soon understood that his frequent traversing of the canvas squares of the great cabin, to and from the privy, had begun to discommode the captain – so to say – and he took to using a chamberpot in the coach. Then again they were obliged to share their meals. Rennie, like many post captains, often preferred to eat his supper alone, but now he felt himself obliged, in order to maintain a show of his courtesy to Mr Tonnelier, to sit at table conversing with him. When they were entirely alone they could converse quietly and easily as friends, but that was not always possible. The steward Colley Cutton could not always be dismissed; other members of the ship's company sometimes needed to come to the great cabin on urgent business; various intrusions into the great cabin could occur at any time in the life of a ship at sea. They could never be entirely at their ease, and all this put a strain on things. James was relieved to think that the voyage would not after all last very long.

To keep himself occupied, and to sharpen his crew, Captain Rennie instigated a rigorous programme of gunnery exercises, feeling that his guncrews remained unproficient. This was abandoned, however, on the second day at sea, when the weather swiftly deteriorated. What should have been an easy little southward cruise of two days became five. Summer storms moved in from the Atlantic, swept up the Channel and ran blustery and turbulent in over the coast of France. Rennie had to beat close-hauled to the west to avoid being driven on a lee shore, beat into the teeth of the storms, and everything and everywhere in the ship was very wet and uncomfortable. The fire in the Brodie stove in the fo'c's'le went out, and cold rations were issued in the messes. Rum was issued to those men who preferred it over beer, and Rennie ordered that those men coming off watch should be given their rum unwatered if they wished it.

Before the storms came, Rennie had obliged James to go into the orlop during the exercising of the great guns, where he would be out of the way.

'Could not I observe on deck? It is only an exercise, after all.'

'Cleared for action, James, as you know very well, there is no place for an idler on deck.'

'Am I an idler?'

'Well well, supernumerary. In effect the same thing, James. No place for you on deck, dear fellow, when we are at quarters and tompions out. Y'must go into the orlop. Spend your time with Dr Wing.'

'Eh? Good God, if you recognised me, surely so will he, will he not?'

'Talk to him in French. He is eager to grow fluent, and he delights in displaying all of his medical instruments and their uses. Like many surgeons he is at heart a ghoul, you know. He will hardly notice who you are – only an interested layman.'

'You will like to make jokes, sir – but supposing he does detect me under my peruke?'

'I'll wager you he won't. Half a guinea, what say you?'

Thus James found himself thrust into the company of Dr Wing in the cockpit. James and Thomas Wing were old friends, and James feared that at such proximity the sharp-eyed surgeon could not fail to see through his disguise. Dr Wing gave no such indication. As Rennie had confidently predicted he wished only to practise his French on the newcomer.

'I hope you will not mind, Mr Tonnelier?'

'No, no, in course not.' Crouching on the stool the doctor had provided in the cramped space.

'I am not yet fluent.'

'I am at my ease.' A tight little smile, half hidden by the beard.

'I fear we are lamentably short of space down here. The chest that is placed between us is for the performance of procedures, should they be required during an action. *Comprendez-vous?*'

'*Ah, oui. La chirurgie.*' A nod.

Dr Wing continued in careful French. He pulled toward him a leather fold, and laid out on the top of the chest his array of surgical instruments: amputating saw, metacarpal saw, catling, bistoury, forceps, scalpel, tenaculum, aneurysm needle. James, in spite of his long experience of the sea, of action at sea and its bloody consequences, began to feel distinctly queasy. He had never before spent any great length of time in the cockpit. In usual, during gunnery exercises, or during action itself, his place was on the deck in the open air, in the bracing stink of powder and flaming wad. Down here in the bowels of the ship the stench of the bilges was today very distinct, and Dr Wing's sedulous descriptions of the tools of his trade began to take their toll.

'Doctor . . .' James, at last. 'I wonder if – if we might discuss something else?'

'*Excusez-moi, monsieur?*'

'Erm . . . *parlons du temps, non?*'

'Ahh . . . ahh . . . *mais certainement, monsieur, naturellement.*' Was there a subdued gleam in his eye as he nodded politely in agreement?

James was almost relieved when the weather worsened, as then gunnery exercises ceased, the great guns were double-breeched in their tackles, and the flintlocks shrouded. Bad weather did not require him to descend into the orlop. He was permitted to remain in the coach, out of sight, and even on one brief occasion to go on deck. Rennie had at first refused. James persisted.

'I am desperately in need of fresh air, sir. I am very stale cooped up in the coach.'

'I do not wish you to be seen on deck, James. At any rate, you ain't dressed for it. Your fine clothes will be ruined in this weather.'

'I was hoping that you would lend me a foul weather cloak, sir, and a hat . . . ?'

'Eh? Oh, very well, very well.' Rennie found his second cloak, and a battered hat, and handed them to James. 'But ye'd better stay close to me, clinging to a lifeline as if you was a terrified landlubber, hey?'

'Very good, sir.'

And presently Captain Rennie and his guest ventured out of the cabin, climbed the ladder, and came up into the streaming, wind-tearing din of the storm. As they trod aft, pulling themselves hand over hand by the lifelines, ducking their heads under their hats against the wind, the lifting mass and swell of the sea surged all around. Pitching and sliding and heeling *Expedient* ran on – shuddering, creaking, groaning. She sank down into a trough, rose again in a pouring flood of water from the rails, and plunged like a wild animal into the thudding fury of the next onslaught.

Smashed curtains of spray fell far over the waist, as far aft as the breast-rail. Four men fought the wheel, two on the weather spokes, two on the lee. James clapped on to a stay and clung as *Expedient* shivered again like a great beast, rolled heavily and thudded with awful force into a freakishly big sea. The deck, angled steep, was wholly and heavily inundated, and swam submerged. James clung and clung and felt his legs dragged from under him by the sheer rushing volume of water. His legs trailed aft a long moment, then his feet found the deck and he managed a semblance of standing. Rennie – knocked bodily against the binnacle – coughed, spat, grabbed another line and hauled himself abaft the wheel.

'How . . . does . . . she lie!' Bellowed to the quartermaster, who was half drowned under his cloak.

'She is sagging off heavy, sir!'

'Someone must go below into the hold!' shouted James, before he could prevent himself. Fortunately nobody heard him, and he turned away toward the rail, keeping his head low.

'We must get a party into the hold, and find out if tiers have shifted!' Rennie, to the sailing master, who now appeared lurching and streaming at his shoulder. 'Mr Loftus, I will like you to take half a dozen strong men with you, and if casks have broke loose secure them without the loss of a moment! Y'will report to me in half a glass! I wish to know if we must retrim!'

'Aye, sir.' Departing.

'Mr Dangerfield!'

The senior mid advanced, clinging to a line and ducking his head. 'Sir?'

'Where is Mr Souter?' Cupping his hand.

'He was took ill, sir, and has gone below!'

'The officer of the watch has gone below? God damn his negligence!' Looking forrard briefly. 'Mr Dangerfield, you will take the con until Mr Loftus returns! I am going forrard!'

'Aye, sir!'

'Mr Tonnelier . . .' Turning to look for James. At that

moment the ship struck another heavy sea, and for half a minute no further communication was possible on deck. Presently, as the ship rose on the great rolling lift, and shook herself free of flood, Rennie gripped James's arm and:

'This was a damned bad notion, after all! You will go below, if y'please!'

'I am quite all right—'

'That ain't a request, Mr Tonnelier! You will get your arse below right quick – if y'please!' A fierce glare.

'Thank you, then I will.'

And James went below, reluctantly went, knowing that to defy Rennie under the circumstances would be nothing but folly.

Later, when Rennie himself had come below, James was witness – by virtue of overhearing most of it from the coach – to an exchange in the great cabin between the summoned carpenter Mr Adgett, and Captain Rennie.

'Now then, Mr Adgett, what depth of water in the well, did y'say?'

'Three foot, sir, and rising.'

'Rising? The pumps ain't adequate?'

'As I say, sir, I am of the opinion that there is a leak forrard.'

'Leak?' A note of concern.

'I cannot locate it accurate just at present, but I b'lieve that is the cause of the ship sagging off and behaving sluggish on the rise of the sea – and not the shifting of tiers, sir, which was very small. Some few water casks did break loose, but they was secured.'

'So that is why the ship is by the head, Mr Adgett. We must double-man the pumps, men to be relieved each half-glass. I shall say so to Mr Makepeace, and Mr Loftus. In the interim you will continue to search for the leak.'

'Aye, sir.'

'If the weather continues severe – we may have to return to Portsmouth.'

'Aye, sir, we may indeed. As I say—'

Over him: 'Find the leak if you are able, and stop it. If y'cannot, report to me again at the change of the watch. Thank you, Mr Adgett.'

'Very good, sir.' And the carpenter departed.

Presently James ventured into the cabin, and anxiously: 'Return to Portsmouth, sir?'

'We must hope not, James, but it may become a necessity.'

'Surely Adgett can find the leak? Surely a repair may be affected at sea? As you are aware, sir, I have only until—'

'James, we have discussed your going ashore in all particulars – save these. Bad weather, and a leaking ship. Even if we find the leak, any attempt to put you ashore in these conditions would be fatal not only to you but to my coxswain and boat's crew. Even to attempt to stand in sufficient close to hoist out a boat and see it safely away would be grossly irresponsible.'

'The weather may perhaps abate. Don't you think so?' Gripping a timber standard as the ship lurched and yawed.

'Abate! Christ's blood, James, you are a sea officer of long experience! D'y'see any sign of an imminent calm!' Nodding toward the part-shuttered stern gallery window, and the heaving sea beyond.

'Yes, sir, forgive me, but I am under a most pressing obligation to—'

'Your obligation is to go into the coach, and stay there.'

'Sir, if I may just—'

'Y'may not. You are in my way, sir.' Pushing past him as the ship again rode deep in a heavy, creaking roll. 'Sentry!'

The sentry came to the door, looking very green about his nose and mouth, and James reluctantly retreated to the coach.

'Pass the word for the first lieutenant to attend me in the great cabin.' Rennie nodded in dismissal and as the sentry departed: 'With my compliments, say to him! If he pleases!'

Fortunately for James – and all aboard – he was proved correct. As night fell over the sea so did the storm subside, and by four bells of the second dog watch calm had descended, the stars and a sliver of moon appeared, and *Expedient* was relieved of immediate peril.

EIGHT

Captain Rennie summoned his second lieutenant to the great cabin, on the fifth day out of Portsmouth, the French coast now mistily visible to the east, in the form of the Côtes des Abers. Porspoder lay some five leagues east of *Expedient*, and the point at which James – Mr Tonnelier – must be put ashore lay some ten miles to the south. The Pointe de Malaise was the westernmost tip of land in the Chenal du Four. Numerous rocky islets lay close in, and the whole coastline was treacherous. Rennie looked up from the chart.

'Mr Leigh, there you are.'

'Sir?' Coming in, his hat under his arm, very correct. He stood in front of Rennie's table.

'You are aware that Mr Souter is took ill?' He did not invite the young man to sit down.

'I am, sir, yes. The poor fellow—'

Over him: 'It means that ye must rearrange the watches between you – you and Mr Makepeace, and Mr Loftus. As you know, in *Expedient* the first lieutenant always takes his watch, so that the second and third are not obliged to keep the deck watch on watch.'

'Yes, sir.'

'Now that Mr Souter cannot take his watch, Mr Loftus must stand in his place.'

'Aye, sir, very good.'

'In course Mr Loftus may at his discretion ask the master's mate Mr Dangerfield to stand his watch, take the con and so forth, if as sailing master his duties call him elsewhere in the ship.'

'Yes, sir.'

'We have a troublesome leak forrard, not altogether pressing, but we must be vigilant as to pumps, trim, and so forth.'

'I am aware of it, yes, sir.'

'Now then. We will approach the French coast, and send in a boat party, Mr Leigh. You will command that party.'

'This is – this concerns our duty of survey, sir?'

'Exact, exact, Mr Leigh. The survey. We will make all the relevant observations, take bearings and prepare, during the hours of daylight. Then the boat will go in at night.'

'At night?' In great surprise.

'You heard me correct, Mr Leigh. At night.'

'D'y'mean, it is – it is like a cutting-out party, sir?'

'Nay, I do not. You will put a man ashore.'

'And this is part of our duty of survey, sir?' Thoroughly puzzled.

'Yes yes, Mr Leigh, it is.' Nodding. 'The survey is to be comprehensive in all distinctions. Step to the table, if y' please, and I will show you on the chart where I wish this to be done.'

Mr Leigh did as he was told, and bent over the weighted chart on the table. It was several years old, but looked accurate in every detail, down to the smallest shoal and rock, marked depths by fathom, the carefully intricate line of the shore, even details of vegetation immediately inland.

'Here is the place.' Rennie pointed to the Pointe de Malaise.

'Good heaven . . .' Involuntarily aghast.

'Yes, you are going to say, are not you, Mr Leigh, that putting a man ashore there is damn' near impossible?'

'Well, I – I would not say quite impossible, you know . . . but pretty near. Sir.'

'Indeed. And that is why we must make our observations with utmost caution, exactitude, and precision, during the hours of daylight. This chart is all very fine, it is a good chart in its way, but we must make observations and take bearings, the situation of every shoal, rock and islet, to a degree that allows of *no error at all*. You have me?'

'I – I think so, sir.'

'Think so?' Sharply.

'I mean, I do understand you perfectly, sir. No error at all.'

'Very well. I will stand in as far as I dare, and then we will hoist out the ship's boats. Mr Dangerfield to command the large cutter, you will command the launch, and Mr Makepeace will command the pinnace. Each boat to carry an Hadley's, boat's compass, sounding lead, long glass, and an accurate pocket timepiece, and of course instrument cases, pens and notebooks, and existing charts, for comparison and alteration.'

'Who will take our watches, sir?'

'Mr Loftus will keep the deck, and I will keep the deck myself, in addition, while we lie at anchor.'

'Very good, sir. Erm, permission to make a suggestion, sir?'

'Well?'

'Do not you think that it will require more than a single day to make all of the observations, sir, and chart them accurate?'

'We have already lost three days to storms, Mr Leigh. There ain't a moment to lose, now. The man must be got ashore tonight.'

'May I ask . . . forgive me, sir, for these questions . . . but may I ask how long this man will remain ashore? Are we to wait for him, while he makes his own observations, or—'

'You will not wait for him at all. You will put him ashore, stand away and return to the ship.'

'We are to leave him there, in France?'

'You are. You will. And before you ask: why? I will say only this: it is all a question of the silk trade.'

'Silk, did y'say, sir? Then the man to go ashore is our supernumerary, Mr Tennelier?'

'Aye, that is the man. And his name is Tonnelier, Mr Leigh. Henry Tonnelier. He is to go in your boat.'

'Very good, sir.'

'He is to meet representatives of the French silk trade ashore, in secret, and try to discover from them how the disastrous falling-off of that trade in France may be circumvented, as a way of preventing a similar falling-off in England. You see?'

'Yes, sir. Well . . . in fact I do not, sir. However, it ain't my business to question the efficacy of such a plan.'

'No, Mr Leigh, it ain't. I shall anchor . . . here. The boats will then be hoisted out, and you will proceed thus.' He designated an area for each boat, drawing lines in pencil on the chart. 'From your observations we will then decide upon which channel your own boat will follow tonight, through the rocks, shoals and islets to the one possible landing place at Malaise – this inlet.' Tapping the chart with his pencil, and drawing a cross at the place.

'Are we to have lights of any kind, sir? I know that local fishermen along much of the French coast use lanterns at night to—'

'There can be no lights of any kind. None.'

'Then – forgive me, sir – how are we to read the chart at night, in order to find our way in?'

'You must commit the final chart to memory, and navigate by dead reckoning. Everything you do in the hours of daylight will be vital to your success tonight.'

'Very good, sir.' Troubled, but determined not to show it.

'No doubt you are wondering, Mr Leigh, why I have not put Mr Makepeace in command of this little expedition tonight, hm?'

'It – it had crossed my mind, sir, since he is the senior lieutenant.'

'Because I want him here with me in *Expedient*, should we need to defend ourselves.'

*

The boats had returned by nightfall, their work accomplished as planned. Now the single boat remaining in the water, close in by *Expedient*'s side, was the second lieutenant's boat, the ship's launch. With a minimum of fuss and notice Mr Tonnelier made his way into the waist and descended the ladder. He was clad in a dark cloak and hat, his face nearly hidden. He nearly forgot to go down the ladder a trifle clumsily, to show that here was a lubberly fellow, but managed to stumble over the thwarts and rock the boat a little as he made his way into the stern sheets.

'Plausibly done,' murmured Rennie to himself as he watched from the deck.

The coxswain stood at the tiller, the man in the bow pushed the boat clear, and the double-banked boat's crew obeyed Mr Leigh's command: 'Give way together!' The launch swung toward the shore in the darkness, and slid from view in a rhythmic washing of oars.

'I hope they don't come to calamity in getting him ashore.' Again to himself, and Rennie pushed himself away from the rail. He sent a boy to ask Lieutenant Makepeace to join him in the great cabin, and went aft. Presently Tom Makepeace joined him.

'Tell me again, Tom, will ye? Y'saw nothing in the way of other ships today?'

'No, sir. Only fishing boats. Bisquines, I believe. Heavy-waled, squat, broad in the beam, lugger-rigged.' With sea officer's accuracy of observation.

'And did they notice you, d'y'think?'

'Well, as I wrote in my report, sir, I think they did – but they did not attempt communication of any kind. We kept to ourselves, and so did they.'

'Yes, very well.' Tapping a chart, rubbing the back of his neck. 'We may only hope and pray that nothing awaits our launch inshore except breakers and rocks and other inanimate delights. Hey?'

'Indeed, sir.'

'Silence is to be the watchword, Tom, all tonight, until the launch returns.'

'I have passed the word, sir.'

'Anchor watches, but we must remain wholly alert. I am not persuaded entire that we shall remain here unremarked. Say to Mr Tangible that he is to be ready to beat to quarters at any moment.'

'I have already done so, sir.'

'Good, very good. Hm, I am not hungry, not at all, but we had better observe the conventions, I expect, and eat a supper. Will y'join me, Tom?'

'Gladly, sir.'

'We will eat, but we will not drink. We must have clear heads.'

*

In the launch James sat in the stern sheets with Lieutenant Leigh, who crouched forward very tense, a hand clutching the gunwale. His voice sounded strained:

'Steady, coxswain, steady . . .'

The man in the bow swung the lead, the line tied with fathom marks, and presently the word came back:

'Fifteen fathom, sand and shell.'

'Very good, very well.'

'You are quite certain of our passage through the rocks, Mr Leigh?' James, in the darkness, in an attempt to be affable. The attempt failed.

'I have it clear in my head.' Curtly, as if to say: do not talk to me.

The boat ran on, driven by the straining backs and arms

of seamen, and double-banked oars. James was aware of a bulked mass against the stars to larboard, and the sucking and washing of waves against rocks, very close.

'That is the larger of the islets,' he said, but not aloud.

During the day he had stood on deck with Captain Rennie, and observed. He saw that the boat would have to pass between two rocky islets, and then through a maze of rocks and shoals beyond. He borrowed Rennie's glass, ostensibly to look at the ship's boats. Through the glass he looked at those rocks, and thought he could discern a way through for a boat – a boat handled with skill. He turned his attentions to the ship's boats, swinging the glass across them. It was all very fine, he had reflected, as he watched the boats' officers making their charting observations, to plot the intended course in broad day; it would be quite another thing to find the way through in the blinding folds of night. Handing the glass back to Rennie:

'My thanks, sir. A remarkably accurate glass, the view is admirably enlarged and clear.'

'Aye, it is a Dollond. The finest ground lenses in London. It cost me a pretty penny.'

James was brought sharply back to the present by a splash of sea water in the face, flung back from the blade of an oar. The bulky mass to larboard was gone, and the boat was again in open water. Ahead lay the most treacherous part of the passage – through the narrow channel and on to the rocky inlet under the rearing headland. James could hear Lieutenant Leigh's harsh, tense breathing, and feel his wound-spring tension beside him. By contrast the rhythm of the oars in muffled thole pins was almost soothing, the blowing breath of the boat's crew like the sighing of a whale. The rippling wash of the oar blades and the gentle seething of the sea were nearly soporific. James shook himself resolutely awake, snuffing in a deep breath of saline air. Soon his attention drifted, and he allowed himself to wonder what lay ahead for him.

He was late – days late – for the rendezvous with his French contact. Would there be anyone there when he got ashore? And what would they want of him, what would they require immediate? He still had no strong idea of why he had been sent, in spite of Mappin's repeated promises to let him know.

'He never did tell me anything of substance.' Muttered under his breath. Another bracing splash of sea water. 'Too late now, I must make the best of whatever I find, and try to do whatever is asked of me.'

All he knew for certain – other than that his journey was of vital importance – was the password he must produce, when challenged: '*Deus ex machina*'.

Suitably theatrical, he thought, and smiled tightly in the darkness. In what way was he a descending god, come to solve the difficulties of hapless mortals? In his head: 'I am only a damned wet sea officer, crouched in a boat and disguised as a someone else. As a bewigged, foppish land-lubber, for Christ's sake.' And not for the first time today, nor yesterday, nor the day before, he shook his head and wondered: 'What am I *doing*, for the love of God? Why on earth did I *agree* to this nonsense?'

'Eh? What say?' Lieutenant Leigh hoarsely, beside him.

'Nay, I – I was merely going over something in my head, you know.'

'Cannot you understand? We must keep silent in the boat.' Curtly.

He was frightened, thought James with a sudden clarity. The young man was desperately fearful, which was why his manners had deserted him.

Abruptly the boat lurched, scraped against something, and Mr Leigh was flung forward. His head struck the roundel of an oar, jutting from a seaman's hand, and he pitched across a thwart senseless.

'Mr Leigh!' James, in alarm.

'He is knocked witless, sir.' A seaman.

The boat lurched heavily again, and there was another juddering scrape. Now the boat drifted clear and began to swing beam-on in the current. Curses, the faint glinting of lifted oars.

'Coxswain!' James turned to the man at the tiller, and saw that there was no one there. All thought of disguise and subterfuge left him now, he stood up, grabbed the tiller, and attempted to pull it sharply over. The timber swung useless in his hand. The rudder had been snapped off.

'You there, larboard number one, pass me your oar! Cheerly, now!'

Astonished, the seaman obeyed, so clearly was that command given in the voice of a sea officer, RN.

James grabbed the oar, moved to where the coxswain had been sitting, and lifted the oar out and down in the water, to act as a makeshift rudder. The boat began to swing back.

'The coxswain has gone overboard!' Careful not to raise his voice too loud, but making it as hard and authoritative as he was able, and as expressions of fear and concern came from a dozen throats: 'We will go about and search for him. Starboard bank, give way together!' And he stood at the makeshift helm, gripping the oar and angling it over to make the boat turn.

Not one of the seamen questioned his right to give orders. They obeyed him without hesitation. The boat came about, but in spite of repeated calls in the rinsing, washing dark, they found nothing. James ordered the boat about again, angled the makeshift helm, and the boat's crew obeyed. Again they found nothing, and by now it was clear to James – to them all – that the coxswain was drowned. Mr Leigh regained consciousness. He groaned, coughed, and was helped to sit upon a thwart by two seamen as James ordered:

'Lay on your oars.'

Mr Leigh was not yet quite himself. He stared about him.

'What has – happened? Where is this place? Are we at sea?'

'You was knocked senseless, sir, when the boat struck a reef.' One of the seamen.

'Are we sinking?'

'No, sir. We are safe. The other gen'man has took command.'

'What?' Swivelling blearily. 'Command?'

'The rudder was broke, sir, and the other—'

'But – I am in command.'

James, clearly and firmly: 'You are injured, Mr Leigh. I will guide us in.'

'But – *you* cannot command a boat's crew, Mr Tennelier. You are a landlubber.' Rising clumsily and stumbling aft. The boat heeled sharply.

'Sit down, Mr Leigh, and be quiet now, will you? I will guide us in, never fear.'

The authority in that voice was unmistakable, even to the stunned and confused lieutenant, and he did as he was told and resumed his seat. The boat righted itself. James gripped the steering oar and:

'Give way together. Cheerly now, lads, while the tide is with us.'

And half a glass after, without further upset, the boat came gliding in on the little sandy beach of the inlet, the great granite headland of Malaise towering black above.

'Oars.'

The oars inboard. A moment, then a sliding crunch.

Men leapt out and held the boat firm as James clambered forrard to the bow. He jumped on to the glistening sand as a wave washed over his shoes. Striding up the slope he turned and in a low, carrying tone:

'Many thanks, lads. We have lost a man, but have come in safe, and you have done your duty. Shove off now, right quick, and get Mr Leigh back to the ship. I must make my way alone from here.'

'But – how will we navigate through all them rocks, sir?' One of the crew, anxiously.

'You must do your best. Row and steer very careful, a man in the bow with the lead. Beyond that I cannot aid you. Good luck to you all.'

'Good luck, sir.' Very subdued.

'Aye, good luck, sir.'

A few moments more and the boat was gone, and James heard the anxious command:

'Give way together, lads.'

The slow, rhythmic splashing of oars as the boat's crew pulled away into deeper water. James could only trust that whoever had taken charge of the boat was capable of steering with an oar. He sighed, turned up the sandy beach, and walked steadily to the rocks beneath the cliff. He smelled wild gorse, the scent drifting on the night air. Now he stood waiting, as Mr Mappin had instructed. Was he too late? Had the moment of rendezvous been kept for the preceding three nights, and now been abandoned altogether? He waited a whole glass, and began to fret.

In darkness he could not hope to find a way up the cliff, nor could he make his way north or south along the shore. On either side beyond the inlet were steep, unforgiving outcrops of rock, rinsed and sucked at by the surging sea. He could see nothing, and hear nothing but the wash of waves.

'Damnation . . .' Muttered.

As if in answer a pittering of rocks from far above. A dull crack as a stone fell nearby. Presently, faintly at first, the scuffing and scraping of shoes on the rocks above. Coming nearer and nearer, descending. A pause, then a voice in French: 'Are you the silk merchant?'

'Erm . . . deus—'

Over him: '*Comment!*' The voice low and urgent.

James thought quickly, decided to take a chance, and: '*Oui, oui. Je suis le commerçant.*'

'*Avancez-vous, monsieur.*'

James went toward the voice, on the opposite side of the

inlet, and was immediately seized from behind, and a blind-folding hood pulled down over his head. Strong arms on both sides lifted him bodily over the rocks, and forced him to his knees in a patch of shingle. The smell of wild flowers, and seaweed. Hard pebbles pressing through his breeches. He shut his eyes in mortal fear, expecting at any moment to hear the click of a cocked pistol, and to feel the muzzle at his head. Instead a second voice said in educated French:

'Tie his arms and pin them behind him, then lift him to his feet.' A brief pause, then close to James's ear: 'Do not attempt to struggle, monsieur, if you please. You are quite safe – if you do not resist.'

James felt his arms gripped again, and soon his wrists were bound tight behind him with strong twine, and he was lifted again to his feet. The voice again, close:

'Will you give me your word that you will not attempt to escape?'

'I can hardly escape, monsieur, when I am blindfolded and bound, on a strange coast.' James, politely enough, but with a hint of acerbity.

'Answer, if you please. Will you give me your word?'

'*Oui, oui, d'accord.*' Impatiently.

'Very good, thank you. If you had not I would certainly have shot you.' A rattle of stones as the man stepped away. 'Take him up.'

James felt a nudge to his spine, and began to walk forward and up a steep path, his breath huffing strained and harsh inside the confining hood, and his arms growing numb behind him.

'*Dépêchez-vous!*' Another nudge. James quickened his pace, stumbled, and climbed on.

*

The boat returned to the ship after a long delay, occasioned by the extreme caution of Mr Leigh, who had recovered his full senses not long after the boat left the shore, and had resumed command. The faint smudge of a June dawn was in the sky to the east by the time the boat bumped against *Expedient*'s side and was tied to a stunsail boom. Mr Leigh reported to Captain Rennie, who had gone below to his bed, leaving Lieutenant Makepeace to keep the deck, with instructions to wake him the moment the boat arrived.

'What? My coxswain is drowned?' Rennie was appalled. He dashed water in his face from the jug brought to him by Colley Cutton. 'How came he to drown, Mr Leigh, good God?'

'We – we struck a reef, or in least fell on some rocks, and lost our rudder. The coxswain fell overboard, as I understand it.'

'As you understand? Was not you conning the boat, Mr Leigh?' Lifting his dripping face to stare at his lieutenant, as the steward slipped discreetly out of the door behind.

'I was knocked senseless by the accident to the boat, sir. I did not see what happened to him.'

'But how could this accident occur, when ye had all the particulars of the channel in your head?'

'The tidal current was very swift, sir, and it was near pitch black, no moon—'

'Did you look for the poor wretch? Did you heave to and search?'

'We did, sir – as I understand.'

'And found nothing?'

'No, sir. Mr Tonnelier had assumed command, and he ordered the search—'

'Mr Tonnelier assumed command?' Then he remembered to add: 'A landlubber?'

'Yes, sir. He did. When I began to regain my senses I heard him give a series of commands.'

Captain Rennie dried off his face, stared away a moment, and: 'Well well, I think you must have imagined that, you know. You had struck your head, and was confused. What you heard was in course one of the boat's crew taking command, an experienced man that—'

'No, sir, no.' Earnestly. 'If you wish, any of the boat's crew will confirm it, sir. Mr Tonnelier took command, and used an oar to steer the boat. I would swear on my oath . . .'

'Swear what, Mr Leigh?' Looking at him.

'That Mr Tonnelier . . . is or was a sea officer, sir, RN. He even ordered me to sit down.'

'Yes yes. Well well.' Draping his towel at his neck. 'Everything and everybody was in a state of confusion in the boat, Mr Leigh, and no doubt Mr Tonnelier, as a man of substance, has wide knowledge of how to govern men, and merely wished to – to protect his life, and yours, indeed, in an emergency. We must be grateful that by a happy chance he was able to do so. Hey?'

'Aye, sir. If you say so.' Unconvinced. 'But I still think—'

Over him: 'At any rate, he was got ashore, and that was our purpose and design. It is a very great pity about the coxswain, but there it is, and nothing to be done. Thank you, Mr Leigh. Y'may retire, and I will send Dr Wing to examine you presently.' A nod of dismissal. 'Cutton!'

*

'Good morning, Mr Mappin.'

'Prime Minister.' A bow.

'Sit down, will you?' Indicating a chair. 'A glass of something?'

'No, thank you, sir.' Sitting down, flipping the tails of his coat on either side neatly.

'No?' Mr Pitt poured wine for himself.

'It is a little early for me, thank you, sir.'

'Ah.' The Prime Minister lifted his glass, and sucked down half of the wine. 'Now, Mr Mappin, your plan is how far advanced?'

'Well, sir, that depends on which plan you mean. I am at work on many and several at once.'

'The French plan.' Looking narrowly at Mr Mappin.

'The frigate plan, sir?'

'Exactly so, Mr Mappin.' Sucking down the remainder of his wine, and refilling his glass. 'How do we progress?'

'He has got ashore into France. To date, to this hour, we have heard nothing more.'

'The frigate has returned to England?'

'No, Prime Minister.'

'An attending cutter, then?'

'There is no cutter with her, sir. The frigate—'

'Then how d'y'know for certain your man is in France? What is his name? Lieutenant...?'

'Hayter, sir. He has gone into France under the name Tonnelier, a silk merchant.'

'Yes, yes, I mind that name. I repeat: how d'y'know he's there, if your ship ain't here?'

'I have received a communication from another source, sir.'

'Do not be obtuse, Mr Mappin, now. Who told you what, how, and when? Hey? I am pressed in many distinctions, and I will like to hear you in plain English.' Another pull of wine, and he drew toward him on the desk a sheaf of documents tied with a ribbon. 'D'y'see these, Mr Mappin? I must go to Windsor, directly, and seek His Majesty's signature. They are... well, never mind what they are, exact. They concern debt, Mr Mappin. Debt. If I am able to persuade His Majesty to take up his pen I shall be grateful. He frets about America still, when matters at home are what concern me. Important matters elsewhere – in France, as an instance – cannot occupy me paramount. But when I do think of them, and ask for enlightenment, I expect to get it, Mr Mappin, I expect to get it.'

'Yes, sir, forgive me.' A tight half-smile. 'The communication was by word of mouth, from a young lady that returned from France yesternight, in the packet-boat. The message had come to her by a horseman, at the port.'

'You trust her?'

'She is Lady Sybil Cranham, sir, daughter of the Marquess of Chalke. She is a confidante of our principal friends there.'

'Then in course she is above suspicion. Where, in France?'

'He is to be taken to the Château de Châtaigne.'

'Where is that?' A slight shake of the head.

'It is near to the coast in the Pays de Léon, north-west of Brest. Isolated, secure, hid away. Our friends believe it is the ideal place.'

'Very well, thank you, Mr Mappin. I will not detain you now. Send word to me, though, as soon as you hear anything further. Will you? Your plan is important, and I do not wish to neglect it.'

'I will, sir, certainly.' Rising.

'Good morning.'

'Good morning, Prime Minister.'

*

'Are we to return to England, sir?' Mr Souter, lying in his cot in his cabin. His breath was foul, noticed Captain Rennie.

'Nay, Mr Souter. As you are aware, we are here to carry out a duty of survey along the French coast, and we shall do so, as ordered. Tomorrow we venture south.'

'We do not call at Brest?'

'We do not. How d'y'fare today, Mr Souter? Any better?'

'I – I endeavour to feel better, sir.'

'What ails you? What does Dr Wing say?'

Rennie knew what Dr Wing thought. Dr Wing had already given his opinion in plain, forthright language, the day previous. 'He is constipated. He don't believe it, and will not swallow the purgative I have prescribed. Won't take his ball pill.'

'You are certain it is simple costiveness?'

'I am.'

'What does *he* think it is?'

'Scurvy.'

'Scurvy! That is nonsense, when we've had fresh produce all the way from Portsmouth until now. There ain't a single scurvy case in the ship.'

'I know it, sir, and you know it. He don't. Or won't.'

'Then I must attempt to persuade him myself. I don't want to lose another man so soon in this commission, Doctor.'

'Then I wish you good luck, Captain. Mr Souter has a certain stubbornness of character and perception that I have noticed before in his race.'

'Have ye, indeed? Leave him to me, Dr Wing. Leave the fellow to me.'

'What does Dr Wing say?' repeated Captain Rennie now in the lieutenant's cramped cabin.

'I do not think Dr Wing knows what ails me, sir. He – pretends that he does. But I am not persuaded. I believe, myself, that—'

'Not persuaded?' Over him. 'I see. Will I tell you something, Mr Souter, about Dr Wing?'

'As you wish, sir.'

'Dr Wing, in my opinion – arrived at from long direct experience of his activity – is very nearly the best doctor-surgeon the Royal Navy has produced in thirty year. He believes you to be costive, Mr Souter.'

'I am certainly not—'

'He believes it, and so do I. The cure is a ball pill. You will oblige me by swallowing it now, without the loss of a moment.' Producing the ball pill from a twist of paper in his pocket. He picked up a glass from the cabinet beside Mr Souter's hanging cot, and held it out with the pill.

'I am afraid I must refuse that request, sir. I have no need for a ball pill. I am suffering from—'

'You are suffering from disobedience, Mr Souter. Y'will swallow this damn' pill right quick, or know the consequence.'

'Captain Rennie, I decline to submit to bullying.' Very pale, but holding up his chin.

'Decline to submit! By God, sir, you are impertinent! You there!'

'Sir?' A ship's boy, attending.

'Find the lieutenant of Marines, and ask him to come to me here, at once, with his sergeant and two men. Jump, now.'

'Aye, sir.' Touching his forehead, running up the ladder.

'You – you intend to place me under arrest, sir?'

'I intend to teach you a lesson, Mr Souter. A lesson ye'll never forget. Unless . . . unless, in course, you wish to swallow your ball pill?'

'And – if I don't?' Still stubbornly defiant.

'You will be marched in full view of the ship's company to the head, and there deprived of your breeches. And there you will sit, sir, upon the seat of ease, until you are eased. Do you apprehend me?'

'I – I do not believe that you would do—'

'You don't believe me?' Looking out of the cabin. 'Ah, there y'are, Lieutenant Melly. Your sergeant is with you, and two men?'

'Very well, I will – I will take the pill.' Mr Souter, sitting up in his coat.

Captain Rennie ducked back inside the cabin, handed the pill to the lieutenant, and the glass of water, and the pill was duly swallowed.

At first light of the following day, *Expedient* weighed and proceeded south through the Chenal du Four toward the Pointe du Raz. The initial part of her mission had been accomplished, but the pretence of survey would have to be maintained for the time being.

*

He woke. The blindfold at last removed, and his hands untied. His captors gone. James blinked in the painful brightness of light, and saw that he was in a simple bedchamber, with plain walls, a high ceiling, a fireplace, and a tall double window with open shutters, overlooking . . . what? He stood up and went to the window. Below lay a stone courtyard, a high wall with a massive gate, and beyond a solid round tower with a conical roof. He rubbed his wrists, and pins and needles prickled through his arms as feeling returned. He pushed open the windows, and smelled hay, sweet chestnut, and roses. Yes, roses, he thought, or perhaps it was another bloom.

He turned to look at the bed on which he had been placed. It was narrow, as narrow as a hanging cot. There was no other furniture, save a commode half hidden by a screen in the far corner. He strode there, availed himself gratefully of the commode, and returned to the window. Peered out and down, and tried to assess where his room was in relation to the rest of the house. Obviously a large house, very large – a château. He put his head out and glanced upward, and saw that the window was in a mansard roof, very steep. Glanced down again, and judged the drop to the stone flags to be sixty or seventy feet. He was high aloft here, and no backstay to clap on to and slide down, nor shrouds neither. To himself:

'Trapped, my boy. Imprisoned. Christ's blood, if these are my friends let me find no enemies here in France.'

He yawned, stretched, and realised now that most of his clothes had been stripped from him. His coat, waistcoat, stockings and shoes. His hat. He clutched at his head. His peruke. He was bareheaded, exposed, chilled, in this great stone house. He was thirsty, and hungry. What o'clock was it? He glanced at the sky, and at the angle of the light across the courtyard, and again sniffed the air. Unless his senses deceived him it was early morning. He had lain here all night. He sighed, stretched his arms above his head, flexed his knees, and then on a thought strode across the chamber to the heavy door. Tried the iron handle. Found it locked.

'In course it is locked, you damn' fool.'

He sat on the bed, and after a moment lay back and mused on the questions Mr Mappin had never properly answered. Why must he go to a remote part of the Breton coast, disguised as a silk trader? Who were the 'friends' in France? Why had he been sent to meet them? What was the true purpose of his task, of all this subterfuge and discomfort?

He had been brought here last night, after two days – or was it three? – in a hovel, or a barn, a place anyway of richly pungent farmyard odours, then a further arduous journey over long distance across fields, and ditches, and then along rough tracks in a cart or trap of some kind. He had been fed meagrely, and given only water to drink. The water he had been given last night tasted of stone, and earth. Well-water. His captors – he was unable to think of them in any other distinction – had refused to answer his questions, had indeed enjoined his silence. His anger, confusion, dismay – all vehemently and repeatedly expressed – had been resolutely ignored. The thought of his treatment at their hands fired his anger all over again, and he jumped up off the cot and strode round the room. There was no looking glass. He had no real sense now of his appearance. He touched his face – and found that his beard had been shaved off.

'Good God, then they have removed all of my disguise. They know I am not Henry Tonnelier, not a silk merchant, and they believe I am a spy. I am trapped here a prisoner, and very probably they mean to execute me. Christ Jesu, what a fool I was to agree to Mappin's scheme. Four hundred a year? You ninny. You bloody blockhead.'

The ratcheting click of the lock, and a woman's voice:

'Le petit déjeuner, monsieur.'

A pretty young woman of perhaps eighteen years, dark-haired and black-eyed in her apron and cap. James took the tray from her, sat on the bed and ate rolls, butter and sweet preserve, and sucked down a large bowl of dark, fragrant, reviving coffee. Presently the girl returned with ewer and basin, face cloth and towel, the water steaming hot.

James smiled at her. '*Merci, ma'm'selle.*'

'*Monsieur.*' A little curtsey and she withdrew, but not before her black eyes met his.

He stripped, washed himself, dried himself with the towel, and pulled on again his shirt and breeches.

'What may I take ashore in the way of baggage?' he had asked Mr Mappin.

'Take nothing.'

'Nothing, Mr Mappin? Not even a valise?'

The eyes closed, the neat head shaken once. 'Nothing.'

'How long am I to remain in France?'

'Mm . . . a short time. Anything you may need will be provided for you. You will want for nothing.'

'Indeed? Not even fresh linen?'

'Not even that. These are civilised people, you mark me? You will be treated handsome on all occasions.'

'Handsome!' With irony, glancing round the bare chamber. He wandered to the window, and gazed disconsolately down once more. And leaned forward. The great gate was open, and a carriage had just come into the courtyard. The echoing clatter of hooves and wheels. The doors of the carriage opened, and the people stepped down. A gust of wind from the open gate sent straw swirling and scattering round their legs, and lifted the ribboned bonnet of the lone woman among them. She clutched at the bonnet, turning away from the wind in her waisted silk jacket and petticoat, and James saw her face. Even at this distance from her, and high above, she was the most strikingly beautiful creature he had ever seen.

'Good heaven . . . who is that?'

And then he turned from the window and looked at the door. Had that girl turned the lock as she left? He did not remember having heard the squeak of the key, and the click. She had carried a large ring of keys at her waist. Had she forgotten to lock him in as she went away?

He ran to the door – and found it locked. And roundly cursed himself.

'You fucking poltroon you! Why did y'not overpower that slip of a girl and make good your escape? Hey? Hey? You are too much the gentleman, by Christ! Instead of admiring her dainty arse, you should have took her bloody keys, y'timid dimwit, and locked *her* in!'

He kicked the door, and stubbed his bare toe. Wincing:

'A fine, upstanding spy you picked, Mr Brough Bloody Mappin.'

James was left alone in the bedchamber until noon, and he lay dozing on the cot because he was still tired after the rigours of the past few days.

At midday he woke to the sound of footfalls outside the door, and sat up. The lock was turned and the door opened, and two men came in, the younger one carrying a plain wooden chair. He placed it in the middle of the floor, and the older man looked over at James and pointed to it. James eased himself warily off the cot and limped to the chair. His toe was still painful. He sat down. The younger man – powerfully built, dour-looking – stood by the door, which he closed but did not lock, as if he and his companion wished James to attempt an escape.

The older man, who was perhaps forty-five, and dressed very plain, with a simple, close-fitted wig, had a gaunt face and an angular frame. In educated French:

'You have hurt yourself, monsieur?'

'No. Yes. I struck my toe, an accident.'

'You wish for a doctor?'

'A doctor? No, thank you. Will you please tell me, monsieur, why I have been brought here, and held captive?'

'I will ask the questions, monsieur, and you will oblige me with truthful answers. Lies I will not tolerate.'

'Ah, I see.' A grimace of a smile.

'How did you arrive in France?'

'How did I— You know very well, monsieur. I came ashore at the Pointe de Malaise in a boat, as arranged.'

'Arranged? I did not arrange it. I have arranged nothing.

You are here because I wish to know why you have come to France.'

'Again, you must know the reason. I do not. I was not told. I am yet at sea, as to that.'

'You do not know why you came? Pfff. Do not play the lackwit, monsieur. It will go very hard with you, if you do not treat me with *respect*.' Cold eyes, a full-lipped, unkind, sardonic mouth.

Fear curled in James's belly, but he lifted his head and stared at his interlocutor defiant, and said nothing.

'What is your name, monsieur?'

'Henry Tonnelier.' Sticking to it, as instructed.

'You, a Frenchman? But no. No no, it is not possible.'

'I never said I was French. I am a silk merchant from England. But your men knew that, didn't they? That is why they asked me on the beach—'

'My people said nothing of silk.' A hint of irritation? Or was it dismay? James watched him.

'They most certainly did, monsieur. I was challenged in those words, exact. "Are you the silk merchant?"'

His interlocutor now removed his wig with an irritated sigh, revealing close-cropped grey hair. James watched him narrowly, and:

'I never saw the faces of the people who seized me on the beach, and yet you have just admitted that they were your men. I do not know if they were the same men that brought me here. I was blindfolded three days, and there were different voices all round me. I do not know this house, neither. I have no idea where it is. But you *know* that I do not. So why do you—'

'Be silent, monsieur. Do not make me angry.'

James now decided that he must attack, and ran out his guns:

'Do not make *you* angry! By God, you arrogant wretch, I will not bear this any more!' He stood up, and at once the young man by the door came towards him. James grabbed up the chair, lifted it by the ladder-back, and faced them both.

'You attempt to do me harm, either one of you, and by Christ I will smash skulls!'

The older man now smiled, and produced from his coat a pocket pistol, which he cocked.

'I think you will not, monsieur. Please to put the chair down, and be seated upon it.'

James saw the futility of further resistance, and did as he was told. But he did not like it, and his face said so.

'Yes, Henry Tonnelier. Perhaps they thought in London that it was a logical name for you, a man born in England with a family background in France. But when we removed your wig, and shaved off your grey-dyed beard, we saw at once that you were not a man in middle life, but a much younger man – in disguise. What is your real name, monsieur?'

'I have nothing more to say to you.'

'I confess I am disappointed. I had thought M. Mappin would send to me a more experienced emissary, wide versed in the art of deception and therefore able to acquit himself well under close questioning. You disappoint me, Lieutenant Hayter.' Uncocking the pistol.

'Eh?'

'You may think you are brave, but had the wrong people took you on that beach you would not have stood up at all well. You would have been broke, and you would have given us away.'

James gave a bitter little chuckle, and:

'The irony is, monsieur, whoever you are – that I know nothing at all, because I have been told nothing.'

'M. Mappin gave you no detail of our business?'

'I have been told nothing, and I propose to say nothing.'

'Ah. Then I must say to you: give me the password.'

'Password? It is . . . *deus ex machina*.'

'Welcome to beautiful France, Lieutenant. And now, we

have work to do. Madame Maigre has come to us this morning, and you must meet her.'

The relief in James's breast gave way to returning anger, and bewilderment.

'But why was I kept blindfolded, if you knew who I was all the while? Why was I made captive, and dragged about the countryside? Why have you treated me so shabby?'

'All will be made clear to you in due course, monsieur, after you have met Madame Maigre.'

'Is Madame Maigre the lady that came in the black carriage?'

'You have seen her? How?' A frown, then: 'Ahh . . . you saw her from the window.'

'I did indeed, yes.'

Something in the way James made this brief reply caused the other man to look sharply at him.

'She is very beautiful, no?'

'Very beautiful.'

'That must be the least of your concern, monsieur. We are here on profoundly important business, and there can be no foolish distraction of purpose. You understand?'

'Very good, monsieur. I shall endeavour to keep that uppermost in my mind, and take notice only of what the lady says to me, when we meet.' With a degree of polite irony. This produced a coldly fierce response:

'Listen to me, Englishman. You are here on sufferance, because my superiors have been persuaded of the need, in our present circumstances, to accept England's offer of help. I remain sceptical. I remain reluctant. Why should we trust the English, a duplicitous race – insular, piratical, uncivilised? What is the reason for your sudden willingness to oblige, to be charitable, and kind?'

'I do not feel in the least charitable, monsieur. Nor do I feel disposed to be kind, neither.' Stung to intemperance.

'No? No, I think you do not.' Holding up a hand as James was about to speak: 'You see, what puzzles me is why M. Mappin would send to us such a clumsily inept and impetuous fellow, with the acuity of a cowherd. Whose disguise would not deceive a dullard child. Whose experience in this exacting field was so obviously . . . offf. Could it be that M. Mappin's heart does not after all beat so very strong in this cause? I wonder.'

'*What* cause? If you are its representative, monsieur, it can have little hope of survival or success, since you will certainly poison it from within.' Further stung.

A long, cold, hostile stare, and:

'You will meet Madame Maigre. She must decide. Her intuition is infallible?'

'Thank you, I look forward to it. Will you tell me your name, monsieur? I will always like to know who my enemies are.'

'I am known as – Félix.'

'Monsieur Félix. I shall remember that.'

'You will do well to remember it, monsieur. We shall see each other again.'

Another cold stare, then he nodded to his companion by the door, who opened it wide. M. Félix swung out of the room, the door was closed in a rush of air that swept over James's face, and the lock turned. Retreating footfalls. Silence.

NINE

As she had proceeded south along the coast, *Expedient*'s leak had grown worse, and soon the duty of survey – or the pretence of it – began to assume a very low priority in Captain Rennie's mind. He called together and spoke to his officers in the great cabin, briefly leaving the ship in the hands of the master's mate Mr Dangerfield.

'Gentlemen, I have decided that we must abandon our duty of survey, and return to Portsmouth. Mr Adgett and Mr Tangible have both told me that the pumps are scarce able to hold their own against the increasing flow of water into the ship, and Mr Loftus is of the firm opinion that was we to encounter more bad weather along this coast we might very probably founder. We will therefore set a course for England, and there undergo urgent repair. It cannot be managed at sea. Mr Leigh.' A glance at his second lieutenant.

'Sir?'

'Assemble the people in the waist, and I will say a word to them.'

'Very good, sir.' Departing.

'Mr Souter. You are quite recovered now, are you?'

'I am, sir, thank you.'

'Very well. Y'may return to your duty as officer of the deck, and relieve Mr Dangerfield.'

'Sir.' His back very straight. His hat on as he left the cabin.

'No wonder he suffers costiveness, the fellow.' Not aloud. 'His arse is so tight never even a fart could escape.' Turning to Lieutenant Makepeace: 'Now then, Tom. I could see you wished to say something. You have a question?'

'Well, sir – I have.'

'Go on.'

'Are we to leave Mr Tonnelier altogether behind in France?'

'Nay, nay, my duty is to return and take him off at the Pointe de Malaise on either the twentieth or the twenty-first day of this month. However, I cannot do so if my ship sinks under my legs. I will make my best endeavour to repair and return by that time, but if I am unable to do it – well, I am confident Mr Tonnelier is a resourceful fellow, and will discover some other means of coming out of France.'

'D'y'mean – that he would hire a vessel of his own, sir?' Puzzled.

'I do not know that. Perhaps he may go independent to a port, and cross in a packet-boat, I do not know. I hope to take him off in *Expedient*. I will do my best for him.'

'May I say one word more, sir?'

'Well, Tom?' Raising his eyebrows.

'With great respect, sir, I wonder if there ain't more to this than simply putting a man ashore, and taking him off again. I was foxed the night you introduced me to Mr Tonnelier, I admit – and was ashamed of myself afterward. Since then I have the strong sense that Mr Tonnelier ain't a silk merchant at all. My feeling is that he is employed official, that he is acting in some distinction for government interest, and not his own – and that is the true reason we came to France, and not the survey, that is no more than sham.'

Rennie looked at him a long moment, then turned away and was silent.

'In course you may very likely say to me that I should mind my own business, sir – but if I may continue ... ?' Finding no response: 'Mr Leigh, after his experience in the launch, is also of the opinion that Mr Tonnelier never was in the silk trade, and is in fact—'

'Yes yes, well well,' Rennie, over him, and he turned to look at him again. 'Ye've expressed your view, Mr Makepeace. I have allowed it, to a point. But I think ye'd better keep your opinion to yourself, from now on. And so had Mr Leigh.'

He took up his hat, and his sword.

'We will go on deck.'

*

HMS *Expedient*, frigate, 36, returned to Portsmouth, increasingly by the head and sluggish in answering the helm, so that she gave Captain Rennie great anxiety in the four days the journey took, and he was always waiting for the first signs of a storm, keeping the deck two and three watches together. By the urgency of her signals as she reached Spithead she was given permission to stand in to the dockyard, where dockyard officers came aboard at her mooring number. She was straightway examined, and the officers, including the master shipwright, allowed that she must be got out of the water and into a dry dock without further delay, and her copper prised up to discover the extent of the difficulty. Her people went into a hulk, and the work began.

Admiral Hapgood was not pleased. He summoned Captain Rennie.

'This is a very dreadful commission, sir.'

'I can assure you, sir, that I have every wish—'

'Nothing goes right with it. You was delayed an unconscionable time. All kinds of troublesome people came and went from London. I was told nothing. And now you return with your duty not accomplished. Nothing accomplished but further delay and expense, and failure.'

Rennie did not see how failure could be an accomplishment,

but he did not say so. He thought it best to say nothing at all.

'Well?' The beetling glare.

'I am as cast down as yourself, sir.'

'Cast down! D'y'say y'are moping, sir, like a damned snivelling maidservant? This ain't a scullery, Captain Rennie, it is a naval port, where sea officers must conduct themselves in a manner befitting their rank and duty.'

Etcetera, etcetera. It was all very vexing and tedious to Rennie, but he bit his tongue and bore it, and came away to the Marine Hotel.

Mr Mappin appeared at the Marine Hotel, where Captain Rennie had been tenderly and joyfully reunited with his wife. He sought an urgent interview. In fact he came direct to their rooms and demanded it. Rennie, in his shirtsleeves, was disinclined to be amiable, his ears still ringing as they were with Admiral Hapgood's round abuse.

'Mr Mappin, I am not ready to see you just now, you know. Ye've called at an incon—'

'You will oblige me by coming to the coffee house in ten minutes.' Mr Mappin, over him, his cane and gloves held tight in his hand. 'Do not fail me.' Abruptly turning on his heel and going away downstairs.

'Christ Jesu . . .' A great sigh. 'Have not I enough to deal with? Bloody dockyard men, and my ship took from under my legs, and bloody Happy Hapgood?'

'Never mind, my darling William.'

'I do mind, though. I must go away from you, just when we . . .'

'You will come back very soon. And I will be here.'

He put on his coat, allowed his wife to tie his stock, kissed her, and went out.

He met Mr Mappin in the coffee house, and:

'How did y'know I was at Portsmouth, Mr Mappin? I have only just arrived this morning.'

'I have been much at Portsmouth in recent days. Nearly all

the time. Why did not you remain in your ship, sailing along the French coast as instructed, after you had put Mr Tonnelier ashore?'

'Mr Who-is-he? Do not you mean – Lieutenant Hayter?'

Mr Mappin regarded him a moment, and: 'How long have you known?'

'From the first moment he came into the ship.'

'He told you? He was given very specific instruction never to—'

'He said nothing. I recognised him at once.' A sniff, then mildly: 'Look y'here now, I have known James Hayter many years, as shipmate and close friend. He is as familiar to me as my own face in the glass. What persuaded you I would not see through his damnfool disguise before he had even opened his mouth? Hey? Good heaven, man. And speaking of my ship, evidently you have not heard of her condition.'

'Condition?'

'She leaked badly following a storm at sea, and the leak got worse and worse. I was obliged to bring her home for repair, else she—'

'Didn't Mr Tonnelier – Lieutenant Hayter – ask you to wait for him? Until the twentieth of June?' Over him.

'He did. But I repeat – my ship was sinking under my legs. I had no choice but to return to England.'

'Had you no thought for your passenger, Captain Rennie? Had you no thought at all for him, and what he had been required to do?'

'Ah, well, I do not know what he was required to do, you see. I was never told. I did my duty and put him ashore, at very considerable risk to my ship and my people. In fact we lost a man out of the boat. A man was drowned, Mr Mappin, in carrying out my orders.' Holding up a hand before Mr Mappin could again interrupt. 'Before you say anything more to me, I will like to remind you of what I said last time we spoke. That if I discovered you in a lie, or a deliberate attempt to hoodwink and confuse me, I would make you answer for it.'

Mr Mappin, usually so moderate in his speech and manners, now had to make an effort to be calm. He shook his head, drew in a breath, and:

'Captain Rennie, above all else you must return to France at the appointed time, the twentieth of June. You *must*.'

'I can promise nothing, I fear. In course I will not like to leave Mr Hayter stranded in France, and I will naturally do my best for him, and for you, in attempting to return by the appointed time. But I cannot work miracles. We may well be delayed here at Portsmouth two or three weeks.'

'Three weeks! That cannot be permitted.' Leaning forward urgently. 'Listen now, what I wish you to do—'

'It ain't a question of what you wish, sir. Fact is fact. When *Expedient* lay in Ordinary her bow timbers had rotted, part of the wale planking in the region of the cant frames and breast hooks, and the corruption was not discovered at the time of her refit. In truth we knew nothing of it at all until the ship began to leak very bad at sea.'

'I know little of the work of shipbuilders, nor of repair. They are not pertinent now. You must take another vessel. I will arrange it. It is *vital* you return to France by the twentieth. You have little more than a week until that date, given the time you have wasted in returning—'

'Take another ship . . . ?' Rennie, staring at him.

'Yes, another ship. I will arrange it with Their Lordships, without delay.'

'Mr Mappin, you have tried my patience very far, sir, and now I will permit you to try it no further. What you propose is out of the question.' Hands flat on the table.

'Captain Rennie, I must tell you something more.' His voice very low and emphatic. 'Lieutenant Hayter will not come out of France alone. He will bring with him a party of persons, who must be got out of France *on that date*. Brought away without remark, nor any attention drawn to them, quietly, discreetly, carefully. You will go there, in the vessel I shall arrange for you, and you will bring them away.'

'Well well . . . I knew nothing of this before, Mr Mappin, nothing at all. You see what happens to fellows like you, when you do not trust honourable sea officers, and keep things from them? You get yourselves in a very pretty fix, and then you expect the Royal Navy to get you out of it. I cannot sail to France in another ship. I am commissioned in *Expedient*.'

'Even if Their Lordships order you to take another ship, you will not obey?' Angrily incredulous.

Rennie sighed. 'Another frigate? Is that what you suggest? How will you arrange that, pray? Do you intend to bring a particular frigate out of Ordinary, refit her and make her ready for the sea, all in a week?'

'There are other frigates here at Portsmouth, lying at anchor. One of those will—'

'Aye, and all of those are commissioned, you know, by and to appointed post captains, just as I am commissioned in *Expedient*. Their Lordships will not take a commissioned ship from under her captain's legs – just like that. Not even the Prime Minister can do it – just like that.' Snapping his fingers in Mr Mappin's face.

Mr Mappin seized Rennie's arm in a powerful grip, and looked right into his eyes. Low and hard:

'The Prime Minister can, and will, and does. I act upon his authority, direct.' He released his grip, and stood up, dropped coins on the table, and: 'Come with me.'

'Eh?'

'We must talk further, and we cannot talk safely here.'

Before an astonished Rennie could ask a single question, Mr Mappin was already away to the door. Rennie hastily took up his hat, rose and followed.

Rennie caught him up and walked with Mr Mappin briskly along the parade toward the fortifications, the castle against the sky in the east. The day was pleasantly sunny and warm, and there was a light topsail breeze. Ships lay moored. A sloop dashed down the harbour, and heeled toward Spithead. Portsmouth had never looked finer or more naval, thought Rennie as he glanced at the flag flying from the tower in the afternoon light. Presently, at the stone wall, Mr Mappin turned and spoke, and within a very few minutes Rennie had been made to understand. He stared at Mr Mappin as that gentleman finished speaking, nodded decisively, and:

'We will not need another ship, Mr Mappin, now that you have made everything clear to me. To take another ship when so much is at stake would be tempting fate beyond all sense. If I go at once to the dockyard and put things in motion, and lift everyone to his duty urgent, we can be ready for sea in a very short time indeed. I will make it so.'

'But if *Expedient* ain't—'

'I will do it, I give you my word. We shall return to France by the appointed date.'

'You are certain . . . ?' Frowning at him.

'As certain as I have ever been about anything, by God. I know my own ship in every distinction, great and small. I will get her ready, put to sea, and complete this task. You have my word on it.'

'Well . . .' Still doubtful.

'There ain't a moment to lose.' Before Mr Mappin could demur, or make further objection. 'Good day to you, sir.'

And Rennie set off down the line of fortifications at something like a run, clutching his hat to his head.

*

Close to, Madame Maigre was even more beautiful than James had thought when he first observed her from his window high in the château roof. He was now aware of the name of the house, Château de Châtaigne – after the large forest of chestnut trees that lay on the estate. M. Félix had not volunteered this information, nor any information. Madame Maigre had told James herself. Their first meeting had been formal, and brief. He had not been taken down to meet her, in one of the grander rooms. She had come to his room, with M. Félix and another gentleman who was not introduced to James, but simply stood clear and waited.

'In course, he is her bodyguard,' said James to himself as he stood and made a leg to the lady.

'Lieutenant Hayter, I am so very pleased to meet you at last.'

'And I you, madame.'

'We will sit.' She indicated that James should again seat himself on the narrow bed, and without her having to signal to him the bodyguard brought her the single chair. James waited until she was seated, and then perched himself on the edge of the bed. A small smile said that she had noted his good manners.

'By God, she is a beauty.' James, not aloud, but struck by her astonishing skin, her wonderful dark eyes, her honey-dark hair, her full, expressive lips. 'Be careful, you damn' fool.' Silently.

'Monsieur Félix has told me that you do not yet under-stand the whole of this affair, Lieutenant.'

'Indeed, madame, I do not understand any of it, to say the truth.'

'Your people in London did not give you even the smallest hint?'

'They did not. Madame, you know my real name, and so I am puzzled as to why the subterfuge of a false one was required. False name, false appearance, false profession, false everything. Forgive my forthright language, but perhaps if you are acquainted with French sea officers you will know that as a race of men we are plain-spoke, and will like others that we find in the world to be plain-spoke also, when we are dealing with them. We are not very fond of disguise.'

Another faint smile.

'You do not find M. Félix plain-speaking?'

'But I am not dealing with M. Félix, madame – am I? I think that I am dealing with you – am I not?'

'Dealing, Lieutenant?'

'Forgive me, madame, I meant no disrespect to you. But I must converse with someone, I must bargain, or transact, or come to terms – with someone. Else why am I brought here? Why have I been obliged to come? You see?'

'Yes, I do see. And very soon you shall have what you desire.' She rose, and James was disturbingly aware of the curve of her bosom, of her figure altogether, in its fine sewn silk, and her ribbon-tied hair. A waft of her scent came to him.

'Can she be seducing me deliberate?' In his head, as he stood up and bowed again.

The day following they had met again, downstairs in a small oval room with a high ceiling and tall windows, simply but pleasantly furnished. The fabric of the room was old and faded, but had been very fine. The view was of a wide, tree-lined garden beyond an intervening stone wall. In this room Madame Maigre had served James coffee and cakes. His clothes had been returned for this second occasion – his coat, shoes, &c. – and he felt himself less a prisoner and more the social equal of this enchanting creature, who leaned forward to fill his cup from the tall silver pot. She seemed slightly ill-at-ease, he thought, which gave her a charming vulnerability.

She began by telling him very briefly the history of the house and estate, and the family.

'Your family, madame?'

'No, not mine.' A nervous smile. 'I am here at the kind invitation of – sympathetic people. Supporters.'

'Supporters of . . . ?'

'Those who are in urgent need of your support also, Lieutenant. Your assistance.'

'My assistance – as a silk trader? They wish me to export bolts of cloth?' Half-facetious.

'No.' And this time her smile was absent, her beautiful face very serious, her gaze direct. 'No, only themselves.'

'Do you mean, madame – that you wish me to take these people out of France?'

'Yes.'

'When the ship that brought me here returns? That is your proposal? That I take them out in a British ship of war?'

'Exact.' Her chin lifted a little.

'I see.' He did not see, but continued: 'Who are they? Will not you tell me, madame?'

'They are in great danger.'

'Well, I do not doubt that many people feel themselves in danger, and wish to flee. Are they aristocrats? Members of a great trading family? Silk merchants, perhaps? I have every sympathy, but why could not they hire their own vessel, or even buy one?'

'Because they are watched.'

'Hm. Surely they cannot be watched so very close. I have begun to hear of many such people in England now, that have fled France—'

'You do not understand, Lieutenant.' A quick breath, that swelled her bosom, and a sigh.

'I confess I do not.' Unable to prevent himself from glancing at her breasts.

'These people are at the very heart of life in France. They *are* the heart.' The direct dark gaze.

And now James knew what she meant. At last understood, and felt the hairs prickle at the back of his neck. He was afloat on a dark and dangerous sea.

'I see.' Softly, a nod. 'Yes, I see.' Looking out at the quiet garden a moment, the shading, quiet trees beyond the lichen-speckled wall. This tranquil view contrasted with the whirl of thoughts and anxieties in his head. Turning to meet her gaze:

'I wonder, madame, if the king and queen wished to escape, why they would not go to Austria, to Her Majesty's brother . . . ?'

'That has been a rumour widely circulated in Paris. The royal family will attempt to flee to Austria. That is why they are held at the Tuileries – so they may be watched.'

'Then if they are watched so close, how will they escape at all?'

'It is to be managed at night. They will travel west through the countryside under escort, as part of a military convoy. No one will even dream that the king would come to Brittany, and go out of France by sea. Therefore, no one will suspect the convoy, which will carry forged warrants from Paris, should it be stopped en route by the National Guard. It will simply be a movement of troops and supplies to help secure the region. You can have no notion of the upheaval and ferment we have faced in France, Lieutenant.'

'Only what I have heard and read, madame, since the revolution.'

'Everything has become even more unpredictable and dangerous in these last weeks. All sympathisers and supporters are now at risk.'

'I have no reason to doubt that, but I must say to you that there will be grave difficulties with this plan, very grave risks.'

'Everything is grave, for the royal family. It would be a grave and terrible risk for the king to remain, and wait for his head to be cut off.'

'The place where I was advised to come ashore is very rugged, the boat was nearly upset, and we lost a man drowned. Again I must say to you that no sea officer can guarantee the safety of passengers going into a boat at that place and proceeding to the ship – which will be obliged to remain well outside the barrier of islets and rocks that line the coast.'

'It is a risk that must be borne, Lieutenant. The place was chosen because it is so barren and remote, and so unlikely. His Majesty—'

'Why does not Count Mirabeau intervene, to persuade the more moderate—'

'Count Mirabeau is dead.'

'Dead? When?'

'In the spring. Robespierre is now in the ascendant, and there could not be a more dangerous and vengeful man, a man more inimical to the king.'

'I had not heard of it. I had not heard of it.' Shaking his head. 'I was – preoccupied at that time, madame, and knew little of the world outside.' Glancing at her. She seemed scarcely to have heard his comment, and continued earnestly:

'All hope of moderation and conciliation died with Mirabeau, and all of us knew it. From that moment it became imperative that the king should escape, and plans were prepared. It has been arranged for the end of the third week of June – a few days from now. The party will come by convoy from Paris. Will your ship be ready? It is arranged for the ship to wait in place?'

'She will be ready, madame. She will stand in on the twentieth of June, and wait for four and twenty hours. Or as near that date as she is able, depending on the weather.'

'Depending on the weather? Are you saying . . . are you saying there is a possibility your ship will not return?' In alarm.

'Oh, she will return, I am in no doubt. But I wish we could have had this conversation just as soon as I came ashore, days since. Because at sea such an arrangement will always be contingent upon the weather, and cannot always be exact, you understand . . . however momentous the plan behind it.'

'We will manage it. It must be managed.' Resolute.

James stood up and stared out of the window a few moments, then:

'I am obliged to ask you again, madame – for the love of God, why was I confined? Why was I led blindfold about the countryside for days together, and then imprisoned here? If you wished me to undertake so important a task – I can only assume that is why my elaborate disguise was arranged – why did not you meet me and tell me all this at once?'

'I am very sorry for all of it, Lieutenant. I do not act alone in this, of course. There are others involved who did not trust you.'

'Félix?'

'M. Félix – and others. They thought – some of them still think – that the British part of the plan could never be anything but a trick. Why should the English help the king of France to escape? England is our traditional enemy.'

'I have simply followed my orders, madame. I knew nothing of the scheme until a few minutes ago, when it came from your own lips. I can only assume—'

'They say that the English intend to deceive us, that they have decided to treat with the new regime in Paris, and that as soon as the king has gone into your ship he will be arrested and returned. Your role in this, your disguise as a silk merchant, established in London, was very typical of British duplicity – an elaborate hoax.'

'I am not a political man, madame, I am a sea officer. But what you have just described is unthinkable. I cannot believe that the British government would ever concoct or be party to so monstrous a betrayal.'

'I did not say that I believed it. I do not.' The dark, serious gaze. 'And cannot.'

'Then, surely—'

Over him: 'I have had to argue very strongly to save your life, Lieutenant. Félix and the others wished to execute you as a spy. You are lucky to be alive, and here talking to me.'

'Then, good heaven, it is madness, the whole thing is madness. If I was not to be trusted, if England was not, then why arrange for the king to come to this part of France at all?'

'Because in the end it was the only plan that had any hope of success, and all doubts had to be thrust aside. We *had* to trust you, or see the king perish. Those of us who believed this have prevailed. And so the convoy will come.'

And now she stood and came to his side, took his hand, and held it in both of hers.

'I hope with all my heart that you will not betray us – betray me, and my trust in you, Lieutenant.' She looked searchingly into his eyes, and he was aware of her with an intensity that made him nearly breathless. Her look, her scent, her touch, her physical closeness. He felt his heart beating in his breast as he said:

'I – I will never like to do anything to hurt you, madame.'

'You will be true?'

'I will be true.'

Her lips parted a little, she closed her eyes, and squeezed his hand.

*

Captain Rennie stood on the deck of *Expedient*, with dozens of dockyard artificers, his own standing officers, and a great mass of yards, parrals, blocks, cable-laid and shroud-laid rope, tar, and tools. The ship had been refloated, and lay outside the great basin, the prised-up sheets of copper on her larboard bow not replaced, and the leak there only patched and caulked.

Rennie and his standing officers faced a frantic twenty-four hours ahead. Her rigging must be rove up, her guns and stores got into her, and her people berthed, everything managed at breakneck speed – reckless speed – if he was to weigh and return to France in time. Even if he managed to depart tomorrow he would almost certainly be late at the rendezvous, but the party that waited on him in France, that depended on him, would surely remain at or near the Pointe de Malaise a day or two, would not they? Given the very grave importance of the enterprise?

'Well well, I will do all I can.' To himself, staring aloft at his half-naked masts. 'I will do all that is in my power. The rest is in God's hands.' A sniff, and aloud:

'Mr Tangible.'

'Sir?' The boatswain, coming from the larboard rail.

'Say to your rigging crews that they are to work alongside the dockyard riggers as if they was their own brothers, you mark me?'

'I have already spoke to them, sir.'

'Make it clear in the plainest language that if any man finds himself in dispute with a dockyard man, he will answer to me. We have no time for that tradition of hostility, nor dispute of any kind. Harmony, Mr Tangible, harmony and hard work will make them speedy.'

'Aye, sir.'

'Mr Loftus.'

'I am here, sir.'

'We have not time to get all her stores in, and she must be trimmed accordingly. The most important items are her guns, powder and shot. Mr Storey will work with you, you are to keep him at your side. Brook no excuse, listen to no plea for delay, nor more time, nor patience. Patience *ain't* a virtue, say to him. Our guns and gunners' stores are to be got into her *today*. We will warp to the gun wharf after the noon gun. The riggers will continue to work throughout.'

'Good God, even while the guns are being hoisted in?' Dismayed at the tangling confusion this could provoke.

'Even then, Mr Loftus. There is not one single moment to be lost, and I will flay the skin off the back of any man that does not know it. We will work all day, and all night, until we are ready for sea.'

'Very good, sir.' Obediently, stifling his doubts.

'Mr Adgett!' Raising his voice to a quarterdeck bawl, calling forrard.

His carpenter came aft along the gangway, shaking his hat free of sawdust, and thrusting a pencil behind his ear.

'Sir?' Stepping on to the quarterdeck.

'What do the dockyard men say, as to the patched repair?'

Grimacing, shaking his head: 'They do not like it, sir. Their work was not near complete when the shores was knocked down and we swam her out. And I confess I do not like it myself, as I say. She has no copper at the patched place, at the wales over the cant frames. That will impair her working going about, and our making headway, I should think.'

'Yes yes, it cannot be helped. What I require to know is – will the patched repair suffice for a week at sea? The caulking will hold?'

'It may do, sir – it might do. If we do not strike no more bad weather. I cannot answer for the safety of the ship in a storm of wind.'

'Very well, thank you, Mr Adgett. D'y'need more men for your own crew?'

'No, sir, thankee. I am reasonable content as I am, as to number of men. But I am not content as to the rest, sir, as I say. Any more than was the master shipwright, earlier today, when—'

'You may leave the handling and working of the ship to me, Mr Adgett.' Over him. 'You will not drown while I am in command.'

Rennie went below to the great cabin, the cracking of mallets and the shouts of artificers echoing behind him. He called for his clerk:

'Mr Tait! Mr Tait, I want you!'

Nehemiah Tait appeared, carrying notebooks, books, paper and ink. He was flustered.

'Are ye ready, Mr Tait?' Rennie threw off his hat and coat, and pulled a chair to him.

'I – I am doing my best, sir. I fear there was an upset in the boat, coming from the hulk, and I have lost my bundle of quill pens, that fell into—'

'Lost? You have no pens about you?'

'I – I fear not, sir. They fell into—'

'Christ Jesu, is there no end to ruthless impediment and vexation in the ship?' Going to his desk, pulling open drawers and finding a bundle of quills tied with twine. He threw the bundle to Mr Tait, who caught it awkwardly, and dropped several items.

'Penknife?'

'I have my own penknife, thank you, sir.' Stooping, gathering.

'Then put it to use, Mr Tait, right quick, if y'please. I must write a letter to Their Lordships.'

'Very good, sir.' Spilling notebooks, papers and pens in a rush on the table. Rennie sighed, blew out his cheeks, and:

'Boy!' Finding no response: 'Colley Cutton!'

'I am just boiling in the spirit kettle, sir.' Emerging from the quarter gallery, the cat Dulcie twining at his ankles.

'Never mind that. Find Mr Makepeace, and ask him with my compliments to come to me at once in the great cabin. Y'will likely find him below, in the hold. Then find Mr Leigh, and Mr Souter. I wish to see them all. I have something of great importance to tell them. Jump, man, jump.'

Colley Cutton touched his forehead, and sidled rapidly out.

'I am ready, sir.' Nehemiah Tait.

'Thank God there is someone in the ship that is, Mr Tait.' A small, grim nod.

A little more than twenty-four hours after, HMS *Expedient*, frigate, loosed her foretopsail, slipped her mooring on the tide, found the breeze off the point, and made sail for France.

TEN

Since being apprised of the nature of their business at Château de Châtaigne, James had been if anything kept under even closer scrutiny than before. However, he was allowed to descend to the small oval room to take his meals, and to converse there with Madame Maigre. He was also permitted to walk and talk with her in the leafy garden, where the air smelled headily of flowers, and the sharp fragrances of herbs, and the sounds were all peaceful – birdsong, and the chirring of insects. On the second afternoon of this greater freedom for James, Madame Maigre turned to him, pausing so sudden that she was almost in his arms as she turned, and:

'Listen to that beautiful birdsong . . .' Closing her eyes as she leaned back her head to listen, revealing the curve of her neck, and the tops of her breasts, and her slightly open mouth. James had to hold himself away with so great an effort of will that he felt his head begin to swim.

She opened her eyes after a moment, and: 'You hear it, don't you, Lieutenant?'

'I hear only the beating of my heart, madame.' Before he could stop himself.

'Oh!' A smile. 'Are you so inward-looking that you have no time for the beautiful creatures of nature?' She turned her head again, drew in a breath and closed her eyes as the melodious notes of the bird – a wren – floated over the lich-ened wall and through the shading branches, giving a poignancy and sweetness to the whole stretching length of the quiet garden, and in that moment he was lost. When she opened her eyes, deep and dark, he took her in his arms and kissed her.

She tried to draw back, to clutch at his arms and break from his embrace, but her resistance was not sustained, grew feeble and was gone, and her own arms were lifted to circle his neck as she gave up her mouth to his, and pressed her body into him.

At last, drawing back her head a little, she murmured:

'Not now. Soon.'

'You will come to my chamber?'

'I will come. And now we must continue to walk, else they will grow suspicious.'

They had been standing deep beneath a spreading tree that hid them from the wall and the house, and now emerged to stroll down the hushed length of the garden. James tried to think of what to say to her, but no rational words would come to him. To himself, as he walked beside her, and glanced casually back toward the wall: 'I cannot say I love her, I scarce know her at all. I must not say it. For the love of Christ I am a married man, married to the most beautiful and wonderful girl. Why did I let myself go just now? Why did I ask her to come to my room? What possessed me? What possesses me yet? You bloody fool, you wretched bloody fool. What are you *doing*!'

At length he said:

'I wish I could say that I care more about why we are here, and my duty, and the great thing we attempt, than I do about being with you – but I do not.' His heart thudding.

'You must not say that to me. Nor let anyone in the house hear you say it.'

'At this moment, here, now, it is simply the truth.'

'Do not walk too close to me, do not take my hand in yours. Monsieur Félix will challenge you if he sees you touch me.'

'He is your lover?' Surprised.

'No. No, he never was. But he wished to be, and still

wishes it. He torments himself with jealous fantasy. That is why he has thrown us together like this, in the garden. To feed the fire of his jealousy, to torment himself.'

'Will not that distract him from *his* duty?'

'For him it is everything, and nothing. He sees me, he talks to me, he is with me – without possessing me. It keeps him on a knife edge, and that is why he is so acute a commander. Every nerve in his body is alert, and tingling. He is alive to every threat, and every possibility. It makes him the best man in France for this undertaking. You see?' A flash of the dark eyes.

'Are you quite certain you never had a regard for him . . . ?'

'He chills me to the bone.' She shivered. 'But he is one of us, he is at the very centre of our endeavour, and we can do nothing without him.'

At thirty minutes to midnight, several days after, as James waited in his locked bedchamber high under the roof, four large covered carts rolled into the great courtyard below, followed by a single plain carriage and a guard of twenty soldiers.

The convoy from Paris had come.

*

In the morning James was brought downstairs to the oval room, but Madame Maigre was absent. Nor had she come to his room during the night. M. Félix was alone in the room, and it was he who briefed the prisoner – as James was obliged still to think of himself. The angular figure turned, and James was again confronted by that gaunt, unforgiving face.

'The party has arrived, as you may know, Lieutenant.'

'I watched their arrival, monsieur, late last night.'

'Their Majesties have expressed the desire to remain completely secluded during their short stay here. Until it is time for them to go into the ship, they will not emerge, nor will they like to see anyone outside their immediate entourage. You understand?'

'Very good. But I must ask certain questions now, monsieur.'

'Questions? There is nothing more you need to know.'

'Well, but there is. How many?'

'Lieutenant?' Irritably.

'How many are in the entourage, and how many of them will be going to the place, to the inlet at the Pointe de Malaise? In addition to Their Majesties? It is vital that I know the number exact, so that I may arrange places in the boat.'

A conceding nod. 'Yes, I see that is important. There will be twenty persons altogether.'

'Twenty! Nay, I had thought perhaps half a dozen, the immediate family only.'

'Their Majesties have particular needs that must be accommodated, monsieur. They cannot be expected to leave France without their principal aides and bodyservants, and various others.'

A quick, impatient nod, and: 'Monsieur, now it is I that must make something clear. We cannot take twenty people in the boat. The boat's crew will be double-banked on the thwarts, to provide sufficient pulling power to get the boat through the hazardous passage. In addition there will be the officer commanding, the coxswain, and myself. There will room, safely, for at most another six persons, and therefore—'

Over him: 'We can reduce the numbers by a few, perhaps – but you will not be going into the boat, Lieutenant.'

'What?'

'No, you will remain with us, until word comes that Their Majesties are safe. That they have reached their destination, and are safe.'

'That is quite impossible, monsieur. If I do not go into the boat, then the boat will not take anyone aboard at all.'

'You cannot mean it.' With open contempt. 'You seriously suggest that you are of greater importance than Their Majesties?'

'I suggest nothing of the kind, in my own right. I am merely following orders. I am to go into the boat, and return to the ship. You yourself, however, have given me sufficient importance to try to hold me hostage against Their Majesties' safety. I don't rate myself so high. I repeat, I merely seek to follow my orders.'

Most of this was pure bluff, and James was unsurprised when M. Félix countered with:

'Your orders have been changed, Lieutenant.'

'By whom?'

'By myself.'

'You have no authority to issue orders to me, monsieur. My orders are issued only in England.'

'Not whilst you are in France, monsieur.' Dismissively, looking out of the window.

'Where is Madame Maigre? I wish to speak to her.'

Turning with a cold stare: 'Madame Maigre cannot aid you, monsieur. She is not in command. Her duties here are now complete, and she will return to Paris.'

'To Paris? Why? When Their Majesties are here, what is there for her to do in Paris, now?'

'There are many others who will wish to leave France, once it becomes clear the king has gone. Madame Maigre will be invaluable in aiding and guiding and assisting them.' A breath. 'You will be returned to your room, Lieutenant, until we are ready for you to go to the inlet and make your signals to the ship.'

'I will make no such signals, monsieur, unless I am permitted to go into that boat.' Defiantly.

'Do not be foolish. I personally would take great pleasure in putting you to torture, if you failed to comply. Serge!'

His dour assistant entered and stood waiting. James glanced out of the window, nodded there, and:

'With your permission, monsieur, I should like five minutes of fresh air. Surely that is not too much to ask, when you ask so much of me?'

A long, bleak glance, then M. Félix nodded. James was taken out into the garden and allowed to walk – with Serge not far behind. James wandered under the trees and snuffed the fragrant shade, but his head was wholly at odds with his tranquil surroundings.

'I must contrive to escape with the royal party. I must contrive to bring Madame Maigre out with me. I will not leave her behind. I will not.' A glance toward Serge, and he wondered briefly if he could not make a dash for the far wall now, and freedom. As if sensing such a possibility, Serge had moved closer.

James paced slowly down the length of the garden, turned casually and glanced up at the high windows of the château. Where was the royal party concealed? In which room was Madame Maigre? A nod to Serge, and he lingered a moment, breathing the soft air.

Il faut que je méchappe.'And he found that he was talking to himself in French saying that he must find a way out. He allowed himself a brief ironic smile. He must think like an Englishman, and try to answer the many questions that jostled in his head in English. What destination had been decided upon for the king and queen? And by whom? Had they decided it themselves? Or had they been advised where to go by the British government? No mention of this had been made to James by Mr Mappin. Mappin had said nothing about the French royal family at all, indeed.

Presently Serge grew impatient, and gestured to James that they should return to the house.

'A beautiful day, is it not?' James said to him, as they set off. '*C'est magnifique.*'

And received no hint of a response.

*

Expedient was not near her own destination as night fell. She lay virtually becalmed some way to the west of the Channel Isles. There was a slow, somnolent, glassy swell in the twilight, and the frigate's sails hung limp. Rennie had paced his deck in an agony of frustration, sent out the boats, then brought the hands back aboard to supper, the boats towed astern. Now, as the watch changed at hammocks down:

'I will go below, Mr Leigh.' To the new officer of the deck.

'Very good, sir. You wish to see the glass-by-glass notations?' Stepping to the binnacle, and removing the noted log under the light.

'No no. There will be nothing in them of the slightest interest, hey?'

'I fear not, sir. Only the lack of progress of the ship.' Returning the notes.

'Indeed. We may only hope for a relieving breeze. Pray for one, will you?'

In the great cabin Rennie sat alone at a late supper, pushed it aside, drank off a glass of wine, and began to write up his journal. The cat Dulcie joined him, leapt into his lap, and fell asleep. Each time he reached to dip his quill in the ink the slight movement caused the furled creature to emit an astonishingly loud purr, like nasal drumming, and to flex her claws against Rennie's legs, to remind him of her affection, lately restored after a prolonged period of hauteur and indifference to his own repeated offers of friendship. Gently, fondly:

'Aye, Dulcie, aye. I am aware of you there, my dear.'
He wrote:

At four bells of the second dog watch, & hammocks down, in light airs & the ship making no headway.
　　At noon she lay at　　3 degrees & 55 minutes W
　　　　　　　　　　　　48 degrees & 29 minutes N
& our progress since has been woeful slow.

The boats hoisted out following on the declaration of noon, & an attempt was made to bring the ship to a breeze, to no avail, & I ordered the boats' crews inboard subsequent to eat their supper, and the boats towed.

Today during the afternoon watch were sighted three Indiamen bound NE at a league & one half distant, very slow, & we did not speak. Chasse-marées & bisquines also, eastward.

The patched repair to the bow remains adequate.

We suffer no sick men, & in consequence Dr Wing is content. I am not. We must reach our design tomorrow, or fail.

WR

'What system of lantern signals had been arranged, Lieutenant?' M. Félix, to James. They were standing in darkness on the rocky beach of the inlet, in the dank tidal whiff of seaweed.

'Three long flashes of a lantern, at regular intervals of a minute, until an answer was observed. Then the boat was to come in.'

'Very well.' He gave an instruction to his assistant, there was a brief clatter of disturbed shingles, and the lantern was produced. 'We will begin.'

After half an hour, when no answering light could be seen to seaward, M. Félix:

'We will wait a further hour, and signal again.'

'Have you a flask with you, monsieur?'

'Flask? No.'

'Perhaps your man has one . . . ?'

'My man?'

'Your servant. Serge.'

'Serge is not my servant, Lieutenant. He is my nephew. And he does not drink anything except water, or goat's milk.'

'Ah. Not even wine?'

'He is very careful of his health.'

'As am I, Monsieur Félix, and the damp air does not aid it.' A breath, he kicked away a pebble from under his shoe, and: 'Has Madame Maigre returned to Paris?'

A moment of silence, then: 'Why do you ask that?'

'I wished to know if she had left the château. I believe that if she returns to Paris she will be in very grave danger, once it becomes known that the king has flown.'

'She will remain here until Their Majesties are safely in the ship – and then she will go.'

'You will not like to consider the danger she may be in, if she—'

'I will not, Lieutenant.' Sharply, over him. 'Your concern is Their Majesties' passage away from France, and nothing else.'

'Yes, in course it is my concern . . . and I do not yet know their destination. I have been told nothing about that. Will you tell me where they are going?'

'When they arrive there, and news of their arrival reaches us here, then you will be free to go. Until then their destination does not concern you, Lieutenant.'

'Why was not I permitted even to see the king and queen? Would not it be sound sense for them to see me before they go into the boat, so that Their Majesties would not be alarmed by a strange face among them on the beach?'

'When the boat comes ashore you will be returned to the château at once. You will not see Their Majesties – who wait separately – and they will not see you, when there is plainly no need.'

'My God, I cannot understand why you wish to treat me so churlish, monsieur, when I—'

'Churlish? Lieutenant, I must ask you to be silent.' Sharply, over him. 'Your questions are irksome to me. In truth I do not enjoy your conversation at all. It is repetitive, whining with complaint, and dull. I thought the English prided themselves on their fortitude, and wit.'

James bit his tongue, counted to twenty, and effortfully kept his temper. The wash of the sea on the rocks, the occasional rattle of a stone as one of them shifted his feet, and the drifting reek of seaweed, and shellfish. They waited a further hour, signalled again, and again found no response.

'The ship will not come tonight, monsieur.'

'We will wait, and try again.'

Further hours passed, the same procedure was followed, and produced – nothing.

As dawn approached James yawned, and stood up – they had all sat down on the rocks long since – and stretched to ease his numb backside and stiff limbs.

'*Expedient* will not come, Monsieur Félix.'

No response.

James rubbed his face, sighed, and: 'The ship is not here, she is delayed. We must return to the château, and wait another day.' To his surprise M. Félix grunted, grumbled, and allowed:

'Hm, perhaps after all you are right, Lieutenant. It has been a long night, and we are all tired.'

They climbed the cliff, and returned to the Château de Châtaigne in a covered cart, a horseman riding ahead. James's blindfold was not replaced for this journey, and he saw that the house was not more than two miles inland, hidden in a vale, and approached by a circuitous route through orchards and woodland, the road little more than a winding lane. When they reached the château they did not go in by the great gate, but came to the rear and a small gate let into the wall under a spreading tree. For the first time James saw the extent and grandeur of the house and surrounds. From this side the château looked almost like a fortress, a place much older than he had at first imagined.

He was taken to his bedchamber, and again locked in. He lay down on the cot and at once sank into an exhausted, dreamless sleep.

When he woke hours later it was to the scraping and

turning of a key in the lock. He heard soft footfalls, and felt someone sit on the end of the bed. For a moment or two he had no notion where he was. At home, in Birch Cottage? Nay, there was no room like this in Dorset. Light from a tall window at the end of the room. Afternoon light, he thought. He sat up, blinking in that light, scratched his head, drew in a breath – and saw Madame Maigre. Heaven, her looks.

He said in French: 'You have not gone away.' Using 'tu'.

'I have not gone away. I wished to see you first.' Softly, using 'tu'.

'I am so very glad.' Heartfelt. All thought of Dorset flying from him.

And now the thing that had been inevitable between them from the beginning overtook them, and they were consumed. It seemed entirely natural to them both to be thus devoured by a force too powerful to resist, and when later they lay side by side neither felt anything but serenity and contentment, and a new intimacy. At first the intimacy was simply of closeness, and quiet, and then it grew naturally and became the intimacy of lovers' talk.

They talked through the late afternoon, and into the softening, fading light of evening. He wished to know her given name.

'What is yours?' she countered.

'I am James. James Rondo.'

'I like Rondo best. It is more gallant, and romantic. I shall call you Rondo.'

A sudden pang, and he frowned. 'I would prefer that you did not.'

'No? Why not?' Amused.

'I – I am not at ease with that name any more.'

Gently, seeing that he was troubled: 'Then I shall call you James.'

'Thank you, I prefer James.' Smiling at her. 'And now tell me your name.'

'Juliette. But I am not Madame Maigre. That is a false name.'

Turning to look at her. 'Ah, you mean – just as my name when I first came ashore was Henry Tonnelier?'

'Yes. We all live and work under these invented names. Thus, if we are ever taken, our families cannot be harmed.'

He was tempted to ask her if she was married – and then did not. She would certainly ask the same of him, and he did not wish to think of his home, and Catherine, and all of his past and future life in England. He did not wish to feel any further regret or remorse, with Juliette's scent in his nose and hair and the taste of her on his tongue. Not now. Not at this moment of languor and easy voices in the quiet magical air.

Presently Juliette: 'Talking of names, do you know Lady Sybil Cranham?'

'No.' Propping himself on elbow to look at her. 'Who is she?'

'She has helped to arrange this escape for us, through her friends in London. Your ship. You yourself.'

'I have never met her. I know nothing about her, except what you have just told to me. She is your friend?'

'Yes, very much.'

'And she will return, after the king has gone?'

'I had better say nothing more.'

'You don't trust me?'

'The less each of us knows about the other the safer we shall be.'

'Those are not your words, though. They are Monsieur Félix's words, are not they?'

'Hush. Let us not talk of these things, when we have so little time left.' She leaned and kissed him, but he drew back a little, and:

'I am greedy. I want more time.'

'My love, we must attend to our duty, and save the king. That is all that—'

'I will like to save you.' And he kissed her, began again to drown in her.

Crack! Crack-Crack! Crack-crack-crack!'

Echoing across the stone wall and courtyard below.

James leapt off the bed, ran to the window, and was shocked by a hole punched through the glass by his head, and splinters of wood flying all round him as the musket ball smashed into the casement. He fell back, and felt stinging where fragments of glass had cut his face and neck.

'James!' Running naked to his side.

'Keep down, keep away from the window!'

Crack! Crack-crack!

Another ball exploded through the window, shattering the entire pane, and ricocheted along the wall with a fizzing whine.

James hopped and stumbled, pulling on his clothes and shoes. 'Have you the key, Juliette?'

She pulled on her own clothes, and he was fleetingly aware of her breasts and unpinned hair as she struggled to button and fasten. Fleetingly but intensely aware of her sheer physical allure. As she found and held out the key, pushing back her hair, he thought:

'I cannot bear to lose her.'

And he took the key, unlocked the door, and ran with her, hand in hand down the long stone stair, as further shots rang across the courtyard. Shouts echoed, the whinnying shriek of a horse in mortal pain, and the screams of men.

Juliette, panting by his side as they ran along a passage into the great hall: 'We must save the king!'

M. Félix met them in the doorway at the far end, his gaunt

face very pale and grim. If he was surprised to see James with Madame Maigre he gave no hint of it. Tersely:

'The National Guard surround the house. Somehow they have discovered that the king is here. There is no hope of fighting them, or even holding them off – they are too many. We will use the passage to go out undetected.' Turning and leading the way along a narrow corridor.

'Passage?' James followed him with Juliette, still holding her hand.

'There is an underground passage leading to the heart of the wood behind the house. We will wait in the passage until nightfall, then come out into the wood, and go to the beach at the Pointe de Malaise.'

More shots from without.

'The gate will soon be smashed down, and the loyal platoon overcome. They must find their luck where they may, we cannot aid them now. The stable is already overrun, and we must go into the passage.'

'Is the platoon well armed?' James, as they hurried to the end of the corridor.

'With muskets and pistols only. There are over a hundred National Guard troops outside the walls. They may well have a field gun, to shatter the gate.'

As they came to the narrow doorway at the end of the corridor, James took M. Félix's arm.

'Juliette – Madame Maigre – cannot now return to the château from the beach, Monsieur Félix. Nor can I. Will you give me your word that we may go into the boat, and then into *Expedient*?'

Pulling free his arm. 'There is no time for that now, for God's sake.'

James seized his arm again, and spun round him with all his sailor's strength: 'Give me your word.' Fiercely.

'Very well, Englishman. You may have it, I suppose.'

*

'Our destination on the coast is three leagues due east, sir, but I fear mist is rolling in from the west.'

Captain Rennie, having kept the deck without a break five watches through, had returned from his cabin after a deep, necessary and refreshing sleep. He glanced to the west, and saw a bank of fog on the water.

'Thankee, Tom.' To Lieutenant Makepeace at the binnacle.

Rennie looked aloft, and again west, and asked for the direction of the wind, the speed and direction of the ship, and what canvas had been bent, or put in the brails, in the last glass or two. His first lieutenant told him, reading from his notations as the duty midshipmen prepared for the changing of the watch. Rennie listened, nodded, again glanced aloft, and paced to the tafferel, where he brought up his long glass. Away to larboard the Pointe de Malaise rose black and clear in the early evening light, and the islets that lay just offshore – but for how long? The setting sun would soon be obscured behind that bank of fog, the fog would roll relentlessly on, and envelop the ship, the surrounding sea, the scene entire. *Expedient* was already late at the rendezvous. Should he risk standing in, now?

'I do not wish to go aground in fog and darkness.' To himself. 'But I must do everything I can to make the rendezvous tonight.'

If the fog became dense, no signals would or could be seen, and the rendezvous must be postponed at least another day.

'We will tack east a further league, Mr Makepeace, if y'please. If the fog keeps pace with us, or indeed overhauls us, then we must anchor and wait.'

'Very good, sir.' To the helmsman: 'Due east, on my command.' Raising his speaking trumpet, and walking forrard a few paces: 'Stand by to tack ship!' And shortly after, calling aft: 'Starboard your helm!'

Expedient duly swung east in a graceful curve. The fog followed. Before the ship had sailed even half a league the fog overtook and enveloped her, and Rennie ordered the ship to heave to, and anchor. She lost way, maintopsail aback, and presently:

'Let go!'

The stopper let go, and the bower falling with a splash and a thrumming whine of cable.

Expedient, her sails brailed up – all but her mizzentop that now lay aback – came to a stop in the shrouded sea, and lay still.

'Mr Tangible.'

'Sir?'

'Y'may pipe hammocks down.'

The echoing notes of the call along the deck, and Rennie took a great sniff of misty sea air, turned to his first lieutenant, and:

'Will ye join me for supper, Tom? And we'll drink a glass or two to keep this damn' mist at bay.'

'Gladly, sir, thank you.'

ELEVEN

The underground passage was low, narrow, and smelled of earthen damp. Tendrils of something James could not identify hung from the curved arch of the roof. Slime? Weed? Cobweb? The royal party was some distance ahead, a huddled group protected by a core handful of troops. The glow of their lanterns was too low for James to be able to make out faces distinct, or even precise numbers. The dripping quiet – down here all sound of battle and invasion was blocked out – was broken only by subdued murmurs of conversation in the dim light.

Presently word came back to the group at the rear – James, Juliette, M. Félix and Serge – that the royal party wished to move forward. The soldier who had brought the message returned to the party ahead, and M. Félix nodded:

'We cannot wait here in the tunnel. We must leave the château at once, and go into the wood. Serge, you will remain here at the rear. I will go forward to Their Majesties, and guide them.'

M. Félix advanced along the tunnel, and with much bowing and murmuring took his place at the head of the royal party. Presently the two groups, still separated by considerable distance, moved ahead. They walked perhaps three or four hundred yards, twice negotiating dog-leg bends, and came to a steep and narrow stone stair at the end. One of the soldiers went up the stairs and was lost to view. Presently all those in the dingy tunnel felt an exhilaration, a sense of immediate relief and release, and James realised that the cause was fresh air. He had frequently experienced the same sensation at sea, coming on deck to take his watch after a prolonged period below in the oppressive air of bilge stink and the odour of unwashed bodies massed together in the hammock rows. The smell in the tunnel was not of too many bodies, but of too many days and months and years of dripping, bricked-in airlessness.

A brief delay, then a message came back. Fog had rolled in from the sea, thick and heavy, and there was no possibility of embarking tonight at the Pointe de Malaise, or even of finding it.

James advanced toward the royal party, seeking to consult with M. Félix. His way was blocked by a soldier with a musket, bayonet fixed.

'No, monsieur, you will come no further.'

'But I wish to speak to Monsieur Félix. It is most important—'

'You may speak to me, monsieur, and I will give him your message.'

Even though this man was in the uniform of an ordinary foot soldier, James was certain that he was addressing an officer. The man's bearing said so, and his educated voice.

'And you are . . . ?'

'Monsieur?'

'Allow me to introduce myself. I am Lieutenant Hayter, RN.'

'Then it is your ship that will take us out?'

'Yes, the *Expedient* frigate.'

A nod. 'You will understand, under the circumstances, that I am not at liberty to reveal my rank to you, Lieutenant, nor my name – but yes, I am an officer in the service of His Majesty.'

'Then you will readily understand, in turn, that we cannot remain here in the tunnel. We must leave the château altogether, and go into the woods. If we remain, the inner entrance of the tunnel will almost certainly be discovered, and we should face certain death. The National Guard have at least one hundred men, well armed. We are but a few, with few weapons.'

'There is a dense mist outside, Lieutenant. We could not find our way to the shore, and your ship will not send a boat in such conditions. We—'

'We must take our chance in the woods, or perish like rats in this dungeon.' Forcefully.

'You may not talk of Their Majesties in such terms, Lieutenant, while I have the honour to protect them.'

'I apologise. It is my wish, as much as it is your own, to protect Their Majesties. We must go up out of this tunnel, and make an attempt to reach the inlet at the Pointe de Malaise. The fog will eventually lift, and then the boat will come. If we stay here, the—'

'You are not in command, Lieutenant.' Over him. 'Kindly allow us to know what is best for Their Majesties' welfare. Please to rejoin your group at the rear, now.' A jerk of the head.

'Do not you see? The fog will certainly confuse those National Guard troops, just as it will hide us from—'

'It is you who do not see, Lieutenant. Be silent, if you please, and allow me to do my duty.'

James was beginning to despair of this officer when he saw M. Félix approaching from the end of the tunnel. He addressed him directly:

'Monsieur Félix, are you in command of the royal party's escort? Of this enterprise altogether?'

'I am.'

'Then I beg you – let us go out of the tunnel now, make our way through the mist to the lane beyond, and on down to the shore. We must make the attempt.'

'The fog is far too thick.' With finality, pointing to the stair, from which eddies of mist could be seen descending in the dim lantern glow. Turning back to James and cutting him off before he could continue. 'We must therefore wait here, below ground. When the National Guard have searched the château without success, they will very likely assume that Their Majesties have already escaped.'

'You assume they will not find the entrance to this tunnel? Do you?' Shaking his head.

'As you saw when we came down, the entrance is concealed behind an apparently solid stone wall. To trigger the sliding mechanism that opens the wall would require direct knowledge of it, or astonishing good luck. The attackers will have neither.'

'Can you really be certain of that, Monsieur Félix? They knew where to come to find the king, exact. Did not they?'

'But they have not found him. They cannot, and will not.'

'Christ Jesu, will not you ask yourself – how came they to this place, hid away on the coast, far from Paris? As out-of-the-way a place as it would be possible to think of in all of Brittany, monsieur. And yet they came here, over one hundred strong, and stormed the house. How? How did they know? Because they had information!'

'We will remain in the tunnel until the mist has cleared.' Stubbornly, firmly.

'Then will you in least allow me to go up and out, and make my own way to the Pointe de Malaise? If the fog lifts, and the boat comes in, I could—'

'No one will leave the tunnel tonight. I have made my decision.' Turning away toward the stair.

James gripped his arm. 'Tell me, monsieur – what does His Majesty think?'

'What?'

'Does His Majesty agree with you, Monsieur Félix?'

'That is not your affair.' Curtly.

'Oh, is it not? But I dispute that, you know. I think it is my business, absolutely. As the officer who will get the royal party into the boat, and aboard the ship, I believe it is my responsibility to inform His Majesty how I intend to manage it. Will you take me to him, monsieur?'

'I will not.' A furious glare.

'Then I will go to him, anyway.' Making to move past M. Félix.

Juliette, who had remained silent until now, took James's arm. 'No, James, no. Not even I am permitted to approach Their Majesties. The bodyguards would certainly shoot you. We must do as Monsieur Félix asks.'

M. Félix continued to glare at him, and at last James:

'Damnation!' In bitter exasperation, knowing he could not persist. He let go of M. Félix's arm, turned to face the other way, and with the dank reek of the tunnel in his nostrils like an omen of the tomb, resigned himself to wait.

*

'There it is! There is the light.'

On the shingle of the inlet Lieutenant Hayter saw the glow of the signalling light from the ship, a league off – one, two, three long flashes in the darkness. A sea breeze, the saline tidal smell of the rocks, the subdued surging hiss of waves breaking on shingle, and sucking in retreat. And now the click of the dark-cover on their own lantern as the answer was made. A confirming series of flashes at sea, and James turned to M. Félix, who said no word to him, but returned to where the royal party remained huddled and separate at the top of the beach, beneath the towering cliff. Serge covered the lantern with his cloak, and waited for further instruction. Juliette had lain down in the hollow of a rock hours since, covered by her own cloak.

'Why do not you join the royal party?' James had asked her. Long hours in the dark, damp tunnel under the château, then the urgent flight through the wood, and in commandeered farm carts along the lanes at dawn, the awkward, stumbling descent down the cliff path, and the subsequent anxious wait through the day at the inlet, had left everyone exhausted. 'They will undoubtedly have blankets and cushions to make themselves more comfortable.'

'I may not,' Juliette had told him. 'It is forbidden.'

'By whom? By Félix? Ain't he free to join them, if he wishes?'

'As their tactical commander and adviser, that is all. Not as equal, or anything like.'

'God's love, are not we all in this together? We are all of us human beings, wishing to get into a boat and escape, and save our lives, are we not?'

'Their Majesties are more than that. It is something that is understood. They are the heart and soul of France, her life's blood and her honour. I am merely a servant.'

'Yes, are you? But even a servant must keep herself warm. Wrap yourself up.' Concerned by her shivering pallor. And she had followed his advice.

Now he straightened up, stretching his aching limbs, and fervently wished he had a flask and a wedge of pie, his usual sustenance on watch through the night at sea. The royal party had had food and drink, he was certain. James and Juliette, and Serge, had had no food in twenty-four hours, and nothing but a little water to drink. M. Félix had very probably eaten when he was with the royal party, James thought. He had made requests, but had been curtly rebuffed.

'Our departure into the tunnel was very sudden, as you know. There was no time to prepare and bring food for us all.'

'Have not Their Majesties ate and drunk?'

'That is not your business.'

'Not my business . . . ? Have you ate, Monsieur Félix?'

No response. James had grown irate. 'Look here, you had better explain to the royal party that we are not beasts of burden that aid them in their escape. We are human beings. If they have ate, so should we have ate. Tell them that, if you please.'

'I will do nothing of the kind, and you will hold your tongue.'

'Then in least let Juliette have something to eat, if you will not feed me.'

'I am all right, James. I am used to hardship now, travelling through France.'

'Damnation to that. I demand—'

But M. Félix had simply walked away from them, and returned to the base of the cliff.

'Could not he in least *ask* for some food for us?' James, astonished and furious.

'He may not. He may not. Their Majesties will assume we have our own food. And he may not importune them in our behalf. And so we must bear a little hunger, a few hours. It is nothing, James.'

'It ain't nothing to me. I never heard of such damned infamous treatment. It would never be permitted at sea.'

'We are not at sea, my love.'

'Not yet.' Savagely.

Soon all this would be forgotten. Soon the boat would come, and they could go into it, and be taken out to *Expedient*. He looked to seaward, hoping to see the lantern in the boat, but saw nothing there but blackness. He sighed, and turned to look back up the beach, and saw the gleam of a light at the top of the cliff. Then another. And another.

'Christ's blood, we are discovered.' Whispered. A moment of hesitation, then he began to run toward the party at the base of the cliff. And stopped, skidding on the shingle. The National Guard clearly knew they were on the beach. What was the point of preserving silence now?

'Félix! Monsieur Félix! The cliff! We are under attack!' In bawling, carrying French.

At once the lanterns at the cliff base were extinguished, as the soldiers of the guard sprang up and readied their weapons. Lights bobbed and danced high above, rapidly descending.

Crack! Crack!

The muskets of the guard, fired at the flickering lights.

James, unarmed, ran to where Juliette lay concealed by a rock, and found her gone.

'Juliette! – Juliette!' Staring round him, then peering up at the cliff again. 'Juliette!' No answer, no sign of her. He twisted to look seaward – and saw the lantern of a boat. Nay, two lanterns, by God. Rennie had somehow read the situation correct, had anticipated their desperate need, and sent two boats in through the dangerous channel. Thank God for a man of action, a sea officer of sharp understanding.

'Boats ahoy!' Hands cupped, bellowing as if through his speaking trumpet on deck. 'Lay out with a will, lads, and take us off! We are under attack upon the beach! Cheerly! Cheerly now, for the love of Christ!' And turning up the beach he bellowed in French:

'Félix! Monsieur Félix! Bring your party down to the water! Our boats have come, and we must go into them!'

The royal party began to hurry down the shingle in the darkness, stumbling and clattering. A puff of sea breeze on James's face as he turned again to the boats. A whistling whirr by his ear, and a musket ball pocked the water beyond. Crack! The sound of the shot, and James ducked down. Crack! Crack-crack! A ball struck a rock in a snap of sparks. Another spun away whining into the darkness. The attackers were firing from on high.

'Hurry! Make haste, for the love of God!' James ran up the beach, slipped and nearly fell, and:

'Juliette! Juliette, where are you!'

Crack! Crack! Crack! Answering shots from the royal guard, fired up the cliff face. One of the lights high above went out, and a moment after a lantern pitched down on to the shingle, tumbled end over end and came to rest in a spill of broken glass.

The royal party came toward James in the darkness, and

he was forced back down to the water's edge by several of the guard.

'I must find Juliette,' he protested. 'I must find Madame Maigre.'

'You will assist Their Majesties into the boat, Lieutenant.' M. Félix, accompanied by the officer James had spoken to earlier. 'Juliette must make her own way.'

'But where has she gone to? I must look for her.' Attempting to push past this officer, who cocked his musket and stood in James's path.

'There is not time. We must get into the boat.' And M. Félix, pistol in hand, forced James backward down the shingle.

'Oh, very well. I will do as you ask, but then I must certainly find her.' And he turned and went down to the water. Cupping his hands: 'Boats ahoy! Who is in command!' In English.

Although the boats were now very near to the beach, and James could make out white paint along the wales, as well as the two lanterns, no reply came from either craft. The ripple of oars was the only sound.

'You there, in the lead boat! Who is in command? Tom Makepeace, are you there?'

No reply, only the rhythm of oars in thole pins, and the splash of the blades. Doubt, combined with fear, coiled and clawed in James's guts. He peered at the boats, and now heard – low but distinct over the water – a voice in French:

'Leve rames!'

'Christ Jesu . . .' Murmured. 'They are French boats.' Turning, bellowing: 'Take cover! Take cover! These are not our boats! They are National Guard boats!'

Crack! Crack!

The royal guard fired past James at the incoming shapes of the boats. Confusion as the royal party retreated. James followed, reflecting briefly that he had never yet got close enough to see any member of the royal family, that they had always been so shielded that his only impression of these demi-gods, whose lifeblood he was attempting to save, was of cloaks and hats and hidden faces, in shadowed light.

Crack! Crack-crack!

Further shots from the guards now, as they fired up at the lights still descending the cliff.

'How in God's name did they know our signal?' James, muttering to himself as he stumbled and slipped on wet shingle, crouching down to avoid being hit by a stray ball. He peered over his shoulder, and saw that the boats were now gliding right in to the water's edge. Soon he, and Félix, and the royal party entire, would be trapped between two superior forces – one from the sea, and the other from the cliff.

'What I would not give for my sword and a brace of sea pistols!'

A shout now behind him, across the water. An unmistakably English shout.

'Ahoy there, ashore! Take cover!' A moment, then: 'Take aim! – Fire! Fire! Fire!'

Followed almost immediately by the most welcome sound James had heard in all the days since this fraught business had begun.

Crack! Crack!

Half-pounder swivel guns, firing canister. Explosions of spray. Splintering thuds. A shriek.

James ducked down, but before he covered his head he glimpsed the boat behind the two French boats, which had now beached. It was *Expedient*'s pinnace, approaching at an angle to enable the best broadside coverage for her little guns.

Crack! Crack!

Canister shot raked the two beached boats in a hail of lethal metal. Further splintering thuds, and the chilling sound of shot smacking into flesh. Horrible screams.

The landing party in the French boats was now in utter disarray. Half of them were killed or gravely wounded, and the others wished only to preserve themselves from further murderous fire. The able-bodied survivors flung themselves ashore, abandoning the boats and their hapless companions, and ran for cover into the rocks on the southern side of the inlet.

A final 'Crack!' and a hissing scythe of shot, then:

'Cease firing! Cease firing!' Bellowed in the pinnace.

James jumped to his feet. 'Who is in command of the pinnace, there!'

'I am Lieutenant Leigh, in command! Who are you?' The voice, like James's, in carrying quarterdeck.

'Lieutenant James Hayter, Royal Navy! Beach your boat right quick, Mr Leigh! We are in desperate trouble here, and there ain't a moment to lose!'

More shots from the cliff, and when James glanced there now he saw that the bobbing lights were more than halfway down. The pinnace came in, and was held in the shallows by two seamen who jumped out at the bow. Lieutenant Leigh jumped ashore.

'You are Lieutenant Hayter?' Peering at James in the darkness.

'I am, Mr Leigh. Formerly of *Expedient*. We must—'

'That was Mr Tonnelier, hey?'

'Yes yes, I was. We must get our party off, as quick as you like. Quicker, by God.'

Merriman Leigh turned his attention to the large party now hurrying down to the water's edge, the guard at the rear firing back toward the cliff. In dismay:

'Christ's blood, Hayter, we cannot take all of these people in one boat. Where are Their Majesties?'

'In their midst, hid and protected. Look here now, we will have to take one of these French boats as well. Are ye double-banked?' Glancing into the pinnace.

'Aye, we are.'

'Then send some of your people into the other boat, and man 'em both single-banked.' Striding to the first French boat. 'This one.' But even as he tapped the bow of the boat with his hand he saw that the starboard gunwale was smashed, and the boat unseaworthy. Turning: 'Nay, we must go into t'other boat.' Splashing to the second boat, his clothes now thoroughly wet. The second boat was sound, aside from splintered timbers here and above the waterline. Groaning and dead men lay slumped on the thwarts, James looked at them briefly, made a face, and:

'Mr Leigh, we must clear this boat of dead and wounded.'

'D'y'mean – just leave them on the beach?' Coming to his side, peering into the boat.

'Mr Leigh, my task – and yours – is to get King Louis out of France. Kindly make this boat ready.' Pushing past him and striding a little way up the beach. Behind him he heard Lieutenant Leigh give the appropriate orders, and was relieved. Mr Leigh had allowed him to assume command without argument. Had Rennie instructed him to do so? James thrust these questions aside, and in French:

'Monsieur Félix! Bring your party down!'

An anxious glance at the cliff. The flashes of muskets there, and the crack of the shots. The lanterns were now reaching the base of the cliff.

The royal party arrived at the water's edge, at the centre a huddled group, faces hidden, surrounded by guards, M. Félix, and Serge. No sign of Juliette.

Merriman Leigh, aghast: 'My God, there is upwards of twenty people here, Hayter.'

'Aye, Mr Leigh. We must get them all into the boats, if y'please, without the loss of a moment. And I must find one more passenger.' Treading away up the shingle before Lieutenant Leigh could protest. Over his shoulder:

'Do not shove off without me!'

But when he rejoined an anxious Lieutenant Leigh three minutes after, just as the cliff party began storming down the beach toward the water, James was alone. He ran, splashed, leapt.

Crack! Crack-crack-crack!

James tumbled into the already swimming boat, and:

'Give way together! Cheerly now, lads! Cheerly!'

And the two boats slipped away from the beach into grateful, disguising darkness.

*

Rennie stood alone at the tafferel, his head bent and his eyes closed, and his right hand gripping his left elbow across his body, the whole of him tensed like a spring. He was not aware of quite how coiled up he was in defence of his thoughts against his immediate surroundings. As soon as he had heard the gunfire from the beach he had ordered the ship cleared for action, had contemplated sending in another boat and then decided against it, had fretted and paced in a fever of anxiety, and had at length withdrawn into himself and gone aft. The ship lay quiet, guncrews waiting in readiness along the sand-strewn decks. Rennie's thoughts – driving out all miserable visions of calamity and disaster at the beach – lay with his wife Sylvia, and she in his imagining lay in their bed at home in Norfolk, under a peaceful starlit sky, to the sounds of owls and nightjars and the distant barking of a fox at the edge of the wood. He could hear these night-wafted sounds quite distinct in his head . . . and now he was brought back. He became aware of someone approaching on the quarterdeck. He opened his eyes, lifted his head with a clearing sniff, and:

'Yes, Mr Abey? Why are you not at your station? Is the boat's lantern in view?'

'No, sir. Asking your indulgence, I – I thought I heard a sound just now.'

'What sound? From the beach?'

'To the west, sir, farther out to sea. Like a kind of clattering, very brief.'

'To the west?' Swinging round, striding to the larboard rail. He brought his glass to his eye and peered into the darkness. Nothing.

'Did ye see a light?'

'No light, sir. Only a very brief clattering sound.'

'Did anyone else hear it?' Raising his voice slightly and calling: 'Mr Souter.'

That officer attended, coming up the ladder and treading aft.

'Did y'hear anything, Mr Souter, out to sea?'

'No, sir, I did not.'

'Very well, thank you. Let me know the moment there is any sign of the boat.'

'Aye, sir.' Lieutenant Souter's hat off and on, very correct, and he returned to his station, pausing briefly at the binnacle to take up his glass and remove it from its case.

Rennie raised his own glass and peered again to the west, and again found nothing in the darkness there. He peered a moment longer, frowned and was lowering the glass when vivid orange flashes lit the sea.

BANG BANG BANG-BANG-BANG BOOM-BANG

Grapeshot smashed through *Expedient*'s larboard rigging in a stuttering, clipping, shredding turmoil of flying metal. At the breast-rail Mr Souter coughed as if punched in the ribs, stumbled, and fell to the deck. The junior midshipman Mr Nicholas, coming aft on the larboard gangway, was spun like a puppet, lost the use of his legs, and pitched into the waist, his hat flying over the side. Ropes and blocks broke and tumbled. Shouts, moans, confusion.

'Mr Abey!' Bellowed.

'Sir?' Half-deafened, a sleeve torn off, his own hat gone.

'Return to your station and stand by! Mr Loftus!' Seeing a powder boy: 'You there, find the master, and—'

'I am here, sir.' Mr Loftus, attending, kicking away a tangle of rope.

'We must cut our cables and beat west, Mr Loftus, and go straight at our opponent. We cannot lie here and allow ourselves be smashed to splinters.'

'Aye, sir.' Turning, bellowing: 'Hands to make sail!' Striding forrard. 'Spare numbers to remain at their guns! Topmen aloft! On the fo'c's'le there! Stand by with sea axes to cut the cables!'

Further flashes, but these from a new direction. From the south, flickering in reflection on the sea.

BOOM BOOM BOOM-BANG BOOM-BANG-BANG

Roundshot zoomed and droned past *Expedient* and kicked up explosions of spray beyond. No shot hit home, and Rennie closed his eyes in a silent prayer of thanks. Had his stern and rudder been smashed, all hope would instantly have been lost.

Within a short space of time – that seemed an eternity to Rennie – *Expedient* swung clear of her cut cables, and caught what little breeze there was to make headway westward. As a roundshot broadside exploded out of the darkness from that direction she was head on to it, and most of the shot went wide of her except for one apparently glancing strike forrard. But she had suffered grievous damage from the first fire, to her rigging and to her people, and Rennie was by no means sanguine she could survive the night, even though she had assumed the condition of a belligerent ship, and stood prepared. A boy had brought a message from the surgeon: thirty-six men wounded, and four killed, including Mr Souter. Attacked from the west, and the south, *Expedient* had only one ally – the dark, that would soon recede as dawn too became her pursuer. Beyond all that, beyond the immediate heavy danger to his ship and the need to fight his way clear, was the fact that Rennie had been obliged to leave the pinnace behind, to abandon that boat and the momentous duty it embodied to heaven knew what peril, alone upon the sea.

'God help them now, for I cannot. I must save *Expedient*, and then return and attempt to rescue them if I am able. That is the only hope for any of us this night.' To the sailing master, now standing at the helmsman's shoulder: 'Cannot we make more headway, Mr Loftus? We must get well clear of the coast to give ourselves sea room. Room to fight, and aim our guns. I cannot even see the enemy plain, only the flash of his broadsides.'

'We could put men into the boats, sir, and pull ourselves—'

Over him: 'Nay, that will not answer, when we have so many wounded, and short numbers on the guns as it is. Find me a wind, Mr Loftus.' Looking aloft at his shadowy canvas, nearly all of it limp.

'I will do my best, sir.' And under his breath: 'Even if I am not God Almighty, for Christ's sake.'

'If you please, sir.' Mr Abey, at his elbow.

'Why are y'not at your station, Mr Abey?'

'I come with a message, sir. Mr Makepeace is gravely wounded.'

'Tom? How bad hurt is he?' Gripping the boy's shoulder.

'He – he is calling for his wife, sir.'

'Dr Wing is with him?'

'Aye, sir.'

'Then he has been got below?'

'No, sir. He is in the forecastle, where the last shot struck. He took a splinter to his breast . . .'

'Christ Jesu.' Quietly.

'Dr Wing wished me to inform you, sir.'

'Very well, thank you, Mr Ab—'

Flashes ahead, making a mirror of the sea, and almost simultaneously to the south.

THUD THUD THUD THUD-THUD THUD THUD

The spanker boom convulsed over their heads with a harsh crack, sending splinters and fragments of rope and metal spraying across the quarterdeck. Blocks fell. The boom sagged and tumbled to the planking, the sail torn loose from its lacing at the foot. The canvas bellied and floated a moment with the force of the shock wave, then hung useless on the thimbles. Farther forrard the tangled crashing of other rigging, yards and sails, and the cries of men in pain.

'Mr Tangible! Mr Tangible!' Rennie, rising from a crouch, his hat and coat covered in debris.

The boatswain did not respond.

'Mr Abey!' Rennie shook his hat free of fragments.

'I am here, sir.'

'Find Mr Dangerfield, and—'

'Mr Dangerfield is below, sir, wounded.'

'Badly wounded?'

'It is his leg, sir, I believe it is broke. His left leg.'

'Then he cannot come on deck ... How old are you, Mr Abey?'

'Fifteen, sir.'

'Well, you are very young, but we are in dire difficulty. I hereby appoint you master's mate, and raise your rank immediate to acting lieutenant. You are now my third, Mr Abey.'

'Oh, thank you, sir.' Astonished.

'Do not thank me, Mr Abey. Your responsibilities are grave, and your work arduous. Are ye ready and willing to do it?'

'Oh, yes, sir!'

'Very well. You will assume command of the gundeck.

Which means that whichever battery is employed – or both – you will give the order to fire. You will double-shot your guns, at reload. And full allowance, you mind me?'

'Aye, sir.' Lifting his chin.

'We must make a reply to that blackguard south of us, and deter him a little. I cannot see him, but we will fire at the flashes of his guns. Stand by to fire as soon as you see them again.'

'Yes, sir.'

'Jump, then, Mr Abey – forgive me. I must not ask an officer to jump. Carry on, if y'please.'

'Aye, sir, very good.' His recovered hat off and on, absurdly formal in the confusion and destruction all about them, and he dashed forrard and down the ladder into the waist.

Rennie suppressed a sigh, and muttered: 'God go with you, lad.' He then strode forrard himself, and pointed at a powder boy extricating himself from a tangled fall.

'You there! Find the carpenter, Mr Adgett, and send him to me! And then find the boatswain!' Turning and coming aft again, kicking aside a twisted mass of rope and a smashed block:

'Mr Loftus! Mr Loftus! We must repair the boom, and bend the driver loose-footed!'

'I am at your service . . .' Bernard Loftus, clutching his side, and white with pain.

'Good God, do not tell me that you are wounded.'

'It is just the wind knocked out of me, sir. I shall be all right directly . . .'

The master clapped on to a stay and clung there a moment, his eyes tight closed.

Another series of muzzle flashes from the south, Rennie swung round to look, and immediately after came Richard Abey's cry from the gundeck:

'Larboard battery, point your guns! – Fire! Fire! Fire!'

The stuttering roar of guns from the southward ship was interrupted by the tremendous shocks through her timbers of *Expedient*'s own great guns, and explosions of flame along her side.

B-BOOM B-BOOM B-BOOM B-BOOM

Concussive, deafening, thudding, and the deck beneath Rennie's feet trembled and shook. The captain sniffed in a deep breath, smelling fiery smoke, and:

'That is more like it! Now we are in the fight!'

*

In the second boat, following *Expedient*'s pinnace, Lieutenant Hayter heard the thudding of guns beyond the rocky islets, and saw the flashes against the sky. He ordered the boat brought level with the pinnace, and brought alongside. He jumped into the pinnace, and consulted with Lieutenant Leigh, both crews resting on their oars. The royal party remained huddled together, their faces hidden, protected by their guard and apparently wishing to take no part in the proceedings, other than to be brought to safety. James doffed his hat briefly in their direction, purely as a formality, and to the lieutenant:

'Evidently the boats coming inshore ahead of you in the pinnace were a cutting-out party from a ship, Mr Leigh. Don't y'think so?'

'A ship that now engages *Expedient*.' Grimly, a nod.

'Well, there is no purpose in proceeding without lights any longer. We are damned lucky to have got this far among the shoals and rocks without coming to grief.'

'Yes, very well, Hayter.' He was about to give the order, then: 'Ought not we to keep well clear of the action, though? With such a valuable party under our care?'

James thought a moment, took a breath, and: 'Yes, you are right. In fact, we had perhaps better anchor here, while we are still sheltered by the islets, and keep our lights doused.'

'Very well.'

When the anchors had been deployed, James:

'Are these swivels loaded, Mr Leigh?' Indicated the swivel guns fore and aft, slotted into the gunwales.

'Aye, we reloaded as soon as they had been fired at the beach.'

'Very good. We may need them should we encounter other boats.'

'Other boats?'

'I think there may well be more than one ship attacking *Expedient*. You hear the sequence of guns? There's three patterns of broadside, all distinct.'

'I had not noticed. I was busy with the marks, you know, as lead boat.' Meaning the soundings they had been taking with the lead in the bow to determine the depth of water under them.

'And if there's other boats scattered about, sent out from these ships, we may have to fight an action of our own.'

'Here, among the rocks? At anchor?'

'Nay, when we venture out to go aboard *Expedient* – or in least attempt it. Dawn ain't far off, and we cannot hide here for ever.'

A further pattern of thuds and flashes beyond.

'If *Expedient* ain't bested.' Lieutenant Leigh, subdued and solemn. 'If she ain't.'

'Damnation to that. If I know anything about Captain Rennie he will never be bested at sea. Ain't a finer tactician in ship-handling and gunnery, in the navy entire. Perhaps y'don't know that, Mr Leigh.'

'I meant only that if she is attacked on all sides, Mr Hayter.' Stiffly, using 'mister' for the first time. 'I meant no disloyalty to Captain Rennie, that you clearly know better than I.'

'He will not sit and wait, you know, to be caught between two attacking ships. He will twist and turn, and take the wind gage, and fall upon them instead.'

'Wind gage? There is scarcely even a waft of breeze.' More than a hint of acerbity.

'We are all tired, no doubt.' James, lowering his voice. 'We had better not bicker like a pair of middies, and discourage our people. Hey? When we reflect on what we are about, after all?'

'Very well, Hayter.' Unbending a little, his own voice instinctively lowered.

'Will you tell me your given name again? I have forgot it.'

'It is Merriman. Merriman Leigh.'

'And how d'y'like to be called?'

'Oh, Leigh will do, you know.'

'Not Merriman? Or Merry?'

'Certainly not Merry, good God. It makes me sound like ten kinds of damned fool.'

James smiled in the darkness. 'Very well. Not Merry.'

'At my school I was called Mabel, of all things.'

'Mabel?'

'Aye, you see? Bloody foolish, altogether.'

'Why Mabel?'

'My middle name is Able. Merriman Able. Mabel.'

'Ahh. Yes. Then I had best not call'ee that, hey?'

'I should be obliged if ye didn't.'

'Plain Leigh?'

'Plain Leigh suits me very well.' A moment, and: 'Will you tell me . . . who was the other passenger you looked for on the beach, but did not find?'

'A lady.'

'Ah. Was she—'

From beyond, interrupting this exchange, a further series of bright, flickering flashes against the sky, followed by many thudding, booming concussions, echoing and reverberating through the rocky islets.

'If I am not mistook, they have reached the decisive moments of the action.' James, half to himself, hunched beside Lieutenant Leigh in the stern sheets.

'I have changed my mind, Hayter. Could not we proceed a little further? And find a safe place to watch?'

'Without great risk to our cargo?'

'Aye.'

'Even if there's other boats?'

'They will not see us if we are careful, and stay hid behind rocks.'

James glanced toward the huddled royal party. 'I do not think we may take that risk, however small.'

'Good heaven, Hayter, ain't the whole business an enormous risk, anyway? What difference can it make to proceed a little way and see how the action goes? Don't it benefit us, in fact, to have a look?'

'Benefit?'

'Indeed, if Captain Rennie is gaining the upper hand, will not we all the sooner be able to get aboard *Expedient* – if we know that he is?'

A nod, a quick breath. 'Yes, all right. Let us weigh and proceed to the last rocky islet and wait there to observe the outcome. Pray God it is the right one.'

'Come, Hayter, I thought ye had absolute confidence in Captain Rennie?'

'I am not God, though.'

'Amen.'

*

The first faint glimmer of dawn, and now Rennie was assailed by a conflicting combination of emotions. He could see his enemy, two ships, one a corvette to the south, the other a frigate to the north, both of them nearly a mile distant, licking their wounds and waiting to move in for the kill. He could see the damage to his own ship, and the drying, crusting rivulets of blood on the decking, half absorbed by strewn sand and fallen canvas. He could see to the sou'-west a gathering of the glassy surface of the sea into ruffles of movements – the wind was rising. He could see how he might best these two vessels, if his luck held, and the repairs to his rigging. He could see the expressions on the faces of his people. They were exhausted, and hungry, and thirsty too, in spite of the boys he had kept running in relays from gun to gun with cans of water during the hours of repeated firing, the guns bouncing in their tackles, burning hot and dangerous to the naked hand. These men had lost shipmates, had seen them fall and been unable to help them, had watched them bleed and gasp away their lives on the gritty, powder-blasted deck in the fury and din of action, their own duty wholly bound up in the survival of their ship. A duty not yet done with, not yet completed, that stared at them in the nascent light – two ships black-resolved to smash their own and kill them where they stood, handspikes and rammers and tackles in hand. Rennie felt both sad and elated – the deep sadness of loss, and the harsh elation of purpose.

'By God, I am proud of my people.' Under his breath. He strode to the tafferel, sucked in a lungful of morning air, and exhaled. Turned, strode forrard to the breast-rail, and went down the ladder into the waist. Looking about him, lifting his voice to carry along the gundeck:

'Now we have them, lads! The wind is rising, and we shall have the advantage! We will smash that bloody little corvette, and then we will have at that damned frigate, and riddle her arse until she begs for mercy! We shall prevail! So let me hear you now, lads! What are we called?'

A ragged, exhausted cry: 'Expedients . . .'

'All the gunnery has made me a little deaf this morning! I cannot quite hear you! What are we called!'

'Expedients!'

'Aye, Expedients all! And today, here and now, as dawn breaks over us – we are the Royal Navy, just as sure as if we was an entire fleet at sea! And by God we will teach those who fire upon an English man-of-war to rue the day their mothers gave them life!' He lifted his hat high over his head. 'Three cheers for England, and King George!'

'Huzzay! Huzzay! Huzzay!' Ragged, but heartfelt.

'Mr Loftus!'

Bernard Loftus limped to the breast-rail above. 'Sir?'

'A double ration of grog for every man!' Further cheers.

'Aye, sir.' The master's hat off and on. Rennie returned to his quarterdeck, up the ladder.

'The rum unwatered if they wish it, Mr Loftus.' Lowering his voice a little.

'Unwatered, sir? Half a pint of rum unwatered?'

'You heard me right, Mr Loftus. Unwatered. I want them fierce lifted up when we come to fight for our lives. Make it so, if y'please.'

'Very good, sir.'

'Mr Abey!' His hand on the breast-rail, above a sand bucket.

Richard Abey appeared below him, his face, hat and coat covered in powder grime. The left sleeve of his coat had been partly torn off the first fire, and now he looked very bedraggled.

'Sir?'

'Are you all right, Mr Abey?'

'Oh, yes, sir.' Climbing the ladder.

'I am going to attack those two ships by beating west into the wind.' Nodding at each ship, then pointing west. 'They will think – both French commanders – that I am running away fearful in the dawn, which is just what, I want them to believe. When we have tacked west half a glass I will come about and run sou'-east straight at the corvette, which is marginally closer to us, and will thus be our first design. When we are within pistol shot I will swing east, and we will then rake her with our starboard battery at point blank. You apprehend me?'

'Starboard broadside, point blank. Very good, sir.'

'You must aim your guns at such an angle on the sprung

breeching ropes that we concentrate our fire on her gunports and shatter them, knock her great guns off their carriages, and kill men. You will then reload with grape.'

'Grape, sir?'

'Aye, you heard me right. By now the frigate will be bearing down, and, will seek to smash us in turn. But I will not permit her commander to do it. I will now tack nor'-east, *straight at him*. We will go head to head, and we, Mr Abey, will have the wind.'

'Aye, sir.' Nodding, beginning to understand the sheer audacity of the plan.

'If I am not mistook, he will break first. He will tack east or west, it don't matter which. As soon as he does we will have him, because the manoeuvre will cost him speed. We will go straight at him as he tacks, and again fire our starboard battery at a severe angle, rake his deck with grape, smash his rigging, and kill men. We will then cross his stern, Mr Abey, and riddle his backside with our larboard battery, double-shotted. That will smash his rudder, and render him helpless. And by God we will have no fucking mercy, come that moment! D'y'hear me?'

'Yes, sir.' Lifting his head.

'Very well. Return to your duty, Mr Abey.'

'Very good, sir.' His hat obediently off and on, and he ran down the ladder.

Rennie peered about him. 'Mr Tangible!'

The boatswain appeared, limping along the larboard gangway from the fo'c's'le. He too had been wounded the first fire, had been taken into the orlop by the surgeon Dr Wing, and been sufficiently patched and restored to come on deck and supervise repair. His face now showed both extreme fatigue, after the rigours of the night, and pain.

'I am here, sir.'

'You are hurt, Roman Tangible.' Concern in his voice. 'I had not realised you was injured so severe . . .'

'Splinters, sir, damn' flying splinters.'

'Your leg?'

'Both of my legs, in truth. Howsomever, I regard myself as lucky.'

'Lucky!'

'Aye, sir, when so many others was wounded very horrible, and the doctor unable to attend to them before they perished, in the heat of battle. I am a lucky man, that can still walk and talk, and do my duty.'

'Well said, well said. Here, take a pull.' Rennie handed him his flask, and the boatswain took a long, grateful draught.

'Thankee, sir, most welcome.' Handing it back. Rennie took a pull himself, and thrust the flask away in his coat.

'And now we must make sail, Mr Tangible. We have hot work to do this day.'

The first burning gleams of the sun showed over the rocky coastline in the east, and the two French ships began to make their converging run at *Expedient* in the lifting wind, as the calls piped echoing across her deck.

TWELVE

In the event Rennie's plan did not go according to his wishes. In fact it did not proceed beyond its formulation in his head, and its explication to his acting third, Mr Abey. 'Anything may happen at sea' is an axiom well known to seamen, from the lowliest idler to the Admiral of the Fleet. It was well known to Captain Rennie, and one he was fond of iterating at dinner, or upon his quarterdeck, or indeed anywhere and at any time it occurred to him. It occurred to him now, as the corvette, far from chasing him as he had hoped, instead swung north and made herself the frigate's close companion on the sea. And then both French ships began to come directly at Rennie, even as he came about to give himself the wind gage.

'God damn and blast those bloody duplicitous Frenchie villains!'

'Sir?' Mr Loftus.

'You see what they are about, the fucking wretches!'

'Yes, sir, I do.' Holding his glass. 'But there is—'

'They mean to flank me, one on either side, and blow me to kingdom bloody come!'

'There is another ship, sir.' Pointing.

'What!'

'Coming up from the south, sir. I think she—'

'From the south?' Raising his own glass. 'Am I to be dogged by every damned ship in the French navy, for Christ's sake!'

'I think she ain't of the same French navy, sir.'

'Eh?' Peering.

'You will see her colours are white, entire. On the corvette and the frigate closing upon us, their colours are white with a red, white and blue canton on the hoist. The colours adopted by the French navy a year since. That means that the attacking ships are loyal to the revolution, don't it, sir, and the—'

'And the ship to the south ain't, by God! You are right, Mr Loftus. I believe she comes to aid us. Hey?'

'That is my opinion, sir.'

'How d'y'make her out? A frigate, would y'say?'

'A corvette, I should say.' Lowering his glass, then raising it and focusing it again, 'Yes, a corvette.'

'Then we are evenly matched against the others – if she does in fact join us, and ain't just shamming.'

'There is a simple way to discover that, sir.'

'Aye, Mr Loftus, there is.'

And presently *Expedient* swung to the south, to meet the oncoming corvette. Who hailed her as *Expedient* came within pistol shot, one glass after, close-hauled on the larboard tack.

'*La frégate anglaise!*' An officer in the bow, with a speaking trumpet. '*Mettrez en panne!*'

Glancing to the north, Rennie ordered his ship hove to. The yards were braced, foresails aback, and she rapidly lost way as she came abreast of the French ship, which had already hove to. This was a risk for both ships, given the pursuit of the two ships from the north, but in Rennie's view a risk worth taking if he had found a true ally.

Richard Abey, as the only quarterdeck speaker of French, was summoned to act as interpreter, as the two ships spoke. He listened, and then translated:

'They are the corvette *La Fidélité*. They ask, have we the king aboard, sir?'

'We have not, say to them.' Rennie. 'We have had to

fight the two ships now bearing down on us, through the night, and have had no time for anything else.'

Presently: 'They ask: do we wish them to assist us?'

'In what sense?'

The question put, and answered, and Richard Abey:

'In action, sir. They oppose the revolution, and wish to aid the king's escape.'

'Ask them, right quick, how they know of the king's attempt to escape.'

Again the question asked, and the reply made.

'They say they have been sent to aid us by the king's loyal friends, and they ask where the king is located at present.'

Rennie, quietly: 'That answer puzzles me, Mr Abey. If they have been sent by the king's friends, why do not they know where he is? Say that we don't know anything, that we await instruction.' And as Richard Abey raised the speaking trumpet to make the response, Rennie turned and:

'Mr Loftus?'

'Sir?' By Rennie's side.

'Pass the word, very quiet and discreet, fore and aft, that we will get under way in two minutes. The signal shall be when I take off my hat.'

'Very good, sir.' And he beckoned a boy.

As Mr Abey finished translating Rennie's reply to the French ship, Rennie spoke to him very low and earnest.

'Now then, Mr Abey. When I tap you on the shoulder y'will slip down the ladder to the gundeck and instruct your larboard divisions by quiet word of mouth to point their guns at the corvette's mainmast. The moment you see me lift my hat at the breast-rail you are to open fire.'

'Fire at the corvette, sir? *This* corvette?'

'Aye, Richard, this one. They ain't our friends, I fear, nor King Louis's neither. I want to snap her mainmast our first fire, and then we will break off the engagement at once, go about, and straight at the advancing ships. Straight at 'em, and pass between them, firing both batteries simultaneous. You have me? You see what I am about?'

'Aye, sir.' A quick nod.

'Very well. Thank *La Fidélité* very polite, bow to them and so forth. And then go down the ladder and wait for my signal.'

'Your signal – your hat. Very good, sir.'

He raised the speaking trumpet, made the reply, and felt Rennie tap him on the shoulder. He ran down the ladder into the waist. As he did so, the master was again at Rennie's shoulder:

'Sir, the two ships approaching from the north are getting dangerous near.'

Rennie glanced at the advancing frigate and corvette. 'Aye, but they will not fire on us so long as we are alongside *La Fidélité*. That would risk damage to her. They will attack only when I fire on her, and break clear. It is essential that we go at them head on, Mr Loftus, to give them only the narrowest possible target. And remember, we still have the wind. We will have the weather-gage.'

A tense few moments. The corvette's officer asked more questions through his speaking trumpet, and received no reply. He repeated his questions, seemed puzzled, then alarmed. He ran aft along the gangway, and at that moment Rennie took off his hat. At once Mr Loftus:

'Make sail! Stand by to go about!' Followed by a flurry of activity, and Richard Abey's cry:

'Larboard battery – *fire, fire, fire!*'

B-BOOM B-BOOM B-BOOM B-BOOM-BANG-BANG

Blasts of flame and great balloons of gritty smoke from *Expedient*'s side, and she shook and shuddered with the thudding shocks of her guns through her timbers. Rennie's ears rang as he saw the corvette's mainmast shiver, teeter, and go by the board, dragging down shrouds, yards, sails, halyards in a creaking, slumping tangle of destruction. The whole little ship lurched and heeled to starboard as the mast crashed down over the hammock cranes and into the sea. Terrible damage had been done to other parts of her upperworks, and men could be heard screaming.

And even as the smoke drifted across the shadowy water between the two ships, *Expedient* began to swing away from the stricken ship, and turn to meet her other opponents.

From the gundeck:

'Re-lo-o-o-o-oad!'

As *Expedient* came on to her new heading, her sails bellying full on the starboard tack, the French frigate fired her two bow chasers – nine-pounder guns. Twin orange flashes, and roundshot droned past *Expedient* to larboard, and kicked up shocks of spray aft.

'Hard at them, Mr Loftus! Let us meet the buggers head on!'

'The corvette is bearing west, sir! She is breaking away to attack us to larboard!' The master.

'Thankee, Mr Loftus. I see her. We will go straight at the frigate.'

The song now of the rising wind in the rigging. *Expedient* pitching a little in the following sea, and rolling. Spray flew across the bow, and sluiced the fo'c's'le. The timeless, pulsing cry of a seabird away to starboard, like a mockery of humankind.

Rennie brought up his glass to look at the second corvette, and saw the flashes along her larboard port strake as she opened fire. A series of spray strikes a cable short of *Expedient* as the corvette's six-pound roundshot fell harmless. At the same moment came the wind-muffled sound of her guns.

THUMP-thud THUMP-thud THUMP-thud

And now a disturbing sight greeted Captain Rennie at the starboard waist ladder. Lieutenant Makepeace, his face ghastly pale, one arm in a sling and his breast bandaged white, came slowly up the ladder, pulling himself up by his free arm on the rigged hand-rope. His undress coat was draped about his shoulders, and his breeches were spattered with blood.

'Good God, Tom . . . you should not be on deck.' Rennie, in dismay.

'As Dr Wing told me, sir. But I know my duty, and it don't lie below.'

'You cannot aid me, nor the ship, by struggling about the deck in your condition, Tom.'

Lieutenant Makepeace did not heed his commander, and came up on the quarterdeck. 'When *Expedient* is attacked we are all attacked, sir. Ain't that so?'

'Aye, but I cannot allow you to risk further injury to your person when you are so badly hurt. Your place is below.'

'Sir, I beg you to allow me the opportunity to defend—'

'Mr Makepeace!' Over him, forced reluctantly to be severe. 'You will kindly go below!'

'Sir, if you will only allow me to—'

'No, sir, I will not. You are in my way, you are an impediment to my fighting the ship efficient.'

'Sir, I—'

'Christ's blood, will you do as you are told, sir!' Very angry with his first lieutenant for obliging him to be severe, when all he wished for him was kind attention and a speedy recovery.

'I am very sorry to have offended you by my honest wish to serve you, sir . . .' The lieutenant had tears in his eyes as he turned away slowly, gripped the breast-rail and took a step toward the ladder.

Rennie moved to assist him, and thought better of it. Probably such assistance would only add to his distress.

'God damn the stupid fellow!' Rennie, in his head. 'He has made me out the overbearing villain, when all I meant to do was save him from himself!'

'Frigate bearing away west, sir!'

As the French frigate heeled on the starboard tack, exposing her larboard ports, which instantly came to life in a flickering of flashes and rushing puffs of smoke.

Grapeshot smacked, fizzed and cut into *Expedient*'s upper-works in a stuttering hail. One of these small lethal spheres struck Lieutenant Makepeace at the top of the waist ladder, spun him round with half of his head chopped away, and flung him across the gangway.

'Tom!' Rennie, in anguish.

The body sprawled on the gangway, then tumbled slack into the waist, the smashed skull pouring blood.

'Christ Jesu . . .' Staring down a moment longer, then turning – only half aware of the destruction all around him – and:

'You bloody wretches!' Bellowing at the still-turning frigate as smoke hung in a long cloud over the sea. 'I will destroy you! I will kill every man of you, and damn your souls to hell!'

From the gundeck, Richard Abey's cry:

'Larboard battery, on the lift . . . *fire, fire, fire!*'

B-BOOM B-BOOM B-BOOM B-BOOM B-BOOM

Flame, and flaming wad, shuddering timbers, boiling smoke. Rennie, who had quite unconsciously drawn his sword, and now held it pointed at the French frigate, saw with a surge of pure malevolent joy the effect of that double-shotted broadside. The whole of the frigate's larboard side took terrible damage, and the mizzenmast was shot away in a great collapsing crumple of canvas and yards. The quarterlights at her stern were punched in with an explosion of glass, and the small boat in the stern davits was torn loose and smashed, the remnants hanging down and trailing in the sea. And clearly across the water, high and thin, as Richard Abey yelled:

'Re-lo-o-o-o-o-oad!'
came a single terrible shriek, repeated over and over, of a
man in transports of agony.

'Aye, *suffer*, you blackguard.' Rennie, savagely. 'All of ye
will suffer, presently.'

As the frigate swung away crippled, the corvette
now came at *Expedient*, and Rennie had to admire her
commander's sheer, crazy courage. She came directly across
Expedient's bow out of the smoke, her starboard side
absolutely exposed, to give herself the maximum broadside opportunity. Flashes, and near instantaneous thuds, as
her six-pounders were fired point-blank. Her guns were
well aimed. Rennie stood rooted to the deck as he saw
a roundshot rocket toward him the length of the ship, a
black increasing ball that seemed to come direct at his
head. He could not duck down, he could not even jerk
his head to one side, so swift did it fly at him. He felt a
terrible blow, and it was as if the skin of his face was sucked
from his jaws and plucked up from round his eyes and
ears, and then he felt nothing more.

Bernard Loftus saw his captain fall to the deck, and feared
the worst.

'Captain!' Running forrard.

A spar fell in his path, and he was entangled in torn
canvas. He wrenched and thrust, and fought his way clear,
and ran to Rennie's side.

'Captain, sir!'

From the gundeck, as the corvette heeled far across to
starboard of *Expedient*, and began to turn north:

'Starboard battery – point your guns! On the lift . . . *fire*,
fire, *fire*!'

And as he knelt by Rennie, Bernard Loftus felt the thudding, quivering shocks of *Expedient*'s great guns. Rennie did
not move, he did not blink, but lay on his side staring at
nothing, his hat gone and his sparse hair standing up in
wisps on his head.

A ragged cheer. Ahead of them, away to starboard, the dashing corvette had been struck with terrible slamming force right through her stern. The width of her stern gallery had been smashed clear away, and the deck beyond swept by a storm of iron. Her rudder, her wheel, and her mizzen has been splintered. A flying fast, bravely handled, beautiful little ship of war had been rendered into matchwood, in a few devastating seconds.

And still Rennie did not stir.

*

The two boats lay in a narrow channel between rocky islets, riding the swell that rose and fell there, sucking against the black walls of rock. They were anchored, and hidden from view, so that if boats came looking for them they would not be easily discovered. Nor could they be seen from the west, out to sea, unless a vessel came directly opposite to their position.

'Not that anyone in those ships will be looking for us at present.' James Hayter, half to himself.

'What say?' Lieutenant Leigh, beside him, lowered his glass.

'Nay, nothing.' James shook his head. 'We must remain here concealed until the action is over.'

'I think *Expedient* has prevailed, Hayter.' Raising his glass again.

James looked seaward, peering under a shading hand, then asked for the glass. Mr Leigh gave it to him, and James focused on the several ships in turn, and the terrible damage all had sustained. Drifting smoke, angled sails, a sense of brief preternatural calm, and foreboding.

'I could not say with certainty that she has prevailed, you know.' Moving the glass. 'The corvette to the south has been took out of the battle, certainly.' Sweeping to the north. 'As has that second corvette. But the French frigate is no worse damaged than *Expedient* herself, and will in all probability attack again.'

'You think so?'

James handed the glass back to Lieutenant Leigh, who peered through it, and:

'No, I think not. Captain Rennie has tacked, and now . . . yes, he means to lay alongside the frigate and board her. Yes! He has loosed another broadside into her! Christ, what a frightful pounding . . .'

And the sound of the broadside echoed deep and heavy across the sea.

THUD THUD THUD THUD-THUD THUD THUD

Smoke boiled and rushed, enveloping the two ships in an angry cloud.

'May I see?' James tapped the lieutenant on the shoulder, and was given the glass a second time. He focused, in time to see an answering broadside from the French ship, just as *Expedient* came alongside. A moment, as the two vessels were again obscured by smoke, and the echo came.

THUMP-THUD THUMP THUMP THUMP THUMP-THUD

'That contest ain't decided.' James, grimly. 'Not by any measure.' Giving Mr Leigh the glass and pointing. 'If *Expedient*'s people was preparing to board at that moment, and if as I suspect the French commander had ordered grape loaded in his guns . . . God knows what frightful slaughter has just occurred.'

'We spoke too soon, hey?' Peering.

'Are you a religious man, Leigh?'

'At moments such as this – I think perhaps I am.' Lowering the glass.

'Hm. Then ye'd better offer up a prayer for *Expedient* and her people.'

'I think perhaps I will, Hayter.' Quietly.

'Aye, and for us, sequestered here. It will be a bloody miracle if we survive this day unmolested ourselves.'

*

Captain Rennie came to himself, and attempted to sit up. 'Has he come about, on t'other tack? Why are the guns not firing?'

'Nay, Captain, do not attempt effortful speech, if you please, sir.'

'Dr Wing . . . ?'

'I am here. And you are not dead, not quite yet. However, if you will oblige me, I should like you to . . .' Restraining Rennie, pushing him gently back down on the hanging cot he had rigged in his cramped dispensary. '. . . just lie back again, will you?'

'I must go on deck. Why are the great guns silent?'

'It will not be wise for you to go on deck. The deck is very bloody and muddled, just at present, and you can do nothing—'

'*Muddled?*'

'Well, yes, that is the word I would use. You may wish to find another. Lie back, and allow me to examine your ears, though I expect – since you can hear me – that the eardrums are not impaired.'

'In course they ain't, good God. I am not impaired at all, Doctor. Why was I brought below?'

'A roundshot near took off your head, you were knocked off your feet by the shock of it passing so narrowly close, and lost consciousness. It is a common thing, in action.'

'Ah, is it? Common, hm?'

'Aye, sir, it is. I have made a little study of the phenomenon.

Perhaps I shall write a paper. The larger the size and weight of the ball, the greater the shock. You were lucky. A six-pound roundshot, I think, from the smaller ship? Had it been an eighteen-pound shot, or a carronade ball, the effect might well have been to shock the life out of you. As it is, you were merely concussed.'

Rennie felt his head and upper body. 'But I suffered no injury at all. I was not hit. Why in Christ's name are the great guns not firing? Was that second corvette bested?'

'So I understand. The action has ceased.'

'What happened to the frigate?'

'The French frigate caused very great damage to us, and we to them. I have brought you here because there was no room to accommodate you anywhere else below. There has been a very great deal of injury, and death.'

And now Rennie saw the condition of Dr Wing's clothing. His shirtsleeves and breeches were caked and slimy with blood.

'How – how many injured?'

'Near half an hundred. And thirteen killed.'

'Hell's flames . . .'

'Aye, that is a closer word than muddle, you are right. The deck is like a corner of hell.' Quietly.

'We must return for the boat, if the action is done. Has the French frigate struck? A damn silly question, hey? She must have done, else the action would still proceed. And now, Doctor, I really must go on deck.' Sitting up again.

'She has not.'

'Eh?'

'The action has ceased – for the moment. The French frigate stood away to the west, bad crippled as I understand her condition, but not killed. And we are left bad crippled ourselves.'

'Then we must return for the boat while the French ship is out of the way.' Decisively. 'This is our only chance of success.'

'Captain, I warn you. Strenuous activity of any kind will be very inimical to your condition.'

'Damnation to that. A headache never killed a sea officer yet. Oooghh!' Clutching his head as his feet reached the deck and he stood.

'Please to lie down again, sir.'

'I will not lie down, damn you! I am the commanding officer of a ship of war, and I mean to prevail. Our boat must be rescued, and the action we have begun today be fought out to the end. Stand aside.'

And he thrust the diminutive doctor away, and went up the ladder.

*

'We will pull toward *Expedient*,' decided James Hayter. 'Stand by to weigh, the pinnace to be lead boat.' Louder, standing up in the stern sheets.

'D'y'really think it worth the risk, Hayter? With the royal party aboard?' Lieutenant Leigh, standing beside him and speaking very low and earnest in James's ear. 'It is a league and more of hard rowing, against a stiff breeze and a lifting sea.'

'It is our only chance, while the French frigate is disengaged.' Speaking quietly and urgently in turn. 'In any wise we shall be needed aboard, Leigh, with so many casualties likely in the ship. Needed to fight her guns, all of us.'

'Yes, you are right.' A nod. 'Very well.' Then: 'Will you go into the second boat?'

'Aye. And then you wait for my command.'

'Very good.' A thought. 'But look here, Hayter, I think perhaps I had better give the commands from now on, you know. After all, you ain't even commissioned at present – in least, not in the navy.'

A brief chuckle. 'D'y'know, I had not allowed that simple fact to enter my mind. I have no authority over you at all, my dear fellow. You must forgive my presumption in behaving as if I was the senior officer present, when I am on the beach, in truth.'

'Thank God you are not still on the beach, in literal truth. Hey?'

'Yes indeed, thank God.' Sobering. 'Very well, I will go into the second boat – and wait for your command.'

Presently, when James had returned to the second boat, and occupied the stern sheets, Lieutenant Leigh:

'Get your oars to pass!'

The oars lifted up from the thwarts.

'Ship your oars!'

The oars in the thole pins, and extended.

'Give way together, lads! Lay out with a will, but let us row dry!'

And the two boats emerged from their narrow hiding place, the pinnace ahead, into the open sea. Three miles distant to the west *Expedient* began to swing limping toward them.

When they were nearly within pistol shot of her, half a glass after, the French frigate came limping in from the west in pursuit.

'Christ's blood . . .' James, in a whisper to himself. '. . . *Expedient* must go about to fight her guns. We are lost, unless . . .'

And aloud, standing up and bellowing in his most carrying quarterdeck:

'In the pinnace, there! We must get under *Expedient*'s lee when she goes about, else we shall be smashed to splinters!'

As if in answer there echoed across the water from *Expedient*:

'Stand by to go about! Starboard battery . . . ready!'

As *Expedient* went about on the starboard tack, the two boats were not close enough to her to find any protection, and were left exposed to leeward on the open sea.

* * *

Aboard *Expedient*, Captain Rennie had made a very bold decision. He was desperately short of guncrew, and his starboard broadside would not now be his standard battery of eighteen-pounder long guns, but his quarterdeck and fo'c's'le thirty-two-pounder starboard carronades, a mere six guns. Six guns – but with a broadside weight of metal of 192 pounds.

'As he goes about in turn, we will smash his foremast.' Rennie, to Richard Abey beside him on the quarterdeck.

'Very good, sir.'

Rennie waited as the French frigate began to make the manoeuvre, in order to bring her own guns to bear. As she tacked to starboard Rennie nodded to Mr Abey, who:

'Starboard carronades – *fire-fire-fire!*'

The thudding explosions of the squat smashers, belching flames. A fiery, sulphurous fog of smoke and fragmented wad enveloped the quarterdeck. As the smoke cleared, Rennie and his young lieutenant saw the result of their attack. The French frigate had taken the full, concentrated weight of shot through her bow and foremast. Her bowsprit, figurehead and cutwater had been destroyed, and her foremast now fell with a rending crash, the headsails snatched fluttering down amid a tangle of stays and shrouds. The ship faltered and lost headway, and was hopelessly crippled.

Rennie lifted his speaking trumpet, the metal glinting in the sun, and:

'Marksmen in the tops, fire at will!'

From *Expedient*'s fore and maintops, Marine sharpshooters directed a hail of musket fire, plus canister shot from half-pounder swivels, across the French ship's decks. The frigate drifted closer.

'Re-lo-o-o-o-oad!'

The carronades rapidly reloaded – sponged, cartridge, shot and wad rammed – and within a minute:

'Starboard carronades ready!'

'Aim using the swivel trucks, Mr Abey. Aim – and fire at will.' Rennie, with a grim little nod.

The carronades turned on their transversible trucks, as Richard Abey:

'Starboard carronades – point and fire at will!'

BOOM BOOM BOOM BOOM-BOOM

Now the destruction of the French frigate was complete. Her mainmast trembled, lurched, and went by the board, and the naked ship was dying in the sea, blood leaking from her shattered strakes in telling red slicks. Screams came from her, and pitiful cries and moans.

Rennie gripped a backstay, felt his eyes fill, and shook his head. To himself:

'But only a little time since, I wished the wretches all the sufferings of hell . . .' Wondering at this spontaneous change of heart, of feeling, of soul. Aloud, as if to purge himself of emotion:

'They have got what they asked for, by God.'

And then he saw young Richard Abey's face as he stood at the rail. He was staring at the French ship in appalled silence. A tear fell on his cheek. He turned to look at Rennie, and there passed between them an apprehension that was at once fleeting and profound, that seemed to say:

'What is this life we have chosen, that brings us to do these things?'

And the moment was gone.

Rennie crossed to the larboard rail, and lifted his glass. He had been aware of the unprotected boats all the time during the bloody culmination of the action, and now, with relief:

'I see Lieutenant Leigh in the pinnace, and our hands at the oars – and at the oars of the boat following. Somehow they have captured a boat.' A pause as he peered, then: 'By God, they have got him in the pinnace . . .'

'Sir?' Richard Abey crossed the deck.

'Lift y'glass, Mr Abey. Y'see that central figure in the huddle of people in the lead boat?'

'Yes, sir.' Focusing.

'That is King Louis. That is the king of France.'

'Yes, sir. But ain't that – ain't that Lieutenant Hayter, in the second boat?'

THIRTEEN

'Tom Makepeace dead?' James put down his fork and stared at Rennie.

'Aye.' A sigh. 'In the action. And my third, Mr Souter, and a great many others.'

'That is sad news indeed.' All pleasure in their reunion now tempered and diffused by this harsh intelligence.

'Aye, it is. This commission has cost us very dear. In least it has not cost you your life, James, thank God though in view of the risks you have took – have been obliged to take – it is a miracle you wasn't killed.'

'I might have been killed, had not I received very kind assistance, as I explained.'

'Ah, yes.' Nodding, a glance. 'Well well, we have done our duty between us, and we have got the king and queen out of France, and safe into my quarters in the ship.'

'But not yet out of French waters. Which brings me again to my request, sir.' Leaning forward over the table. They were in the gunroom – Rennie's cabin being occupied by the royal party – sitting at one end of the mess table over a snatched meal. From above and without came the clatter and crack of mallets and chisels, and scattered splashing as battle detritus was heaved over the side. Rennie poured wine into their glasses, and now shook his head.

'No no, James. Do not iterate that request, if y'please. I have more than enough on my mind—'

'We cannot weigh until rudimentary repair is completed, you said so yourself, sir. While we lie here, let me take the gig and go ashore, and bring Madame Maigre away – if I can find her. There is no need of a boat's crew, I can manage the gig on my—'

'It's out of the question, James.' Over him. 'We must proceed as soon as we are able.'

'But, surely—'

'On any number of grounds, out of the question. As I've already said to you.'

'I know all the grounds, all the objections. I am willing to take my chance. Leave me behind, if you have to. I will follow you home to England.'

'Sail to England in a bloody gig! Are y'mad, James? Has living in disguise addled your brains?'

'Greater things have been done in boats.'

'You cannot mean – Captain Bligh?' An incredulous frown.

'If he could sail a thousand leagues in a launch, I can sail an hundred in a gig, sir.' Defiantly.

'Don't be such a damned fool.' Sternly, then, tilting his head: 'Who is this woman, James? What does she mean to you, exact?'

'Without her protection I would certainly not be sitting here now. Further, she is part of the king's entourage. It would be the cruellest indifference to abandon her altogether, do not you—'

Over him: 'James, James – I am very sorry, but if she has not been took, she is dead.'

'We cannot know that for certain.'

'The attacking party was already advancing from the cliff down the beach by the time you embarked with the royal party, yes? She must've been took then, don't you think so, or killed by a musket ball? Unless . . . unless . . .' Raising his eyebrows.

'Unless what?'

'Unless she was one of them, all along. A revolutionist.'

'Eh?'

'Had not you considered it?'

'Nay, I had not!'

'But good heaven, you described to me the events leading to your escape from the château with the royal party, through the lanes to the inlet. How did the National Guard know that the king was hid at the château? How did they know to follow you to the inlet? They must have been told. They must have been given information from within, so to say.' He shrugged.

'You cannot think that Juliette would—'

'Juliette?'

'Madame Maigre. You cannot believe that she would be so duplicitous. It's – it's impossible.'

'Why?'

'Well, you do not know her, in course, else you would not suggest such a thing. Forgive me, but it is just infamous bloody nonsense.'

'Why?'

'What d'y'mean *why*? I know her. I know her loyalties and beliefs. I know to a certainty that she could never—'

'Y'know nothing of the kind, James.' Over him, shaking his head.

'What?'

'It is wrote all over your face, it is in your eyes. You are infatuated. The woman has took you in, hook, line and gaff.'

'I am sorry you should think so little of me, sir, when I have done my part as honourable as I could. I reject everything you have said about Madame Maigre. You do not know her.'

'Well well, I will not like to add to your distress, when ye've been so cleverly duped.' Raising a hand as James began furiously to reply. 'Nay, do not let us argue, if y'please. Whatever she may have accomplished, we have left her behind now, and that is the end of that.'

'Very well, if you will not allow me the gig I will take the French boat instead.' Standing.

'What did y'say?' In turn growing angry.

'I am not under your command, I think. I am not commissioned in the service. I am acting as an independent agent in this, under the distant command of Mr Mappin and the Fund. I have brought that second boat to the ship, and I have decided independent that I will take it away.'

'You will do no such fucking thing, sir!'

They glared at each other across the narrow table. From the deck above:

'Boats approaching from the east! And two sail of ship from the so-o-o-outh!'

The two officers ran on deck. Two fishing boats could be seen approaching from the east. James looked at them only briefly, but Rennie peered at them through his long glass. He lowered the glass, stepped to the other rail, and focused the glass on the two ships to the south. A moment, and:

'Now then, Mr Hayter.' Lowering his glass and turning.

'Sir?'

'We must set aside all difference, agreed? Under the circumstances?'

'In course, yes, agreed.'

'You are willing to forget all about going ashore, and to return to duty as a sea officer?'

'I am, sir.'

'Very good. I am appointing you my lieutenant.'

'Under Mr Leigh?'

'You will replace Mr Makepeace, and act as my first. My clerk will write it down later.'

'Very good, sir. I have no blue coat.'

'Damnation to dress regulations, Mr Hayter. They have never troubled you in the past, and you have a natural authority as an officer. All I ask is that you apply it on my quarterdeck. We are attacked from the east, and from the south, and will soon be fighting for our lives.'

'From the east? But surely we have seen these boats before, along this coast. They are only bisquines, are not they? Fishing boats?'

Rennie thrust his glass into James's hand, and pointed. 'Aye, bisquines, but they are full of troops.'

James peered through the lens and saw that Rennie was right. The two bisquines had been commandeered. He swung the glass to the south, and peered at the two approaching ships. They were frigates. He returned the glass to Rennie.

'I beg your pardon, sir. Shall we beat to quarters?'

'We will first cut our cable and run due west, Mr Hayter. As soon as we are under way we will then clear for action. I hope that's the last bower I lose, I'm running short.' Moving aft to the tafferel.

'Very good, sir.' James strode to the breast-rail, and lacking a speaking trumpet cupped his hands at his mouth, filled his lungs and bellowed:

'On the fo'c's'le there! Cut away the bower! Cut the cable!' A moment, then turning: 'Hands to make sail! Topmen aloft!'

The boatswain's call echoed along the deck. All around him James saw and heard the familiar, pulse-tightening rush and flurry of the ship coming alive. Even in her half-smashed, half-crippled condition *Expedient* was a man-of-war, and lifted herself to that imperative with a heartening surge of purpose. All activity of repair was abandoned, topmen jumped aloft, sails were loosed and set, and yards braced. The ship swung free, gathered herself and stood west into the wind.

The master Bernard Loftus ran up the ladder from the waist, stopped short and stared at James in wonder.

'By God, it really is you, James.'

'Aye, it is.'

'I heard you was aboard, but could scarce believe it.' Brushing at his shirt and pulling on his coat. 'I was in the orlop assessing damage with Mr Adgett. How came you—'

Over him: 'Long story, Bernard, best told when we are at ease, which we ain't just at present.'

'You are right. We are not.' And he hurried aft, putting on his hat, and calling back as he went: 'Welcome back!'

James was about to raise his cupped hands to his mouth a second time when Rennie left the tafferel and came forrard to join him.

'Two things occur to me, Mr Hayter.'

'Sir?'

'Before we beat to quarters, the royal party must be got below into the lower deck. They cannot remain in my cabin during an action. Second, how many soldiers protect the king?'

'Half a dozen, I should say . . . Ah, I see your design, sir. Guncrew.'

'Aye, we are going to need every man we can muster. I fought the last action against the frigate with carronades alone, but that will not answer against two frigates now. We must man as many of our guns as we are able, short-handed as we are. You and I, and Mr Loftus, must take our places at the tackles. And the middies, too. Idlers, waisters, any man that is on his legs.'

'Unless we can contrive to outrun those frigates, sir. Crowd on sail, beat west, and then run north to England.'

'We are in no condition to run, only to limp. The chase would be short, and end in disaster.'

James glanced aloft, then forrard. 'Very good, sir. We must gain the wind, turn and fight.'

'Aye, we must.'

'What of the other frigate, though? There is no possibility she will return to the battle?'

'None. She was dismasted, and drifted away. Her people attempted to tow her with boats, but she drifted inshore away to the north, behind the islets.'

'Ah. Then there's only the two frigates approaching need concern us.' A faint smile.

'Aye, those.' Grimly, lowering his voice. 'I cannot pretend that I am sanguine as to the outcome, James. Do not forget those damned fishing boats.'

James, lowering his voice in turn: 'We have been in dark

places before this, sir, with all the odds against us, and we have always prevailed.'

'Perhaps not today, though. I cannot help feeling – this ain't our fight, James.'

'Not our fight . . . ?'

'Well well, perhaps with the cargo we carry it ain't the time to say so, you are right. If we are attacked in one of His Majesty's ships then it is our fight whether we like it or no, and we must lift our heads and hearts, and do our best.' A moment, then: 'I will like to shake your hand, James.'

James held out his hand. 'Good luck, sir.'

Rennie gripped the hand, shook it, and: 'God bless you, my dear friend.'

*

Lieutenant Hayter, coatless and with a kerchief tied round his head, ducked below the hammock cranes as a chopping hail of grapeshot smacked into rigging and timber just over his head. Splinters and frayed fragments of tarred cable spun and scattered. A fragment cut his cheek, and another nicked the corner of his eye. He winced, sucked in a breath, and stumbled to his feet. Tears streamed from the cut eye, mingled with drips of blood.

'Re-lo-o-o-o-ad!'

Crack! Crack! Crack-crack!

Canister shot sang, and bit into everything it hit, thudding, pocking, lethal.

James ran aft, and found Rennie standing with apparent calm by the binnacle, holding his glass under his arm. Ducking as more shot fizzed and whirred across the deck, James:

'Sir, I must ask leave to put a proposal, before it is too late.'

'It is already too late, Mr Hayter.' Calmly, grimly.

'No, sir, no. I think not.' Ducking again. 'Will not you crouch down, sir?'

'I will not.'

James felt himself obliged to stand up straight on his legs. He was half-blinded, and he felt dazed and sick, but he would not allow himself to display weakness before his captain.

'Sir, I think I must take the royal party out of the ship, and away in a boat.'

'In a boat, good God! Why is your mind so fixed on boats? It is madness in an action such as this. I will not even consider it.'

THUD THUD THUD

Expedient's remaining larboard carronades. The deck shuddered underfoot, and a fog of smoke and grit swirled about the two officers.

'Sir, if you please, I must press—'

'I will not hear any more! Return to your station, sir.'

'Christ's blood, will not you listen! It is their *only chance*!'

Lieutenant Hayter had spoken with such vehemence and conviction that Captain Rennie turned to look at him, as smoke boiled all round. And was forced to admit to himself that the lieutenant was probably right.

'Sir, we must strike very soon, else be blown to pulp and matchwood. If I can get away in a boat with the king, hide among the islets, and then make for England, there is hope for His Majesty yet. If he is took, there will be none. He will be executed.'

'Nay, James.' Shocked. 'Not even the revolutionists would commit so foul a crime as regicide.'

'Would not they? Then why has the king fled? Because he does not like their manners?'

'I imagine because he wished—'

James, over Rennie: 'They meant to kill him, if he had stayed in France. They mean to kill him if they take him a prisoner now.'

Rennie looked at him a long moment in the hanging smoke, and at last sniffed in a breath.

'Very well, James. I must accede to your wish, since you have been in France and know the condition of life there better than I. We will go about and haul in one of the boats lying astern, and get you and the royal party into it. We will fight our guns long enough for you to slip away under our lee.'

'Thank you, sir.' With evident relief. 'Will you then strike?'

'And be took ourselves?'

'Surely that is better than being smashed and killed? With the king gone out of the ship, then it really ain't your fight any more – is it?'

'I will decide when ye've gone, James. And I'd be obliged if ye'd go right quick. There ain't a moment to lose.'

'Very good, sir. I will say goodbye.'

'I hope not permanent, James.' A nod, and he went aft through the smoke.

The orders given, and *Expedient* came about. The boat brought in. *Expedient* continued to fight her guns, and the two French frigates pressed home their attack, while the bisquines hovered beyond the fighting ships.

Expedient loosed two further broadsides, and under cover of the dense smoke the royal party went into the boat – the pinnace – and James and a small crew pulled away toward the islets. James went with a heavy heart. He knew that his scheme had little hope of success. He knew also that when – not if – Rennie struck his colours, *Expedient* and all in her would likely suffer very hard at the hands of their vanquishers. *Expedient* had done very great harm, in French waters. She had destroyed a frigate and a corvette, and damaged the two present frigates, whose people would wish to exact payment.

'Even if we slip away under cover of the islets, they will certainly come looking for us. And to reach England we would have to break cover and head for the open sea.' James to himself as he stood at the tiller in the stern sheets. 'What chance can there be for us?' Looking over his shoulder at the continuing battle, and the heavy clouds of smoke hanging over the sea.

'What chance?' Aloud, unwittingly.

'Sir?' The seaman nearest him, bending over his oar.

'Nothing. I said nothing. Lay out with a will, there.'

The echoes of the action followed them, muffled now by smoke and increasing distance.

THUD THUD THUD BOOM THUD

The ripple of the oars, and the huffing breath of the oarsmen, then:

'Sir? I think *Expedient* has struck, sir!'

James looked, and saw that her red ensign had indeed been lowered. The two French frigates were already flanking *Expedient*, starboard and larboard, and the troop-laden bisquines had begun to close her. All gunnery ceased, and as if embodied in the drifting pall of smoke a threatening silence spread over the sea.

In the pinnace the hunched figures of the royal party – reduced to a mere dozen souls – remained mute in their cloaks and hats, all powdered finery hidden, all authority fled. A thought came to James as he glanced at them. It occurred to him that he had never really seen the faces of the king and queen, that these people seated in his boat, under his charge of protection, were no more significant in the vastness of the world and the totality of the human condition than anonymous beggars huddled at the alms-house gate, waiting for the beadle with his lantern and keys, and his parochial contempt.

'And what are they to me, any more than to the beadle?'

In his head. Rennie's words rose to follow that question: 'This ain't our fight, James.'

A breath, and he thrust such thoughts aside. He must rise to his responsibilities and his duty. Now that *Expedient* was lost, this boat was all that remained between its occupants and disaster. he must do his utmost to save Their Royal Highnesses – and himself. Aloud:

'Monsieur Félix?'

No response.

In French: 'Monsieur Félix, will you come aft over the thwarts, if you please? I wish to discuss my plan with you.'

No response.

'Is Monsieur Félix not here?'

No response. And now in English James:

'Lay on your oars, there!' The crew ceased rowing, the oars lying horizontal in the thole pins. The boat drifted to a halt, riding the swell.

Again in French: 'I must respectfully ask Your Royal Highnesses to allow Monsieur Félix to speak. I must discuss my plan with him, my proposal to escape these waters.'

No words. No sound. Nothing. He could not understand it. Surely Monsieur Félix had come into the boat with the royal party? He had seen him on the side ladder . . . but had he seen him in fact come into the boat?

'I did not. By God, he has stayed behind.' To himself. 'But *why*?'

'Sir?' The seaman nearest him, nodding aft past James.

James turned and saw with deep dismay that one of the bisquines had detached itself from the mêleé and smoke, and now approached the pinnace with speed and purpose.

'Give way together!'

The boat's crew gripped their oars and bent their backs. Droplets and rinsing splashes flew from the blades, and the pinnace began to move briskly through the water. But even as they came up to their best speed, James could see over his shoulder that the bisquine was gaining, five and twenty soldiers aboard. In half a glass – less – the bisquine would overhaul them.

'It is hopeless.' He did not say the words, nor even whisper them, but in his head and heart he was certain of their truth.

FOURTEEN

James woke in darkness, and for a moment thought he was returned to the underground passage at the Château de Châtaigne. The air was similarly dank and confined, and there was the same smell of stony damp. He stirred, and felt leg irons bite into his shins. Manacles bit into his wrists. There was the dull, gritty clinking of chains on the stone floor. His head ached severely, and there was a foul taste in his mouth. He was very cold, and felt that he had been wet, and was now clammily half-dry. He was wearing only shirt and breeches, and his feet were bare. Now he heard another set of chains as someone stirred nearby in the darkness.

'Who is there?' His voice echoing against a low ceiling.

'Christ, but my head aches . . . ohh. Is that you, James?'

'Aye, sir, it is.'

'Thank God. I feared when I woke that I was alone in this place.'

'You are not alone, sir. And I too have a headache. Did they give you cold tea, when you were took? That is what they gave us to drink.'

'I was blindfolded when they took me out of *Expedient* – and yes . . . yes, I was given cold tea.'

'And I remember nothing after. We were drugged, sir, both of us, to be brought here. But where are we, though? Is it a dungeon?'

'Don't know that, James.' A further clinking of chains.

'And you do not know what has become of the king, sir?'

'I fear I do not. What happened in the pinnace?'

'One of the bisquines overhauled us, and we were obliged to surrender without resistance, to protect the royal party from immediate injury. The soldiers outnumbered us, and were armed very heavy, and we had no weapons above pistols, and a musket or two.'

'Y'did right, James, y'did right. There was no choice. Nor for me – I struck my colours.' A sigh.

'Yes, sir, I know.'

A long moment, then Rennie: 'We are certainly in a fix this time, James.'

'D'y'think they will hang us?'

'Put us on the gallows with the king? Make a show of executing us with him?' A mirthless chuckle. 'I doubt that. We are small beer, James, in this affair.'

'You think they will simply imprison us, then?'

'Ha. They have done that already.' Clinking his chains.

'I meant – permanent.'

'Very likely we shall be left to rot, in least for the time being.'

'But first there will have to be a trial, and that will give us time to—'

'Trial? My dear James, why should they dignify us with a trial? We are interlopers and pirates, who smashed French ships in French waters, when we are not at war. No no, they will leave us here until we have been made thoroughly frightened and miserable, and then when they are ready they will hang us right enough. Not in course from the yardarm of the French flag at Brest, nor even in a public square, with a roll of drums. No, it will be done in a little sullen courtyard, hid from view, and our corpses dragged away on handcarts to the burial pit.'

'Unless we escape.'

'Escape!' The word bounced dully off the ceiling.

'We must always think of it, sir, while ever we have our health and wits.'

'Ever the optimist, hey, James?'

'I will never like to give up my freedom gladly.'

'As if we had a choice. Christ's blood, we have nothing to "give up". We are shackled in irons in a stone chamber far below ground. We might as well be in Hades.'

'Did you say below ground, sir? I do not think so.'

'Eh?'

'Listen. Ain't that the sound of . . .'

They both listened. Distantly, much muffled, the hollow booming sound of waves bursting in over rocks.

'The sea.' Rennie, softly.

'Surely we could not hear the sea unless we were near to the shore, and above it. On a clifftop, as an instance.'

'You think we are in a castle?'

'Or a fort, sir, on a headland.'

'Fort? Where?'

'Somewhere near to Brest. There are fortifications all along the northern reaches of Brest Roads. We studied them on the charts, if you recall, when we came here in *Expedient*.'

'Aye, you are right, we did.'

'And if we are held in a fort, then likely our ship is in the harbour – or in the dockyard, repairing.'

'You think they will repair her, James? When she has done such damage to them? Will not they wish to break her up?'

'No, sir, I do not think so. She is badly injured at present, but beneath her wounds she is an oak-built, Chatham-built, stout and sturdy sea boat. There is no better frigate afloat.'

'There is no need to sing her praises to me, James. I am well acquainted with her virtues, you know.'

'Then y'will like to renew that acquaintance, will not you, sir?'

'What, from a stone cell in a military fort? Ha.'

'From a boat, sir, with a cutting-out party, at night.'

'Yes yes, well well . . .' A sigh. 'It don't do to speculate on the impossible, James.' A clinking of chains. 'I wish to God they would relieve us of these damned irons. They cut into the flesh very painful.'

'Which is why we must always think of escape, sir. Of freedom.'

'Freedom?' A breath. 'Even if we could be free as you suggest, and retake our ship by some fantastic circumstance – a miracle – and then escape to England, what would we face, at home? The king of France has been snatched from our care, and returned to his fate at the hands of the revolutionists. We have failed, James. The commission is a dismal reverse in every distinction.'

'All the odds were against us from the beginning. We have done our best – and very nearly succeeded, too.'

'Very nearly don't answer in a case like this, as you know very well.'

'I will never like to despair, sir. It ain't a condition befitting a sea officer in the Royal Navy.'

'Ah. Hm. You wish to stiffen my sinews, hey? To remind me of my oath, and so forth? Yes?'

'Well – yes. It ain't like you to lie down and die without a murmur, sir.'

'You prefer me to stand up on my legs and die, do you?' Not harshly. 'Shouting my love for freedom as the noose is tightened at my neck?'

James made no reply. After a few moments he said:

'Our people are very likely held in this same fort. As a military establishment it must function by military rules and customs. One of those is certainly that prisoners should be allowed exercise from time to time – released from their confinement and brought into the open air to march about. If I am not mistook, they will be guarded by a small number of troops. Now then, if we could get a message to our people, there is a good chance they could rush and overpower their guards, and get their hands on a set of keys.'

'Ahh. Keys.' Without enthusiasm.

James began to crawl across the uneven stone floor, dragging his chains with him. He was at the limit of their length when his outstretched hand found a door. A heavy timber door, studded with nails. His fingers scrabbled over the surface of the timber – and found a lock.

'One of which will fit this door.'

'James, my dear friend – you are grasping at straws. Straws in the wind.'

'Nay, I am not, sir. My hand is on the very lock that will release us. That is what I grasp.'

'Yes yes, ye've found the door, and the door is provided with a lock. Very good. Excellent.'

A groan, off to one side in the darkness, and a stirring of chains.

'Good God, who is that?' Rennie peered unseeing.

A cough, then a croaking voice:

'I – I am here, sir. What is—'

'Who are you?' Sharply.

'Lieutenant Leigh, sir, at your service. Are we in the orlop?'

'No, Mr Leigh, we are ashore. In a dungeon.'

'Dungeon?' The chains. 'I don't recall being . . . ohh, my head!'

'Yes, Mr Leigh, we are all in the same boat.'

James smiled in the darkness, then:

'We believe we are held in a military fort, Leigh, that overlooks the harbour at Brest. Our wish is to attempt an escape, and retake our ship.'

'Hayter, is that you? But how can we escape, when we are held in irons?' Further clinking.

'You may well ask that, Mr Leigh.' Rennie, with a sniff.

They were all silent a moment, then James:

'Sir, we are three resourceful sea officers, of long service and experience. Surely, if we put our heads together, it's not impossible we could devise between us a scheme to gain our freedom . . . ?'

'You really have got such a scheme, James? But is it practical, hey? That is the question. Or merely a fantasy, concocted gorgeous and elaborate in your head by the action of the drug we was all given?'

'No, sir, I did not say that I had a plan wholly formed, only that perhaps we might discuss ideas severally among us, and—'

Over him: 'Oh, very well, in least it will pass the time. Go on, then, James – you begin.'

'Thank you, sir.' And he began.

*

Heavy footfalls thudded outside the door, and there was the rasping squeak of a key in the lock. A creaking sound as the door swung open, and a breath of less stale air from the passage beyond. And light. Light from a lantern held up at the open door. The gleam of a ring of keys, the dim bulk of the man behind the light, and his harsh, penetrating voice:

'Your time has come, messieurs.' In French. 'You will be blindfolded and released from your chains – but you will remain manacled.'

'What does the fellow say?' Rennie, peering at him.

James glimpsed a chevron on a sleeve, and asked in French: 'Where do you take us, Sergeant?'

'Silence!'

'I merely wish to—'

'You will be silent, or you will be gagged!' The sergeant advanced.

James made one more attempt:

'Are we to see the commander of the garrison?' Again in French.

The sergeant advanced further into the cell and struck James full in the face with the heavy bunch of keys. James fell back with a gasp, blood dripping from his nose and cheek, and dropped dazed to his knees.

'You bloody wretch!' Rennie snarled at the sergeant, who raised the keys to him. 'Yes, strike me too, you villain! And by God I will live to see you disembowelled!'

The sergeant now placed the lantern on the floor, and Rennie saw his face. An ugly moon face, with a bulbous nose. A thatch of dark hair. There was another figure in the passage outside. The sergeant straightened with a grunting sigh, and swung the keys in a sudden vicious arc at Rennie's head. At the same moment Lieutenant Leigh rose from the darkness at the side, looped his chains about the sergeant's neck, and jerked. The sergeant grunted, struggled, and was pulled off his feet. He and Lieutenant Leigh crashed over on the stone floor in a furious clinking rattle of chains. The second guard now rushed into the cell, brandishing his bayoneted musket. Rennie kicked his feet from under him, felt an agonising pain in his ankle as the leg iron bit into it, and he too fell. The musket flew from the guard's grasp, and sent the lantern skittering away across the floor. It tumbled against the far wall, tipped over in a crash of broken glass, and went out.

Black dark.

A moment of utter silence.

Then furious activity erupted. Shouts, grunting breaths, heaving, struggling bodies, and the chinking rattle of chains and irons. Rennie grappled with the guard he had tripped up, and found him powerful, and powerfully fierce. Lieutenant Leigh kept his wrist chains clamped under the sergeant's chin, and dragged them back into the fellow's throat. Demonic thrashing, and hands scrabbling at the chains, and at last the sergeant slumped and was still. Lieutenant Leigh heaved and kicked his way clear. Rennie reared back, blindly aimed his held-together fists at his opponent's skull, and felt the twin manacles at his wrists thud home. A grunt, and Rennie felt the guard go limp.

James Hayter, down on his knees, shook his head and felt blood splash on his hands. He stumbled to his feet.

'Sir? Captain Rennie? Are you all right?'

'I am all right.'

'As am I.' Lieutenant Leigh.

'We must get hold of those damned keys, and free ourselves.'

A frantic search for the ring of keys, in the jostling, chain-clinking darkness. At last Lieutenant Leigh located the ring by the sergeant's outstretched foot. And in blind, fumbling and cursing haste he tried to find the correct key for his irons, and could not. James crouched and searched the pockets of the sergeant's coat, and found a tinderbox. He stretched to the farthest extent of his chains to where he thought the lantern had fallen. And could not find it.

'Christ's blood, where is it!'

Stretching, straining, his fingertips swiping and scrabbling over the filthy stone floor. A squeak as his hand touched a slippery tail, and he heard the rat scuttling away along the wall. And now his fingers found the tip of the bayonet on the guard's dropped musket. With great difficulty he managed to grasp the bayonet and pull the musket toward him, cutting a finger on the razor edge of the blade. At last he had the musket in his hands, and with it probed for the lantern, located it, hooked the handle with the bayonet and dragged it toward him.

A moment, a light struck with blood-dripping fingers, and the lantern was lit. The glass of one facet was broken, but the lantern stayed alight, and in a few moments more they had found the correct keys for their manacles and leg irons on the ring. The three Expedients were free. But only free, as they were obliged to acknowledge, within one section of a large fort.

'A change of plan,' said James now. 'Since we are no longer obliged to wait until we could be brought out of the cell and took before an officer, and then attempt our escape – as I'd originally proposed – we can now proceed of our own volition.'

'Yes, by all means, James. There ain't a moment to lose.' Rennie, rubbing his wrists and moving to the door of the cell.

'With a proviso.' James held up a finger.

'Eh?'

'We must proceed – in disguise.'

'Disguise? Good God, you are wedded to disguise!'

'Not quite, sir. She is merely a mistress of convenience. Mr Leigh and I will be sergeant and man, and you will be our prisoner. So you will not have to go in disguise, only your two lieutenants.'

'Ahh.' A nod. 'Very good, very good.'

'However, I must ask you, I fear, to . . .' Picking up a set of irons.

'What, put those damned things back on?'

'If our subterfuge is to be convincing, sir, you must. Just as Lieutenant Leigh and I must shift into these stinking, sweaty uniforms.' Nudging the prostrate sergeant with his foot.

'God damn me . . . ohh, very well.' And Rennie held out his hands.

Presently the three officers quit the cell and ventured into the low-arched, echoing passage, which proved to run in one direction only, away to the left. James and Lieutenant Leigh, dressed in the boots and uniforms of the sergeant and guard, followed the manacled and shackled Captain Rennie. The sergeant and his companion they left behind, bound and gagged on the floor of the cell.

At the end of the passage the three officers came to a gate of iron, plated, strapped and studded across. Lieutenant Leigh found the appropriate key on the ring, after moments of anxious fumbling, and unlocked the gate. Cautiously he pulled it open. Sunlight streamed like molten metal into the passage, and the three men blinked and shaded their eyes in the glare. A moment, then the gate was pulled open all the way, and they stared out. The gate gave on to an empty cobbled court-yard, a long oblong space surrounded by high stone walls. The smell of fresh horse dung drifted over the walls, and the saline smell of the sea. In the open air the booming thud of waves was more distinct. A brisk wind was coming in from the west, from the sea, and all three men turned their faces instinctively in that direction.

'Topsail breeze,' murmured Rennie, sniffing it. 'Fine topsail breeze.'

Shouts of command now echoed over the opposite wall, and the solid rhythm of marching feet.

'A drill?' wondered Rennie.

'Perhaps a parade?' James. 'Or simply the changing of the guard.'

'What o'clock is it, I wonder?' Lieutenant Leigh, shading his eyes and looking toward the sun.

'About noon, I should say.'

As if in answer there came the thudding boom of a cannon, and further bawled commands.

'Aye, noon.' Rennie.

For a moment or two the prisoner and his two guards stood irresolute at the open gate, then the gate on the far side of the courtyard was thrust open with a rattling clank, and Rennie and his companions were obliged to act. Lieutenant Hayter gave a series of hoarse, hectoring commands in French, and pushed Rennie forward on the cobbles, Lieutenant Leigh bringing up the rear with his musket. From the far gate emerged a long line of prisoners, all manacled, and at once Rennie recognised them as *Expedient*'s crew. They looked very dirty and downcast, and were dazzled by the sunlight, but otherwise unharmed.

'Do not show any sign of recognition,' murmured Rennie over his shoulder. 'Do not look in their direction.'

The large party approached the centre of the yard as the small party marched briskly toward them, and the far gate. There were three guards with the large party, all armed with muskets. These guards now herded their charges toward the long wall on the north, where they began to trudge in disconsolate lines up and down. Several of them clearly recognised Captain Rennie, and drew him to the attention of others.

But Rennie ignored them, holding himself stiffly erect as he was marched away over the cobbles by his escort. The three guards with the other prisoners barely glanced toward them. Two of them stood against the wall, their muskets leaning beside them, and lit their pipes. The third turned to the wall, opened his breeches and urinated.

'Those men will not trouble us, if we are decisive.' Rennie, over his shoulder. 'Give the order to wheel about, and march me back toward them.'

'Eh?' James, immediately behind him.

'We will rush them.'

'Christ's blood, sir. They are all armed.'

'Surprise, Mr Hayter. The essence of an action. We will rush them as soon as we are level with their position.' All muttered urgently over his shoulder. 'Mr Leigh.'

'Sir?'

'Bayonet the man that is pissing. Aim at his throat. Mr Hayter, you will seize his musket, and bayonet the guard next him. The third fellow will surrender at once.'

James sucked in a deep breath, and gave the order in French to turn about. The little group duly wheeled, and began marching back across the square. As they drew level with the three guards standing at the wall, Rennie:

'Now!'

Lieutenant Leigh raised his musket, dashed straight at the guard turning from the wall and buttoning his breeches, and ran him through the throat. The guard fell with a desperate throttled gasp, blood spraying from his neck.

James ran at full stretch straight toward the musket leaning against the wall, snatched it up as the second guard began to react, and plunged the bayonet straight into his heart. The man stared at James appalled, then sight vanished from his eyes. He coughed once, and slumped, and the steel blade slipped bloodily free.

The third guard stumbled back along the wall, knocked over his musket, and:

'*Non . . . non . . .*'

He slid down the wall in a terrified crouch.

'Tie him.' Rennie. 'And for Christ's sake untie me.' Holding out his manacled hands.

A ragged cheer from the ship's crew, now crowding round.

'Silence!' Rennie, forcefully but not loudly. 'We must go very quiet and careful now, lads, if we are to get out of this with our lives.'

Lieutenant Leigh unfastened the manacles and leg irons, and Rennie rubbed his wrists.

'Three of you will shift into the uniforms of these guards. You, there. And you. And you.' Pointing. 'You will then take up their muskets, and with Mr Hayter and Mr Leigh escort the rest of us. You there, Whittle.' To another seaman. 'What lies beyond the far gate, lad?'

'A parade ground, sir. A great square, upon which the garrison soldiers make their duty to their commanding officer, in marching ranks. And the cliff and sea is directly beyond it, sir.'

'How many soldiers?'

'I do not know, sir.'

'At a guess, then.'

'Above an hundred, I should say. Maybe an hundred and a half.'

'And how many are we?'

'There is seven'y-four of us, sir.'

'So few?' Glancing round. 'What became of all the others?'

'They's all dead or wounded, sir. And the stan' officers is held in another place, I b'lieve, sir.'

'Dear God . . .' Quietly, then turning: 'Where is Mr Abey?'

Richard Abey pushed his way to the front of the group. His coat had gone and he was filthy dirty, but unhurt.

'I am here, sir.'

'I am right glad to see you, Richard. I am glad to see you all. Now then, Mr Hayter and Mr Leigh, and the other lads – jump now, shift into those coats – will escort the party out of that gate, and across the parade ground in the direction of the cliff. Should anyone intervene, or question what we are about, Mr Hayter will answer in French.'

'Very good, sir.' James, stoutly.

'And by the by, ye'd better fix that clear in your head, before we go out of the gate.'

'Yes, sir. Fix what in my head, exact?'

'What you are going to say if we are stopped. In French.'

'Ah. Yes.' Nodding.

'Well well, what are you going to say, Mr Hayter?'

'Latrine duty, sir.' Confidently.

'Eh? D'y'know where the latrines are, in this fort?'

'No, sir. But there's always latrines to be dug, or dug over, at a military establishment. I shall say: "Fatigue party of prisoners, for the new latrines!" I'll warrant it will not be questioned, sir, not even for a moment.'

'Pray God you are right.' A breath, another glance round, and: 'Very well, let us proceed.'

'Sir?' Lieutenant Leigh. 'What are we to do when we reach the cliff, sir?'

'Go down it, Mr Leigh, and find boats.' As if stating the obvious.

They were not stopped. The noon parade had dispersed and the parade square was deserted when the party of prisoners and their escort marched diagonally across it and arrived at the top of the cliff. Here the wind was stronger, and whistled over the clifftop in buffeting gusts. Beyond lay Brest Roads, to the south the Pointe des Espagnols, and the harbour and dockyard to the east. A forest of masts stood in the harbour, and it was there that Rennie looked, shading his eyes. He glanced back at the bulk of the fort, and the long stable block away on the north of the square. A flag snapped and rippled against the sun, high on the pole above the signal gun on its mound of earth. All seemed quiet, and orderly.

'They are at their dinner,' murmured Rennie to himself.

'That is why we are unmolested.' He ignored the pang of hunger that rose from his belly at the thought of food, and looked instead to the immediate task. And saw to his surprise and relief that there was a path cut into the cliff, leading down to the shore. There were iron stanchions and hand-ropes.

'Escort your prisoners down, Mr Hayter.'

They proceeded down the cliff to a rocky, shingled stretch of shoreline. Beyond the headland to the west was the open sea. To the east Brest Roads and the harbour. But there were no boats anywhere to be seen, and the whole of the shore-line away to the east was rocky, treacherous and difficult. Cliffs jutted, and outcrops of rock against which the sea dashed itself.

Rennie detached himself from the party and stood looking east a few moments, then walked along the shore to where waves heaved in and thudded themselves into spray against jutting rocks on the west. He stared out to sea, at the scud-ding whitecaps there. Presently Lieutenant Hayter joined him.

'Yes, James?' Over the booming of the sea, and the whistle of the wind.

'The people wish to know what we are to do, sir.'

'What have their wishes to do with anything, hey? It ain't for them to press me. Nor you, Mr Hayter.'

'Very good, sir.' Formally correct, his back straight.

Rennie squared his shoulders, sniffed, and: 'We will walk to the east along the shore. Under escort, in course, just as before. A party of prisoners.'

'Along the shore, sir?' Glancing there.

'Yes. Yes. Along the shore, Mr Hayter.'

'Forgive me, sir, but it is very rocky indeed beyond this section. Waves pound the whole of that part of the coast.'

'As I can see with my own eyes, that are perfectly good. We will proceed east, Mr Hayter, without the loss of a moment. We must discover boats if we are to penetrate the harbour and reclaim our ship.'

'Shall I give the order, sir?'

A long glance at his lieutenant, then Rennie: 'Nay, I will talk to them a moment, James, and urge them to their duty. We are all tired and hungry, and we cannot afford to lose heart. Must not, under any circumstance. I mean to prevail in this, and they must understand me, and follow me willing and in good cheer.'

*

When they had gone less than a quarter of a mile along the broken shore to the east, Rennie and his party were obliged to pause. There was no path beyond the next cliff, which plunged straight down into the sea. Lieutenant Hayter consulted his captain, the two men standing away from the main group, many of whom now lay down, tired and hungry as they were.

'Surely we must go back, sir . . . ?' James, keeping his voice low.

'Retreat? Don't be a damned fool. D'y'think they will take kindly at the fort to what we have done there, hey? It can only be a matter of time before those dead guards are discovered, and the alarm raised. We must proceed, and find and commandeer boats.'

'Aye, boats. But where, sir?'

'Boats abound on these shores, I am in no doubt.'

'I do not think they are quite so plentiful ashore as you suppose, sir . . .' He broke off, staring past Rennie. '. . . However, they are numerous enough at sea.'

Rennie turned to look, and saw a large, three-masted chasse-marée running east into the harbour, not more than two cables off. She was transom-sterned, rigged with lugsails, and a headsail on her flat-steeved bowsprit. They could see men on her deck. She was almost as large as a naval cutter.

Rennie nodded. 'She is just the vessel for us, by God. Hail her, Mr Hayter, if y'please.'

'Yes, sir. Erm, what should I . . . ?'

'Say that we are a party from the fort, stranded by the tide and the pounding sea, and so forth, and ask them to take us off. When we are aboard, we will overpower them.'

'Very good, sir. Only I will not tell them that.' James cupped his hands at his mouth, and in bawling French:

'Ahoy, the chasse-marée! We are from the fort, and we are trapped by the tide! Please aid us, and take us off!'

The chasse-marée lost way. An indistinct hailing shout, in answer. James repeated his plea, and to his great relief saw that the vessel was altering course, and standing in toward the shore. But she did not sail all the way in, and James was entirely understanding of her master's reason. The shore was very rocky and dangerous, there was a stiff breeze and a heavy chop, and to attempt to bring the chasse marée any closer in would risk her safety.

'I fear he cannot take us off, sir.' Aside, to Rennie.

'Don't be so damned womanish, Mr Hayter. Y'must convince the fellow to take the chance. We are desperate, say to him, and will drown if he don't save us.'

James did not like to be called 'womanish', but he did as he was told, and renewed his efforts. In English, urgently, to the group on the shore: 'Remain lying down, as if injured.' And in French, hailing the chasse-marée: 'We have injured men, and they must be treated or they will die! Please help us, and take them off!'

Presently a small boat was hoisted out and lowered, and two men and a young officer began to pull toward the shore, the boat pitching and tossing hazardously.

'This will not do,' Rennie said, in a low, urgent tone. 'A small boat will not answer. You must induce them to bring the vessel itself—'

Over him, very firmly, James: 'If several of us get into that boat, sir, we can overpower the crew of the chasse-marée by a surprise assault. As we did at the fort with those guards. That is all we may hope for under the circumstances.'

'But you will need all four of you that have muskets. How will you explain—'

Again over him: 'No, sir. One guard, myself, with a musket. And three men posing as injured – with hidden bayonets. Whittle, Thoms, and Denton.' Indicating three young and strong able-seamen.

As the boat neared the shore, Rennie hesitated, looking at the boat and then at his people. A breath, and then he nodded. 'Very well. That must be our plan, then.'

The three supposedly injured men – who were very dirty and wet, and looked suitably bedraggled – were given bayonets to hide in their clothes and carried limp by their shipmates down to the boat, that had now beached. James explained the situation in rapid French to the young officer, and helped get the prostrated men into the boat, then got into the boat himself. With seven men now aboard the little boat was laden very heavy, and nearly capsized as it headed out through the waves to the chasse-marée, which had anchored, her head to the wind.

Rennie watched them go and was filled with trepidation and doubt, which he concealed.

'Will they succeed, sir?' A voice at his side. Richard Abey.

'Yes, Mr Abey, in course they will.' With stout conviction, lifting his chin. 'I have every confidence in Mr Hayter.' Turning to the assembled men. 'We shall prevail today, never fear.'

They all watched the boat as it neared the chasse-marée.

'Mr Abey.'

'Yes, sir?'

'What became of our standing officers? D'y'know where they are held?'

'They were kept separate from the rest of us after we surrendered, sir. I do not know why.'

'Could they have been held in the ship, I wonder? Could they have remained aboard?'

'Perhaps that is possible, sir. I think they were marched forrard to the fo'c's'le.'

'Very good. Thankee, Richard. If they was still aboard – luck may be with us.'

On the beach they waited when the boat reached the chasse-marée, and the occupants went aboard, the injured lifted and carried. Long moments, then a furious eruption of activity on deck, men running and clashing, and the *crack* of a single musket shot.

Silence, and the chasse-marée rode the lifting sea. Those on the beach stared motionless. And at last came a voice.

'We have her! We have took her!' Lieutenant Hayter, appearing at the starboard rail.

'Thank God.' Rennie rubbed his hand through his sparse hair. 'Thank God he has done it.'

'We are going to bring her in as far as we dare! Wade out to us, and we will throw you lifelines, so that you may haul yourselves aboard!'

FIFTEEN

By the time all of *Expedient*'s people had been taken aboard the chasse-marée, it was mid-afternoon, and Rennie was anxious to depart the vicinity of the fort. He had ordered the crew of the vessel bound hand and foot and taken below. It was very cramped below, and with so many men now aboard the vessel she was low in the water and sluggish in answering the helm. Rennie was anxious that naval order should obtain, as soon as they were under way, and having discovered what little food was aboard, he ordered a late dinner, and then instituted a system of watches.

Lieutenant Hayter had ascertained, in conversation with the master of the vessel, that she was attached to the dockyard at Brest, and had been sent to the landing place of the fort, beyond the headland and the cliff which the Expedients had descended. The chasse-marée had carried a party of dockyard artificers, who were to make repairs.

'Repairs?' James had asked him. 'What repairs could naval artificers carry out at a military fort?'

'Well . . . they were to repair the gallows there, I understand.'

'Good God. So they meant to hang us?'

'I do not know, Lieutenant.'

'Is our ship in the harbour at Brest?'

A brief hesitation, then: 'Yours is the frigate?'

'Yes, the *Expedient*.'

'She is there, moored near to the dockyard. Many people

at Brest wished to see her burned and destroyed, but she is to be repaired, I believe.'

James conveyed this information to Rennie, in the cramped space he had taken as his 'great cabin' below, beneath the low framed skylight. Rennie nodded, eating a slice of blue cheese, and came to his decision. He had found the master's charts, and now tapped the largest.

'We will sail east, then double the Pointe des Espagnols, and run south into the depth of the roadstead, as if we had business at some farther landing place there. Then in the second dog watch, as the light fades, we will come about and run north, creep into the harbour itself, and find *Expedient*.'

'Very good, sir. You like this cheese?'

'It is very fair, as cheeses go. You do not care for it?'

'It is food, in least.'

'What is the fort called, where we was held? Did the master tell you, James?'

'He did, sir. It is called the Fort du Diable.'

'The devil it is.' And he chuckled. 'Very good, very good. Did you require the master to give you his hat and coat, as I asked?'

'They are here, sir.' Giving them to Rennie.

'I will just shift into them, and we will go on deck and sniff the wind, hey?

'Very good, sir.'

'I want you there with me in your present disguise, in case we should meet another vessel and be obliged to speak.'

'Then – shouldn't I wear the junior officer's coat, sir? A military sergeant on the deck of a dockyard vessel will not look—'

'Yes, yes, I had not considered that.' Over him, with a frown. 'Change coats with the young man, and then join me on the deck right quick.'

'Very good, sir.'

* * *

Evening, and the chasse-marée ran north toward the thickets of masts in Brest Harbour, the headland of the Pointe des Espagnols to larboard in the fading light. They had seen other vessels during the afternoon, but none wished to speak, and they had sailed unmolested to the limits of the roadstead.

Lieutenant Hayter, dressed in the uniform of the young lieutenant, peered through that officer's long glass.

'Can y'see *Expedient*?' Rennie, at his side.

'Nay, I cannot. She is concealed among many mooring numbers, sir.'

'Hm. But we will find her, I am in no doubt.'

'Yes, sir. But I wonder how we will safely approach her, when night falls? We have no boats – well, only a very small gig – and this vessel is too large to manage in so crowded an anchorage, in darkness. We will likely get athwart hawses, or even fall aboard other ships.'

'We will brail up our canvas and deploy the sweeps, and proceed very careful. There ain't a density of cloud, and there will be moonlight beside, and riding lights. We shall find her.'

'There will likely be an armed crew aboard her, don't you think so?'

'We are many, and they will be few, James.'

'We have four muskets and as many bayonets, against who knows what odds?'

Rennie turned to look at his lieutenant, and grew severe. 'I don't understand you, Mr Hayter. You have took to womanish ways. Doubt, hesitancy, caution. A desire to see calamity and misfortune, where none exists.'

'Really, that ain't quite fair, sir, when I—'

'Not *fair*! We have a task before us that requires clarity of purpose, and a stout heart. I will not have petulant maid-servant's talk in my hearing. Mr Leigh and Mr Abey will attend me and remain at my side, if you will not stiffen your spine, and speak manly and sensible.'

'I . . . I . . . very good, sir.' And he had to bite his tongue, tremulous with rage.

Expedient's people were assembled on deck to double-man the long sweeps, eight on each side. Rennie ordered the lugsails and yards lowered rather than brailed up or reefed, and the chasse-marée proceeded by manpower alone.

Night had fallen as they approached the anchorage, and when the chasse-marée was hailed from the decks of various moored ships – as she was several times during the next glass – James simply replied:

'Dockyard vessel! Artificers aboard!'

Which response was in every instance satisfactory, since the vessel was allowed to pass without hindrance deeper and deeper into the harbour.

James grew increasingly uneasy as they went. He wished to say to his captain that the alarm must certainly have been raised hours ago at the fort, and very probably the chasse marée herself missed by now, and that if they continued to move about the harbour they would almost certainly be apprehended, and dealt with very severe. However, James had no wish to be called 'womanish' a third time, and so he kept quiet.

A few minutes after, it was Rennie himself who voiced those very fears. Now from the shore could be heard the sound of great activity. Platoons of soldiers marching, the barking of dogs, and shouts of command. Lights flickered along the harbour wall.

Rennie took a deep sniffing breath, peering anxiously at the shore, and:

'We must find *Expedient* right quick, or be took ourselves.'

They had by now traversed the nearly entire width of the anchorage, narrowly avoiding a dozen ships. A shape loomed out of the blackness, and James, in a hoarse, carrying whisper:

'Oars!'

The sweeps lifted from the water, and the chasse-marée gliding with barely a ripple.

'I know those lines.' Rennie, quietly.

'Aye, sir.'

It was their ship. It was *Expedient*. The chasse-marée glided right alongside the greater ship, fended herself off with sweeps, then was manoeuvred in under the starboard chains. Now from above, a French voice:

'Who is there? Who are you?' A face appeared at the rail, in the glow of a lantern.

'Dockyard,' called James.

'*Ah, oui.*' The face and the lantern. 'You are very late. Too late.'

'We were delayed by all the upheaval ashore. Some kind of search, I don't know.'

'*Alors*, they never tell us anything out here. But you are too late now. Come back tomorrow, will you, when we are ready to start dismantling the rigging?'

'We have been sent to come aboard tonight, so we may begin work at first light.'

'First light? Why so early?' Grumbling.

'Because that is the arrangement made by the shipwright! *Mon Dieu!*'

'Oh, very well. Come aboard. There is nothing to eat, you are too late.'

'Well done, James.' Rennie, in his lieutenant's ear, all irritation with him forgotten.

With the chasse-marée moored alongside, tethered to a stunsail boom, Rennie, James, Lieutenant Leigh and the other Expedients all went aboard. As they came up the side ladder into the waist, Rennie whispered to James:

'Let us first ascertain how many they are, and then decide how to tackle them.'

'Very good sir.'

The guard aboard the ship consisted of a sergeant of the militia – the man who had hailed them – and a platoon of irregulars. The sergeant appeared to be resentful of this duty. His men – in his view – were the flotsam and jetsam of the port. In a brief conversation with James – as the Expedients assembled on deck – he described himself as protecting 'a worthless hulk'.

'Worthless? Nay, that is why so many men have been sent. To commence the repair.'

'But surely the repair has been cancelled?' Puzzled. 'As I understood, the whole damned ship was to be stripped out, the rigging and masts dismantled, and then she was to be broke up.'

'Broke up? Then you have been misinformed, Sergeant. Tell me, have her powder and shot, and her stores, been removed?'

'Well, that is all to be commenced tomorrow, as I thought you knew . . .'

'*Oui, oui*, of course. Where are your men, at present?'

'They are below.'

'*Ah. Bien.*' A bayonet to the sergeant's throat. 'You will oblige me by keeping silent, and you will not be harmed.'

'Christ, who are you!'

'Keep silent.' Pressing the tip of the blade into the sergeant's throat.

James beckoned to the others who were armed, and the sergeant was bound and gagged. Presently the armed party went below, and took the platoon of irregulars entirely by surprise at their supper. Plainly these were not men who had ever expected to make up a guard in anything but name.

'Why was she not better protected, James?' wondered Rennie, as they came on deck and went aft.

'The dockyard lieutenant who commanded the chasse-marée said she was to be repaired, I am certain of it.' Glancing up at the rigging. 'Sir, should not we inspect the ship below, first? Make an assessment of—'

'Yes, yes, presently.' Rennie crossed from the starboard rail to the larboard on his quarterdeck, and peered aloft. Then: 'Yes, the navy, and the whole maritime organisation here at Brest, is plainly in a condition of disarray and division,

James. One faction don't wish for what t'other does. That is the confusion, I think. And I should say that was so throughout the port.'

'And – that will aid us, will it not?'

'To escape? Aye, certainly. While they search for us in confusion ashore, little dreaming we are afloat in our own ship. Aye.'

'Sir? Captain Rennie?' Richard Abey, ascending the ladder from the waist.

'Well?' As his acting lieutenant came aft.

'We have found Mr Loftus, sir, and the other standing officers. They were confined in the orlop.'

'Very well, thankee, Mr Abey. That is welcome news.'

'They were supposed to assist with the repair, sir, then the decision to repair was lately overturned, and they were locked away.'

'In irons?'

'No, sir. But they were bound up very painful, and left in the sail room without food or water.'

'Is Dr Wing with them?'

'Yes, sir. He is attending to them now, sir.'

'And his own condition?'

'He is very furiously angry, sir. Raging angry. "It is infamous – wretched infamous!"'

'Ah. You have his voice very accurate, Mr Abey. But he is otherwise unharmed?'

'His wrists are very chafed, and his ankles – but he ain't really hurt, sir. Only angry.'

'We may thank God they all survive. Where is Mr Leigh?'

'He is inspecting the hold, sir.'

'Very good. You will join him.' And as the youth made his obedience and turned to go: 'Mr Abey . . .'

'Sir?'

'Take care not to mimic the doctor anywhere proximate to him, hey? In fact, ye'd better not do it at all, any more.'

'Very good, sir.'

As Richard departed, Rennie turned to James. 'We should release those fellows in the chasse-marée. They will be damned uncomfortable by now, trussed up below.'

'D'y'mean release them from their bindings, sir, or let them go altogether?'

'Good God, we can't just let 'em go, James.' A sniff.

'Then – how may we safely untie them, sir?'

'Well well – they had better be made comfortable, in least. I don't wish us to be seen as tyrants and torturers. That ain't our way, in the Royal Navy.'

'I will see what can done for them.'

'Very well. But first there is the more pressing matter of the overall condition of the ship. Ask the boatswain to come and see me. I want him to tell me whether or no we are able to weigh and make sail, with the ship so badly damaged and in need of repair. I pray God he will tell me – yes.'

'Aye, sir.'

And I will like to hear a report from Mr Storey about our guns, and gunners' stores. Say so to him, will you?'

'Yes, sir.'

'Then we'd better have a report from Mr Trent about our victualling stores. Oh, and by the by, impress upon the people they must move about the ship as quiet as mice, no loud talk.'

'Very good, sir. Erm . . . anything else?'

'What? No no, James. Carry on, if y'please.'

James touched his hat, and went below, and Rennie paced aft, looking aloft, a post captain once more in command of his ship.

The wind had died to nothing, and now the hush of the anchorage was broken only by the distant shouts and tramping of boots ashore – and a great confusion of activity along the harbour wall.

Rennie peered there, found a glass at the binnacle, raised it, and:

'In course . . . in course . . . they are getting into boats to search for the chasse-marée.' He lowered the glass and hurried below.

Presently, in the great cabin, Rennie addressed his hastily summoned officers.

'We will take aboard the crew of the chasse-marée, then scuttle her. When we slip on the tide early tomorrow, we will set her crew adrift in a boat. Mr Hayter, you will take a party aboard, and bore holes in her hull. As quick and quiet as you can, if y'please. Mr Leigh, you will take charge of the crew, and bring them into the ship. Mr Abey, you will observe the activity of the searching boats, and report their movements to me glass by glass.'

'Aye, sir.'

'Very good, sir.'

'Very good, sir.'

'Yes, Doctor?' As the surgeon appeared at the door. 'Come in, come in.' And Dr Wing did come in, as the other officers departed, and he made a detailed report, with a written list.

Of the 260 souls of *Expedient*'s original complement, fewer than 100 remained. Of those coming under Dr Wing's interest, the dead had been buried at sea, and the many wounded had been taken ashore. In answer to Rennie's question:

'No, sir, I do not know where ashore, exact. There is a good naval hospital here at Brest, I believe. We may hope they have been carried there, but nothing is certain. The navy here – indeed authority altogether – is sadly lacking in direction and order. Take as an instance the shameful way we were treated, tied hand and foot like common footpads, nothing to eat or drink—'

'Yes yes, well well, we have all suffered considerable inconvenience of late, Doctor. You will perhaps like to consider the damage we ourselves have inflicted on the French. And to reflect that we are all of us fortunate not to've been took out on a public square and shot. A possibility still, if the boats coming from the shore should find us.'

'Do you think they will find us, Captain?'

'I hope not. I hope not. With so broad a harbour to traverse, so many ships, so little discipline . . . perhaps they will grow weary and desist. After all, they have got back their king, have not they? I expect that counts for everything with them, now.'

'You mean, sir, do you not – that they mean to execute their king?' Quietly.

'Nay, I mean nothing of the kind, Doctor. We made our best endeavours to bring him away, at great cost to ourselves. Our ship is gravely damaged, and we can only hope to limp home as it is. We cannot allow ourselves to dwell on the present circumstances of the French king, nor speculate as to his future, when it ain't in our hands. That is a matter for the French, now.'

'Then – forgive me, sir – if it is only a matter for them, why did we come here at all?'

Rennie glared at his surgeon, and for a moment was very angry with him. Then he sighed, and shook his head.

'This is our fourth commission in *Expedient*, Thomas, and I think Their Lordships know we will never shirk our obligation to face hazard, in whatever form it may take. But I tell you plainly – this commission is the most improbable of success that I have ever been obliged to accept. I have done my utmost – we all have – but I am not God Almighty, nor even one of his saints, that can work miracles. I am only a sea officer, mortal flesh and blood, my ship is but a little wooden world, and we have both been nearly destroyed in a cause that could never find a favourable end, that was clearly doomed from the beginning.' A breath. 'Why did we come?'

'Indeed . . .'

'Because we was ordered. Because it was our duty. I will always like to do my duty – if I am able.'

'Again, forgive me, but that don't quite answer the question, sir.'

For a moment Dr Wing thought he had gone too far, and that Rennie would turn on him in a fury, but now he saw that Rennie's taut silence as he stood at the table was not scarce-contained anger, but scarce-contained grief. A tear fell on his cheek, and quietly:

'I cannot bring myself to look close at your list . . . and the names of all those we have lost. All those young lives, gone for ever. Tom Makepeace, the best and most loyal of men . . . I wish to God I knew the answer to your question, Doctor, I wish I did. Alas, I do not.'

SIXTEEN

An hour before dawn. The tide had turned, and was now on the ebb. Very quietly, all hands under strict orders to remain silent, *Expedient* slipped her moorings. She needed neither wind nor towing boats to make headway, but could proceed purely by the force of the receding water. At Brest, as everywhere along this coast, the tides were extreme in their ebb and flood. As she began to move there was no further sign of the searching boats.

Expedient was not in what her officers would call a seaworthy condition. She had been battered, her masts and rigging were far from sound, and her people were sadly few. It could not be helped. With everything at stake she would have to do. The crew of the sunken chasse-marée were now placed bound and gagged in the vessel's boat, and released to drift.

'They will be discovered soon enough, I expect,' Rennie said to James as they watched the boat slowly spin and bob in their wake, and drift away at an angle. 'Our task now is to remain *un*discovered, hey?'

'Indeed, sir.'

Expedient's mooring lay at some distance from the dockyard and wall, but with many ships lying outside her. A passage had been left clear of ships between her and the western side of the roadstead, so that dockyard vessels might come and go. This was the passage *Expedient* slipped through now, gliding west across the harbour toward the narrow entrance, the fort to the north, and the Pointe des Espagnols to the south. They had a bare hour to accomplish their escape before daylight rode up like a fiery enemy to pursue them. Rennie had his carronades run out, with two-man crews standing by. To James:

'We cannot fight our long guns so short-handed. We must afford ourselves some protection, however, and our smashers will provide it.'

'What will become of our wounded ashore, d'y'think?'

'Do not ask me that.' Quietly.

'I'm sorry, sir.'

'The only thing that should make us glad is that we are tolerable well provisioned for an hundred souls – I am not glad, though.'

'Nor I.' Thinking of Juliette, whom he now believed – in his heart – was dead.

'But neither am I sad, James.' Lifting his chin. 'I am resolved.'

Expedient reached the point immediately south of the fort, and Rennie ordered topsails loosed and the beginning southerly wind harnessed. He sniffed the wind, and the sea, and began to believe – where before he had only allowed himself to hope – that *Expedient* really would make her escape. He squared his shoulders in the first faint greyness of dawn, and felt the sturdy planking beneath his feet.

'My ship is under my legs again, and—'

BOOM BOOM BOOM

The guns of the fort, high on the cliff. Spray erupted white to starboard, half a cable short of the ship.

'Christ Jesu . . .' Rennie stared at the black wall of the cliff. Further flashes there.

BOOM BOOM

'Mr Tangible! Courses and t'gan'sails! We must run for our lives!'

'Hands to make sail! Topmen aloft!' And the calls.

'We will all bear a hand, Mr Hayter. Every man that is on his legs.' Rennie, moving to take up a place on a halyard. 'You too, Mr Loftus.' Beckoning his sailing master from his place by the helmsman at the wheel. Spying a boy running forrard: 'You there, boy! Clap on to this fall! You ain't of a size, but y'must pull your weight today, all the same.' And to the carronade crews: 'Leave those smashers for now! Bear a hand!'

BOOM BOOM B-BOOM

Fountains of spray over the deck.

'They have got our range now, God damn and blast them, the villains. Cheerly now, lads! Let us get clear of these damned guns, and break for the open sea!'

'What a pity hhh it is a clear dawn hhh and not a grey and gloomy one . . .' James, heaving at a fall.

And now came a sound even more chilling than the crash of guns. Rennie had sent a man into the main crosstrees as his sole lookout, and now that man called:

'Two ships in pursu-u-u-uit! One mile astern of us!'

Rennie abandoned his position at the halyard, snatched up a glass as he ran aft, and focused from the tafferel. Silhouetted to the east against the fiery ingot of the rising sun, the masts and sails of two ships of war. Frigates.

'Christ's blood . . .' Whispered. 'How have they repaired so soon? I thought I had damn near crippled them, as they near crippled me.'

BOOM BOOM BOOM B-BOOM

Roundshot whirred past *Expedient*, and flung up spray to larboard. The creaking and straining of yards, rigging and timbers as the ship heeled with the lifting wind on the larboard tack, heeled and pitched in the swirling suck of the tide, and ran west under her canvas towers.

Rennie jumped up into the mizzen shrouds, careless of his safety, and focused his glass ahead. Ten miles to the open sea. Hooking an arm through a shroud he swung round and peered at the following ships. Were they gaining? By God, they were. Soon they would begin to fire chasers, and attempt to smash his rudder. His already damaged rudder, that was hanging on its pintles by mere good luck. One accurate shot with a long nine and the ball would render *Expedient* helpless. He would have to devise a defence. A defence that would allow him time to reach the open sea – say an hour.

'The best defence is to attack, ain't it?' In his head. 'Can I attack while I am running away?'

He jumped down on his quarterdeck, and clamped the glass under his arm. He paced and paced, back and forth across the deck, head down, as his ship heeled and groaned and quivered under him like a frightened animal. Presently, to the helmsman as he went forrard past him:

'Just so, Whittle, hold her just so.'

To James, who now stood at the breast-rail, his crewing work done:

'Mr Hayter, a word with you, if y'please.'

James came aft, and Rennie beckoned him close. 'I have a notion to fire a carronade, James.'

James glanced astern. 'But they are far out of range of our carronades, sir . . .'

'They are gaining rapid, though.' Taking his arm and guiding James to the lee rail. 'They are gaining, but we cannot turn and face them.'

'Then how can we—'

'Listen, now. If we was to take a carronade off the gunport, right out of its breeching rope, and fix it on the deck just about – there – at the tafferel, how high could you elevate its aim?'

'Well, sir, not overly high. You mean – to fire it through one of the chase ports?'

'Nay, I do not. You will secure it with tackle rings, but the essence of it is – hammocks.'

'Hammocks . . . ?'

'Hammocks filled with sand, several of them togther, placed under the carronade carriage and elevating the muzzle to fire in a high trajectory at those damned ships in pursuit.'

'Firing roundshot, sir? Thirty-two-pound roundshot?'

'No, no, no.' Impatiently. 'A mortar bomb, James. A lethal projectile that will fall on one of those frigates and cripple her, and deter the other.'

'We don't possess such bombs in the ship, I fear.' Shaking his head.

'No, but we can *make* one, or even two. Mr Storey has got in his stores four-pound grenades, has he not?'

'I think so, yes.' Beginning to see. 'Yes, I'm sure of it.'

'Very good. I want him to make me a stick of them, bound together in a sleeve of canvas and tied up with stout chain, the topmost grenade to have a long fuse.'

'Yes, I see, yes. A stick of say half a dozen, placed in the elevated carronade, and fired in a high arc.'

'Exact. To fall on the leading frigate, at her fo'c's'le, and explode with lethal effect.'

'Shall I send for Mr Storey, sir?'

'No, James, you will set about placing the carronade as I described. I will speak to Storey myself.'

One glass by the bell, and the preparations in hand. *Expedient* now clear of the fort, but the two pursuing ships appreciably nearer, the sun climbing in a great dazzle above them.

A droning whine and a spew of spray to larboard. Then a distant

THUMP

The action had begun.

The 'bomb' carronade was in position, secured by a system

of fore-and-aft and thwartwise tackles to rings in the deck and the tafferel, and supported by a mound of sand-filled hammocks – clewed and tied off – to give the muzzle extreme elevation, exactly like a mortar.

The frigates, one slightly astern and to larboard of the other, had each commenced firing bow chasers in a steady rhythm. Each pairing of nine-pounder shots came closer to striking *Expedient*, sending fans of spray over her decks as they struck the sea. When the frigates had overhauled *Expedient* to within a quarter of a mile, Rennie ordered the first of the grenade-bombs loaded. Mr Storey had supervised the entire procedure himself, and had made three bombs in all. He had calculated everything – the height, parabola, distance, and timing required for the fuse. Now he stood by the carronade to fire it, waiting for Richard Abey to give the direct command.

Richard Abey lifted his hand high. 'On my signal . . .' And dropped his arm.

BOOM

A fluttering whine as the bomb flew up in a rush of smoke and flame and fragments of wad, tumbled end over end in a blur, higher and higher and smaller and smaller, then dropped, trailing a corkscrew of smoke. The bomb fell out of sight, and for a moment Rennie believed it had fallen into the sea. Then there was a series of flashes at the bow of the leading frigate, her bowsprit flew to pieces, and the forestay snaked up in a great flailing curl.

CRACK-CRACK-CRACK-BANG BANG-BANG

A moment of quiet, then the frigate's foremast shuddered, tipped and went by the board. She lost way at once, slewed in a half-turn and began to burn. Sails caught fire on the fallen mast, and soon the whole head of the ship was enveloped in fiery smoke.

On *Expedient*'s quarterdeck the carronade had slewed to one side with the force of the discharge, and one of the hammocks had burst, spilling sand over the planking.

'Re-lo-o-oad!' Richard Abey.

Mr Storey and the carronade crew, aided by seamen of the afterguard, righted the carronade, and another grenade-bomb was loaded. Mr Storey aimed the squat gun as accurately as he could, and stood by.

'Wait . . .' Rennie, his glass focused on the second frigate, which had now tacked to larboard and was preparing to fire her starboard battery of guns.

'Wait . . . very well, Mr Abey.'

'On my signal . . .' And Richard Abey dropped his arm.

BOOM

The second bomb flew up, tumbling and spitting fuse smoke, reached its zenith against the dawn, and began to fall. A flickering flash, and the bomb exploded in mid-air. The cracking thuds of the multiple explosion. The sea stitched ragged all round the second frigate. Clouds of smoke drifting high on the wind.

'Bugger the poxy thing!' Mr Storey. 'The fuse burned too quick!'

'Wait . . .' Rennie watched through his glass. Presently: 'Your bomb was not wasted, Mr Storey. The grenades bursting above the ship have done great injury to the men on her deck. They meant to fire a broadside at us, but they've been interrupted in that purpose.' He lowered the glass.

'Shall I load the last bomb, sir?'

'Nay, Mr Storey, thankee. Your work is done for today, and very well done, too. Neither frigate will wish to pursue us now. They have had a nasty taste of Hades, and it has discommoded them.'

'Very good, sir.' Touching his hat.

'Mr Hayter.'

'Sir?'

'We shall replace the carronade at the gunport, if y'please, and rerig the breeching ropes. Thankee again, Mr Storey, there is no need for you to oversee the work. Y'may go below.'

'You wish me to take the last bomb with me, sir?'

'Indeed, Mr Storey, take it with you, and keep it as a curiosity, hey?'

A glass. Another glass. And now *Expedient* was clear of Brest and the immediate coast. She had left the frigates behind and was heading into the Atlantic. Rennie had inspected his ship, and thought that she could limp home to England safe enough. He went aft to his quarterdeck in a relatively buoyant frame of mind.

'Mr Hayter.'

'Sir?' James, dressed now in a version of his favourite working rig, with a kerchief tied round his head. He wiped his hands on a scrap of cloth. He was very dirty, having been deep into the cable tier at the boatswain's request.

'What d'y'say to breakfast?' Thinking that his lieutenant looked like the worst sort of ruffian in a gin-and-sawdust drinking den.

'I should welcome it, sir, indeed.' He balled up the filthy cloth and threw it over the lee rail.

'Then let us eat it together, hey?'

'I'll just wash my face and shift into my coat—'

'Never mind, never mind.' Magnanimously. 'I don't care how you look, my dear James, when we have beat the French at sea, and will not be troubled by them any more.'

But Captain Rennie had spoken too soon.

*

Expedient at sea, west of Ushant, at 5 degrees and 29 minutes west, 49 degrees and 29 minutes north, the wind from the south-west. At four bells of the afternoon watch the ship preparing to bear north for England, having tracked far enough west into the Atlantic to be clear of all French difficulty. Lieutenant Hayter the officer of the watch, his appointment as replacement first lieutenant now confirmed by Rennie's written warrant.

'De-e-e-e-ck!' The lookout in the main crosstrees. 'Sail of ship two leagues due east, beating west toward us!'

'What manner of ship? A merchantman?' James, through his speaking trumpet.

'She has the lines of a frigate, sir!'

James focused his glass astern and found masts and sails. To himself: 'A frigate?' To the middy on duty: 'You there, go below to the captain's cabin, and say—'

'I am here, Mr Hayter.' Captain Rennie came on deck, seating his hat firm on his head, and carrying his long Dollond. 'I heard the report. Jump up and have a look, will ye?'

'Aye, sir.' James slung a glass on his back, jumped into the mizzen shrouds and went aloft. He was used to such requests from his captain, who had a lifelong aversion to heights and seldom ventured above his quarterdeck. Rennie strode to the tafferel and lifted his glass. Presently James bellowed from the mizzen crosstrees:

'French frigate! Cracking on!'

'Thankee, Mr Hayter! Return to the deck, if y'please!'

James stepped off the crosstrees and plunged to the deck by a backstay, careless of the smears of tar on his makeshift working clothes.

'That second damned frigate was not crippled after all, James.' Rennie, leaving the tafferel.

'But why in God's name does her captain pursue us? We are beyond French waters, now.'

'Vengeance?'

'You think so, sir?'

'Perhaps we killed a brother officer in our last attack. Perhaps he simply hates the English.'

James glanced astern. 'Well, whatever his reasons, he is there. If he wishes to destroy us we must run or fight – even though we are not at war.'

'Not at war? If those blackguards really do wish to kill their own king, James, as you believe – and Dr Wing thinks the same thing – then how long before they will like to kill ours? It is only a matter of time.'

James looked at Rennie, and thought of why they had come to France, of why they were pursued now.

'I believe that may likely be so, yes.' Quietly.

'We cannot outrun him, James, in our present state of repair. We will have to fight.'

'With another grenade-bomb, sir?'

'Nay, we cannot expect that ruse to work again. He will not come close enough for a bomb to be effective. Even if he did, we have only one further bomb, and no more grenades. If that should miss, or explode short . . .'

'Surely we must try?'

'Nay, the Frenchman will attempt to injure us at long range with his bow chasers. We'll run west as long as we can, then when he believes he has us at his mercy, we will go about and run straight at him. He must either continue to run straight at us, or tack away to bring his great guns to bear. We haven't guncrew enough to fight our own long guns, but if we can close the distance between us to carronade range – then we may have a chance to prevail.'

'Very good, sir.'

*

Expedient ran west, deeper and deeper into the Atlantic, but she was limping and slow. A glass, and the French frigate nearer by half a league. Another glass, and now Rennie sniffed the air, and felt a cold puff of wind against his cheek, from a new direction. Was the sky just a little darker? Within moments:

'De-e-e-e-ck! Stormclouds far to the south-we-e-e-st! Very dark and heavy!'

James jumped again into the shrouds, and confirmed the report. Rennie reached a decision almost at once. He paced aft, turned, then loud enough for all on deck to hear:

'Mr Hayter, we will sail into the storm.'

'Sail into it, sir?'

'Aye, that is our best chance to elude the fellow, and then run north to England. If we don't absolutely have to fight, damned short-handed as we are, then by God we will not.'

'Sir . . . if you please . . .' James moved close to Rennie, and lowered his voice. 'Our standing rigging ain't sound, nor our upper masts. And that persistent leak is only patched. Even in heavy weather, bruised and battered as we are, it would be a close-run thing. But in a fierce storm—'

'We face a storm either way, Mr Hayter. A storm of wind, or a storm of metal. I prefer the wind. We will steer sou'-west.'

*

Expedient met the first squall head on. The onslaught was fierce, blustering and capricious, and very dangerous to a ship in *Expedient's* condition. Her only hope of survival in the hours before her was to keep her head to the wind. If she faltered, even in these first huffing, puffing blasts, if she so much as lost her footing a moment and fell to her knees, she was lost. The wind rose briefly to a shrieking whistle.

'Four men at the wheel, Mr Loftus! Two on the weather spokes, two on the lee!' Rennie had to cup a hand to his mouth and bellow in the master's ear to make himself heard.

'Aye, sir!'

At first the swell was merely beaten down by the sweeps of wind, with flurries of spray whipped and scattered over the rolling sea, the surface itself dimpled and scoured beneath the swirling spray. Then the swell began to lift and run before the increasing madness of the wind, to heave and seethe and ride up in blue-black masses. Horizontal rain slashed and beat like liquid metal against the ship, and men on deck had to duck their heads. Lightning stood on the sky like a great sudden tree of light, and a branch darted and danced across the trucktops of the masts. An immediate head-numbing concussion, and repeated thudding aftershocks.

Rennie had ordered all his guns double-breeched, hatches battened down, and sail reduced to a bare minimum to keep the ship's head up.

'If I live through this it will be a miracle,' murmured James. The tied kerchief was torn off his head by the wind. His hair thrashed all over his face, and the wind seemed to suck his thoughts out of him and fling them away over the tafferel. 'If any of us lives, we will be blessed.'

'Mr Ha-a-ayter!'

The master Mr Loftus, clinging to a backstay. Ducking his head, then lifting it:

'Ca-a-asks loose in the ho-o-old! I ne-e-ed a party to secu-u-ure them!'

'Very we—'

A huge sea smacked into the bow, buried the bowsprit and inundated the fo'c's'le. The shock of the impact nearly knocked James off his feet. He clung to a stay, and felt Bernard Loftus lifted bodily against him as the sea surged aft over the hancés and half-buried them together.

The ship did not lose her footing. She rose steady and sure, shook off the excess water and strode on. But all was not well within her. Deep in her innards she was disturbed, and uneasy.

'Mister A-a-bey!' James, in his most carrying quarterdeck.

Richard Abey, swathed in heavy-weather oilskins, lurched to James's side. 'Sir?'

'I am going belo-o-ow with Mr Loftus! You will take the co-o-on! Keep her head up!'

'Very good, sir!' Like an otter with water streaming all over him.

'Come on, Be-e-ernard!'

And the two men fought their way forrard, gathered a small party of able men, and went below.

In the hold, the belly of the ship, James saw the extent of the difficulty in the swaying lantern light. There was a great sloshing lake of water. Whole tiers of casks had come loose and were jostling, surging and smacking together in that water. A dead rat floated toward him, and was carried away as the ship rolled. There was the stink of spoiled meat, and other things. With each heavy movement of the ship more casks shivered and squirmed together in the tiers, and it was clear to James and Mr Loftus both that if the loose casks were not replaced in the tiers, and the whole of the tiers secured, the trim of the ship would soon be compromised, and the ship placed in mortal peril, particularly given the depth of water in the hold. She was already injured and weakened without, and if her internal difficulty increased she would grow sluggish, her head would begin to droop, and in the full severity of the storm to follow – she would certainly founder.

'Mr Loftus, we will begin by securing all loose casks, if y'please. I am going up to report to the captain. I will rejoin you in a few minutes.' And he went up the ladder. In his head he told himself: 'That depth of water is the greater fear. If she is leaking this bad now, what will she be like in an hour, when the storm is at its height?'

There were relays of men already at the pumps, but even with all pumps manned and worked continuously at full capacity the depth of water below was horribly dismaying. The fury of the wind as he came on deck and went aft was tempered by his relief at being away from the foul smell of the hold.

Rennie was snatching an hour of rest in his sleeping cabin, suffering from a bout of severe headache – an intermittent condition that was the result of a blow to the head during one of the earlier engagements with the French. Dr Wing had advised him to rest a full watch through, and given him physic, but Rennie was determined not to succumb. He was awake in his hanging cot when James came to his door. James made his report in clear, concise, seamanlike language.

Rennie sat up, rubbed his forehead, and: 'Very well, thankee. Do what y'can to secure the hold, and report to me again. As to the depth of water, well well, we must keep the pumps working and hope for the best. Is Mr Adgett there below?'

'He is engaged on another repair, sir.'

'What repair? Oh, d'y'mean the boats' tillers, that was broke?'

'Yes, sir.'

'But that ain't vital work, James. He must follow your direction, and aid you in the—'

'He is following my direction, sir. If we founder, the boats may be our only hope.'

'Well well, we will not founder. That will not happen. Who has the deck?'

'Richard Abey, sir.'

'Very good.' A nod, and he rubbed his forehead again. 'The boy has come up to his new rank very well, has not he?'

'Indeed, sir.'

'Cutton! Colley Cutton! A can of tea!' Swinging his legs to the deck, and clutching the side of the cot as the ship rolled. He nearly fell.

'Sir, are you sure you are well enough to—'

'Yes, yes, yes. I am.' Over him. 'Kindly return to the hold, and report to me again in one glass.'

James found Mr Adgett, who had completed repair of the boats' tillers, and took him below to the hold.

'We will have to find this second leak, you know, and stop it. The pumps cannot keep up.'

'I will do my best, sir, as always. But as I say, with all these casks heavin' about loose, I cannot be certain of success.'

'We will secure the casks. How many men have you in your crew, now?'

'I am desperate short-handed, sir. There is only my mate and me.'

'Mr Loftus!'

Bernard Loftus joined them on the platform of the orlop.

'How long before we are secure in the hold?'

'Another glass, at least. We are having great trouble in getting casks returned to their tiers, because we cannot tell if the damned ballast is shifting under the ground tier. And if water casks in the ground tier have been stove in, and the water has escaped—'

'Yes, I understand – it will make unstable all tiers above. Christ's blood, what a mess. What depth of water in the well?'

'Five foot, and rising.'

'It was madness to sail into this storm, sheer bloody lunacy . . .' Lurching and stumbling as the ship pitched and slewed heavily through another tremendous sea. 'Very well, do all you are able. I must consult the captain's opinion.'

James returned to the great cabin, and found that Rennie had gone on deck. James climbed the ladder. The wind roared along the deck, whipping and snatching and tearing at everything in its path. The poles of the masts creaked and sighed in their restraining shrouds and stays. Night was descending over the sea, and the remaining light showed only the lifting dark hills of waves, now tall over the ship as she slid into a trough, now surging at an equal height beside her as the ship rode up shuddering and groaning, and spray flew over her bow.

Captain Rennie stood forrard of the wheel, clinging to one of the lifelines rigged fore and aft along the deck. He was wearing an oilskin and a battered hat, and in the near darkness his face had an alarming pallor. His voice was strong.

'What is the matter, Mr Hayter? Why are you here on deck?' Over the wind.

'Sir, do not you think that we must lighten ship?'

'Eh? Lighten ship, did y'say?' As if this were a suggestion entirely without merit.

'Sir, there is a second serious leak, and five foot of water in the well. Unless we lighten ship, it is likely she will founder. In my own opinion—' Ducking under a heavy smash of spray. 'In my opinion, sir, the—'

'Lighten ship! What d'y'propose?'

'I think we should throw the great guns overboard, sir.'

'What!' Staring furiously at his lieutenant, gripping the lifeline.

James thought that Rennie's eyes were too bright, and his face too livid. He had the look of a madman on a hilltop, intoxicated by height and distance, and the piercing conviction that he could fly. James opened his mouth to repeat what he'd said, and Rennie:

'How in the name of Christ d'y'propose to fight the enemy without *guns*, you fool!'

'Sir, our enemy is not that French frigate. Our enemy is the storm. Unless we—'

'You have took leave of your senses! Go below, sir, and lie in your cot!'

'Sir, I cannot abandon my—'

'Did you hear me, you mutinous blackguard!' Shouting over him. 'You are in the pay of the French, by God! It is that damned woman, she has turned y'head! You are weak, sir, weak! And a traitor, in the bargain! Sentry! *Sentry!*'

'Sir, you are not yourself. Let me help you to your quarters.'

'Stand away from me! *Sentry!*'

The ship rode to the height of a wave, quivered and strained a moment in blasts of wind, and heeled as she began to surf down into the trough. An ominous grinding and creaking.

'I cannot keep her head up!' One of the men at the wheel, desperately.

A long, shuddering moment, and slowly the ship righted herself.

'Sir! We must get those guns overboard!' James, gripping Rennie's arm.

'Take your traitor's hands off, you damned scoundrel!'

James glanced around, saw only the four men gripping the wheel – all concentrated wholly on keeping the ship's head to the wind – and made his decision. He sucked in a breath, swung his fist and knocked Rennie unconscious. As Rennie collapsed, James caught him, lifted him on his shoulder and carried him below. Rennie was a spare man, not heavy to carry, but in the conditions James had great trouble in getting him down to the great cabin.

Rennie's steward Colley Cutton helped to get the captain into his sleeping cabin.

'He has fainted on deck,' James said. 'Thank God I was there to break his fall, else he would have been swept overboard.'

'Fainted, sir?' Anxiously.

'Yes, the captain was not himself. He – he talked very quick, and then his eyes rolled up in his head. Hold the cot at the corner, while I get him . . . that's it, thankee.' James heaved the limp form into the hanging cot, then: 'How long had he been intemperate in his language?'

'Intemp . . . ah yes, I see, sir. Loud and daft. Well, since ever he rose out of his bed, I should say. It's them headaches which makes him strange, but he will not lie still when they comes on. He must get up and drink tea with a splash of rum to lift hisself.'

'You gave him rum?'

'He demanded rum, sir.'

'But that is the worst possible thing for a severe headache.' Thinking that he should not have struck Rennie, after all. Was not *that* the worst possible thing?

'Hit ain't for me to tell him that, sir. I do as I am told.' Holding the cot as the ship rolled.

'Surely Dr Wing has forbidden him rum?'

'Dr Wing ain't his steward, sir. He ain't here when such demands is made. Alls I can do—'

'Yes yes, very well, Cutton, thank you. I will say a word to Dr Wing myself.' And he left the steward to attend to Rennie, and hurried on deck to begin the arduous and dangerous task of jettisoning the great guns. As soon as he came on deck he heard a cry, whipped thin by the blasting air:

'Starboard number three gun loose on de-e-e-ck!'

A rending, grinding sound forrard, and a thudding crash. James felt the deck timbers shake under him. Another cry, high and terrified:

'The gun is sending across the de-e-e-ck!'

Rumbling, then a further thud, and a horrible scream.

The ship yawed as she rode down the slope of a tremendous sea. Spray flung in a drenching sheet across the fo'c's'le, and foam seethed along the larboard rail. James lurched forward, clinging to the lifeline. As the ship came up on the rise of the next sea, further rumbling and grinding, a further thudding shock. Another scream, tailing off into nothing.

'Mr Tangible!' bawled James. 'Roman Tangible! Gun loose in the fo'c's'le!'

James fought his way through a thunder of sea along the gangway, and reached the fo'c's'le.

A man lay sprawled just aft of the fo'c's'le, half-submerged in a draining flood of water, his left leg twisted and broken. Blood leaked into the rinsing water, and the man's body slid and nudged against the forehatch coaming. Beyond him in the fo'c's'le the number three gun, trailing rope, lay at an angle against the broken gunport, the breeching bolts wrenched clear of the ship's side. The Brodie stove, long since cold, had been struck by the loose gun, and the felled man caught there as he tried to clap on to loose tackle. It was nearly dark in the fo'c's'le, and James could hear the terrified bleating of beasts in the manger forrard. He ran to the felled man, and saw that he was dead. His chest had been crushed.

The ship lurched to larboard, the gun lurched with it, the trucks squealing, and abruptly plunged away from the gunport, diagonally across the deck, directly toward James. He had a split second to leap clear, and the gun smashed into the waist ladder, and splintered it.

'Roman Tangible!'

'I am here, sir!' A breathless voice.

'Thank God. Party of men, Mr Tangible, to secure the loose gun.'

'Aye, sir.'

'Bring hammocks! Hammocks to choke the trucks!'

James kept well clear of the gun, knowing that at any moment it could again hurtle across the deck, and crush out his life.

The boatswain returned with a party of four men, and half a dozen hammocks.

'Four men ain't enough, we need—'

'Four men is all I could muster, sir.' Over James. 'There's more men injured below, and these is all I have.'

'Very well. We must make do. Now then, lads! On the next rise, when the gun runs away from us, we must follow!'

'Follow a loose gun, sir?' Mr Tangible, aghast.

'I saw this same thing my first commission. The only way we could secure the damned thing was to choke the trucks with hammocks, then haul on the tackles and lash the gun fore and aft to the side. We must do the same—'

'Look out, sir! It is running wild again!'

Again James had to leap clear as the gun lumbered, not back the way it had come, but slewing in a semicircle, and plunged laterally, smacking against the hatch coaming, and spinning heavily away.

'Christ Jesu . . .' Roman Tangible. 'We must send ropes over it, somehow.'

'Nay, the hammocks will answer!' Seizing two hammocks. 'Follow me!'

SEVENTEEN

It was only after the rogue gun had been secured – braked and choked off by hammocks under the trucks, and hauled and lashed up alongside the gunport, a further five men having been summoned from the hold to aid the original four – that James saw the futility of his plan to jettison all of the great guns. He had not the means to do it. The emergency crew that had secured one loose gun were now urgently dispersed. Five had returned to the hold, the other four to the pumps. To heave guns overboard efficiently required careful assembling of tackles and men, and he had neither. He was even more short-handed than before the storm. Men had broken bones falling, men were seasick, and there could be no proper system of watches, now.

The position was desperate.

Pacing on the water-blown, wind-lashed deck, clinging to the lifeline, he had to make the most terrible decision. He could keep the ship's head to the wind, and continue to defy the storm. Or he could bring the ship about, and attempt to run before the wind. Either way he risked everything.

Lifting his head, half-blinded by flying spray, he saw his purpose:

'Reefed forecourse, and reefed driver. And we may by the merest glimmer of providence survive this night.'

Turning his head from the blasts of wind and water, sucking a breath:

'Mr Ta-a-angible! Stand by to go about! Hands to make sa-a-ail!'

Presently the call, snatched at and made ghostly by the storm, and a handful of able men answered.

Half a glass, and moments of pure terror as the ship wore, heeling and heeling, the sea boiling up round her stern, seething up along her side. Her masts tipped, as if like falling trees, everything creaking and groaning and grinding, cables and ropes dangling, a block swinging wild, and at last she lifted herself, wallowed and wallowed and lifted herself . . . and was running free.

Mr Tangible, clinging to the rail at James's side:

'Oh Christ's love, sir . . . oh by God, I thought we was done . . .'

Another half-glass, and Bernard Loftus on deck. 'We have secured most of the casks, I believe. And the pumps are holding at four foot and a half.'

'They have gained, then? That is well . . . that is well . . . thankee, Bernard.' Glancing about. 'Where is Mr Abey . . . ?'

'I could not say – I have been below all the time.'

'Take the con, will you? I must go below and see the captain.'

James went below, and found Rennie awake.

'Who is that? Where the devil is my steward? Cutton!'

'He is fetching you some tea, sir.'

'James? By God, I could not see who it was. Why are we not beating west, into the storm? We are running before, now, ain't we? What has happened?'

'Yes, sir, we are running before. You fainted on deck, sir, and were carried below. It was my judgement that—'

'Your judgement? You ordered the ship about?' Frowning at him.

'I did, sir, yes. Else we should have foundered. The—'

'Foundered? What fucking nonsense is this! I gave no such order! Ohh . . .' Clutching his head.

'A gun broke loose in the fo'c's'le, sir. It was touch and go before we could secure it. Casks had broke loose in the hold at the same time, and the pumps were unable to gain against the leak.' All very quickly and forcefully, before Rennie could interject again.

'Loose gun? Leaks? Why was I . . . why was I not kept informed? Ohh . . .' Rubbing his head.

'We have survived, sir. The storm continues, but the immediate danger has passed, and we are no longer in dire peril.' Firmly.

'Well well – I do not like it.' Swinging his legs to the deck, and lurching. James took his arm and aided him to keep his feet as the ship rolled heavily, yawing as she righted herself.

'Kindly don't attempt to coddle me, so y'may soften me toward your conduct.' Pushing James away, and immediately falling down. James helped him up on his legs. 'Did not ye hear me!' Again angrily pushing James away. 'We are heading east, direct for France, when we should be westing!'

'In fact not due east for France. We are running before the wind, nor'-east and a point east – sir.'

'D'y'mean to contradict me, sir? Hey!' Glaring, his face deathly pale.

'In course I do not wish it. I merely—'

'Then why d'you talk over me, like a damned impudent middy that has took too much wine!' Clutching at his hanging cot, and wincing as his head gave him further pain.

'I am very sorry, sir.' Stiffly.

'You ain't, though, by God. I see it in your eye, and in the cast of your mouth, too. You wish that I had not woke and found you out. That is what you wish, sir. Well well, I have woke, and I have found you out. Who has the deck? Mr Abey?'

'No, sir. Bernard Loftus. I do not know where Mr Abey is, at present. I have not seen—'

'Ah, yes. Yes, I sent him below when I came on deck myself. He was not fit for duty.'

'Not fit, sir?'

'Do you wish to contradict me again, damn you! I will go

on deck, and we will go about. The ship will go about, and beat west.' Staggering as the ship rolled and pitched.

'Are you quite well enough, sir?' James, in near despair. He could not strike his captain again, for fear of causing him severe injury. As it was, he had been guilty of a mutinous act, an act punishable by death – should he have been discovered in it. How could he prevent Rennie from going on deck and undoing all the healing work that had lately saved the ship?

'What d'y'mean, am I well enough?' Rennie peered closely at James. His breath was stale, James noticed. 'And when you say I fainted on deck, what d'y'mean by that? Hey?'

'I was obliged to carry you below, sir.'

'Because I fainted?'

'Indeed.'

'How did I faint, exact? Did I slip from consciousness very sudden, like a scullery maid with the vapours? Or did I groan, stagger, and so forth, and then slump down slow? Which?'

'You went down very sudden. I caught you, and carried you below – sir.' Affecting indignation now. 'I thought I was doing right, aiding a fellow sea officer.'

'Fellow sea officer!' A huff of stale breath. 'You are merely a lieutenant, sir. I am a senior post.'

'Indeed.' Icily polite.

'And I think that I did not "faint", as you are pleased to describe it. I think I was *felled*.'

'I do not understand you, sir.'

'Don't ye? Don't ye?' Glowering. 'Well well.' A near-contemptuous sniff. 'If I thought for one instant that you had allowed a falling block to strike me, or some other loose object flying about the deck, and then had pretended—'

'Ship's lights ahe-e-e-ad! Two points to starbo-o-o-ard!'

A cry from the deck.

Both Rennie and James ran on deck, all differences forgotten. As they came up into the rushing air and flying spray of the storm they saw the lights, very near on the starboard bow.

'Starboard your helm! Hard over!' bellowed Rennie at once. Running aft to the wheel. 'Starboard your helm, d'y'hear me!'

Four strong men at the wheel, and the ship answered as the wheel was spun, heeling and yawing as the lights ahead ran closer and closer, and became in the glimmering darkness a looming shape – the shape of the French frigate, beating into the teeth of the wind, and clearing *Expedient* with only a few feet to spare.

'By Christ, the bugger has chased me right into the heart of the storm!' Rennie, astonished. Recovering, and growing fierce as he stared after the retreating lights in the blackness: 'So he really does intend to smash and destroy me, does he, God damn his soul! I will show him what that entails, the fucking blackguard! I will catch him by the arse, and blast him to Kingdom Come! – *Stand by to go about!*'

The only thing James could do was clap on to a stay and stand appalled as the command was obeyed, and all his work of bringing the ship to a safe course, and the greater probability of survival, was dashed to pieces.

'God help us. God help us all.' As the sea battered the turning bow, surged over the lee rail, and swept aft in a swirling flood.

*

Within moments of going about *Expedient* fell on board the French frigate. That ship had also begun to turn in pursuit, and the two commanders, intent on destroying each other, thus nearly achieved their design without firing a shot.

Expedient struck the French frigate amidships on the starboard side. A heavy, grinding crash and shudder, and *Expedient*'s bowsprit speared at an angle across the French ship's waist. Her cutwater smashed into the wales and gunports. Shards of timber splintered away and dropped into the boiling sea. Netting hung torn. Both ships lost momentum and began to be carried by the wind and waves nor'-east with the storm. The French frigate had been weakened by the shock of the collision, and had sprung serious leaks below. Her light, lean lines were ill-constructed to withstand such a thudding impact. *Expedient* – oak-built at Chatham – was a sturdier, stouter sea boat, and she withstood the concussion better, but not unscathed. Already damaged and limping before the storm, she was now in mortal danger. Both ships would founder if they did not extricate themselves from this awkward, tangled embrace. Already the French frigate was swinging beam on to the full fury of the storm, and as she was brought to the full peril of this condition she would likely – if she foundered – drag down *Expedient* by the head.

This did not happen.

The force of the wind swung the French frigate with such surging power that *Expedient* began to be carried astern, and this movement caused her to wrench clear. She lost her spritsail yard, her figurehead and her boomkins, and her hawse holes were torn open on the starboard side. A great part of her beak and her cutwater were severely mauled. But she was free.

Expedient staggered away, staggered into a fortuitous wearing movement, pitching and sluggish, and Rennie and Hayter – gifted a moment of pure good fortune – bellowed instructions fore and aft, and succeeded in making chance into deliberate action. *Expedient* wore, and again ran before the wind. Astern of her the French frigate lay wallowing and crippled, beam on to tremendous seas. Within a few moments she disappeared in the darkness, and *Expedient* was again alone in the storm. A last, desperate wail came from far astern, borne on the rushing air.

'They are calling for help, sir.' James, cupping his hand to his mouth.

'I hear nothing.' Rennie, turning his face to the wind, beads of water flying from his cloak.

'They will founder . . .'

'There is nothing can be done for them, Mr Hayter. We must save ourselves, now.'

'Aye, sir.' And to himself: 'Thank God, thank God.'

'Five foot of water in the well, sir!' Bernard Loftus, ducking his head as he came on deck to make his report. 'I do not reckon the pumps can keep up! She has sprung a further leak forrard with the force of the impact, and she is by the head!'

'The pumps must keep up, Mr Loftus! The pumps will keep up! We will all stand our turn, every man that is on his legs! Half a glass each man, Mr Hayter, turn and turn about! You will go with Mr Loftus and take your turn immediate! Both of you! Jump!'

Neither man thought to object or bridle at this instruction. To tell an officer to jump was a fundamental breach of sea etiquette, but etiquette was not the question now. The question – pounding and echoing in every man's head – was: 'Will I survive? God's love, will I live through this night?'

Hours of frantic, exhausting toil at the pumps, and below in the hold Mr Adgett and a small crew did their utmost to plug and caulk and seal. The water in the well rose to six foot, six foot and a half – and then slowly began to fall. *Expedient* was deeply by the head, dangerously so as the following sea lifted her stern and pushed her damaged bow below the surface. She was sluggish in answering the helm, but she was alive. And slowly as the pumps gained, the storm drained itself of all its ferocity and strength, and blew itself out.

At dawn the sea was a rolling grey wilderness, but it was no longer gale-whipped and terrifying. The grey sky, low overhead, added nothing of cheer to the scene, but in least there were no flashes of lightning, no crashing broadsides of thunder. Cloud scudded and roiled over the heaving dulled sheen of the sea. *Expedient* dipped and sluggishly rose under triple-reefed topsails, and ran on.

On the quarterdeck a pale, unshaven Rennie glanced aloft, then turned and stared at the riding sea astern. Presently:

'We can bring her home, now. She will swim to England, now.'

James wiped his sleeve over his forehead and face. Scarcely above a whisper:

'Aye, sir. Home again.'

Three long and difficult days and nights followed, the pumps clanking and sluicing by the hour, and bone-weary men growing so exhausted they fell down stupefied and numb, and had to be carried below to Dr Wing. The lighter wind continued, and on the morning of the fourth day *Expedient* sighted the Isle of Wight. She rounded the Foreland and sailed into Spithead just after noon. Rennie made his signals but ignored the responding signalled instruction to take up a mooring number. Instead he sailed right on into the harbour and the dockyard, fearful that if he remained far out at Spithead his ship would sink under him.

He was fortunate in that the tide was favourable, a dry dock was available – a seventy-four having just been released into the Great Basin – and *Expedient* was floated in, was secured, and the work of dismantling her rigging begun. Sick and injured men were sent over to Gosport and the Haslar Hospital in boats. The remainder – the pitiful remainder – of the people went ashore. Captain Rennie and Lieutenant Hayter made their way to the port admiral's office to make their duty to him, and finding him absent repaired to the Marine Hotel in the late afternoon.

At the hotel Rennie wrote a letter to his wife Sylvia – who had gone home to Norfolk with the proviso that she would return at once to Portsmouth should Rennie wish it – saying that he would come to Middingham as soon as he was able. He gave a shilling to a boy to take it to the evening mail coach, and then joined his lieutenant, who was preparing to take that same coach to London.

'You go up at once, James? Tonight?'

'I think I must see Mr Mappin without delay, sir. First thing tomorrow.'

'You have secured a seat in the coach?'

'Here is the porter, now.' He took the paper ticket, and gave the man a coin.

Rennie nodded, sniffed, and: 'Yes. Yes. I think I had better come with you. That will be best. Waiting here to see Happy Hapgood ain't a good scheme. He will do nothing but admonish and complain, and blame – when he has no comprehension of anything.'

'You go to the Admiralty . . . ?'

'We will make our duty to Mappin together, and give our report direct to him.'

'*Our* report, sir? Surely—'

'Our report, James.' Firmly. 'About this damned nearly impossible task we was given. And then I have a great number of questions I wish to put to Mr Mappin. He has not told me the truth, nor even half of it, and I mean to know the reason.'

'Sir, I do not wish to tell you your duty, but now that we are ashore in England mine is to the Secret Service Fund, while yours is surely to Their Lordships – ain't it?'

'Mappin is the man behind the commision. He has arranged it all. We will go to him together. You there!'

'Sir?' The porter, returning.

'Here is a guinea. Go to the George Hotel, and get me a seat in the mail coach.'

'Tonight, sir? I don't know as I can, sir. The coach is nearly always—'

'I will add another guinea when you bring me the ticket. Go on up to the George. Jump, man, jump!'

At precisely six o'clock the two sea officers, one in civilian clothes, the other in his dress coat, stepped up into the

London coach outside the George Hotel in the High, and settled in their seats. The cries of ostlers clearing the way. Coaching horns. The horses took the strain under the whip, turning and clopping on the dusty cobbles, and the coach swung north along the street, swaying on its springs.

*

James came awake, and saw through the open window a wide green space, and the sky. At the horizon the sky was a dull pale pink, merging into pale yellow, merging into pale pure blue above, against which a stand of trees spread delicate and intricate, in a host of subdued greens, gently shimmering in the early light. This early moment of the day, mute except for the soft twittering of birds, was the only true moment of peace in life, he mused. Soon the activity of man would break in and over it, and quiet tranquil glory would vanish. Man must always disturb and destroy such halcyon moments; by his nature he was both urgent and clumsy, however particular or fine-honed his purpose.

James turned his shoulder toward the window a little further, and attempted to sit up. At once he was assailed by dizziness, and fell back on the pillow. He attempted to suck in a lungful of pure air, and was reduced to panting for breath. His head ached, he felt suddenly cold, he found that he was trembling.

'Good heaven, I am fevered . . .'

Again he attempted to sit up, clutched at the window sill, and succeeded in lifting himself into a leaning position against the wall by the window, the bedcovers falling from him.

'Whhhh . . . I am cold . . . whhhh . . .' Shivering violently. He clutched at the covers, and pulled them up round one shoulder. He looked out of the window.

'What is this place?'

Beyond the trees now, the crowing of a cock. Answered a moment after by another, at a distance. Soon the cocks were in echoing conversation, each celebrating the other in the dawn.

'Where the devil am I . . . ?'

The lowing of cattle away to the left of the trees, and the flat clanking of cowbells, then the call of a cowherd, urging them on.

A footfall outside the room, and the clatter of the latch.

'James?'

'I am here . . . wherever that is . . .'

'Y'don't recall? Coach threw a wheel, and we was put up at this farmhouse.'

Rennie came in and stood at the window. He was already shaved and dressed, carrying his hat. Peering out:

'Pretty enough country, but we must be on our way out of it in five and twenty minutes. Show a leg, James, hey?'

'I am not quite myself, I think . . .' Passing a hand over his forehead. It was damp and cold with sweat.

'Eh?' Turning from the window.

'I think perhaps I have a touch of fever . . .'

'Nonsense, it's the cider we drank last night. A glass too many. Two glasses. I felt the same until I swallowed a quart of tea, and now—'

'I tell you, I am fevered! I am shivering cold, and yet my head is on fire inside.'

Rennie looked closely at his friend, saw the sheen of moisture on his face and neck, and the dazzled look in his eye, saw the trembling of his limbs, and was dismayed. He betrayed nothing of this, and instead:

'We'll get you to London, and you will feel better. The coach—'

'London! I cannot go there. I cannot go anywhere. Whhh . . . so damned cold. What o'clock is it?'

He slipped, his back to the wall, struggled a moment – and fell face down in the bed.

'James . . . ?'

Rennie came to the bed, reached out a hand, then

withdrew it. To himself: 'Nay, I had better not touch him.' And aloud:

'I'll just call down for hot water, and so forth.' Moving to the door.

James rolled over in the bed in a heavy flailing heave, half sat up and fell back. And now he was trembling uncontrollably.

'Whhh-hhh-hhh . . . I heard shots! We must go . . . go into the tunnel – whhh-hhh . . .'

Rennie left the bedroom and clumped down the narrow stair. He found his way to the farmhouse kitchen, where the farmer's wife was preparing breakfast.

'Is there a doctor hereabouts? A local man?'

'A doctor, sir?' Breaking eggs into a bowl. 'Are you poorly?'

'Nay, I am not. Your teapot revived me. But my lieutenant is . . . he is a little unwell today.'

The woman frowned, concerned. She wiped her hands on her apron, and:

'There is Dr Denfield at Headley Down, but that is near five mile . . .'

'Five mile? Well well, I wonder if your husband could lend me a horse?'

'I'm sure he will.' Nodding. 'I will just arst him.' Coming round the table. 'He is in the yard.'

Rennie did not ride to Headley Down. A boy was sent, and an hour later returned to say that Dr Denfield would come as soon as he was able, he was attending a confinement. The coach, wheel repaired, had left half an hour ago, and Rennie – reluctantly, anxiously, fretfully – had remained at the farm.

'I should have gone on to London, but I could not leave the poor fellow lying here so ill with no friends.' As he waited for the doctor in the farmhouse parlour. 'Dr Denfield is a good man – is he?' Anxiously. 'A reliable man?'

'Oh, yes. We have known him near twenty year. He will always attend prompt, if he can.'

'Yes? Very good, very good. Hm.' Nodding, twisting to peer through the window.

'Will you like to eat a breakfast now, sir?'

'Eh? No no, thankee, madam. I am not hungry.'

'I has plenty of eggs left, look.' Kindly.

'No doubt you are fatigued from cooking for so many this morning, and so early.'

'Lord, sir, I am used to cooking early. A farm rises with the sun.'

'As does a ship, indeed. I will just climb the stairs again, and look in on my friend.'

'Are you sure I cannot aid him in any way? I will gladly—'

'It will be better if he is not disturbed.' Rennie, rather more sternly than he had meant, and he saw the look of doubt in the woman's eyes. He had told her that James was suffering from colic, but now he saw that she did not quite believe that any more.

'Very well, sir. I shall not interfere.' Politely.

'You are very good, very kind.' Rennie smiled at her, and went up the stairs.

James lay on his back on the bed, the covers thrown off on the floor. He was unconscious, and his breathing was rapid and shallow. Sweat dripped from his forehead on the pillow, and sweat had soaked through the bedding. His whole body trembled and shuddered.

Rennie bent to pick up the fallen covers, then held back. They were now contaminated. He glanced round, saw a cupboard, and found blankets. He heaped blankets over his shivering friend. James did not wake, and the shivering did not diminish.

Rennie stood anxious at the window, breathing the fresh air. Presently he heard the sound of hooves and wheels approaching, and he clumped rapidly down the stairs. He met the doctor coming up. A cramped mutual introduction on the narrow staircase, and Rennie took Dr Denfield up. He hovered in the doorway as the doctor examined the patient. Presently:

'Well, Doctor? Is it typhus?'

Without looking at Rennie: 'No, Captain Rennie.'

'It ain't . . . ?'

'No, it is a returning bout of a tropick fever, I think. Your friend has been in the tropicks recent?'

'We have served together in tropick climates, but not recent. The fever he suffered was yellowjack, at the West Indies.'

'Yes?' A brief glance at Rennie. 'I cannot agree with you. He suffered a bout of malaria, and took it for something else. Had he suffered from yellowjack he would not be lying here. He would be dead.'

'Could he die of this – now?'

'He could, but I don't think it likely. Has he been under a very great strain of late? An arduous voyage?'

'Very arduous.'

'That is the reason. We need seek no further explication. Malaria is a returning disease, very capricious and vengeful, that may strike at any time, but in particular when the patient has been under strain. He must be kept quiet, fed very light, and then only fluids. Plenty of fluids.'

'Is he – a danger to others?'

'It will be as well to keep him separate. As a precaution, you apprehend me? I will say so to Mrs Temple, and to her husband in his field, as I depart. They must be told it is fever, but I will reassure them it ain't typhus. Typhus we *do* fear, rightly so.'

'His son died of it.' Quietly.

'The patient's son?'

'Aye.'

'When?'

'Some little time since.'

'I see. Yes, I see. That is why you asked me if . . .' Nodding briskly. 'This ain't typhus, thank God.'

'You are certain, Doctor?'

'Quite certain.' Another nod, and a quick little confident

grimace. He rose from the chair he had pulled beside the bed, and came downstairs with Rennie. He spoke to Mrs Temple about the patient, reassured her, and explained the necessary requirements of diet and rest. He gave her a flask of physic. To Rennie:

'I will call again on the morrow, Captain Rennie. You will in course stay here at the farm?'

'In truth I ought make my way to London. I go there on very urgent business. I should like to summon his wife from Dorset to nurse him, you know, but she has been very ill herself.'

'Cannot your business in London wait a few days? You were travelling there together, were not you?'

'We were.'

'Listen now, it will aid him in recovery to see a familiar face when he wakes.'

'I expect you are right, Doctor, yes. The business in London must wait a day or two. In truth it cannot make any great difference now, in any case.' This last half to himself, with a sigh.

The doctor glanced at him curiously as he went out of the door into the yard, but said nothing. He climbed into his gig and was away. Only when the doctor was out of sight beyond the trees did Rennie recall that he had not offered payment.

'I am filled with embarrassment, Mrs Temple.' To the farmer's wife. 'What must the fellow think of me, that I did not offer to settle his fee?'

'But did he arst you for it, sir? Dr Denfield will never arst for payment until he is satisfied with his patient, look.'

'Ah.' A little rictus. 'Ah.' A breath. 'I am greatly obliged to you, madam, for allowing us to impose on your goodwill a day or two longer. Until my friend is able to get up on his legs.'

And he settled that obligation by placing a guinea on the

sideboard, so that there should be no embarrassment as to board and lodging.

Rennie lay in his little bedroom under the eaves, and was restless. He had looked in again on James after supper, and found him sleeping peacefully. The tremors and sweating had gone, and he had felt easier about his friend. Rennie's own headaches, that had recently plagued him, had receded now, and his head was clearer – but that only added to his wakefulness and unquiet contemplation.

The commission had been a hopeless failure in all distinctions. His ship was so badly damaged that she would probably have to be sold out of the service, or broken up. He had lost more than half of his people and his officers. To what purpose?

'Young Souter, that I never liked, poor fellow. And cheerful, steadfast Tom Makepeace, that I have known since *Expedient* was first commissioned. What am I to say to his widow? I should have wrote to her as soon as we made landfall, and have not. So many letters I have neglected, in my rush to get to London. What for, in God's name? What am I to say to Their Lordships? I do not care anything about Mappin, in the end, the fellow. His whole purpose is to conceal, and obfuscate, and omit. But what am I to say to Their Lordships, who wrote my warrant? I have lost the most valuable passengers that was ever in a British ship of war. They will wish to lay the blame for what has happened . . . and their eyes will fall on me. I *will* be blamed.'

This bleak realisation weighed heavily in on him now in the darkness, and for a moment his head buzzed and he could not get his breath. He sat up.

'I see it quite clear, by God. I was always meant to take the blame. In course, they will like to pretend that they wished to save King Louis, and they will say that through my miserable ineptitude I have cost France everything. Her last and only hope and I have wrecked it, and now only disaster can follow. They *meant* to have a scapegoat from the beginning. I will be cashiered, that is certain. And afterward . . . after all that . . .'

The feeling that he was being crushed alive drove him from his bed. He rose and stumbled to the window. The cool night air on his face was no comfort.

'Who will employ a disgraced post captain, even in the humblest merchantman? And what will become of my darling Sylvia? I shall lose my Norfolk home, and everything I value. What will become of poor James, if he lives? He will likely be cashiered himself. Christ's blood, has not he suffered enough?' Leaning his head on the window frame.

'And young Leigh, that I placed in command of what is left of my people, and my ship – what will become of him? Even with all his family interest and connection, will not he find his career broke and destroyed by the sheer ill-fortune of having served under Captain William Rennie?'

He breathed deep in an effort to calm and comfort himself. An owl hooted in the solemn dark, the sound carrying through the wood. Long silence. Another deep, sniffing breath, and now he did feel a little better. He was about to turn away from the window when from the wood came the sudden shrieking cry of a small creature caught in predatory talons. He tilted his head, listening. The cries rose in a desperate crescendo, and were cut off. A moment, and:

'Aye.' Whispered. 'Aye, that is life on this earth. Timid and lost in the scurrying dark, blind and fearful and lost – and sudden painful death.'

He stared into the blackness.

'Why are we given life at all, when it is only harshness and suffering? Why?'

A tear fell on his cheek. Another, and another, and he wept.

'Oh, Christ . . . I am lost . . . lost . . .'

All the destruction and horror and strain of the past weeks beat in on him now, and lashed him like a storm of wind.

He bent his head, and was so overwhelmed that at first he scarcely noticed a light brushing movement against his leg. Again something nudged him there, and trod light over his foot. He dashed tears from his eyes, and peered down. And heard a distinct thrumming purr.

'Good God . . .'

He bent down, felt about him blindly and found the creature, and lifted it up.

Presently he returned to his bed, and lay quietly back against his pillow with the cat on his breast, its head bumping against his chin and the thrumming of its pleasure in his ear. He stroked the animal, and felt misery and sadness retreat. Softly:

'You are not Dulcie, my dear, but you are a very great comfort to me in my hour of need.'

Soon after he drifted peacefully down into deep relieving sleep, and did not wake until the sun stood broad in the sky.

*

Dr Denfield came and went twice more during the course of the next two days, and James slowly regained his senses, and his sense of self, so that on the third day he was able to sit up in bed, take broth and a little solid food, and converse with the doctor, who told him:

'On the morrow, Lieutenant, y'may rise and walk about.'

'Not today?'

Dr Denfield held up a hand, closed his eyes against further interruption, then continued:

'Walk about, breathe the air, and measure your strength. If you no longer feel faint, nor queasy, then on the *following* day y'may safely go to London, if you wish.'

'Yes, thank you, Doctor. Thank you indeed for all your kindness in attending to me.'

The doctor inclined his head, and encouraged, James continued:

'But ain't it possible that I could rise later today, walk about and so forth – and then go to London tomorrow? It is very urgent that I should go, d'y'see.'

Dr Denfield took a breath. 'You are a sea officer, sir, as are my uncle and cousins. You are a very singular race of men, not much given to heeding medical advice. I have given you mine.' A very direct gaze. 'What you do with it, once I have driven away in my gig, I cannot govern.'

'Thankee, Doctor. I am in your debt.' Reaching for his purse. 'Erm . . . may I settle that part of it that is monetary, sir?'

'Y'may.' A nod, a half-smile.

And when the doctor had gone, James drank off the dregs of his broth, stretched his arms over his head, and lay back.

'I will rise presently, and go outside.'

He fell asleep at once, and did not wake until the evening. And found when he did wake that his spirits were low. Dreams had troubled him, and the mood of the dreams lingered now – anxiety, and gloom, and a sense of foreboding. He tried to shake off the mood by attempting to rise and wash his face, but as he got up on his legs and reached for the ewer and basin he felt himself weak and faint, and had to lie down again.

As he lay there on the bed in the deepening shadow of evening, he began to reflect on everything that had recently happened to him. At first his thoughts were tumbled and jumbled together in a maelstrom of moments and images; then as his weakness and faintness retreated his thoughts grew more ordered, until he was able to discover in himself a kind of sombre understanding.

'I have changed . . .'

He had changed. A few years since – nay, a few months – he would never even have thought of embarking on a new life with a woman like Juliette. Yet he had begun to do so, and had continued until she was lost at the inlet. Never before would he have thought of leaving his beloved

Catherine – no matter her continued wan listlessness and melancholy. In a few months the world he knew had seemed to change so much, not only his private world but the world at large. It seemed to him now that everything was darker and less certain, less accommodating of his private self – of any individual man. It was as if all manner of new and barbarous things were possible, and probable.

He sighed, and looked at the light waning in the window, the last sunken glow of the sun. It was not that the seasons had altered, nor the birds that came and went with them, soaring on the sky, nor the shape of the hills and the spires of churches across the undulating quiet green fields of England. But that now over it all lay a long shadow, a gathering storm in the still of the evening and the hush of dawn. When the substance of that shadow would come rolling darkly over the land he did not know, but he was certain now it would come, and would carry away on its black tide all of the things he had known and trusted and loved, and render them into mud and ash.

'A few months ago none of these things would have entered my thoughts.' Murmuring in the quiet air of the little room. 'My God – I would never have dreamed of striking my captain, no matter how compelling the reason, nor dire the circumstances. And yet I did do it, without a moment's hesitation, because I thought I had the right to save the ship – and in course myself. Six months ago my home was the centre of my life, it was my life's blood. How could I wish to see it spilled away? How could I wish for such things? The storm ain't just out there . . . it is gathering inside of me, in all of us, and making us into selfish madmen, loose guns on the deck of the world.'

Returning sleep allowed him respite from these heavy things, at last.

*

Recovered, Lieutenant Hayter made the proposal that he and Captain Rennie should hire horses and ride to London. He was vociferously opposed and contradicted by Dr Denfield, Mr and Mrs Temple, and Rennie himself. He took James aside.

'Good God, ye've only just got up on your legs. Have you the smallest notion how far it is to London?'

'Erm . . . where are we exact?'

'We are five or six mile from Haslemere, and fifty mile from London. A very exhausting ride for anybody that has lately been ill. Pray do not again think of riding there, if y'please.' Sternly.

'Ohh, very well, just as you like.' A shrug. 'We must try for seats in one of the turnpike coaches, I expect, at a post inn.'

And that was what they did. The farmer carried them to the inn in the early morning in his cart, and was duly thanked. James was accepted inside the coach – which was already very full – by virtue of his recent debility, and Rennie was obliged to ride on top under the open sky – which soon became wet. The journey to London was long, with several stops at inns – this was not a fast mail coach, after all – and several showers of rain, and when at last they arrived at their destination Rennie was monosyllabic with cold, despair, wretchedness, and loathing for the world and all its works. James, on the other hand, had slept most of the journey, and arrived refreshed, comfortably dry, and in equable humour.

'Shall we take chairs, and go to Mrs Peebles's hotel?' Looking about him in the noise and bustle and smell of the London evening.

'Chairs!' Ferociously.

'Well, yes . . . you do not suggest that we should walk there, do you, sir?'

'Walk!'

They engaged chairs, and were conveyed to Bedford Street.

Rennie had a hot bath, and was restored. James lay down to rest, and woke in returning gloom.

At a late supper in the dining room, he said:

'We must arrange the interview with Mappin, I suppose. We must tell him our bad news.'

'No supposin' about it, my boy. We are already late, and we must arrange it, right quick.'

'Tomorrow, then?'

'Why not now?'

'Tonight? I – I am still feeling a little faint, you know. Tomorrow will answer, surely?'

'First thing, then. We should go to him first thing after breakfast. Hey?'

'Hm.'

But when they met again in the morning over the breakfast table, Rennie's brief mood of uplift and optimism had drained away, and he was apprehensive, pallid, and had cut his chin with his razor.

'You are bleeding, sir.'

'Eh?'

'Your chin.' James tapped his own chin, and nodded as the girl brought his bacon and eggs.

'Damn the thing.' Rennie dabbed at the cut with his napkin, and when his own eggs came: 'Nay . . . I am not hungry today.' And he pushed them aside.

Presently James too lost his appetite, laid aside his knife and fork, and settled for a cup of strong coffee.

Rennie sucked down hot black tea; sniffed, sighed, grimaced. 'Damn the fellow.'

'Sir?'

'It is all his doing, that will be our *un*doing. He is the same kind of wretch as Greer, the fellow.'

'We must face him, all the same.'

'Aye . . . I cannot cut him with my sword, but by God I shall cut him with my tongue, James.'

*   *   *

Captain Rennie and Lieutenant Hayter decided to go to the Admiralty to enquire after Mr Mappin, since they had no other address. The address of the Secret Service Fund – if such an address existed – had never been vouchsafed them. They made their way to Whitehall on foot, but when they came to the Admiralty and went in under the arch, they could discover nothing. The whereabouts of Mr Mappin were unknown. His name produced frowns of unrecognition in the Admiralty officials, who obliged the two sea officers to wait in a small side room downstairs until they were summoned.

'Summoned?' Rennie.

'By a representative of Their Lordships.' The clerk who attended on them, bleakly.

'Ah.'

The brusqueness of these instructions was lost on neither man, and each began to be privately and deeply apprehensive. They had been engaged in momentous international events in one of His Majesty's commissioned ships of war, and had failed. The most telling words in any officer's warrant of commission, plainly written out, were these:

Hereof nor you nor any of you may fail as you will answer the contrary at your peril.

Even though Rennie alone presently had a warrant of commission, neither man was in any doubt that both now faced that peril – in its own implacable way greater and more formidable than all the dark and stormy perils of the sea. James's involvement was as whole as Rennie's, commissioned or no, and his entire future was equally in jeopardy.

In the event they faced only the Third Secretary, Mr Soames. They were shown into his stuffy office, and seated upon plain wooden chairs. Presently Mr Soames came in, dressed as ever in black coat and white linen, and exuding wafts of astringent cologne.

'Captain Rennie. Lieutenant Hayter.'

Both officers stood up and bowed.

'Mr Soames.' Rennie, politely neutral.

'Sir.' James, equally polite.

Mr Soames motioned them both to sit down, and sat down himself at his desk. He adjusted the position of the inkwell, glanced into a drawer, made his expression agreeable, and:

'Now, gentlemen, how may I assist?'

Rennie and James glanced at each other.

'Assist, Mr Soames?' Rennie. 'Do not you wish us . . . to assist Their Lordships?'

'In what distinction?' Eyebrows politely raised. He dabbed at his lips with his lace kerchief, and returned it to his sleeve. A further waft of cologne. 'Hm?'

'Well well . . . in the question of . . . in the matter of . . . of the commission, and so forth. The coast of France?'

'France?' Glancing from one to the other.

Rennie took a breath, and:

'Perhaps, Mr Soames – you yourself cannot assist us, after all. We had wished to see Mr Mappin, Sir Robert Greer's successor at the Fund. You are acquainted with him, I am in no doubt?'

'Mapple? No.' A little shake of the head.

'Come come, Soames. Mappin. Mr Brough Mappin.'

'Hm.' Another little shake of the head. 'Since Sir Robert's unfortunate death I have been privy to none of the deliberations of the Fund, none of its activity.'

A knock on the inner door of the office. Mr Soames turned his head there.

'Come.'

A clerk entered, and came to Mr Soames's desk. A brief whispered exchange, and the clerk gave Soames a document, and retired. The squeak of the door-hinges, the click of the latch. Soames felt for his spectacles in his coat, spread open the document and perused it. Presently, lifting his head to look at his visitors:

'Hm. A preliminary report of inspection, concerning your ship, Captain Rennie. Quite why it has come to me I could not say. But since you are here in my office, perhaps that is why. So far as I can gather . . .' tapping the document '. . . your ship is in a parlous condition. I am not unfamiliar with dockyard language, in course, but the injuries to the fabric of the ship listed here are too great in number to allow of immediate whole comprehension.' Glancing again at the document. 'However . . . it would appear that the quartermen that wrote out this report have concluded that your ship must probably be broke up.'

'Broke up! *Expedient?* Nay . . .' James, in angry astonishment.

'My dear Lieutenant Hayter – it ain't my decision.' Soames, mildly.

'I don't believe it! Broke up? The notion is absurd.' James had stood up, ignoring Rennie's warning look, and now advanced to the desk. 'May I see the report, Mr Soames?' Holding out his hand.

'I notice you ain't in uniform, Mr Hayter.' Soames, again mildly.

'Well, no . . . we came from Portsmouth, and I had not time—'

Soames, over him: 'In fact, you are not presently commissioned – are you?'

'Well, no, but I am—'

'Not attached to HMS *Expedient?*'

'Well, not official, but I—'

'Then the report cannot possibly concern you. To speak plain, it is not your business. Is it?'

James bit his tongue, made his back straight, took a deep breath, and obliged himself to say:

'You are right, in course. Strictly speaking, it ain't my business. I beg your pardon, Mr Soames.' He bowed, and resumed his seat.

But Rennie had now stood up again, and he said to Soames: 'You deny knowing Mappin, do you, Soames?'

'I do not know him.'

'Then we need trouble you no more. Our business is with him, and he is not here.'

'Forgive me, Captain Rennie, I had thought you said your business was to assist Their Lordships. Since none of Their Lordships is presently available – I am here.'

'Good day t'ye, Soames.' Rennie took up his hat and put it on, motioned to James to join him, and strode from the room.

EIGHTEEN

In a coffee house in the Strand Rennie drank off a second cup of tea, and:

'Well, James, we have made our attempt. We have done our duty.'

James looked at him a moment, then leaned forward earnestly. 'Sir, with respect – we have not. In least, I have not. I have given no report to Mr Mappin, that charged me with this task. I have wrote no letter, made no explication. I have discharged nothing of my final obligation.'

'No letters was to *be* wrote, James. That was the strict understanding, good God. Nothing to be wrote down official. In that way no lies could be nailed, and we was lied to from the beginning. What did they expect from us! Hey! That we alone should save France!'

'Sir . . . we should not discuss this too loud, in a public place.'

'Yes yes, very well.' Rennie lowered his voice, and now he too leaned forward. 'Listen now, we have done everything that we honourably could, short of giving up our lives. So now let Mappin seek us out, if he wishes. We will remain at Bedford Street one further day – four and twenty hours – and then go home.'

'Home! You mean – to Norfolk? To Dorset?'

'I do.' Turning and lifting a hand to signal for more tea.

'But, surely, sir . . . you cannot neglect your ship, nor your people, at Portsmouth . . .'

'James, James . . . my career in the Royal Navy is at an

end. I know that full well. If Mappin and Their Lordships will not say otherwise to my face, here in London – and I am certain they will not – then I shall go home to Norfolk and write my letter of resignation. Mr Leigh is at Portsmouth. He is a sensible young officer. He can undertake all that is required in paying off, and so forth. And then "my ship", as you call her, will be broke up. She ain't mine any more. She ain't even a ship. She is just a few hundred ton of timber and ballast, lying dry and purposeless.'

James looked at Rennie, and saw resigned weariness in the deep lines of his face and forehead, and pain in his eyes. His thinning hair and exhausted pallor emphasised the sense of a man near to despair.

'Sir, let us remain here in London not one day longer, but two.'

'Nay, my mind is made up.'

'Then, will you wait two days – for my sake? So that we may be entirely sure?'

'Sure of what, for Christ's sake? That we are defeated? We know that certain, both of us.' Looking at James very direct.

'I do not.' Stoutly. 'Not quite yet.'

Rennie took a breath and looked away across the coffee house. He did not see anything of the animated groups at other tables, the waiters threading through those tables, trays held high, nor hear the ripple and murmur of conversation and laughter in this convivial place. He saw only darkness, and all of the dark things that had thronged his mind at the farm, and made him so low he could find no way out. He held his breath in, as if to shut the darkness out.

The serving maid brought Rennie's fresh tea. He did not see her, and just as she leaned to place the tray on the table, Rennie turned abruptly in his chair to say something to James, and the tray was knocked to the floor with a crash. The girl slipped and fell, and gave a cry as hot tea splashed and scalded her arm.

Rennie sat a moment as if stunned, and James jumped up from his chair, assisted the girl to her feet, and wrapped a linen napkin round her burned arm.

Rennie fumbled for coins, dropped them on the tablecloth, and rose from his chair. Without a word he walked away to the door and out into the crowded Strand, leaving James to apologise to the girl in Rennie's behalf, and follow him outside.

James caught Rennie up, and in silence – through the bustling crowds and traffic of the Strand – they made their way to Bedford Street. When they reached Mrs Peebles's hotel, James suffered a brief fit of shivering, his head buzzed thickly, and he was obliged to sit down on a hall chair. Rennie was concerned.

'My dear James, I am a selfish villain, rushing you through the streets when ye've been so ill. You there!' To a startled maidservant. 'Fetch the porter.'

'Yes, sir.' The girl bobbed, and ran to the rear.

'I am all right, sir, really . . .' James, attempting to stand.

'No, you ain't.' Rennie put a hand on his shoulder. 'We'll just get you upstairs, so y'may lie down and rest. I'll send for a doctor.'

'No, sir, no. I am not ill – just a little fatigued.'

Rennie got James upstairs with the porter's assistance, and saw him to bed. James's pleas to be left free of further medical advice were ignored. Rennie descended the stairs and obliged Mrs Peebles to send for a local physician.

'Well, sir, I don't know which doctor to recommend.' Mrs Peebles, in her little parlour. 'We has a surgeon that will stop in for cases of over-indulgence, like . . . or there is an alt'gether grander gen'man, that will come for the higher type of case.'

'Yes? Who is that?'

'The grander gen'man?'

'Yes yes.' Impatiently.

'Dr Robards, sir. Dr Glendower Robards. But I don't know as he will come at once, just like that.'

'Send for him, if y'please. Say that the patient is a very distinguished naval officer.'

Dr Robards came – tall and dignified in his black coat – after half an hour, and was shown up to James's room. James was most reluctant to be examined, at first. But his visitor was so obviously at the higher side of his profession that James soon submitted.

Dr Robards took his pulse, examined his tongue, looked into his eyes, examined his neck and chest. He asked questions with calm insistence, and to each reply nodded:

'Mm-hm . . . mm-hm . . .'

Then, at the end of the examination, a further nod.

'Mm-hm. A tropick disease, malaria I should think. A recent recurrence.'

'Yes, but I am quite recovered.'

'Are ye?' A quizzical look.

'Oh, indeed.'

'No, y'are not. Y'must lie abed two days, in least. Three, for preference. My preference. Light diet. No excitements of any kind. No *London* life, d'y'take my meaning?'

'I – I don't know that I do, Doctor.'

'No wine, no excursions, no . . . companions.'

'Good heaven, I am a married man.'

'As most of us are, sir. But we are also men of the world. No London life. Y'apprehend?'

'Your meaning is quite clear to me.'

'Very good, Lieutenant.' Closing up his instrument case.

Downstairs Dr Robards said to Captain Rennie:

'I came at once because I was told he was a very distinguished sea officer. Is your friend very distinguished?'

'He has the very highest connections.' Rennie, knowing that he sounded pompous, but feeling it was necessary.

'Ah, has he?'

'His father is Sir Charles Hayter of Melton House, in Dorset.'

'Ah. I fear I do not know the name. And you are . . . ?' Politely.

'I do beg your pardon, Doctor. We was not properly introduced when you came in. I am Captain William Rennie, RN.'

A frown of recall. 'Captain Rennie . . . of HMS *Expedient*?'

'The same. Have we met before?'

'No no, but now I do recollect . . .'

'Recollect, Dr Robards?'

'The late Sir Robert Greer was my patient. He mentioned your name more than once, Captain Rennie. You were evidently much in his thoughts – toward the end.'

'Good God.'

On the second afternoon of Lieutenant Hayter's period of enforced rest, Mr Mappin came to Bedford Street. Captain Rennie, having agreed to delay his departure to Norfolk, had gone out to 'clear his head', unable to bear his gloomy thoughts in the confined space of Mrs Peebles's hotel any longer, and James was dozing in bed upstairs.

Mr Mappin came quietly into the bedroom, and sat down beside the bed in the only chair, his back to the window. Downstairs he had given a coin to the porter.

'Do not announce me. I will go up and find him.'

'Sir, the gen'man ain't well – he should not be disturbed.'

A second coin.

'Very well, sir, you knows best. I shall not interfere. Second door on the left.'

Now he sat beside the bed patiently, studying the face of the young man. He did not shake him awake. He had no wish to startle or discommode him. Presently James stirred, and opened his eyes.

'Good afternoon, Mr Hayter.'

'Who is it . . . ?' Blinking, peering at the figure silhouetted against the light from the window.

'Brough Mappin.'

James struggled with the covers, and sat up. Blinked again.

'Mr Mappin – you have come.'

'As you see.'

'We sought you at the Admiralty, but they—'

Over him: 'Yes, I know. I have been out of town, else I should have come sooner. I was sorry to hear you had been ill.'

'I am all right. It was just a brief return—'

'Of malaria, yes.' Again over him. 'Not a thing to be trifled with. Y'are right to lie abed until it is over and done.'

'Who – who told you I had malaria?'

'I keep my ear to the ground, Lieutenant. Naturally, I will always like to know how my associates go on.'

'Yes, well . . . you will not like to hear what I have to tell you, Mr Mappin.'

'There is no need to tell me anything.' A brief shake of the head, and he brought a small silver snuffbox from his pocket, and took a pinch. Seeing James's glance:

'You notice this snuffbox, hey? Yes, it belonged to Sir Robert. He made me a gift of it.'

'I think I must inform you, Mr Mappin, that the very grave task you commissioned me to undertake . . . has been a hopeless failure.'

'Yes, yes . . .' Mildly, putting the snuffbox away in his coat, and dabbing his nose with his kerchief. 'I have known all about it for some little time.'

'You have . . . ?'

'Oh, yes. Yes, the intelligence came to us through Lady Sybil Cranham. The royal party was retook by the National Guard, after ye'd brought them off at the Pointe de Malaise. That is old news.'

'Ah. Oh.' A breath, sitting up straight. 'I had wished in course to come at once to London, the moment we landed at Portsmouth, but I was took ill on the journey, and—'

'Yes, yes . . .' Holding up a hand, closing his eyes briefly. 'Don't distress y'self, Lieutenant. I know all about it.'

'I am very sorry indeed that we were not able, in spite of our best attempts, to save Their Royal Highnesses.'

'No. Well. You could not have saved the king and queen, even had you brought the party out of France, you know.'

'Not saved them . . . ?' James stared at his visitor.

'Nay, y'couldn't. You see, the king and queen were took at Varennes.'

'Varennes? Where is that? D'y'mean, they had escaped again, when—'

'Varennes is north-east of Paris on the road to Montmédy, near the Luxembourg frontier, where there are large Austrian forces. Alas, King Louis was recognised en route, and the National Guard summoned.'

'But – how could they have come there, Mr Mappin, when they were captured on the Breton coast?'

'They never were at the Breton coast, Lieutenant. Never anywhere near.'

'Eh . . . ?'

'The party you and Captain Rennie so gallantly attempted to rescue was a troupe of Parisian theatricals, cleverly disguised.'

James stared at him in mute disbelief.

'In short, they were decoys, sent to that far coastline deliberately to put the National Guard off the scent, while the real royal party made ready to flee to the queen's brother, across the border to the east. Count Axel von Fersen – an intimate of the queen – had arranged that flight. Lady Sybil Cranham, among others, arranged the flight to the coast, and we did the rest.'

'We . . . ?'

'You and I, Lieutenant, and Captain Rennie – and others.'

James stared at him, and saw Mr Mappin's silhouette dissolve into a blur, attended by a thick, bilious buzzing. He fell back against the pillow, his face waxy and damp with sweat. Mr Mappin stood up at once and poured a glass of water from the jug on the cabinet. He bent over James, carefully and gently lifted his head, and brought the water to his lips.

'My dear fellow, I do beg your pardon. The truth was too much for you, when you have been through so very great an ordeal. Here, drink a little more.'

When James had recovered his colour and his composure, Mr Mappin said to him:

'Never think you have failed, Lieutenant Hayter. You and Rennie acquitted yourselves admirable well. The fact that the overall design was a failure was not your doing.'

'We have lost above half our people killed and wounded . . . and our ship is to be condemned.'

'I know. It is very regrettable. But never forget – you acquitted yourselves flawless and brave. That is the thing to grasp, and hold on to. You are not to blame for Varennes. Hm?'

'Flawless, and brave?' Drinking off the water remaining in the glass.

'Indeed.'

'In course . . .' Musingly, half to himself. '. . . neither Captain Rennie nor I could've had any real notion of the depth of duplicity we faced.

'Necessary duplicity – will not you agree?' Taking the glass from him, and returning it to the cabinet.

'Mr Mappin.'

'I am here.'

'I will like you to leave me alone, now.'

'In course, in course. You've had a shock, and you are tired.'

'Nay, not because I am shocked, nor tired neither. Because I cannot bear your company a single further moment.'

'Ah. Very well.'

'This ain't the end of it, though. When I am on my legs, we will meet again.'

'I hope so, Lieutenant.'

'Face to face on open ground, with pistols. God *damn* your blood!'

*

The following morning Captain Rennie was summoned to the Admiralty, where he was interviewed *in camera*, in the nearly empty boardroom. It was not a comfortable interview. Beside himself there were present the First Naval Lord, Admiral Hood, the First Secretary, Sir Philip Stephens, and a clerk, who took minutes. Rennie was permitted to say very little in his defence, in fact very little at all. The First Naval Lord made clear his own view:

'The whole enterprise was damnable nonsense from the beginning, Captain Rennie. I don't like subterfuge, and half-truth, and reckless forays in the dark. This business, this intrigue, was nothing higher than a damned courtesans' masquerade.'

'I am wholly—'

'Save the king of France? This scheme was as likely to save him as soaking him in spirits of wine and setting him on fire, for Christ's sake.'

'Well, yes, sir. But we—'

'Kindly be silent, sir. I am not finished.'

'I – very good, sir.'

'When I approved this scheme I was told it entailed no more than an enquiry into the condition of the silk trade, in France. I had no idea of its underlying purpose. Had you, Sir Philip?'

'I had not.' The First Secretary shook his head. 'No, sir.'

'None of us knew anything about it, in whole, nor even in part. We was persuaded that the silk trade was of sufficient importance to the nation's interest and prosperity to warrant our assistance. Had we known the *real* nature of—'

Rennie again opened his mouth. 'I did not know myself, sir, until—'

'Had we known, we should have stopped it. You fired on and destroyed French ships, in French waters, when we are not at war with France. You have cost the lives of fifty of your people, and lost another hundred wounded and took. Your ship is so badly damaged she will likely have to be condemned.'

Rennie stood silent, miserable and angry and powerless.

'As it is, the whole lunatic thing has achieved – what? King Louis has not escaped. He has been arrested and returned to Paris. The entire business has been futile. Utterly and wholly worthless, and if the French will like to make trouble for us, damned embarrassing in the bargain.'

Rennie said nothing. Let them condemn him. He would not defend the indefensible, even if he had not been the cause, only the instrument.

'The truth is, Captain Rennie, you could be broke for this. Court martialled, cashiered and ruined. You and that damned young fool Hayter, that allowed himself be persuaded to act as a spy. We had no notion the man you would put ashore in France was a sea officer. No inkling at all. What business has a sea officer to enlist as a spy, behind our backs. Hey?'

Rennie looked straight ahead at the weather telltale at the far end of the room, and bit his tongue. It seemed to him that these high men, these powerful official men, were attempting to distance themselves from any culpability at all, by placing all of it at his door, and that he had no choice but to stand and listen.

'You have brought the king's service, all the traditions of the Royal Navy, into disrepute of the most dismal kind. You acted with a belligerence and aggression far in excess of your instructions and your competence. Your actions could have brought us to a condition of war, sir, d'y'realise? May do so yet. Who can tell?'

The First Secretary now cleared his throat, gave a little lift of his head, and glanced at Lord Hood, who:

'Yes, Sir Philip?'

'Ought not we . . . to bring matters to a conclusion, sir? In fairness?'

'Yes? You think so?'

'In all fairness, I do.'

'Very well.' Again turning to Rennie, who had stood throughout with his back straight, since he had not been asked to sit down. 'Captain Rennie.'

'Sir?'

'I am obliged to acknowledge that you y'self may have been misled in this. That don't excuse your conduct at sea, mind you. Your conduct was recklessly unwise, in nearly all distinctions. However . . .'

He let the word hang in the air, and Rennie waited, with the faintest stirring of hope in his breast, for the words that would follow.

'However . . . we have concluded that no good purpose would be served by bringing you to court martial.'

'No, sir?' Glancing into Hood's deep-set eyes, his stern face.

'No. You have suffered very severe, and while we cannot condone what ye've done, we cannot condemn you entire, neither. In short you have been lied to, Captain Rennie – as have we ourselves at the Admiralty – by a person without scruple in his undertakings and machinations, the fellow.'

'Do you mean – Mr Mappin, sir?'

'I do, sir. I may say to you candidly as one sea officer to another that was it in my power to have the bugger flogged, then by God I would make it so!' A deep sniff. 'It ain't in my power, Captain Rennie. Mr Brough Mappin has very high connections, very high protection. He has cost the Royal Navy very dear, but he cannot be touched. And given that he cannot, that was at the heart of this whole wretched affair, then I cannot in all conscience punish you, sir. Nor Lieutenant Hayter, neither.'

'I am – very greatly obliged to Your Lordship.' A bow.

'You are, by God.' Turning to the clerk, who had been

sedulously making his notes at a corner of the table. 'Mr Bunt.'

'Sir?' Laying aside his quill.

'I have changed my mind. You will keep no minutes nor notations of this interview, after all. You will destroy them forthwith.'

'Very good, sir.'

The clerk gathered up his notes into a bundle, took them to the fireplace, and carefully deposited them on the fire, where they burned bright an instant, and in another instant became ash. Rennie watched, and for the first time in many days felt his heart begin to lift.

He was not sure whether or no the First Naval Lord knew all of the facts – that the king had not been captured off the Breton coast but far to the east at Varennes – but Rennie did not care to enlighten him if Hood did not know. All he cared about was that he could now, today, walk out under he the arch of the Admiralty with nothing beside his name but his rank, and the name of his ship. He did not yet know any of the detail, but he was quite certain that a way would be found to exonerate him – and James Hayter – in everything connected to recent events in France.

'Will it save *Expedient*, though?' Muttered to himself as he stepped out into Whitehall, a few minutes later. 'Will it save my ship?' He glanced along the broad thoroughfare, and thought of engaging a chair to take him to Bedford Street, and then decided to walk there. He sniffed the air. The day was warm, and the cloacal stink of the river wafted across Whitehall.

'Bilge reek at sea is a thing I abominate.' As he strode along toward the Strand. 'But by God London is putrid foul by compare. I would not wish to spend my life in such a filthy stench.' Stepping out to cross the street. 'Nay, I would not.'

NINETEEN

James woke with a little start, his breath catching in his throat. There was someone in the room. He listened, turning his head on the pillow, and heard a movement in the darkness, a brief rustling sound. He eased himself up against the pillow into a sitting position, and reached for his pistol case. And remembered that he had no pistol case. Remembered that he was lying ill in a London hotel, defenceless.

Again the faintest movement, as if the air itself had whispered.

'Who is there?'

And now a whispered reply:

'James?'

A woman's voice.

'Who is it? Who are you?'

'Juliette.'

'Juliette!' Jolting back against the bedhead.

'Shh! We must be quiet.' In French.

A light struck, and the glow of a candle. Juliette's beautiful face in that glow.

'My God, it really is you . . .'

She placed the candle on the cabinet, and came to him, into his arms. Her warmth, her scent, her lips on his. His heart swelled and thudded, his head whirled, and he felt he would fall senseless, yet at the same moment he had never felt more intensely alive. A long, fervent, kissing embrace. And at last:

'Oh, my darling, my darling . . .'

'Shh ... shh ... I am here.'

'I thought I had lost you. I thought you were killed ...'

'At the beach?'

'Yes. My God, I looked for you everywhere. I thought you had been shot, and had fallen among the rocks. I could not find you, and when the royal party came down to the boats, I had to go with them, and leave you behind.'

'I hid myself, and escaped afterward.'

'Why did not you come with us! Why did not you—'

'Hush, my love.' Fingers to his lips. 'I could not follow you, because I was caught between the National Guard troops and the water. I saw you go, and I was desolate – but I could do nothing.'

And now James gripped her hands in his, and looked into her eyes. 'Did you know the party we rescued in the boats was *not* the king and queen?'

A sigh. 'Yes – I knew.'

'And yet you said nothing to me! You allowed me to think it was all entirely real! Why did not you tell me the truth, Juliette!' In real anguish.

'Hush ...'

'In God's name, why?' Quietly, intensely, still gripping her hands.

'My love, you will break my fingers.'

'I am sorry.' Releasing her hands. 'The last thing I would wish to do is harm you. But you must tell me why you deceived me. You must!'

'I was under the greatest constraint from M. Félix. I could tell you nothing. He could have had me shot if I had said a word of the truth to you, or to anyone. You had to believe absolutely in the rescue plan.'

'That was all a lie.' Bitterly.

'My love, what could I do ... ?'

'Yes, what could you do? Your only choice was to make me believe you – by seducing me.'

'At first it was only that – until I fell in love with you.'

'At first! So you make a practice of seducing gullible men, to make them believe!'

'How you wound me when you say such things. These are desperate days in France, and we must all do desperate things . . . but I fell in love with you, my darling.'

'Can I believe that, now . . . ?' Looking at her, wishing with all his being that he could believe her.

'Why would I have come to England to find you, if it were not true? My darling, my love – look at me. Why would I come, at such risk, if I did not love you?' She tried to look into his eyes, but he sat back against the pillow, and looked away toward the window, so clearly in torment that now it was she who took his hands in hers, and held them tight.

'My love, my dearest, I came because I could not bear to think I would never see you any more.'

And now he did look at her, and very soft:

'How did you find me, Juliette?'

'A message came to me, with this address. I was able to escape to England at the very last moment, when all of us who took part in the deception to help the king escape are under sentence of death, and sought all over France.'

'But who sent you this message? How could—'

She shook her head, and put her hand to his lips. 'Forgive me, I do not know . . . I do not know.'

'What d'y'mean – you do not know? Do you wish to deceive me further! Captain Rennie and I have both been grossly deceived, and a great many men killed! I don't know that I am able to forgive anyone that!' Growing desperately and miserably agitated.

'You do not forgive me?' Looking into his face.

'I don't know what to believe, any more. I don't know who to trust.' Looking away from her. 'There is no honour left in anything.'

'My darling . . . did not you wish to aid us in helping the king to escape? What difference does it make how it was done? We were all part of the deception. If the plan had succeeded, would you now feel so bitter? Would you say such wounding things to me?'

'Oh, d' you mean, if the king had escaped to Austria, or if the party we attempted to rescue had been brought to England? Which? Neither happened! We were *deceived*.'

'Yes. You were deceived. In a noble cause.'

'The cause may've been noble. To deceive honourable men was not.'

'Do you wish me to go away?'

'What . . . ?' Looking at her.

'I admit it . . . I was just as guilty of deceit as all the others, just as culpable. Will you send me away?'

'I   I do not wish it.'

'Why not? If I am guilty?' Softly, leaning closer.

'I – I could never send you away.'

'Why not? Tell me . . .'

'Oh, good heaven, you know why. Because I love you, my darling, I love you . . .'

And he kissed her, feverishly, breathlessly, helplessly, and they clung to each other and sank down on the bed. Soon there was no more talk, only the timeless, wordless language of sighs and cries and gasps that all lovers speak untutored in the flooding dark.

*

'Captain Rennie, you are alone at breakfast, I see.'

Brough Mappin stood perfectly groomed in front of Rennie's table in Mrs Peebles's dining room. Rennie looked at him and was in no way inclined to be welcoming. An insult lurked under his tongue, and then he left it there. Instead:

'I am. I prefer to eat breakfast solitary.'

'Why not in your room, then, off a tray?' A smile. His cheeks were smooth-shaven, his stock flawless, everything about his person perfectly arranged.

Rennie did not care for that smile. It was a little too complacent, a little too self-assured for this hour of the day.

'D'ye want something of me, Mappin?' Deliberately omitting 'mister'. 'I am surprised y'have the effrontery to face me, after—'

'Indeed, I wish to say a word to you, Captain Rennie.' Over him, easily. 'May I join you in a cup of coffee?' He pulled out a chair, and made to sit down.

'Y'may not. I never drink coffee.'

'Ah. Then – tea?' And he did sit down. Rennie scowled at him, and cut off the top of an egg.

'Or d'you take chocolate in the morning?' Mr Mappin was determined to be affable.

'Chocolate! I do not.'

'Is Lieutenant Hayter recovered, I wonder? He was ill, poor fellow, when last I was here, and that had made him . . . captious.'

'He is better, I think.' Grudgingly.

'Good, good. I am glad to hear it.'

'I have not seen him today.'

'No? At any rate, it is you I wished to see, Rennie.'

'I think we can have nothing to discuss.' Rennie attacked his egg, wounding it deep with his spoon. Yoke spilled. 'I will say to you candidly that my opinion of you—'

Smoothly, over him: 'I will like you to come with me to meet a certain person, this morning.'

'Certain person?'

'Indeed. A private interview, that will greatly aid your understanding – of late events.'

'Late events, hey? A very pretty description. Well well, who is it?'

'It is a person you will in course know at once, when you see him.'

'D'y'mean that I'm already acquainted with the fellow?' Frowning.

'You will certainly know who he is.'

'Christ's blood, Mappin. It is the early part of the day, and I am *trying* to eat my breakfast. If you are going to speak to me, speak plain, or leave me in peace.'

Mr Mappin made himself smile again, and: 'I have a carriage. I think after all I will not drink tea. I will wait for you outside. Ten minutes?' And without waiting for a reply he stood up and stepped away quickly out of the room.

Rennie sucked down hot tea, and called for more toast. He would make Mappin wait fifteen minutes, at least. And when his toast came:

'Nay, twenty, the damned presuming bugger.' Muttered.

'Beg pardon, sir?' The servant girl.

'Nothing. I was clearing my wind.' And when the girl had gone: 'Even then I may not go with him, if I don't feel like it. After all he has put us through? Who the devil does he think he is, ordering me about ashore?'

But in the end his curiosity got the better of him, and he did go.

In the carriage – a plain black conveyance, no coat of arms, no embellishment – Rennie said to Mr Mappin:

'If you will not tell me who it is, in least tell me where it is, hey? Where do we go?'

'Be patient.'

'Be patient with you? By God, you ask too much, sir.' An exasperated sigh, but he did not press Mr Mappin further. Instead he settled back in his seat and was content to watch the passing scene. They crossed a square crowded with carriages, and carts, and then they were in streets of tall houses. The carriage turned down one of these streets, proceeded to the far end and stopped. Mr Mappin and Rennie descended.

'This house.' Mr Mappin indicated a house with columns, the lamp glasses freshly polished, the step pristine, the door glossily painted.

'Whose house is this . . . ?' wondered Rennie aloud, but he got no answer.

Mr Mappin pulled the bell. The stamping of the horses' feet behind them, echoing in the quiet street. A brief wait, then the heavy door swung inward, and they went in. Liveried footmen, a grand mirror, a long portrait at the head of the stair. They were led across black-and-white-chequered stone, their footsteps clicking, and through a panelled door into a tall, book-quiet room.

'Mr Mappin.'

'Prime Minister. May I introduce Captain William Rennie, RN, of HMS *Expedient*.'

'Good God . . .' Rennie, under his breath.

'Captain Rennie.' The Prime Minister came forward and shook Rennie's hand. The grip firm. The face of a young man but the eyes older. A brown coat, a high-tied stock, no wig. Wine fumes, very distinct.

'I am very glad we are able to meet, so that I may thank you.'

'Thank me, sir . . . ?'

'Indeed, Captain Rennie. In private circumstances, away from the trappings and formalities of office.' He led the way toward chairs, and a side table. Turning:

'A glass of wine?'

Rennie very nearly refused, so early in the day, and then thought that to refuse would be impolite – impolitic – and he accepted. Inclining his head:

'Thank you, sir. You are kind.'

He was given a glass of port wine. Mr Mappin also accepted. Glasses were raised, and tipped. The wine was a little rich for Rennie's taste – he preferred the subtler flavour of Madeira – but he swallowed it willingly enough. His glass was at once refilled.

'Gentlemen, shall we sit down?'

They sat down. Light from the tall window at the end of the room fell glancing on a desk, a snuffbox, and the high glass of an Argand lamp. Mr Pitt turned his direct, friendly gaze on Rennie, and:

'You have done us proud, you know.'

'Eh?' Before he could stop himself, then: 'Erm . . . thank you, sir.'

'Y'may not think so, now. When you have lost so many brave men, and your ship lies broken, you may not think so. But what you did was very remarkable.'

'You flatter me, sir, I think.' A polite half-smile.

'I know you were not told the whole truth, at the beginning. We could not tell you. Eh, Mappin?'

'We could not, sir.'

'The plan of diversion and decoy might well have failed, had you not believed in it, entire.'

'I – I think that it did fail, sir . . .'

'Not through want of British effort, though. Not through any lack of British endeavour and determination. Your determination, sir, and courage, and skill. We did everything that was in our power to aid King Louis to escape – through you, Captain Rennie. England can never be blamed, King George can never be faulted nor blamed nor held to account for *want of desire*. We did everything that was humanly possible. You did, Captain Rennie. Your actions were heroic. Aye, that is the word. Heroic. I have read the whole of the report.' Nodding.

'I – I have submitted no report . . .'

'Lieutenant Merriman Leigh was advised that a report should be forthcoming as soon as he was able to furnish it, from Portsmouth.' Mr Mappin, to Rennie. 'He did so, in your absence.'

'He did? Ah.'

'And now I will like to make the loyal toast.' Mr Pitt refilled his own glass, and raised it. He stood. 'Gentlemen, the king.' Rennie and Mappin stood in turn.

'The king.'

'The king.'

They drank, and the Prime Minister remained on his legs. 'A further toast, if I may.' He held up his glass to Rennie. 'To you, Captain Rennie.'

'Indeed – Captain Rennie.' Mappin held up his glass.

They drank, and in spite of himself – in spite of all his doubt and guilt and sense of failure – Rennie found himself moved. A moment, and he cleared his throat.

'You are very good.'

The Prime Minister nodded benignly. 'However . . .'

'Ah, now.' Rennie, in his head. 'Here it comes, at last. Now I shall discover my fate. Yes, by God, that damned word. However . . .'

'However, Captain Rennie, you will understand, I am in no doubt, that no word of this may ever be made public.'

Rennie thought it best to say nothing. He waited.

'We cannot be seen to have interfered, nor even to've attempted to interfere, with the intimate internal arrangements of another nation. The domestic disturbances in France are not our business. The fate of the king – much as we deplore his arrest, and confinement – does not lie in our hands. These things are altogether a matter for France. Should there be any repercussion as to your actions at sea – everything will be denied.'

'But – should there be such repercussion, sir – will those denials be believed? We was obliged to fire upon and destroy several ships. We was very plainly a British ship of war.'

'I have read the report.' Nodding again. 'And should those events ever be raised between our two nations, I shall say the French were fighting among themselves – opposing factions – and that any attempt to besmirch Britain's name would be took very ill. The Royal Navy was never there. *You* were never there, Captain Rennie.'

'And . . . what of the prisoners, sir? Many wounded men were took into Brest, and are held there.'

'Discreet attempts – through commercial channels – will be made to free them. Certain moneys will be made available, at Brest. Bribes, to be candid. The families of your men that lost their lives will also be took care of. You have my word.'

'Thank you, sir.' A bow. 'You are kind.'

'As to you yourself, Captain Rennie, I shall say a word to Lord Hood, at the Admiralty. And to Lord Chatham, in course – but it is Hood that manages things, in truth, not my brother. I will like to reward you, and – what is the lieutenant's name?' Turning to Mr Mappin.

'Lieutenant Hayter, sir.'

'Ah, yes.' Turning back to Rennie. 'Aye, Captain Rennie, I will like to reward you and Lieutenant Hayter both. You should be moved up. You deserve it.'

Thank you, sir.'

Presently the meeting came to an end, and Rennie and Mr Mappin took their leave. As they reached the door of the room, Mr Pitt called after them:

'Captain Rennie?'

'Sir?' Turning.

'Your most grateful servant, sir.' And he bowed.

But when Captain Rennie had been returned to Mrs Peebles's hotel, and Mr Mappin had departed, lingering doubt remained. Rennie thought about all the Prime Minister had said, and found that in truth he had no greater 'understanding' of anything, in spite of Mr Mappin's earlier assertion. Rennie was puzzled and confused, he was – at sea.

'Whose plan was it, in fact? Was it Mappin's, or Mr Pitt's, or mostly a French one, formed and arranged by French loyalists – with British advice and assistance? Was our own king part of it? Was Mr Pitt obliged to advance the plan at the king's insistence – to aid his fellow monarch?'

He thought long and deep, sifting through all possibilities and likelihoods, and could find no satisfactory answer. At last:

'I shall never know the whole truth, nor even half of the truth.' A sigh, then he recalled the Prime Minister's promise – perhaps made to deflect such questions:

'I will like to reward you, Captain Rennie, you and Lieutenant Hayter both.' Well, that was clear enough, by God. Clear and unequivocal. Their careers in the Royal Navy were safe.

'I must say a word to James, at once. It will lift him.' And he hurried along the corridor to James's room. Knocked, waited, knocked again. No reply. He waited another moment, then called:

'James? Are you awake, dear fellow?'

No response. Rennie knocked once more, then when he heard nothing he tried the handle, and found the door unlocked. He opened it.

'James?'

The room was empty. The bed had been stripped, and cupboards stood open and bare. A footfall behind him, and Rennie turned. A maidservant, her arms laden with fresh bedlinen.

'Oh, sir – I thought you was gone. I was jus' about to turn out your room.'

'Turn out my room?'

'Yes, sir. The other gen'man – your friend – paid his bill and went away this morning, sir. I thought you was certain to've gone with him.'

'Paid his bill and left . . .'

'Yes, sir, with his lady friend.'

'Lady friend?' Rennie stared at the girl. 'D'y'mean – his wife?'

The maid blushed, and shifted the linen from one arm to the other.

'Perhaps it was his wife, sir. I – I do not rightly know. She was a French lady, I think.'

'French!' Brushing past the maid, knocking folded sheets to the floor. 'The damn' fool!'

Rennie ran down the stair and confronted Mrs Peebles in her parlour.

'When did Lieutenant Hayter leave?'

'About half an hour after you went out yourself, sir. He paid his bill, and—'

'And he did not leave word where he was going?'

'No, sir.'

'The lady that accompanied him, was she French?'

'She was a lady cert'nly. And yes, I b'lieve she was French. They was talking French as they went out.'

'And how long have they been gone? An hour?'

'Really, Captain Rennie, you must not distress me so with all these questions. I don't care for upset in my house, I do not. This is a quiet, decent house, for gentlefolk.'

'Yes, I do beg your pardon, Mrs Peebles. Was not the matter very urgent I should not trouble you so insistent.' He put down a guinea on the table.

'You wish to settle your bill, Captain Rennie?' Carefully polite.

'I wish you to aid me, Mrs Peebles.' Looking at her very direct. 'Now then, which way did they go?'

'I think they may have turned down toward the Strand, but I cannot be certain.'

'They had no carriage?'

'I don't think so, no. They cert'nly never sent for one from here.'

'Very well, thank you, Mrs Peebles.' Rennie stared down the passage a moment, and rubbed the back of his neck.

'Will you be leaving us yourself, sir? Now that your friend has gone?'

'Yes. No. I – I am not quite certain, just at present. I will let you know – later.'

'Thank you, sir.' She smiled, and discreetly removed the offending guinea.

*

'Where do you take me, James?' Juliette, looking out of the windows of the carriage he had secured for them.

'To my brother Nicholas, at Lambeth. We should probably have gone there last night.'

'To your brother? Why not to another hotel?'

'Hotel staff may be bribed, and guests observed coming and going.'

'You think we are watched?'

'Listen now, my love, and attend me very close.' Looking behind through the oval window, then leaning near to her, and looking at her intently. 'You are sought in France. You came here by clandestine means. I will not ask how, nor with whose aid, but I do not trust anyone with connection to this affair. My brother has lately moved to Lambeth from his apartments at Lincoln's Inn, where he practises the law. He wished to be very private at his new house, and has told only close members of the family where it lies. People who would wish to find you, and me – and do us harm – cannot possibly discover us at Lambeth.'

'You think we are in such danger – even here in England.'

'I do, by God. You and I have been engaged in attempting to smuggle King Louis out of France, have we not? You know that you are sought in France, but why not here, also? Will not the revolutionists wish to discover and take vengeance upon those in England who aided the attempt? We can afford to trust *no one at all.*'

'Not even each other?' A little smile.

He did not reply, but simply glanced at her as if to say that making jokes now was foolish.

This mute response did not entirely satisfy her as the carriage turned and rattled over Blackfriars Bridge, and her face said so. James was too preoccupied to notice.

'We are going the long way round to Lambeth.' James, as they passed over the wide brown river. 'We could readily have gone by a closer bridge . . .' Again glancing behind through the oval window '. . . but I wished to be careful.'

The carriage passed down Great Surrey Street and into Lambeth Road. James began to relax a little, and ceased peering behind. They came to Paradise Walk, and open fields. The carriage turned down a lane toward a stand of trees and a substantial low-built house, set well back in a wide garden. James signalled to the driver by tapping on the inside roof, and the horses were pulled up. A moment of quiet.

James opened the door and got out, and folded down the step for Juliette. To the driver he said:

'Wait here a moment.'

He led Juliette through an arched gateway and along a path. A covered portico, and a bell-pull. James rang the bell, and presently the red-painted door was opened by a maidservant.

'Good morning. Is the master at home?'

'You wish to see Mr Sacheverell, sir?'

'Erm, no . . . Mr Hayter. Who is Mr Sacheverell?'

'He is the other gen'man that lives here, sir.'

'Ah. Thank you.' A quick glance at Juliette, then: 'Will you say to Mr Hayter that his brother James wishes to see him.'

'Well, sir – that is why I arst. Mr Hayter ain't here at present. Only Mr Sacheverell. You wish to see him, sir?'

'Erm . . . yes. Yes, certainly. Mr Sacheverell.'

'Very good, sir. Will you come in, and wait in the library?'

James and Juliette were shown into a small green pleasant room, lined on three sides with bookshelves; on the fourth a window gave on to a green garden. Library steps stood in a corner. Near the window were a standing globe and a small leather-topped desk. On the desk, a silver inkwell, a pouncebox, a bundle of quills. The faint scent of cologne on the air.

Five minutes passed. Ten. A bracket clock pinged the quarter hour. Then the door was opened, and in stepped Mr Sacheverell, striking in a quilted green coat, black britches and black silk slippers. In a neutral, not quite languid tone:

'My apologies for having kept you waiting, but Nicholas

did not warn me you was coming. I am Handeside Sacheverell. My friends call me Handy.'

James bowed. 'Lieutenant James Hayter, RN. May I present you to my friend Madame Maigre?'

The formalities, and they all sat down.

'How may I assist?' Mr Sacheverell turned his languid gaze on James.

'Well, in fact I wished to see Nicholas, Mr Sacheverell. I see now that—'

'Handy.'

'Yes, I beg your pardon. Handy. I see now that I should have gone to his chambers at Lincoln's Inn, where he—'

'Oh, he ain't there.'

'No?'

'No no, he is at home.'

'Home . . . ? You mean, he is at Melton?'

'Yes, he has gone down to Dorset for a week, to see his mother. Forgive me, she is your mother too, in course. Lady Hayter.'

'Yes, hm. In truth I had wished to stay here with my brother a few days. But this is your house, Mr Sacheverell. Handy. And I could not impose on your—'

'It ain't my house, you know. No, I share it with Nicholas, but it is his house.'

'Then, I wonder if it will be an imposition to ask . . . ?'

'By all means, stay as long as you like. There is plenty of room. You came in a carriage?'

'Yes, it's outside, in the lane.'

'Then Jeffers will bring in your bags, and ask the driver to wait.'

'The driver needn't wait.'

'Oh, but surely—'

James, over him: 'Mr Sachev— Handy. Please don't think me impertinent, but what is your situation here? My brother has never spoken of you. Are you yourself a lawyer?'

'Nay, I am not.' Easily.

'Then – are you my brother's man of business?'

'Not that, neither. Nor his amanuensis. I am simply – his friend. We are neither of us married men, and it suits us very well to share this house.'

James glanced out of the window. 'Yes, it is a very pleasant house, in a pleasant setting. I can see why my brother took it.'

'Very pleasant, and very private. We are not disturbed here.'

'I – I hope that we will not disturb you.'

'We?' A quick look at Juliette. 'Ahh – you mean that you and Madame Maigre *both* wish to stay here?'

'Well – yes.'

'Ahh . . .'

'Just for a short time, you know. A day or two, until . . .'

'Until?' Again glancing at Juliette.

James leaned forward. 'You are my brother's friend, so I am going to be candid, and trust you. We wish to hide here.'

'Hide?'

'Yes, we wish to hide because—'

'We are pursued, monsieur.' Juliette, over him. 'You understand?'

Mr Sacheverell again looked at her, more appraisingly this time, and gave a little grimace of comprehension.

'Yes, you are lovers. You wish to be lovers undetected. I do understand, I assure you. You will be quite safe here with me. – Jeffers!'

He rang a bell. A manservant appeared and Mr Sacheverell instructed him to bring in the visitors' bags. James gave the man money for the carriage, and told him to send it away.

Presently James and Juliette were shown to their adjoining rooms, with the invitation to join Mr Sacheverell for a 'light luncheon' at one o'clock.

'James, what will we do . . . afterward?' Juliette, her hand on James's. They stood in the open connecting doorway between their two rooms.

'Afterward?'

'*Oui, ensuite*. When we have stopped running away.'

'Well – we will find a house.' With a confidence he did not feel, patting her hand. She withdrew her hand.

'Where?'

'Somewhere in England, I expect.'

'But you have a wife in England.'

'Yes, thank you for reminding me. My brother will no doubt see her when he is in Dorset. She is living at my father's house at present.'

'You will go back to her, will you not . . . ?'

'Why do you ask me these things, Juliette, when our circumstances are difficult enough? I might equally ask whether or no you intend to return to France.'

'I cannot go back there. I can never go back, now.!'

James was silent a moment, and the quiet of the house, broken only by the silver notes of birds, rising and floating across the quiet green garden outside, emphasised their solitude and seclusion. Juliette touched James's face, and he turned his head to look into her eyes. A breath, and she said:

'I am sorry. Forgive me. We will live day by day together – until we are free.'

*

At luncheon Mr Sacheverell happily conversed with Juliette in French, on trivial subjects. He made it clear to her, politely but firmly, that he wished to know nothing of the present difficulties in France, nor of her own particular circumstances in that regard. They discussed the benign climate of the south; provincial manners compared with Parisian manners, &c., &c.; French cooking; wine. After luncheon, when Juliette had gone to rest, Mr Sacheverell took James's arm and they went into the garden. As they walked under the trees:

'Nicholas has engaged Laidlaw to transform the lower

half of the garden. It is two acres, nearly two acres and a half. You know Laidlaw?'

'I confess I do not.' Slightly uncomfortable.

'No? He is the coming man. Not perhaps at such a premium as Brown, or Kent, or Repton, nor on the same scale of landscape – but on the smaller scale, a few acres, he is sublime. I will show you the drawings afterward, if you would like to see them?'

'I should like to very much.' For something to say.

'And now I must broach another subject.' Pausing and turning to James. An intake of breath. 'What am I to say to Nicholas?'

'Say to him?'

'Now, now, James – I may call you James?'

'In course you may – Handy.'

'Good. Now.' Again the pause, and the glance. 'You and I both know that I cannot pretend that you was never here, when Nicholas returns – hey?'

'Nay, in course you cannot. Why should you?'

'Exact, exact. I must tell him everything. So. What shall I say about your friend Madame Maigre? After all, you are a married man.'

'Be candid.'

'Ahh. Candid. Candid . . . entire?'

'Yes. Yes.' Nodding. 'I should not wish you to dissimulate. You must tell my brother everything, as you said.'

'But your wife is at Melton, ain't she? Nicholas will have seen her there, and they will have talked of you, will not they?'

'I expect so.'

'Yes. I see that you do wish to speculate as to his feelings on the matter, when he learns that you have been here with another woman. Hm. Hm. But you see I know Nicholas very well.' Tapping his chin with a finger. 'He is a curious amalgam of emotions and attitudes, your brother. On the one hand generous-spirited, humane, the least censorious of men – and on the other . . .'

'Yes, I know. A prig.' An uncomfortable half-smile. 'About certain things he is quite unbending.'

'So, you see, I am in something of a dilemma.' Mr Sacheverell. They walked on a little way, and at last James:

'Handy?'

'I am here.'

'Since we are being candid about my own circumstances, may I dare to be candid about your own?'

'Mine?'

'Indeed. What is your relationship with my brother?'

'Relationship?' A sharper glance, and a tightening of the languid tone.

James looked at Mr Sacheverell, and tilted his head on one side a little, and waited. Presently Mr Sacheverell sniffed in a breath, and with a tight smile:

'We are the closest of friends. You follow?'

Again James waited, and said nothing. Mr Sacheverell:

'You are a sea officer, often away from home for long weeks or even months. Surely you must find, at sea, that there are other officers – perhaps one in particular – with whom you think yourself more in sympathy than with anyone else? Yes?'

'Well, I suppose so . . . yes.'

'It is like that with Nicholas and myself. We are companionable. We are in sympathy.' A sharp little glance, and a slightly arched brow. 'You understand?'

James saw that he must go very carefully, now, else provoke disaffection or even outright animosity. In all delicacy and decency and good sense he could probe no further. The friendship between Mr Sacheverell and Nicholas was almost certainly more intimate than Mr Sacheverell was prepared to admit.

'However, it ain't my business.' James, in his head. Aloud he said:

'Forgive me for presuming to press you about your friendship with my brother, Handy. I had to be certain, you apprehend, that you would not wish unfavourably to influence his opinion as to my own circumstances. That you would wish to make him understand, in light of your own friendship, that this is not a fickle, foolish affair. Madame Maigre – Juliette – is very dear to me, and I must find a way through that will be least painful for all concerned. You see?'

Had he put it both tactfully and clearly enough? Without appearing to threaten? Had he?

Mr Sacheverell put a hand on James's hand, looked at him very direct, and nodded.

'In course I do see, my dear James. Yes, certainly.'

Mr Sacheverell nodded again, and withdrew his hand, and they walked on down to the lower two acres to see the progress of the work there.

TWENTY

Captain Rennie fretted at Bedford Street, wrote a further letter to his wife Sylvia in Norfolk, and waited one day longer – in the hope that James would either send word, or return. No word came. In the evening Mr Mappin came to the hotel. He was not his usual calm, assured, urbane self.

'I have had intelligence from France that a certain party is here in England, which can only mean grave danger for Lieutenant Hayter. Where is he?'

'Is this party – female?'

'Nay, it is a man. Can I assume from your question that Lieutenant Hayter is with a woman?'

'He has gone away with her. A Frenchwoman. When he has a wife.'

'Yes, so he will will not have gone to Dorset, that is certain.' Glancing down into the street from Rennie's window. 'If he and the woman are still in London, they are in very grave danger indeed. We must find them.'

'Aye, that's all very well to say, Mappin. London is very big and wide, and we are two men of a million in that bigness. How in God's name of d'y'propose to find them, hey? Or even to begin the search?'

Mr Mappin, turning from the window: 'We must make the attempt. We know that he will not go to Dorset with her, when his wife is there. Has he any particular friends in London that you know of?'

'Nay, I don't know.' Shaking his head. 'If he has, I've never met them.'

'At Portsmouth, then?'

'Only shipmates.'

'Hm. We must hope he has not gone there. Agents of this man will be watching there, I am in no doubt.'

'Agents? Who is this fellow?'

Mappin moved again to the window and glanced down anxiously into the street. Over his shoulder:

'It was thought he was an absolute loyalist, but now there is contrary intelligence. It appears that he has had a change of heart, and has joined the revolution.'

'Good God. Was he involved in the—'

'Yes, he was.' Over Rennie. 'He was intimately connected with the plot to bring King Louis out of France. He goes under the name of Félix.'

'I think I heard James mention that name. Yes, in fact – in fact it was to do with the woman he has now run away with.'

'You have met her? You know her?'

'Nay, I don't. She is called Juliette, and he is infatuated with her. That's all I know.'

'Aye, Juliette. Madame Maigre. She should never have come. She is in mortal danger from Félix, as is the lieutenant, and all of us that have been party to the plot.'

'Well well, I am not averse to danger, you know.' Rennie, getting up on his legs. 'I have faced danger on many—'

'At sea, Captain Rennie.' Mr Mappin, over him grimly. 'You have faced danger at sea. But we are not at sea now. We are on land, in a great dark city, and in any doorway, round any corner, there may lie in wait deadly peril.'

'Then I am ready for it.' Rennie took up his sword.

Mr Mappin raised a finger. 'Lieutenant Hayter has two brothers, has not he?'

'Two older brothers, yes.'

'One of whom lives in London, yes?'

'You are right, by God, he does. He practises at law.'

'What is his name?'

'Thomas, I think. Nay . . . Nicholas.'

'Where are his chambers?'

'At Lincoln's Inn, as I recall.'

'We must go there at once.'

'At night? Surely there will be nobody there at night?'

'There will be a watchman or a clerk that can tell us where Nicholas Hayter lives. Lieutenant Hayter may have gone to him to seek refuge. That is our best hope. I have a carriage. Let us go down. Nay, do not encumber yourself with that damned sword, Captain Rennie. You have pistols?'

'Pocket pistols, aye.'

'Bring them.'

*

They found Nicholas Hayter's chambers at Lincoln's Inn by asking directions of a watchman, in the open square, and a second watchman pointed them to the correct stair, but added:

'You will find no one there, gen'men. Chambers is all locked up a-night.' Holding up his lantern to show them the entrance. He allowed his staff to rest against the wall, an indication of his confidence that he was not about to be attacked by these late callers. His rattle jiggled at his waist.

'Surely there is a clerk?' Mr Mappin.

'Aye, but he don't sleep 'ere, sir.'

'Then where does he sleep?'

'He will not 'ppreciate being disturbed at night, gen'men.'

Rennie spoke now, in a voice tutored by command: 'We are officers in His Majesty's service. We must speak to this man at once. The matter is urgent. Show us where he lives.'

'Show you . . . ?'

'Take us there, man!'

The watchman took them, grumbling under his broad hat, and coughing, and sniffing. Presently they came to the dwelling, a tenement house in a courtyard, and Mr Mappin knocked.

A delay of a quarter of an hour before the clerk could be brought from his bed, and persuaded to talk to the visitors. Rennie fretted, paced, swore. Mr Mappin fretted but was still. At last the clerk appeared in his nightshirt. Mr Mappin addressed him, having got his name from the watchman.

'Now then, Mr Baldry—'

'Baldock, sir. William Baldock. It is very late, and I—'

'We wish to know where Mr Nicholas Hayter lives.'

'Mr Hayter? Oh, I could not tell you. I could not say.'

'D'y'mean that you do not know?' Sharply.

'That is – correct. I do not.' To the watchman, who was preparing to return to his duty: 'Did you not tell them I don't know where he dwells, Hill?'

'They said it was urgent, Mr Baldock.'

'Well, I cannot say, all the same.' Nodding at Mr Mappin.

'I think you mean – you will not say.'

'I mean, sir, that I—'

And now Captain Rennie again felt obliged to take charge. Stepping forward to the doorway:

'I am Captain William Rennie, RN, and I wish to find and speak to Lieutenant James Hayter, Mr Nicholas Hayter's brother, on a matter of the greatest urgency.'

'Well, I – I know nothing of Mr Hayter's brother. I am only a clerk. I tell you, I do not know where—'

'So urgent that I have been given authority to pay for information.'

'Pay!' Beginning to be indignant. 'You mistake me if you think—'

'Ten guineas. Ten guineas in gold, payable at once, into your hand.' Taking his purse from his pocket, and shaking coins into his palm.

'Good heaven . . .' Mr Baldock's eyes grew wide.

The watchman cleared his throat, and lifted his lantern

the better to see the gold. Mr Baldock recovered himself, and assumed an expression of wounded dignity. Dismissively:

'It is of no avail, it is of no avail. Mr Hayter ain't even in London, he is away in the country, in Dorset.'

'Damnation!' Rennie, turning away.

'Wait, though.' Mr Mappin. 'Even if Nicholas Hayter is away, that don't mean his brother has not gone to his house in London. Eh, Mr Baldock?'

'I tell you. I told you. I know nothing of his brother.' The clerk closed his eyes, and shook his head.

'But you know where that house lies, do not you? What place, what street?'

Mr Baldock opened his eyes, sighed heavily, looked from one to the other, and at last: 'Will you give me a solemn undertaking never to trouble me again? Will you go away, and never come back – if I tell you?'

'We will.' Rennie, with authority.

'Will you promise never to mention my name in this distinction? Will you give me your word, solemnly give it, as to that?'

'We will. Here, take the gold.' Holding out the coins.

And Mr Baldock took the money.

*

They came to the house in the dead of night. There was no moon, and the carriage lamps did not well illuminate the lane outside. Mr Mappin had provided himself with lanterns, and he and Rennie each took one as they approached the house, leaving the carriage and driver waiting under the trees in the lane. As they approached along the path, Mr Mappin – in the lead – abruptly came to a halt, and Rennie came up against him.

'What is it? Why d'y'stop, Mappin?'

'Just a sense that all is not well here . . .'

'What d'y'mean? You saw something?'

'Nay, nothing. But everything is too quiet, almost as if the darkness itself was holding its breath. In my trade I have learned that such a sense, such an instinct, should not lightly be ignored – and never at night.'

'I have seen nothing, nor heard nothing, neither. Ain't you being fanciful?'

They were speaking in very subdued tones, and now in spite of himself Rennie felt a shiver of unease run through him.

'I am never fanciful, Captain Rennie.' Mr Mappin. 'And if I am right . . .'

'Then we had better raise the alarm, by God.' Rennie, pushing aside timidity and striding forward toward the house. 'I will pull the bell, and knock, and let them know—'

'Nay! Nay!' Mr Mappin, in a warning whisper, catching Rennie's arm. 'Do not!'

'What the devil d'y'mean?' Rennie, *sotto voce*, furiously. 'If my friend is in peril in that house, I will not stand by and allow him be slaughtered in his bed, d'y'hear?' Shaking his arm free of Mr Mappin's grasp. But Mr Mappin gripped it again, even more forcefully.

'Listen now, if villainy is afoot as I suspect, and assailants are attempting to gain entry to the house, they will likely do so at the rear. It will be better for us – and Lieutenant Hayter – if we go to the rear ourselves, and take them by surprise. Yes?'

Rennie was obliged to admit that this made perfect sense, and he nodded: 'Yes. Very well.'

'You have your pistols?'

'I have them.'

'Cover your light with your coat, and follow me.'

And Rennie did that very rare thing for him, after many years of command – he did as he was told, and followed.

They made their way cautiously down a side path to the rear garden, the bulk of the house dim on their right, their part-covered lights showing them only the ground immediately ahead. They came into the wide garden.

There was no glimmer of light anywhere in the garden, nor from inside the house. Mr Mappin held up a warning hand, and whispered:

'Wait. Very, very still . . .' A moment, and they heard a clicking, fidgeting sound, coming from the rear of the house, subdued but clear in the hushed darkness of the garden.

They had reached a clump of bushes and paused there, and now Mr Mappin turned to Rennie and whispered:

'Wait here, will you? I am going forward to investigate.'

'Wait here? Nay, Mappin . . .' But before Rennie could protest further Mr Mappin had slipped away in the darkness, leaving Rennie alone. Long, anxious moments, and Rennie crouched down, waited, and heard no more of the fidgeting, clinking sound. Presently, cautiously, he rose on his legs. And was at once struck a blow to the head from behind. A rocket burst of stars exploded in his skull, and he slumped senseless on the dew-moist grass.

*

When he woke it was in a well-appointed, well-lit room, to the sound of voices and the smell of coffee and tobacco. A tall, slim man was leaning over him, peering down with a cheroot in his hand. Smoke curled up against the light.

'Who are you?' Rennie demanded, and felt an instant searing pain in his head.

'I am Handy Sacheverell, and you are in my house, Captain Rennie.'

'Who? Where? Ohh . . .' And he clutched at his head, felt a bandage, and was further bewildered. Had a block fallen from the rigging and struck him? But he was not at sea . . .

Mr Mappin's concerned face now appeared beside that of Mr Sacheverell.

'Good God – Mappin. You are here, too.'

'I am here.'

'I – I begin to recall, now. We came in search of James.' The light blurring at the edges, the faces above him blurring, then clearing into sharp focus.

'Aye, we did.' Mappin's grim little nod.

'To a house at Lambeth . . .' Concentrating on Mr Sacheverell's face. 'Your house, sir, did y'say?'

'In truth the house belongs to Mr Nicholas Hayter – but it is where I live, yes.'

'Where is James? And his companion?'

Now Mr Mappin shook his head. 'Gone.'

'Gone! Ohh . . .' Again clutching at his bandaged head, which he felt would split under the bindings.

'They have been took. I was too late. By the time I reached the house the assailants had got in at a window, and dragged Lieutenant Hayter and Madame Maigre from their bed, and escaped through the front door of the house.'

'I fear I slept through it all.' Mr Sacheverell, with a little apologetic shrug. He puffed at his cheroot, and exhaled smoke. 'I sleep very sound in usual, I confess.'

Rennie sniffed camphorated tincture under the tobacco smoke, and knew the reason. And now he attempted to sit up, holding his fragile head.

'They cannot have gone far, surely. We have a carriage. Let us—'

'They have took my carriage.' Mr Mappin, very matter-of-fact. 'Clearly they had lookouts posted, who saw our arrival, and when we went to the rear of the house one of them followed us, and the other sprang upon my driver and overpowered him. I found him lying in the lane. He is dead.'

'Good God.'

'So y'may consider y'self lucky, Captain Rennie, that y'did not suffer the same fate. That you will live through this night with only a sore head.'

'My head ain't so damned sore that I cannot make some attempt to save my friend – and even that damned woman, that has got him into this trouble.' Sitting up properly, and fighting off waves of dizziness.

'We can do nothing before daylight. They have got clean away.'

'You made no attempt to chase? None at all?'

'My dear Rennie, they were escaping at the front of the house before I had even gained entry at the rear. You had been felled by what was clearly intended as a fatal blow. Only your hat saved your life. By the time I had found my coachman dead, and found and recovered you into the house, all hope of hot pursuit was lost. Indeed, for a time – while your head was being examined by Mr Sacheverell – I thought that perhaps we had lost you.'

'You bandaged my head, sir?' Rennie, to Mr Sacheverell.

'I have a passing knowledge of wounds.' A little shrug, a puff of the cheroot.

'You are a doctor?'

'Nay, I am not. I had some little experience of campaigning in the late American war. You should not get up on your legs just yet, you know. Rest is advised, after a severe blow to the skull.'

'I am very grateful to you, Mr Sacheverell, for your kindness. But we have no time for rest.' And he forced himself upright. As soon as he did so, he staggered, a wave of fainting weakness washed up from his belly into his head, and he fell back down on the sofa on which he had been lying. Presently, as the fainting spell passed, he heard Mr Mappin outside the room:

'I am nearly certain they will make for the coast, to take ship for France. May I leave Captain Rennie in your care, Mr Sacheverell? I must return to Whitehall at once, and raise the alarm.'

And Mr Sacheverell's reply: 'In course I am happy to oblige. I am only sorry we keep no horses here when Nicholas is away. He has took the carriage . . . alas.'

'I will go on foot, running.'

'Running?'

'I was a champion at the paper chase in youth, and I am still very fast, even now.'

The voices receded, and there was the sound of the front door thudding shut. Rennie pulled himself up into a sitting position, and slowly got to his feet. The dizziness had passed, and he felt able to walk.

'I cannot wait here. I must proceed on my own. There ain't a moment to lose.'

TWENTY-ONE

'For God's sake release us from these bindings,' pleaded Juliette. 'We cannot escape from a carriage moving at such speed.'

She lurched on the seat as the carriage bounced through a dip in the road. The jingle of harness and the flinty clatter of hooves under the spinning rhythm of the wheels as they flew through the night. The night shut out by tasselled blinds at the windows, the interior lit by a single lamp.

'I have removed your gag, Madame Maigre,' said M. Félix beside her, 'so that you may reply to my questions. But I am not quite so gullible as to set you free altogether.'

All in French. M. Félix glanced at the seat opposite, where James lay bound hand and foot, and gagged. Only the movement of his eyes, from one figure to the other opposite him, indicated that he was alive and conscious. A gash on his forehead, that had bled into one eye, was evidence that he had not been captured without a struggle. M. Félix returned his attention to Juliette.

'Why are you with this inadequate man – this boy of a man – in England? Have you forgot that you are a citizen of France?'

'A citizen? Is that what I am? Is that what you are? A citizen of the revolution?'

'Yes, of course. That is the reality of life in France, now.'

'But – what of all our work, our mission? All of our painstaking planning and effort and risk, to help the king escape? Does it mean nothing to you?'

'Less than nothing, madame. Such things are beneath contempt, now.'

'So you are a turncoat and a traitor, then. It is you that is beneath contempt now, monsieur.'

She spoke the words almost softly, and allowed the scorn in her eyes to burn into his a moment, then turned her head away against the green upholstered back of the seat. M. Félix reached and gripped her chin with his strong fingers, and turned her head back toward him. In a lower, more intimate tone:

'Did you really think I could let you go just like that, Juliette? You know the depth of my feelings for you. That is why I am taking you back to France, where you will be safe, where I can make you understand and care for me, over time.'

'I will never care for you, monsieur.' Trying to twist her head free of his grasp.

'While he is alive . . .' Aiming a sharp kick at James that caught him in the crotch. '. . . perhaps you are distracted a little by his boyish devotion. But when he has been dealt with, and despatched, and you have only me to contemplate and grow fond of . . . you will change your mind then, madame. You will come to see me as the centre of your life, that saved you out of the deepest and fondest love and regard for you.'

'Love! When I am kidnapped at pistol point, bound and gagged and flung into a carriage, and taken away a prisoner at night! You fool!'

And her eyes flashed all the Gallic scorn of that word. 'Idiot!'

For answer M. Félix smiled and kicked James again. James's eyes stared in fierce agony, and he grunted again and again through the tight gag. Sweat broke out on his forehead and mingled with the drying blood, and dripped on the upholstered seat.

'Where are – where are the other men, that came with

you to the house?' Juliette, in an effort to distract M. Félix, so that he would cease his vicious assault on James. She succeeded.

'They have horses, they will follow us to the coast, my dear.'

'Where?'

'You will see the place when we get there. I have a vessel waiting.'

'Do not – do not you fear detection, if we arrive at a port in daylight?'

'The place is not frequented. It is on a quite remote part of the coast, on the empty sands. Nobody will see us arrive there, nor depart.'

'What will become of Lieutenant Hayter?' After a moment, very quietly.

'He will receive his reward for his part in the late abortive plot – when he has told me what I wish to know.'

'What can he possibly tell you? He was not—'

Over her: 'He will tell me the name of the man that is behind the English part of the plot. The man M. Mappin obeys, that calls into being all such things in England – spies, schemes, intrigue abroad. The man always with ample moneys at his disposal to pay for information in a dozen countries. The man that is at the heart of all British secret intelligence – who controls the Secret Service Fund.'

'And if he does not tell you?'

'Ohh . . . ohh . . . he will tell me, I assure you. Have not you observed, my dear? Lieutenant Hayter cannot endure even very moderate pain.' Leaning forward so that his face was near to James in the swaying, jolting carriage. 'He knows very well that I can provide far greater pain than the paltry twinges he has thus far experienced.' Lowering his voice to a menacing whisper. 'Pain so great, so piercing that the strongest man alive will whimper like a child in begging that it should cease. Yes, yes, indeed . . . he knows it, poor wretched fellow.' Sitting back and turning to Juliette conversationally:

'And so you see, he will tell me almost at once.'

'Why have you turned against us so?'

'I am only against your association with him, my dear. Never against you yourself.'

'I did not mean James and me. I meant the whole of the royalist cause in France. What did the revolutionists promise you in return for your treachery and betrayal?'

'I am tired now. I think I may rest a while, until we come to the coast.' M. Félix yawned. 'Perhaps you should do the same, my love. We have a long way to go, after I have conducted my little inquisition.'

'What did they promise you?' Bitterly.

'Sleep. Sleep. It will refresh your beauty.'

He settled back against the upholstery, and closed his eyes.

They came to the coast at mid-morning, and Juliette was aware that they had passed through marsh country only because – a little after dawn – M. Félix had raised one of the blinds to peer out of the carriage. A stretching, watery landscape under a wide sky, the glassy reflecting water divided by long earthen banks, marching into the distance. She had shivered in the chilly air. She was dressed only in a shift, and James in shirt and breeches – clothes M. Félix had taken up from a chair and brought with him when he dragged them naked from their bed. They had been obliged to scramble into these clothes as they were put into the carriage in the lane.

Now the carriage drew up in stunted scrub at the end of a long track, above a wide beach of sand and shingle. The vessel M. Félix had spoken of – a small brig – lay at anchor a cable offshore, a single topsail bent to aid the anchor. A boat lay beached at the shoreline, but there were no seamen with the boat, nor anywhere in sight. James climbed out of the coach, hobbling painfully, his legs and his mouth gag untied by the coachman. M. Félix had already untied Juliette's hands and feet. James was ashen pale, dried blood staining one side of his face. Blood was crusted on his shirt. Juliette watched him anxiously as he hobbled to the top of the beach. He winced as he went, and twice nearly fell. Juliette moved to help him, but was at once prevented from doing so by M. Félix, who held her arm.

'Stay away from him. Your life is with me now, my dear.'

'Will you not give us something to eat and drink?'

'We will eat when we go aboard the ship.'

An onshore breeze blowing over his face gave James some relief, and he recovered sufficient to call to M. Félix:

'Will you untie my hands a moment, monsieur?'

M. Félix barely glanced in his direction. 'Nay, I will not.'

'I wish to make water, and cannot unbutton.'

'Then you must either hold your water – or be made wet, like an infant.'

'This is intolerable!' Juliette flashed at M. Félix. She moved toward James. 'I will aid you.'

M. Félix strode after her, gripped her arm and restrained her. Bending fiercely to her:

'Do not go near to him now, nor ever again! Do you hear!'

And Juliette twisted and spat in his face.

A terrible gleam came into his eye, and without wiping the spittle from his face he struck her a sharp, knuckled blow to the side of her head, sending her reeling to her knees with a cry.

James saw that the coachman was distracted by the horses, and he ran at Félix from behind, stumbled and nearly fell over a tufted mound of earth, and crashed heavily into M. Félix with the full weight of his body. M. Félix pitched over with a grunt, and Juliette leapt clear of him. Catching up a flat, heavy stone she dashed it against his head. He grunted again, tried to get to his knees, and James stumbled up and kicked him with all the force of vengeance as hard as he could in the crotch.

The coachman, hearing the commotion of the assault, ran round from the front of the coach, a bridle in his hand. Juliette scrabbled in the pocket of M. Félix's coat, found a pocket pistol, and snatched it out. As the coachman advanced, dropping the bridle and pulling a pistol from his waistband, Juliette cocked her weapon, raised it and

crack

shot him through the forehead. His head snapped back, his knees buckled, and he fell dead.

James, glancing toward the boat, and away along the beach:

'There are seamen somewhere nearby ashore, that came in the boat. They will have heard that shot. We must take the carriage and escape before they come.'

'Yes, we must get away.' Nodding, and glancing at the ship.

'We'll take him with us.' Nodding at M. Félix, who lay doubled up, gripping his crotch in agony. 'He wished to ask me some questions, and certainly I will like to reciprocate, and ask some of him. And now, my love, for the love of God untie me so I may go behind the coach and unbutton.'

But before Juliette could untie James's hands, four horsemen came at a gallop along the track toward them. In desperation Juliette raised the discharged pistol, pointed it at them, and then let it fall from her hand. In moments she and James were surrounded and helpless, the leading man had dismounted and helped M. Félix to his feet, and fate had again reversed itself.

*

Rennie had managed to hire a horse from a stable at Lambeth, and ride to the Admiralty in Whitehall. His purpose was to obtain aid from Their Lordships, by one means or another, to rescue Lieutenant Hayter and his companion. He believed that their captors would seek to escape to France in a small private vessel. His view was that Mr Mappin would also seek to mount a rescue, but through the Secret Service Fund, not the Royal Navy.

He was proved wrong. When he came to the Admiralty he found Mr Mappin already there, with exactly the same purpose.

'We can aid each other, Captain Rennie, and thus aid our friends. I have had great difficulty in persuading the clerk to allow—'

'They will never give us a commissioned ship, you know.' Over him, on the stair where they had met, leading up to the boardroom and other offices.

'But we *must* have a ship. How else are we to prevent—'

Again over him: 'This ain't an Admiralty matter, strictly speaking. From the beginning it was subterfuge, and intrigue, with dubious intent. To date, it has not met with great success.'

'Dubious intent! To save two of our bravest—'

'My dear Mappin, I am with you, I am with you. But we must approach the thing correct. Never forget that when it comes to ships, the men that occupy this building will never like to agree to dubious intent. Not twice, in the same cause. We must find the right man – Commodore Maxwell.'

'Maxwell? Never heard of him.' Shaking his head impatiently, gripping the banister.

'He looks after the official charts, you know. He's an old friend of mine, since the late American war. Bravest man I ever knew. Lost a leg in '82, and has found his place here ever since.'

'Charts! What can a man that husbands charts do for us in this emergency, good heaven!'

'Mr Mappin, you are agitated. Pray calm y'self, sir, and attend me. Commodore Maxwell will give us our warrant, d'y'see?'

'Warrant?'

'Aye.' Greatly more at ease in these surroundings, in these circumstances, than the usually imperturbable Mappin. 'Toby Maxwell will write out a warrant enabling us to seize a private ship in His Majesty's name, in an emergency, in the nation's interest.'

'But can he do that? How? On what authority? What has it to do with *charts*? Listen now, we must find the First Secretary, and ask him to arrange—'

'Mr Mappin!' Harshly, fiercely, as they reached the top of the stair.

'Eh?'

'There ain't a moment to lose! Cease jabbering, sir, and follow me, will you!' It was not a request.

They found Commodore Maxwell drinking coffee at the table in his little office, his crutch resting on the back of his chair. Presently, having been introduced to Mr Mappin, and listened to Rennie's rapid explanation and request:

'In course I am not permitted to accede to any such wild and irresponsible notion, you know.' Writing out the warrant, and sealing it with wax.

'In course, in course, my dear Toby. Understood. And thank you. Come on, Mappin! We must go to Dover right quick, as soon as we've found you a horse!'

'Dover? Portsmouth, surely?'

'Dover!' Already out of the door.

*

Juliette was made to wait in her shift, with the four men, at the boat. Their horses, and the carriage horses, had been turned loose. Three seamen had also appeared, returning from far down the beach to the west with a musket and a brace of rabbits. All of them were now obliged to wait on M. Félix's pleasure, while he interviewed Lieutenant Hayter in the carriage.

The leader of the four horsemen, a lean dark man with sour breath, said to Juliette:

'Why does he not question the prisoner aboard the ship? We are wasting time lying here, when we could have weighed by now and put to sea, out of reach.'

'You do not think I am a prisoner?'

'We are returning you to France, but you are not an enemy, madame.'

'A prisoner, but not an enemy. You see no contradiction, monsieur?'

'We are instructed to give you every protection, madame.'

'Pfff. If I tried to run away, you would shoot me down.'

'No, indeed, madame. Even though you have shot one of us, we would never shoot you.'

She turned away from him, and lifted her face to the sea breeze. And glanced anxiously at the carriage, where it stood isolated above the beach, the dead coachman lying beside it.

In the carriage. M. Félix regarded James with a nearly detached stare. James's ankles had again been bound together, and his hands bound behind, and he sat opposite M. Félix on the upholstered seat. Although he was determined to show no sign of weakness nor humiliation, he was feeling very wretched and fearful. He feared the pain of torture. He feared a lingering, agonising death afterward. He feared for Juliette, and what might become of her when they took her back to France. Presently, M. Félix:

'You are going to tell me the name of the man that is above M. Mappin.'

James was silent, staring at his captor with what he hoped was clear contempt. He now drew breath to speak, and then did not.

'Yes. Yes, I see. You do not intend to submit. It is a principle with some men – warriors, seafarers such as yourself – always to be heroic. Yes. They are simple-minded boys, these men.'

From his coat he produced a small silk bag, from which he extracted a finely made pair of sewing scissors.

'What I will do – unless you decide to tell me the name – is cut away the lids of your eyes.'

James stared at him, and willed his breathing to grow slower. He could not stop the thudding of his heart.

'You are wondering, I expect, why I do not take you aboard the ship, and deal with you there?'

He moved suddenly to the seat beside James, who twisted and writhed away from him.

'Yes, well, I could not perform the task delicate enough, afloat. The movement of the ship would cause additional injury.'

A quick, jabbing movement, and one of the blades cut James's cheek. He winced with pain, gasped, and thrust himself as far into the corner of the seat as he could. M. Félix jabbed again, and caught James just above his ear. Drops of blood.

'Like that, you see. Perhaps causing the loss, not just of the lids, but of the eyes . . .'

James shut his eyes, forcing himself to be steady, drew breath, and:

'Very well, very well, I will tell you. The name of the man is Sir Robert Greer.'

'Ah. Sir Robert Greer. Thank you, Lieutenant.' He wiped the scissors on his kerchief, opened the silk bag, and held the scissors poised over the little gaping silken mouth. 'But, you know . . . I am nearly certain I heard that Sir Robert Greer . . . had died.'

A bleak smile, and he let the bag fall empty on the seat. It made no sound. Now he held up the scissors like tiny crossed swords.

'You are a fool, Lieutenant. Sir Robert Greer would never have sanctioned the English part in the plan to save King Louis. He died, and the new man – the man you and M. Mappin obey – arranged it. You see? I know almost everything about you English . . .'

The smile left his face as if a mask had fallen.

'. . . except that name.'

Another lunge, and James turned his head desperately away. From the distance outside:

crack-ack

The unmistakable, echoing report of a long-barrelled musket.

Shouts on the beach, and the sound of running feet. A pounding on the carriage door.

'Monsieur Félix! Monsieur Félix! We must get into the boat, and escape!'

M. Félix opened the door and snapped:

'Who attacks us? How many?'

The leading horseman, panting and pointing:

'They are English revenue men, I think. A dozen or more, coming from the marsh. All armed.'

'Then we must go.' Decisively, a quick nod. 'Bring him.' Jerking his head at James, exiting the carriage and running down the beach toward the boat.

A distant shout now: 'Stop! In the king's n-a-a-a-me!'

The sound of another warning shot, and for a brief moment James was inspired by the hope that the Excise men would take M. Félix and his party, and rescue Juliette and himself. The hope was soon dashed. The horseman dragged him bodily from the carriage, slung him over his shoulder and carried him at a staggering run down to the boat.

The boat was dragged into the shallows and shoved off. All on shore jumped, tumbled and heaved themselves into it, it wallowed heavily, and was under way, every able man at an oar. James was able to glimpse the Excise party as they reached the carriage. Two or three musket balls kicked up little spurts of spray, but none was near the boat, and as the echo of the shots drifted away the boat rounded the brig and was under the lee, and bumping in under the chains on the swell, where it was secured with a line.

Under his breath James muttered bitterly:

'And now we are certainly lost.'

He slumped in his bindings, his feet dragging in the sloshing water at the bottom of the boat.

Presently he and Juliette were taken up the side ladder and into the brig, and they put to sea.

*

'Hard down with your helm, and keep your luff!' bellowed Captain Rennie in carrying quarterdeck. The helmsman of the merchant brig *Puffin* scowled at Rennie, and brought the vessel a point closer on the larboard tack as they ran down the Channel from Dover. There was a sharp chop running, kicked up by the southerly wind, and the little ship heeled steep, spray smashing up and fanning across her bow, and the rigging a-hum. Her pennant streamed and snapped from the trucktop of her main, and Rennie glanced aloft, bracing his feet on the angled deck.

'What is our speed, if y'please?' To the boy running out the logship at the tafferel.

'Five knots, sir.' Gripping the knotted line at the mark on the rail.

'Ain't enough! Braces, there! And bowlines! Cheerly, lads, cheerly! Look lively, in the name of the king!'

'Mr Mappin joined Rennie abaft the wheel, staggering as he tried to find his balance on the sloped planking. He was distinctly green in the face.

'So far as I am able to ascertain . . .'

'Eh? What? Can't hear a word y'say, Mr Mappin!' Tilting his head.

'So far as I am able to ascertain, there is only the signal gun aboard, Captain Rennie!'

'Never mind, never mind. We had no time to be selective when we came to Dover. I would have wished for a cise cutter, with ten guns, but there was no such vessel available. We was obliged to take what we could get, and we have got *Puffin*, all 140 ton of her. Is there powder, Mr Mappin?'

'Eh?' Lurching as the bow dipped into the chop, and a smash of spray swept over the deck.

'Powder! For the signal gun!'

'I could not say. I expect so.'

'"Expect so" will not answer at sea, Mr Mappin. Discover it, yea or nay, and report to me, if y'please.' Striding under the brigsail boom and gripping the lee rail as he glanced again aloft. Sea water swirled at his feet, and spread in an angled wash across the deck. Mr Mappin saw this swirling water with queasy eyes, tried to quell the horrible disquiet that was rising within him, and only just managed to point himself seaward over the rail before disquiet became a violent cascade.

'God preserve me from lubberly men.' Rennie, but in his head. Aloud: 'Stand by to tack ship!' Striding to the wheel. 'Stations for stays!'

The brig's small crew at their places, beginning to respect this hard disciplinarian for his seamanship, and readier now to do his bidding.

'Ease your helm down – handsomely, now!'

Jib sheets eased, the brigsail boom amidships. Rennie peered, craning his neck, was satisfied, and:

'Helm's a-lee!' A long moment. 'Off tacks and sheets!'

As sails spilled air and the brig came through the eye of the wind:

'Maincourse haul!'

And as she came round, foresails aback:

'Let go and haul!'

Yards braced and sails trimmed as she swung on to the starboard tack and began to run true, heeling into the wind.

'Well done, lads! Handsomely done!' And to Mr Mappin, still clinging to the rail:

'We'll catch 'em yet, hey, Mr Mappin! What say you?'

But Mr Mappin was unable to express an opinion, or indeed say anything at all.

'Aye, we'll catch 'em – if they are at sea.' Half to himself, nodding. By God but it was a pleasure to be back in his element, in command of a ship at sea, the clean smell of that sea in his nostrils as she beat to windward, the sun on his face as he looked aloft and trod the deck. Never mind the outcome on this day, never mind if it came to blood and fear. Here, now, he was as wholly alive as it was possible for him to imagine, and it made his heart sing.

Almost gently to the helmsman, but not quite:

'Luff and touch her, lad. Keep her up.'

And a great sniffing breath, hands braced behind his back.

Mr Mappin staggered away to the companion hatch, and went below. As his head disappeared Captain Rennie began to sober a little. If Mappin could not fight, that left only himself to do so. These merchant seamen – able enough in handling a ship along the coast of England – were not fighting men, and could not be expected to transform themselves into warriors at a moment's notice, in service of a cause they could not be expected to understand. Further, he had no guns. Well, a signal gun that would make a bang or two – provided powder could be found, and made into cartridge – but nothing else. Mappin – blast the fellow – had enjoined him to leave his sword behind at Bedford Street, and now he had only two pocket pistols, and an old cutlass he'd found in the captain's quarters.

Puffin's captain was not aboard. When Rennie had arrived at Dover and commandeered the brig with his spurious but impressive-looking warrant, her captain had been absent on an errand at Deal, and was not expected to return before the morrow. The mate had gone with him.

'Two pocket pistols and a rusty hanger. Well well – we must do our best.'

But his mood had fallen from its recent height, and a frown settled on his forehead. He must busy himself. He must apply himself to practical things.

'You there, boy.'

'Sir?'

'Who is the best lookout among the people? Find him, and send him to me.'

*

The French brig – with James and Juliette gagged and bound, and hidden away behind the breadroom – had been at sea barely one glass when she was pursued. Members of the Excise party ashore had signalled by red rocket to an Excise cutter lying offshore – the *Peregrine*, ten guns, captained by Commander Warren Hunt – and she had given chase. As she did, a second brig appeared from up Channel, and fired a gun.

Commander Hunt at once altered course to intercept the second brig, believing the two were a pair, seeking to aid each other. He accordingly fired a warning shot across the second brig's bow, but as he came within hailing distance he heard:

'*Peregrine*, there! We are *Puffin*, I am Captain William Rennie, RN, in command, and I order you to chase, stop and detain that damned French brig, in the king's name!'

'RN . . . RN?' Commander Hunt said to his second officer. 'Unless I have lost my senses that brig cannot possibly be a commissioned naval ship. It is a ruse.' Through his speaking trumpet he bellowed:

'Heave to, *Peregrine*! I am going to board you!'

'The French brig will escape! We must stop her! Stop her!'

And indeed the first brig was now beating away south into the wind, but Commander Hunt felt there was time enough to deal with her – when he had dealt with *Puffin*. Raising his trumpet:

'You will heave to, or be fired upon!'

Rennie had no great guns, and with enormous irritation was obliged to heave to. He did not wait for Commander

Hunt to come to him, but had *Puffin*'s boat hoisted out, and went to *Peregrine*, bringing with him a slightly unsteady but compliant Mr Mappin. As soon as Rennie came aboard *Peregrine* he introduced himself and Mappin, showed Commander Hunt his warrant with the Admiralty seal, and:

'Commander, I will be very much obliged to you if y'will pursue that French vessel at once, for Christ's sake.'

'I was in pursuit of her, when you fired a gun, Captain Renn—'

'At once, if you please.' Over him. 'Mr Mappin here has seen a certain person upon her deck, and recognised him. He is a man called Félix, a very dangerous fellow. He has a British prisoner aboard, a sea officer, RN. It is my urgent duty to rescue that officer, and yours, Commander.'

'Is this true, Mr Mappin?' Commander Hunt, as Rennie stalked to the rail with a sigh, and peered at the retreating French brig.

Mr Mappin was still rather nauseous, but ready to aid Rennie.

'It is true. Captain Rennie drew my attention to a figure on deck as we came down the Channel, and I took his glass and observed the man. I was amazed we had come upon him, but it is the man we seek, without question.'

'We are wasting time!' Rennie, in a fury of exasperation.

'And are you a naval officer, Mr Mappin?' Commander Hunt.

'Nay, I am not. I am in – another branch of His Majesty's service.'

A frown. 'D'y'mean – the Board?' Meaning, the Board of Customs.

'Nay, nay.' Shaking his head.

Rennie, striding from the rail: 'I will vouch for Mr Mappin, I will vouch for him.' Pointing at the brig. 'That is the ship we must pursue, without the loss of a moment. A British naval officer is certainly confined somewhere aboard her. Well? Well?'

Commander Hunt glanced again at Rennie's warrant, and then at Rennie. A breath, then a brisk nod.

'We will pursue her. D'y'wish to return to *Puffin* first?'

'No no, I will remain aboard your cutter. You are armed, *Puffin* ain't.'

'Very good.' To his second officer: 'Mr Tulkinghorn! Hands to make sail!'

Within moments *Peregrine* heeled into the wind, leaving *Puffin*'s boat bobbing on the swell, and the chase began.

TWENTY-TWO

Peregrine was a fast, weatherly vessel, and soon overhauled the French brig. A further warning shot was fired, but to Rennie's surprise – and Commander Hunt's – the brig made no attempt to come off the wind and heave to, indeed gave no sign that the shot had even been heard.

'Give her another gun,' Commander Hunt ordered his gunner. 'Aim close, so he cannot fail to see the shot strike the sea.'

The gun was fired, and the roundshot sent up a fountain of spray just ahead of the brig. Now something happened that astonished both Rennie and Commander Hunt. The brig swung to larboard off the wind, and revealed a line of four previously concealed gunports, and four squat guns run out.

'By God! By God, he has got carronades concealed aboard!' Commander Hunt, outraged and dismayed.

As soon as he had said the words, orange flashes lit the gunports, and a moment after came the concussive sound of the guns:

THUD THUD THUD-THUD

Twelve-pound roundshot whirred past the cutter, uncomfortably close, and spray shot up immediately aft of her.

'What are your guns, Commander?' Rennie. 'Four-pounders, ain't they?'

'Aye, a mere twenty-pound weight of iron broadside. His broadside is near fifty pound.'

'Then we must run straight at him, and board him.'

'Eh?'

'Sheer bloody aggression is the only tactic that will answer today, Commander.'

'But I cannot nearly match him, Captain Rennie. This is plain damn' foolishness.'

'Plain damn' death, if we don't attack! You wish to die directly, Commander?'

'Nay, I don't!' Stoutly.

'Then be guided by the will to live! The will to prevail!'

Commander Hunt stared at Rennie a long moment, then:

'Mr Tulkinghorn! We will go straight at the brig as they reload! Prepare to board! Cutlasses and pistols for every man! And grappling irons forrard!'

The two vessels closed, and at the last moment the brig came about, presenting her starboard side to *Peregrine*. Another four gunports, and what Rennie suspected were the same four carronades, worked on pivoting transverse carriages. Carronades, by contrast with long great guns, were a fraction of the weight, and thus much more easily fought – loaded, run out and fired – by much smaller guncrews. This time the aim of those crews was better.

THUD-THUD-THUD THUD

Two of the four twelve-pound roundshot struck *Peregrine*, and struck heavy. Her bowsprit was smashed and her forestay snapped by the first. The second whirred lethally the length of the deck, struck and severely wounded her mast, broke the tiller and killed the helmsman. An eighteen-inch splinter pierced Commander Hunt's chest, and he fell dying. Rennie was knocked off his feet by the shock wave of a third ball that did not hit anything, but droned away astern. He was otherwise unhurt. He got up on his legs, his ears ringing, and found himself effectively in command.

Mr Tulkinghorn, Commander Hunt's second-in-command, was dazed, and his face speckled with blood, but he was still on his feet. Before he or Rennie could issue any commands, the cutter's momentum brought her to a direct collision with the brig, which she struck amidships. *Peregrine* shuddered right through her, yawed and swung, and her whole length collided with the brig's starboard side in a grinding, rending crash. Rennie found his voice.

'Grappling irons fore and aft!' Bellowed. 'We will board her, lads! Mr Tulkinghorn forrard, and I will lead aft! This is a fight to the death, lads! Show no mercy to these damned blackguards, that have fired on an English ship in English waters! Cut them down! Cut them down!'

And with a roaring yell he leapt up on *Peregrine*'s rail, and clambered into the brig, followed by bellowing men made dangerous by the rage that follows terror. *Peregrine*'s crew outnumbered the brig's crew two to one, and they were better armed and better trained. Although fighting was briefly fierce, resistance soon ceased, and the Frenchmen laid down their small-arms to preserve their lives.

He had been wrong about the carronades, Rennie noted. There were in fact eight all told, four a side, cleverly concealed beneath false decking and hatchways amidships. As he made this inspection he found to his surprise that Mr Mappin was by his side, a sea pistol in his hand.

'Good God, Mappin, I did not know you had come with us in the assault.'

'In course I came. I should have felt a damn' fool else, or a poltroon.'

'But I did not expect you to take part, when you was ill.'

'Pish pish. As soon as the action began all sickness

vanished. Pure self-preservation set in, and what better way to preserve one's life than by fighting for it, hey?'

'That is well said, Mr Mappin. I am in your debt, sir.'

When Rennie had formally accepted the French master's sword in surrender, he took a small party of Excise men below, leaving Mr Tulkinghorn in charge on deck. Mr Mappin came below with him.

'You think they are still alive, Captain Rennie?' Quietly, as they went down the ladder.

'I most fervently hope so. It will be a bitter end to this day if they are not.'

'Indeed.'

Rennie and Mappin both called James's name repeatedly as the search was conducted, and at last, as they came to the breadroom aft, Rennie heard what he thought was a muffled thud from within. The breadroom door was wrenched open, and Rennie had one of the Excise men tap the rear bulkhead with his musket butt. Hollow.

'Prise it off with your bayonet.'

The bulkhead was prised open, splintering as it came, and as soon as it was removed Mr Félix leapt out of the cramped space and fired a pistol point-blank, shooting dead the man with the bayonet. Rennie raised his own pistol at once, then lowered it.

Félix advanced, holding a young woman in a torn shift in front of him, an arm round her throat. She stared in terror at Rennie and the party of Excise men. M. Félix had brought a second pistol from his coat, and now held it at the young woman's head.

'You will allow me to go free, or I will kill her.'

Behind M. Félix Rennie could see James Hayter, bound and gagged in a crouched position. Only his eyes, frantic and desperate, gave him animation.

Rennie stood back a little, the rest of the small party behind him with Mr Mappin.

'I will not impede you,' he said to M. Félix. 'If you wish to go on deck, you may do so.'

'You will go on ahead of us, monsieur, and warn them on deck to let me go free.'

'May I not release Lieutenant Hayter?'

'You may not. You will do exactly as I tell you. Walk to the ladder, and go up. Tell them on deck to stand well clear, and let me go free. And remember – I have only to pull the trigger, and Madame Maigre will die.' Jerking his arm tighter round her neck so that she flinched and shut her eyes.

'Very well.' Rennie pushed his way to the ladder past the Excise men, nodded to Mr Mappin, and went on deck. Presently he called down.

'Come up! It is quite safe!'

Waiting on deck, with the rest of the Excise crew standing well back, Rennie saw first Mr Mappin emerge, then the small party of men, now deprived of their weapons. A cautious M. Félix followed, holding the young woman as tightly as before, the pistol at her head. He began issuing instructions at once.

'Stand very still! Nobody will move until I say so! A single movement from anyone will cause her instant death!'

Utter silence on deck, broken only by the uneasy creaking of the two ships together as they rode a passing wave.

'That is good, very good. Now, you English will hoist out the boat, and go into it.' Pointing at the boat in the waist.

Silence. Uneasy glances between members of the Excise crew.

'Do as I say! Or I will scatter her brains!' The pistol.

Mr Tulkinghorn, in a low, anxious tone, to Rennie: 'What shall we do?'

'Stand fast, Mr Tulkinghorn.' Rennie, equally low. Raising his voice: 'Now then, monsieur, why not be a reasonable man?'

'Do not provoke me!' The pistol.

'We are many, you know, and you are but one man alone.'

'Release my people! Release them at once!'

'Stand fast, Mr Tulkinghorn.' Rennie, again very low. Louder: 'No, monsieur, I don't think you understand me.' And he walked deliberately aft toward M. Félix.

'Stop! Stop, or I will shoot her!' Pushing the muzzle of the pistol against his prisoner's temple.

'Nay, you will not, I think. If you did, you would in course be cut to pieces at once. We do not want more bloodshed, neither of us.'

'*Stop!*'

And Rennie did stop. He opened his mouth to speak.

But before he could say anything else, one of the Excise men snatched up his musket, and fired at M. Félix. The ball struck him in the left eye. He gave a cry and fell, dragging his prisoner with him, and as he fell his pistol discharged. A thin *crack*. A puff of smoke. Blood poured in a red stream over the deck. It did not come from M. Félix, whose wound bled little. It came from his hapless prisoner, shot in the temple. Her lifeless body fell from his grasp and lolled on the planking, her red-soaked hair clinging to her head and neck.

Rennie ran to her, saw that he could not aid her, and kicked the pistol from M. Félix's hand. In a fury he turned on the Excise man who had fired.

'Who ordered you to shoot! You have killed her, damn you blood!'

He ran at the man, snatched the musket from him, and flung it in a violent tumbling arc away over the side.

'I'll see that you are court-martialled and hanged, you bloody wretch!'

Mr Mappin now moved to Rennie's side, took his arm, and:

'Nay, nay, what's done is done. The man acted impetuous – but we have achieved our aim.'

'Achieved our aim! Achieved it! The poor woman is dead, for Christ's sake!'

Earnestly, drawing him aside: 'And that is a very great pity. But Lieutenant Hayter is alive, our enemy is dead, and our work is done.'

Rennie looked at him, took in the sense of what was being said – and anger died in his breast. He sighed, and sniffed in a breath. As always after a fierce and bloody action, weariness and melancholy began to descend on him. Another glance at Mappin, and he nodded once, stepped away, and began to issue orders. The bodies were removed from the deck, and presently Rennie went below. He released Lieutenant Hayter from his bindings, and helped him up the ladder. As they came on deck, James:

'Where is Juliette?'

'My dear friend – she is gone.'

'Gone? You mean, he has escaped with her?'

'Nay.' A breath. 'She is dead.'

'Dead . . . ?'

'A shot was fired, and she was killed. I am very sorry.'

James stared at him a long moment, and said nothing. Then he turned and walked aft to the tafferel, and stood looking away at the riding sea. He heard the wash of the sea under the counter, and the rinsing slap of waves against the rudder, simple sounds he had heard a thousand times, sounds that in usual he would scarcely notice at all. Yet now they seemed to take on a significance so desolate and implacable and bleak it was as if they spoke directly to him, and he could not ignore their meaning.

Rennie looked at James standing there alone, and made to follow him and comfort him, and then did not. To himself:

'He is better left alone, just at present.'

One glass after, Captain Rennie set the brig free of the half-crippled *Peregrine*, having obliged the brig's crew to tip the carronades over the side. He then jury-rigged and sailed the limping cutter north to rendezvous with the *Puffin*, went back aboard her, and took *Peregrine* in tow.

*

At Dover, when they came ashore, Brough Mappin returned at once to London to make his report, and Rennie took rooms at a small waterfront hotel in order that Lieutenant Hayter might rest and recover from his ordeal. But James was both too agitated and too cast down to rest.

'I had not thought to ask you this before, but how did you discover us, sir? You had intelligence about the brig?' Turning from the window.

'Nay, I did not. I came direct to the coast – very much against Mappin's advice. And yet he came with me all the way, he does not lack courage, the fellow.'

'So – so it was luck, then?'

'Well, as you know, I don't believe in luck, James. Guesswork, perhaps. I will allow it was guesswork, inspired by my profound desire to see you safe and sound again in England.'

'Yes – well. I thank you for that, sir. But I . . . I think you have wasted your time on me.'

'Eh?'

'I don't mean . . . I don't mean that I ain't in your debt. I do thank you for what you did, with all my heart.'

'We are shipmates, James.' Simply. 'I could never have looked at myself in my glass again, had I not strained every sinew to save you. I don't think I would call that a waste of time.'

James shook his hand warmly, nodded, tried to say something more, and was prevented by a rise of tears. Presently he regained his composure enough to say:

'I am a selfish blackguard to've said what I did. Forgive me.' And then he fell silent, and was lost in his thoughts, working his hands together as he sat on the corner of the bed in the little room.

'Will ye not lie down, my dear friend, and rest?' Rennie, presently. He did not like to leave him alone, now. He did not feel easy about it.

'I do not think I shall ever rest again.'

'You are overwrought, in course. It is natural, after what has happened. But in time—'

'Time will do nothing. Time will not answer anything.'

Rennie was silent. He made a face, walked to the window, stared out at the sea. And presently came to a decision.

'I must say a word about our friend Mappin, James.' Turning.

'I had wished Mappin dead, but no longer. He is nothing to me now, and I will not like to hear any more about him.'

'I must tell you, all the same. It may make a difference to your view of this whole matter, when you have heard what I'm going to tell you.'

'Oh, as you please . . .' Rising from the bed, and sitting on a chair. 'I will not swear to listen.'

'Mappin has told me that Lady Sybil Cranham is dead – she that helped mount the spurious rescue of the king.'

'She is dead, too?' Dully.

'Betrayed by Félix, in course, before he came to seize Madame Maigre.'

'Juliette.'

'Aye.'

'Whom I loved.' Half-sad, half-defiant.

'Aye.' Quietly, a nod.

'What happened to Lady Sybil?' Distractedly. 'How did she die?'

'He exposed her to the authorities, if that is how they can be called, when they are only dogs.'

'So – they hanged her?'

'She was put to the guillotine.'

'Put to the what?' Looking at him.

'I had never heard of it, neither, when Mappin told me. It is a new and very horrible device, a kind of heavy axe hoisted on a tackle between two posts, and dropped from a height of twenty feet upon the neck, severing the head.'

'Christ in heaven.' Softly, then: 'My poor dear Juliette did not live, but in least she was spared that.'

'As were you, James. Had Félix succeeded in taking you into France, that would almost certainly have been your own fate.'

'Aye, very like.' Again quietly, then, half to himself: 'I think that he was right, after all . . .'

'Right? Who was?'

'Sir Robert Greer. D'y'remember, he said long since that the revolution would mean a new Dark Age across all of Europe? I did not quite believe him, then. But now I do.'

'I am glad. I am glad. Because what I must tell you now will be very unwelcome to you.'

'How so?' Frowning.

'Mappin believes – nay, hear me out, please,' as James shook his head at the further mention of Mappin's name, 'Mappin believes – and I cannot in all conscience say that I do not – that Juliette came to England upon Félix's instruction, deliberately to seduce you anew, and obtain from you information vital to the French about the activities of the Fund, and British military preparedness, in the event of war.'

'That is damned nonsense! Mappin believes! But he cannot know for certain!'

'He has not told me everything, even now. I learned a little more from him only after we had rescued you. I can only assume—'

'Assume! Assume! I cannot bear to hear another word.' Bitterly, and as Rennie drew breath to continue, James rose and crossed to the window. 'No! No! I will not listen!'

'I know you don't trust Mappin, James, and was I in

your place perhaps I should feel the same. But I must tell it all to you, James, it is my obligation.'

'Sir, I am very grateful to you for everything you have done, but if you wish to remain my friend, pray do not say another word against Juliette!'

Rennie, undeterred: 'He believes that she acted under duress, to protect Lady Sybil.'

'But how could Juliette protect her, for God's sake, when she had been put to death!'

'That was concealed from her, in course.' A moment. 'There is something else.'

'What?' Running a hand through his hair.

'They was cousins. An intimate connection, since childhood. So, you see . . .'

James looked at him, stared out of the window, looked at Rennie again.

'Are you saying to me . . . that she never loved me?'

'No, I cannot say that absolute . . .'

'Then what *are* you saying, sir? You and Mappin between you?'

'I think it very probable that she was torn between two affections, James. Her love for her dear cousin – and her love for you.'

'You are saying absolutely that she betrayed me! That everything was deceit! All of it!'

Rennie was silent, not trusting himself to find the right words. He looked away.

'Are you not!'

At last, quietly: 'My dear James, you are my greatest friend, and I will not lie to you. I think you have been caught up in a very dark circumstance, in which no one could find happiness. We was all caught up in it, and swept along unknowing, or half-unknowing, toward the gloomy hush that is now upon us, and lies all around.'

James stood at the window, and for a long time said nothing. Then, presently:

'All I know . . . all I know is that I loved her, and have lost her.'

Darkness fell on Dover, and Rennie returned to James's room, where he had left him fitfully asleep. James was again awake, standing in his shirt and breeches at the window, leaning forward with one hand on the frame. He turned as Rennie came in.

'I have engaged our rooms overnight, James. Then we can depart in the morning, refreshed.'

'Depart. Hm.' A little shake of the head. 'Where will you go, sir?'

'Go? I shall go home to Norfolk, to my wife. Thanking God that I can.'

'Ah. In course, I cannot go home. Not now, nor ever again.'

Rennie pulled his flask from his coat, poured brandy into a glass, and crossed the room. He handed the glass to James.

'Here, drink this.'

'I don't want anything.' Shaking his head.

'Drink it, if y'please.'

And James took the glass, looking at Rennie. He drank off the spirit, and coughed.

Rennie reached for the glass, and poured another generous measure. 'Drink that, too.' Handing back the glass. 'If y'please.'

James drank.

'Now, then.' Rennie. 'I will like you to listen to me—'

'If you are going to say that I should go home, sir, in spite of all that has happened, you are mistaken.' Over him. 'I have lost my son, my only son, and I have deserted my wife. Beyond that I have lost Juliette. Cannot you understand? Cannot you see? I am utterly wretched. I have lost everything that has mattered in my life. Everything.'

'You damn' fool!'

'Eh?' Shocked out of his misery.

'Ye've been spared, for Christ's sake! To live another day, and make the best of things! The world may not be very lovely just at present, but we must lift up our heads and hearts in it, and face whatever it may bring. You have a home. You have a wife. Go to her! Go home to Catherine, and tell her that you love her! Or by God, James, I will never be your friend again!'

HMS Expedient

Peter Smalley

1786: Captain William Rennie and Lieutenant James Hayter are on the beach and on half pay when they are given a prime commission: *HMS Expedient* is a 36 gun frigate which is to be sent to the South Seas on a scientific expedition.

But there is something odd and disturbing about the nature of their task. They sense that they are not being told the whole truth about the forthcoming expedition? Why is their voyage through the Atlantic dogged by sabotage and why are they followed by a mysterious man of war? And what are the secret orders which may only be opened once they round the Cape of Good Horn?

The answers lies on a beautiful uncharted island, in the remotest corner of the Pacific immensity, to which the storm-battered Expedient limps for desperately needed repairs. Soon the dangers of the voyage will pale in comparison with what the crew discover there, across the limpid waters of the lagoon.

'Smalley has written a real page-turner, engrossing and enthralling, stuffed with memorable characters. Highly recommended.' *Daily Express*

'Following in the wake of Hornblower and Patrick O Brian . . . there is enough to satisfy the most belligerent armchair warrior: cutlasses, cannibals, as well as a hunt for buried treasure. All this plus good taut writing gets Peter Smalley's series off to a flying start' *Sunday Telegraph*

arrow books

arrow books